DANNY PHANTOM™

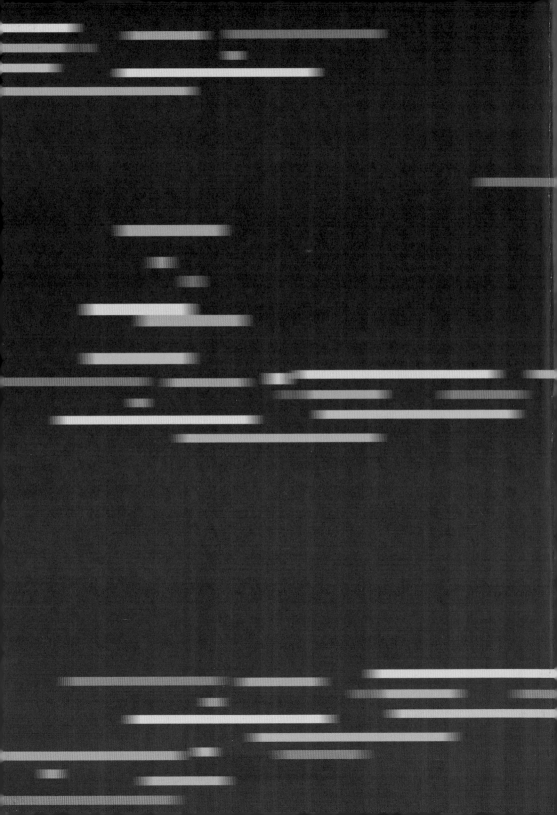

DANNY PHANTOM™

A GLITCH IN TIME

WRITTEN AND ILLUSTRATED BY
GABRIELA EPSTEIN

BACKGROUNDS AND COLORS BY
KILLIAN NG

nickelodeon™

AMULET BOOKS • NEW YORK

PUBLISHER'S NOTE: This is a work of fiction. Names, characters, places, and incidents are either the product of the author's imagination or used fictitiously, and any resemblance to actual persons, living or dead, business establishments, events, or locales is entirely coincidental.

Library of Congress Control Number 2022945353

Hardcover ISBN 978-1-4197-6054-9
Paperback ISBN 978-1-4197-6055-6

@2023 Viacom International Inc. All Rights Reserved. Nickelodeon, Danny Phantom and all related titles, logos and characters are trademarks of Viacom International Inc.
Based on the TV series Danny Phantom™ created by Butch Hartman
Text by Gabriela Epstein
Book design by Brann Garvey

Published in 2023 by Amulet Books, an imprint of ABRAMS. All rights reserved. No portion of this book may be reproduced, stored in a retrieval system, or transmitted in any form or by any means, mechanical, electronic, photocopying, recording, or otherwise, without written permission from the publisher.

Printed and bound in China
10 9 8 7 6 5 4 3 2

Amulet Books are available at special discounts when purchased in quantity for premiums and promotions as well as fundraising or educational use. Special editions can also be created to specification. For details, contact specialsales@abramsbooks.com or the address below.

Amulet Books® is a registered trademark of Harry N. Abrams, Inc.

ABRAMS The Art of Books
195 Broadway, New York, NY 10007
abramsbooks.com

To Emily & Ben—thank you for being funny.

And to my parents—thank you for going to Burger King for a week straight in 2006 to get all the Danny Phantom toys.

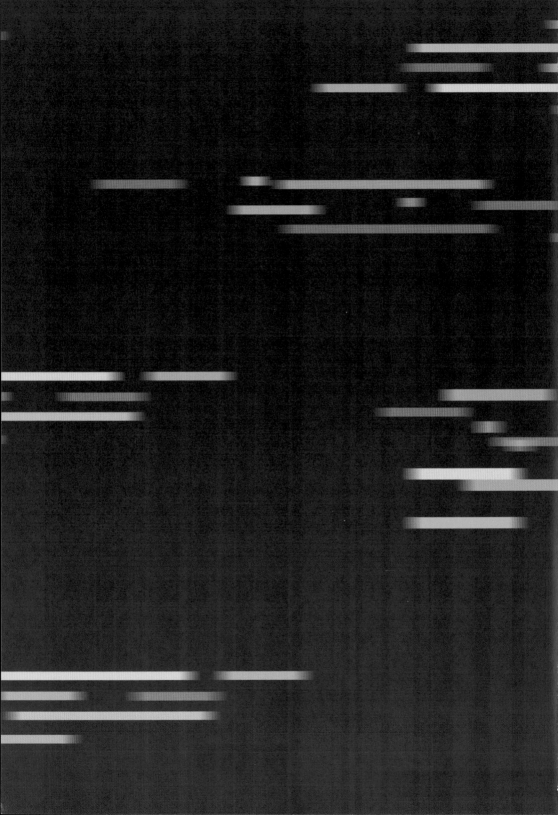

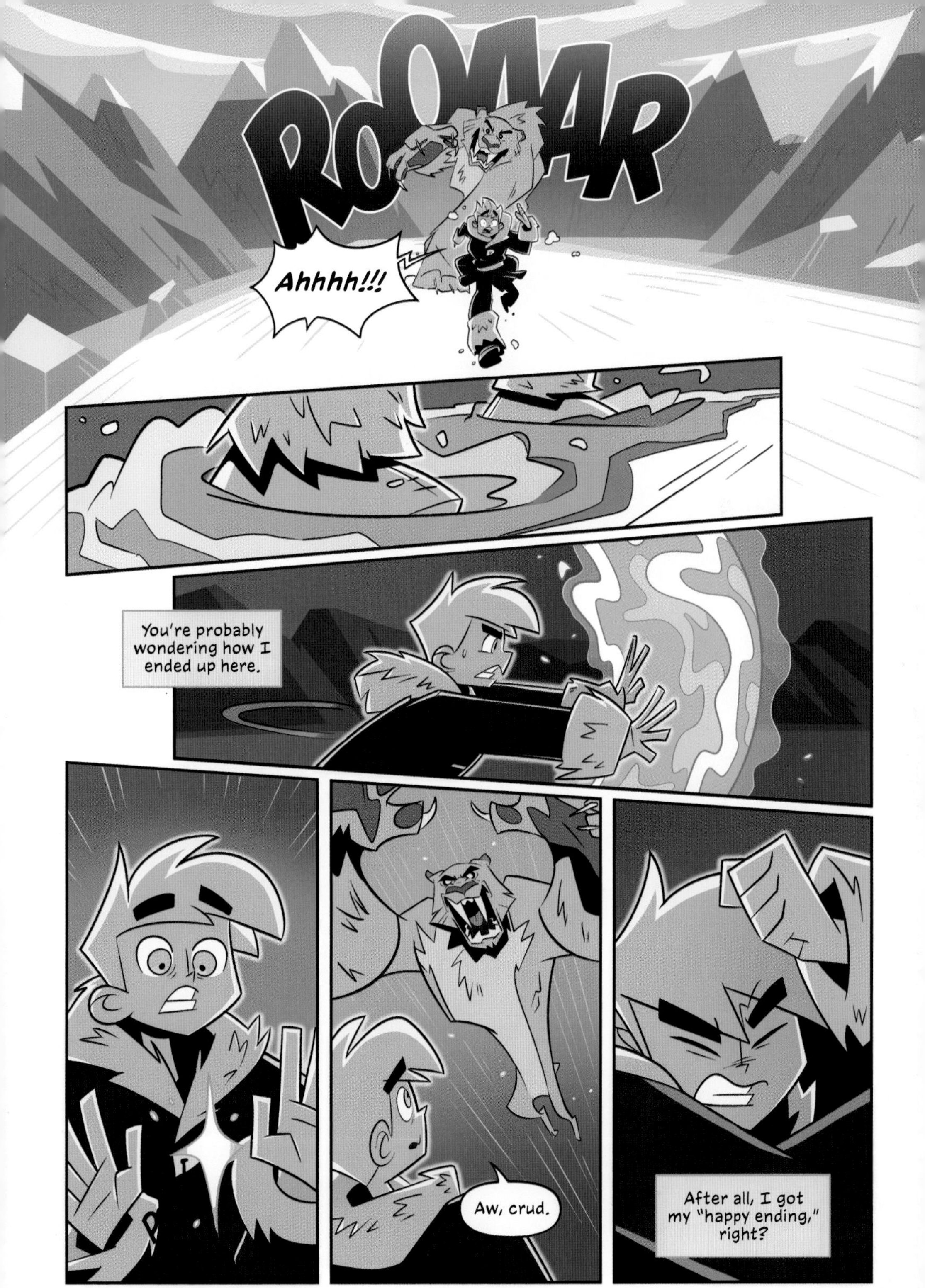
ROOOAR
Ahhhh!!!
You're probably wondering how I ended up here.
Aw, crud.
After all, I got my "happy ending," right?

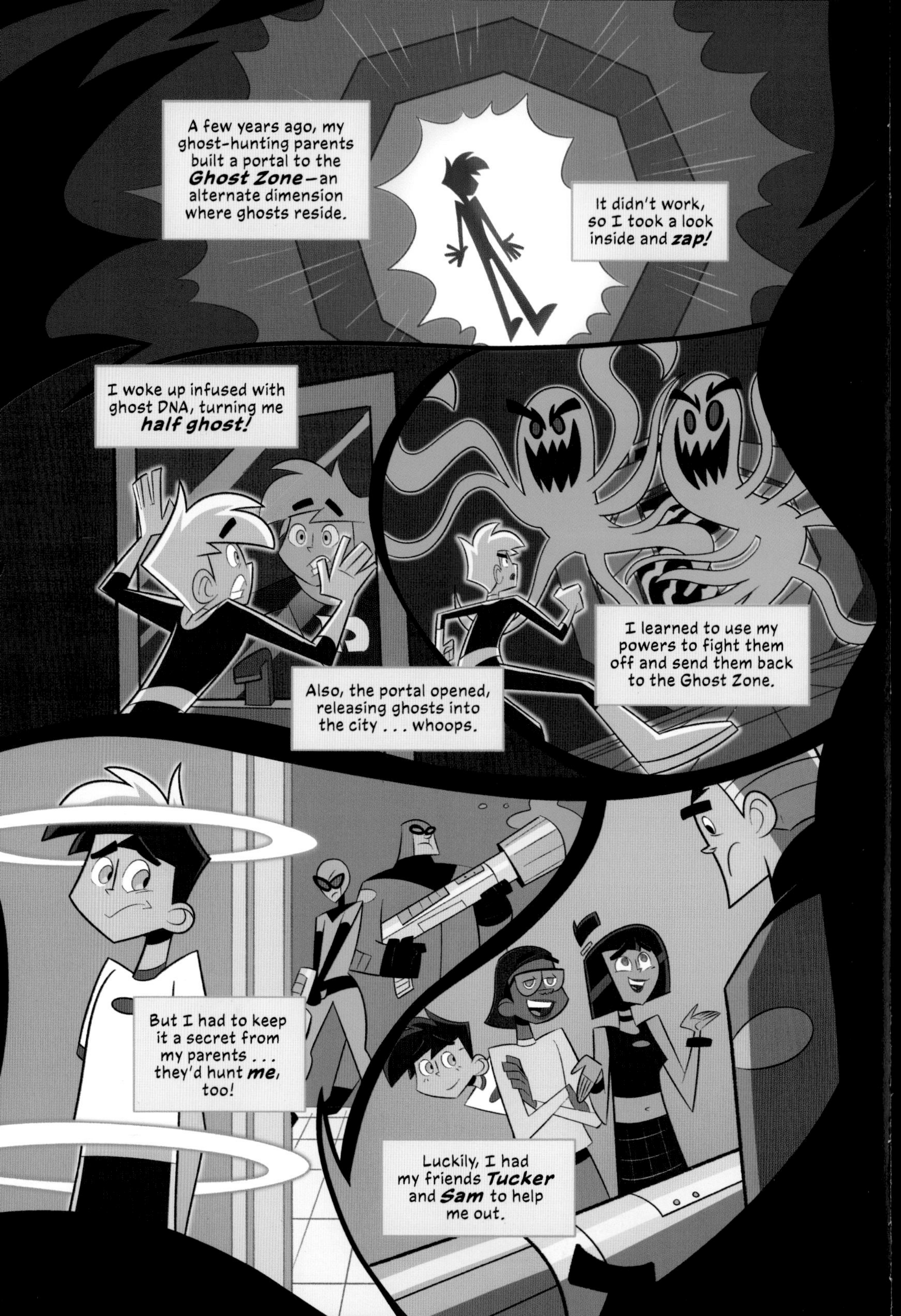
A few years ago, my ghost-hunting parents built a portal to the *Ghost Zone*—an alternate dimension where ghosts reside.
It didn't work, so I took a look inside and *zap!*
I woke up infused with ghost DNA, turning me *half ghost!*
Also, the portal opened, releasing ghosts into the city . . . whoops.
I learned to use my powers to fight them off and send them back to the Ghost Zone.
But I had to keep it a secret from my parents . . . they'd hunt *me*, too!
Luckily, I had my friends *Tucker* and *Sam* to help me out.

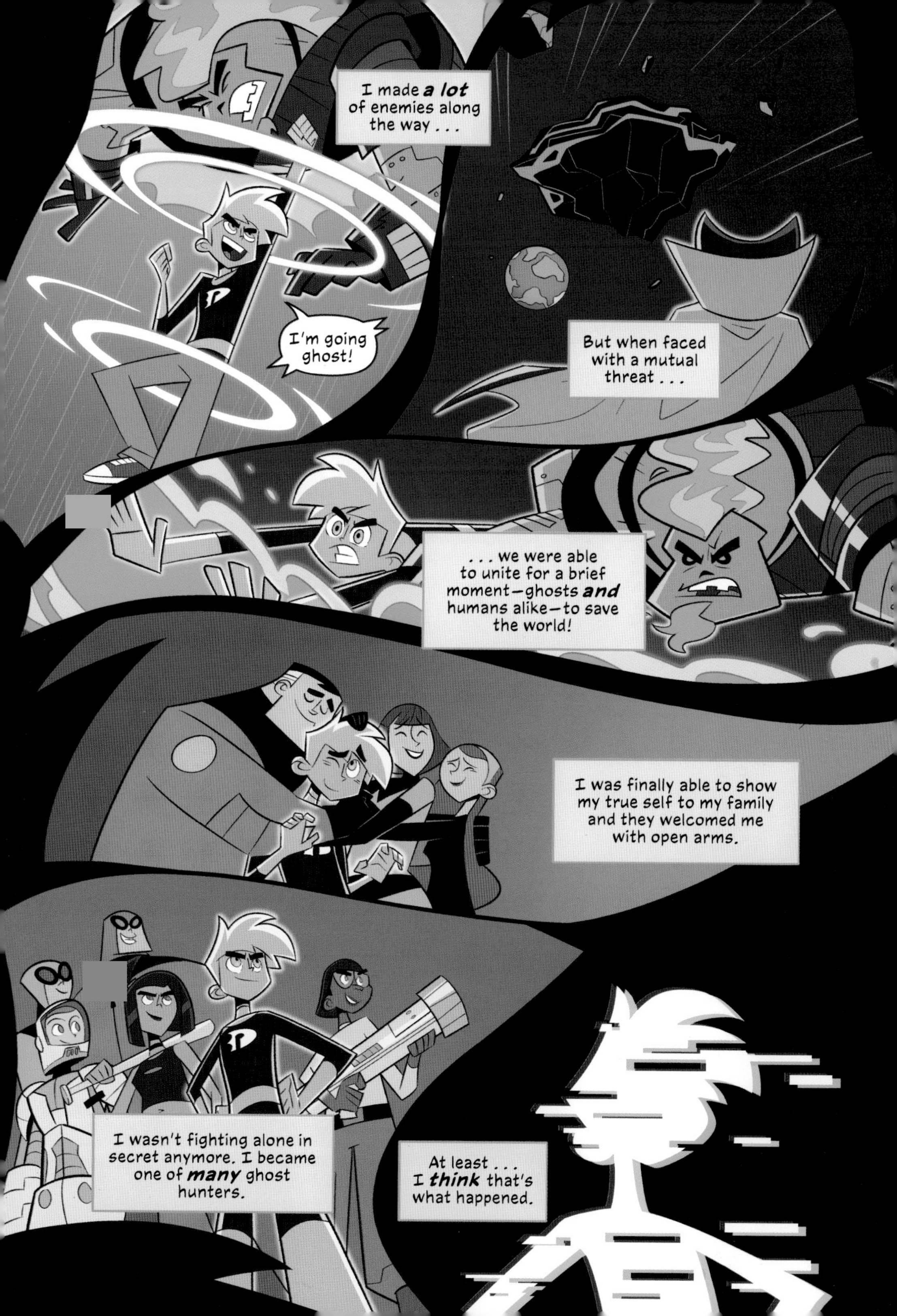

I made ***a lot*** of enemies along the way . . .
I'm going ghost!
But when faced with a mutual threat . . .
. . . we were able to unite for a brief moment—ghosts ***and*** humans alike—to save the world!
I was finally able to show my true self to my family and they welcomed me with open arms.
I wasn't fighting alone in secret anymore. I became one of ***many*** ghost hunters.
At least . . . I ***think*** that's what happened.

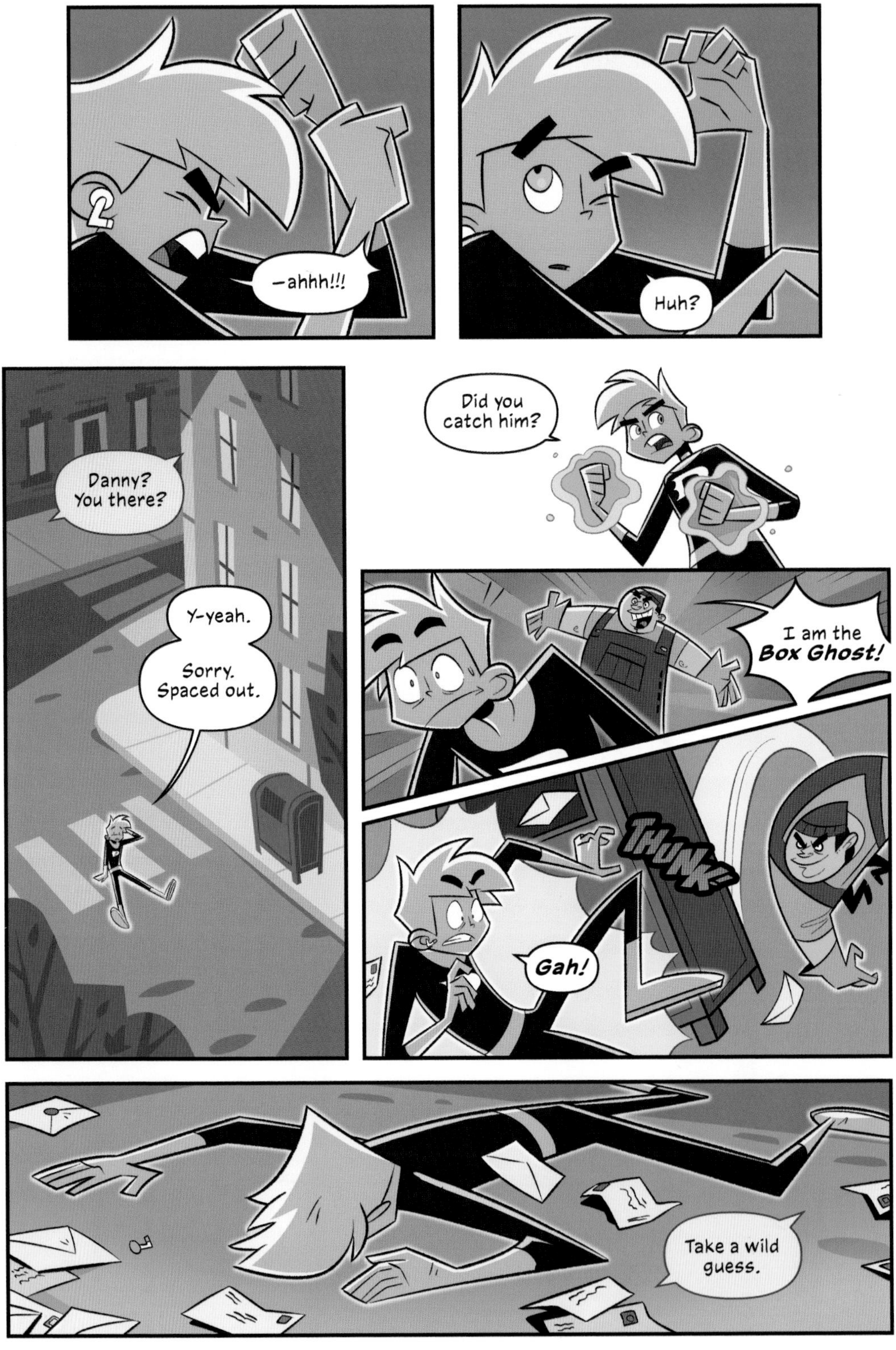
—ahhh!!!
Huh?
Danny? You there?
Y-yeah.
Sorry. Spaced out.
Did you catch him?
I am the *Box Ghost!*
THUNK!
Gah!
Take a wild guess.

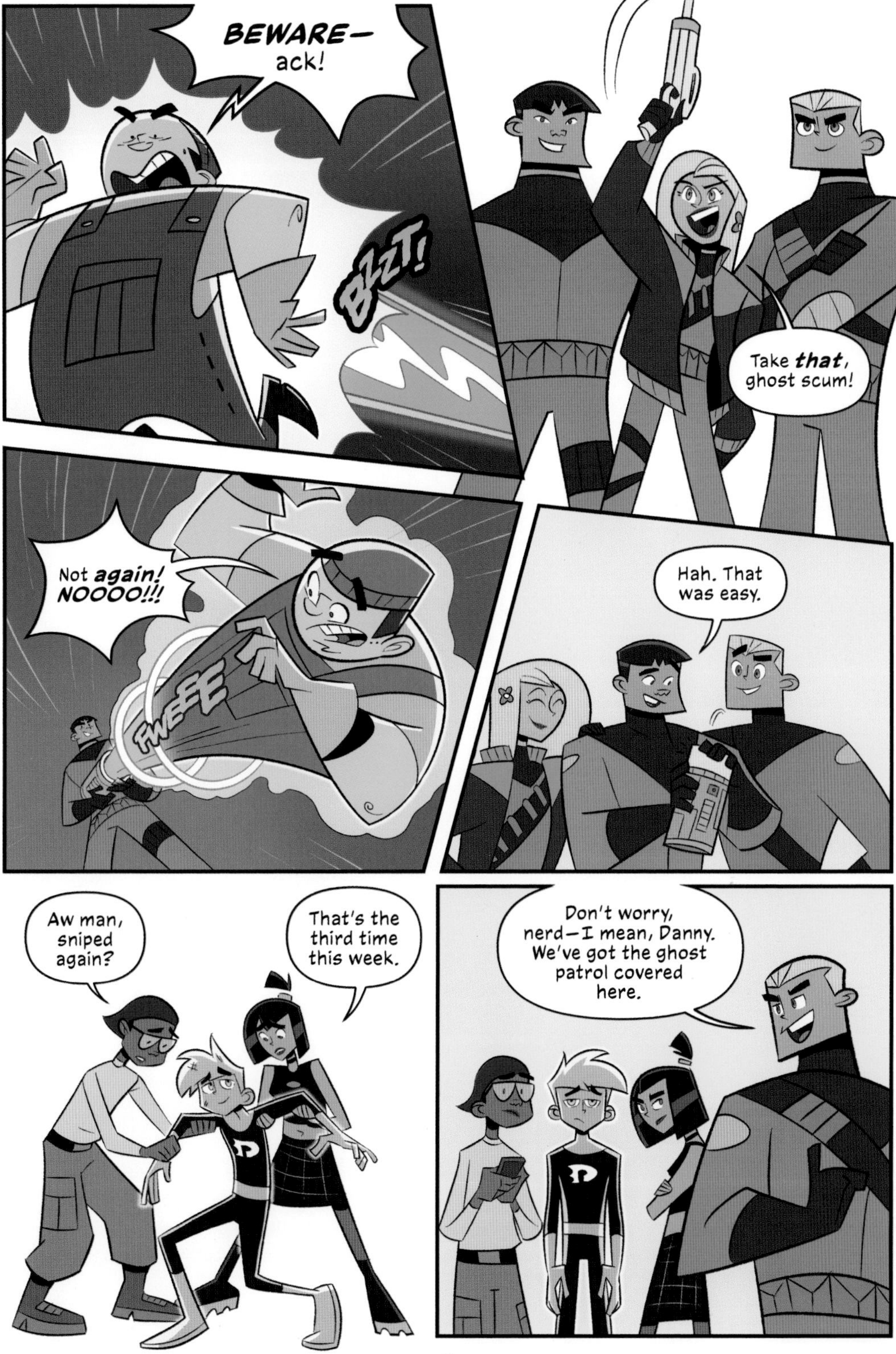
BEWARE—
ack!
BZZT!
Take **that**, ghost scum!
Not **again! NOOOO!!!**
FWEEE
Hah. That was easy.
Aw man, sniped again?
That's the third time this week.
Don't worry, nerd—I mean, Danny. We've got the ghost patrol covered here.

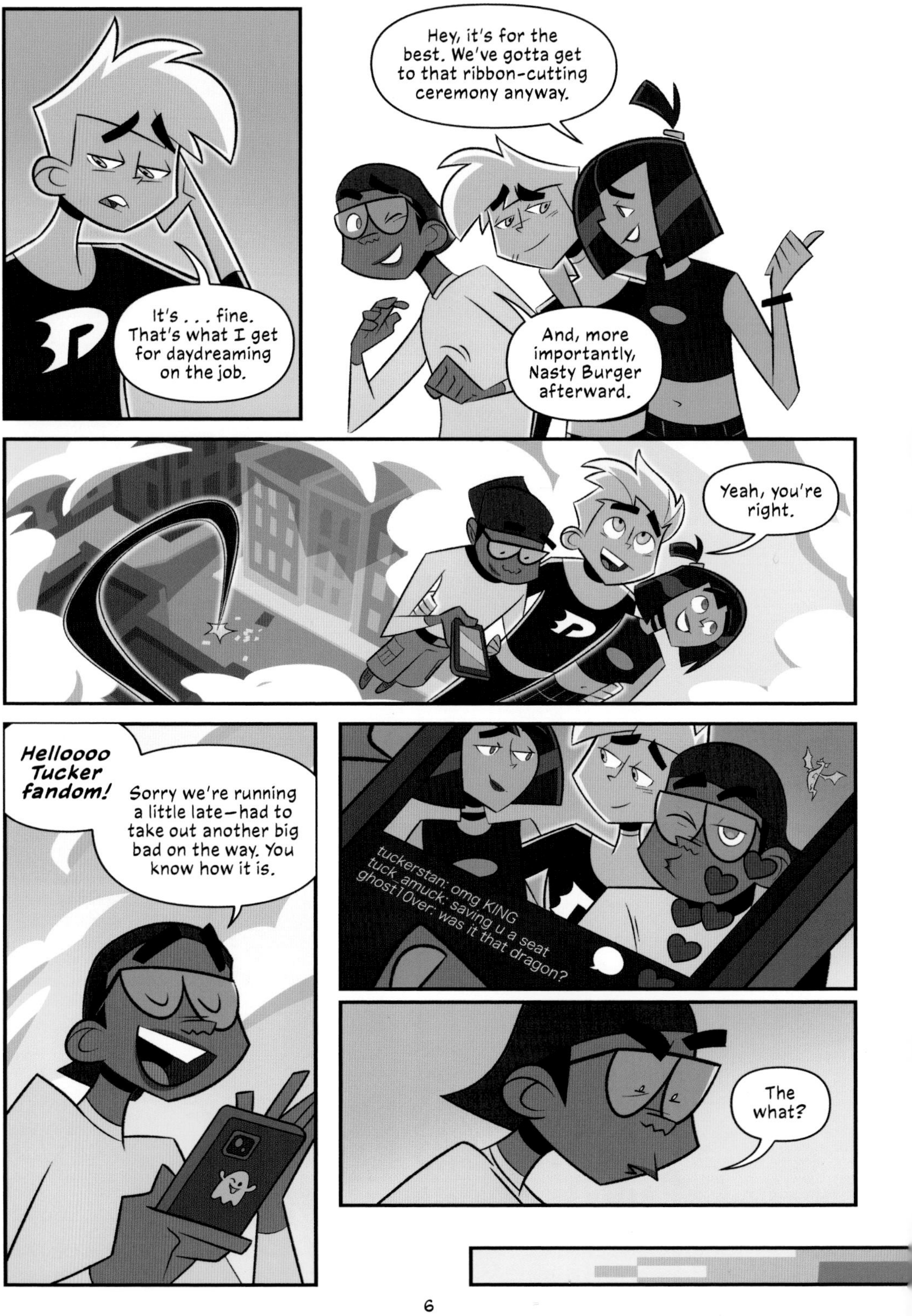
It's . . . fine. That's what I get for daydreaming on the job.
Hey, it's for the best. We've gotta get to that ribbon-cutting ceremony anyway.
And, more importantly, Nasty Burger afterward.
Yeah, you're right.
Helloooo Tucker fandom!
Sorry we're running a little late—had to take out another big bad on the way. You know how it is.
tuckerstan: omg KING
tuck_amuck: saving u a seat
ghost10ver: was it that dragon?
The what?

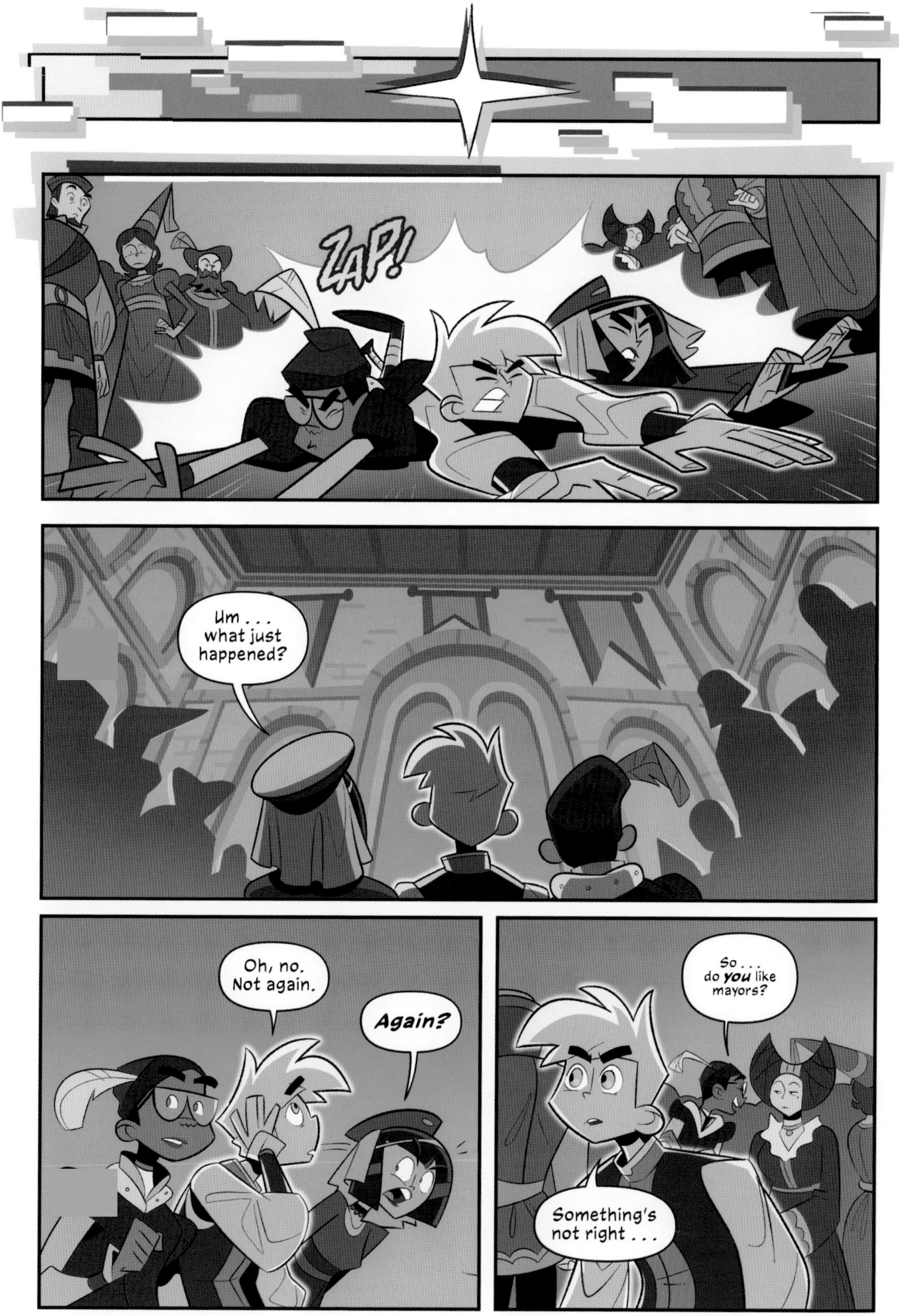
ZAP!
Um . . . what just happened?
Oh, no. Not again.
Again?
So . . . do you like mayors?
Something's not right . . .

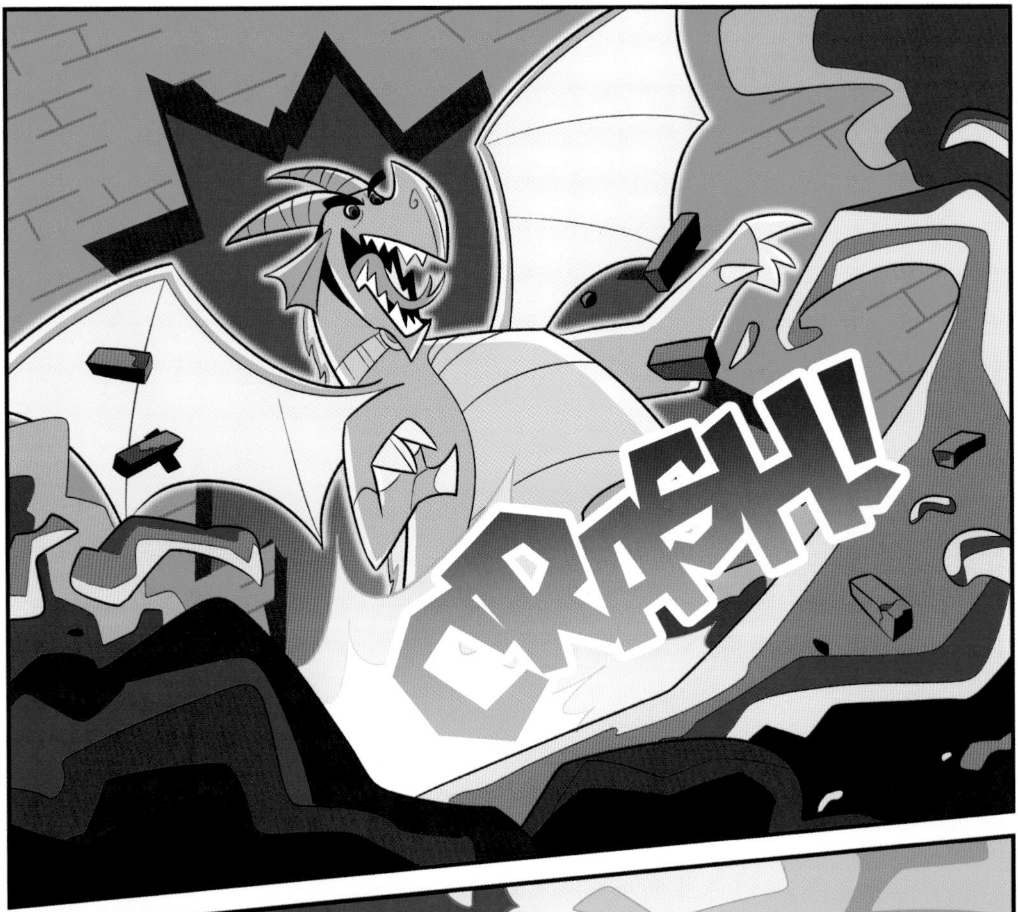
CRASH!

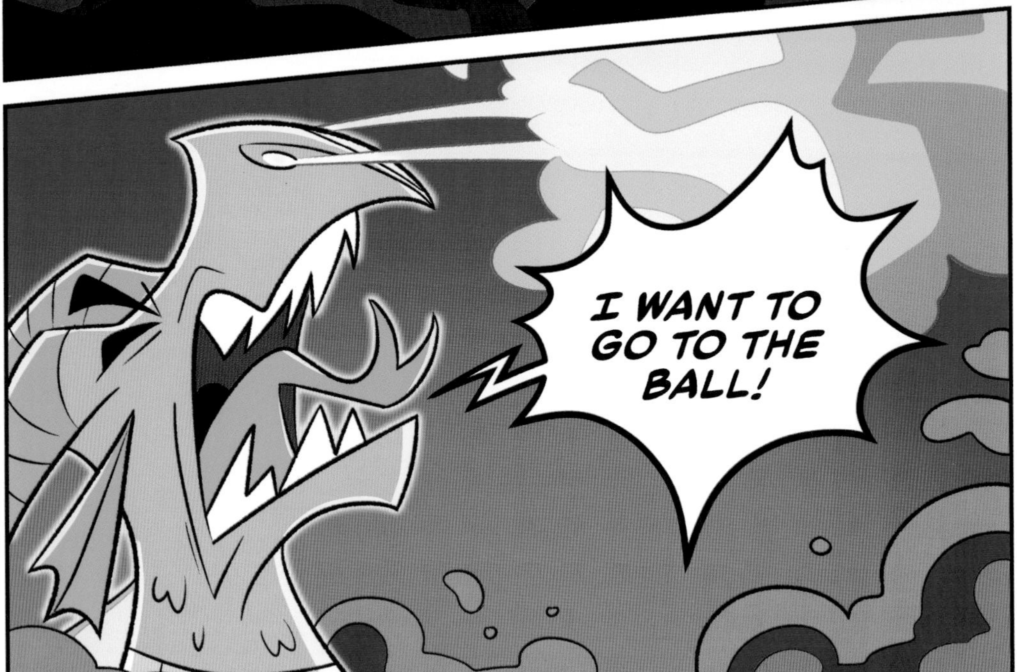
I WANT TO GO TO THE BALL!

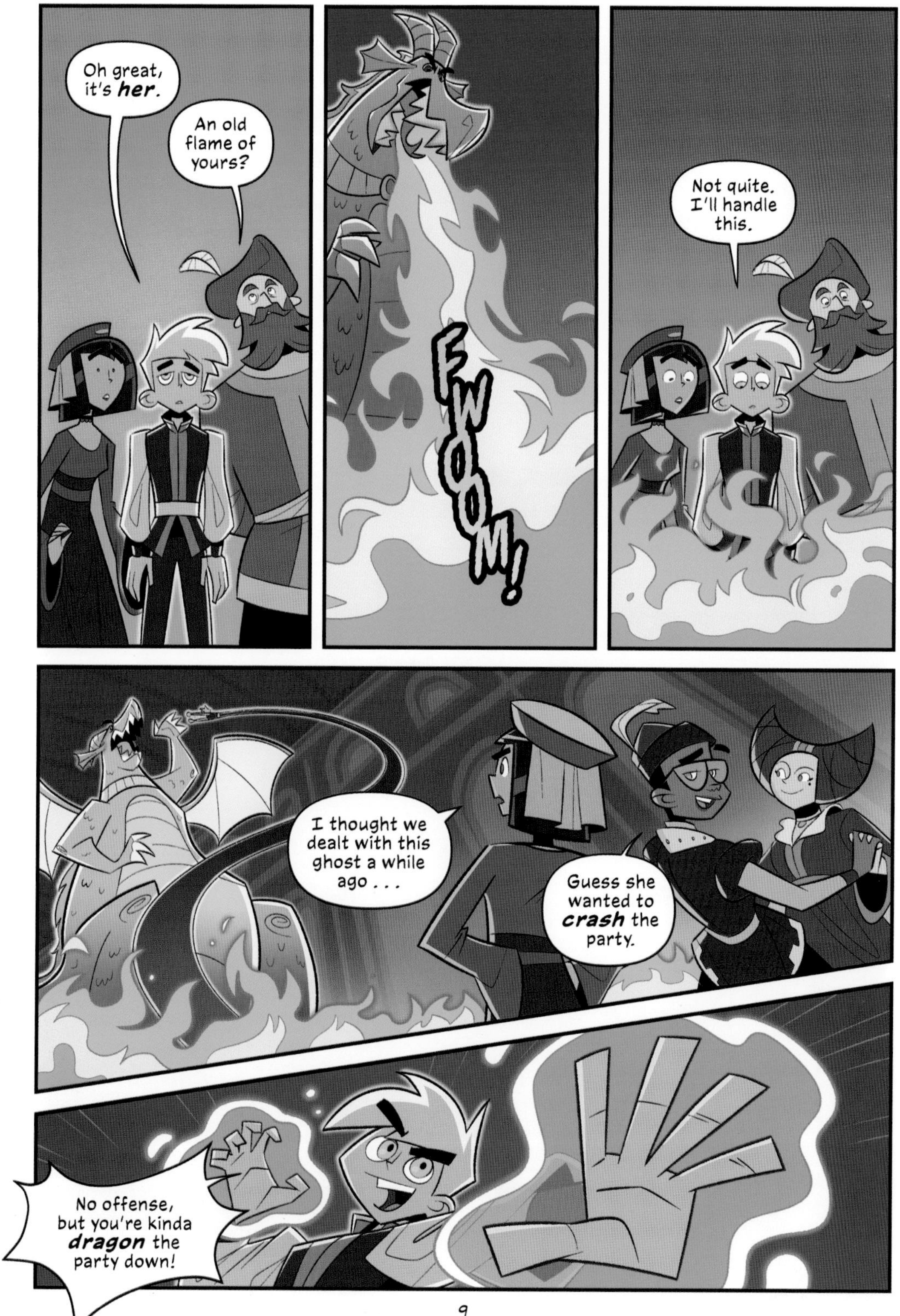

Oh great, it's **her**.
An old flame of yours?
FWOOOM!
Not quite. I'll handle this.
I thought we dealt with this ghost a while ago . . .
Guess she wanted to **crash** the party.
No offense, but you're kinda **dragon** the party down!

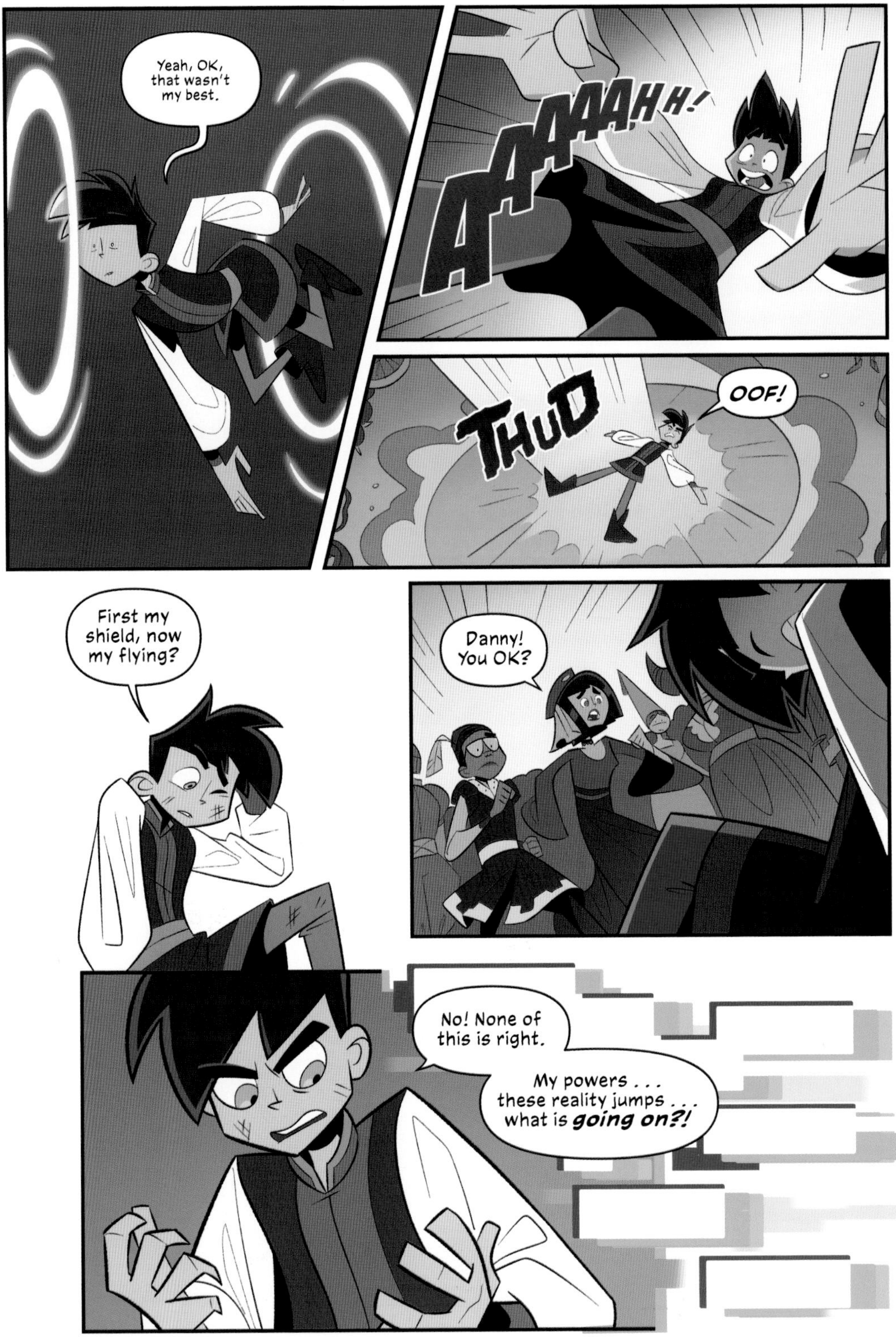
Yeah, OK, that wasn't my best.
AAAAAAHH!
THUD
OOF!
First my shield, now my flying?
Danny! You OK?
No! None of this is right.
My powers . . . these reality jumps . . . what is **going on?!**

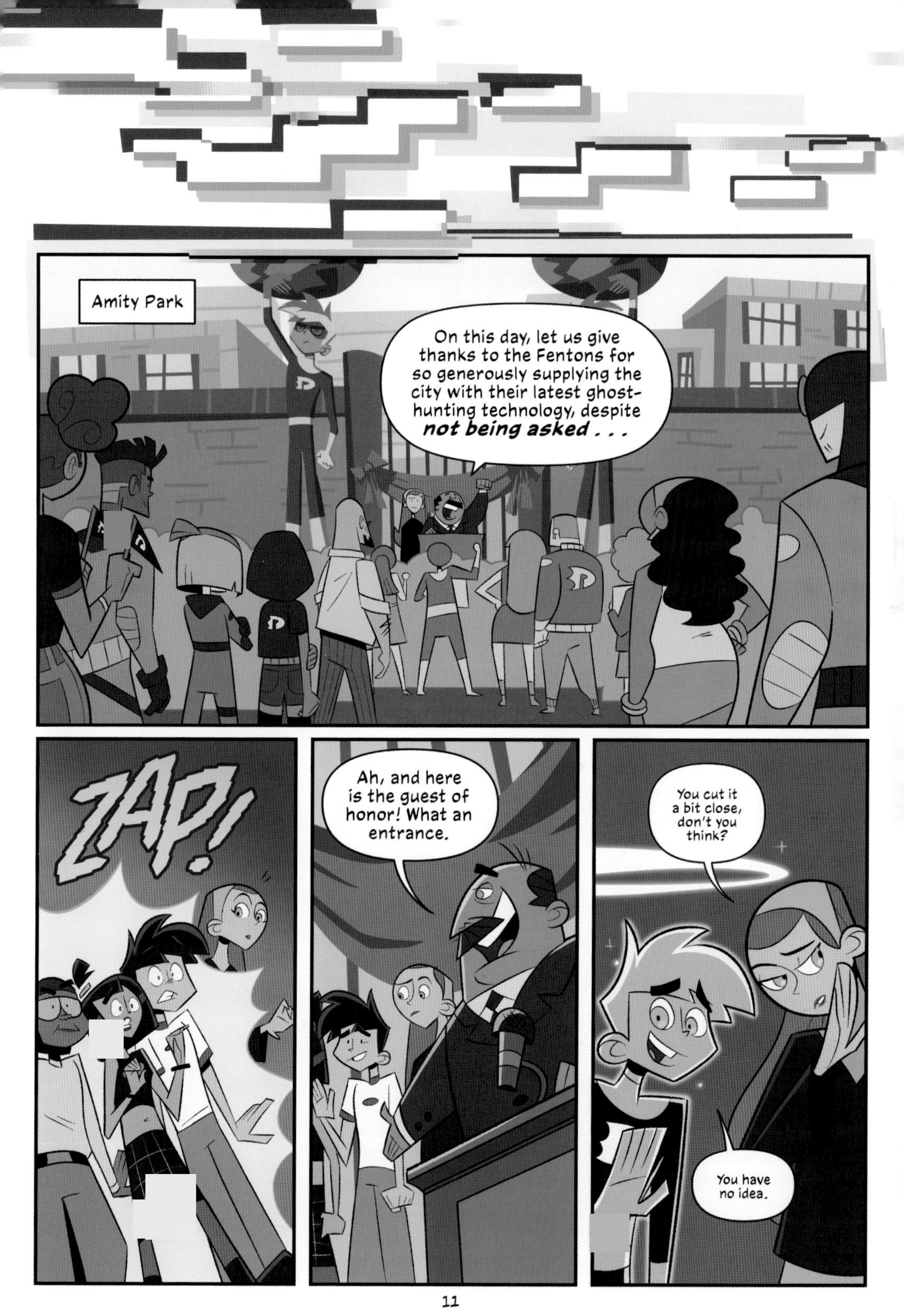
Amity Park
On this day, let us give thanks to the Fentons for so generously supplying the city with their latest ghost-hunting technology, despite ***not being asked . . .***
ZAP!
Ah, and here is the guest of honor! What an entrance.
You cut it a bit close, don't you think?
You have no idea.

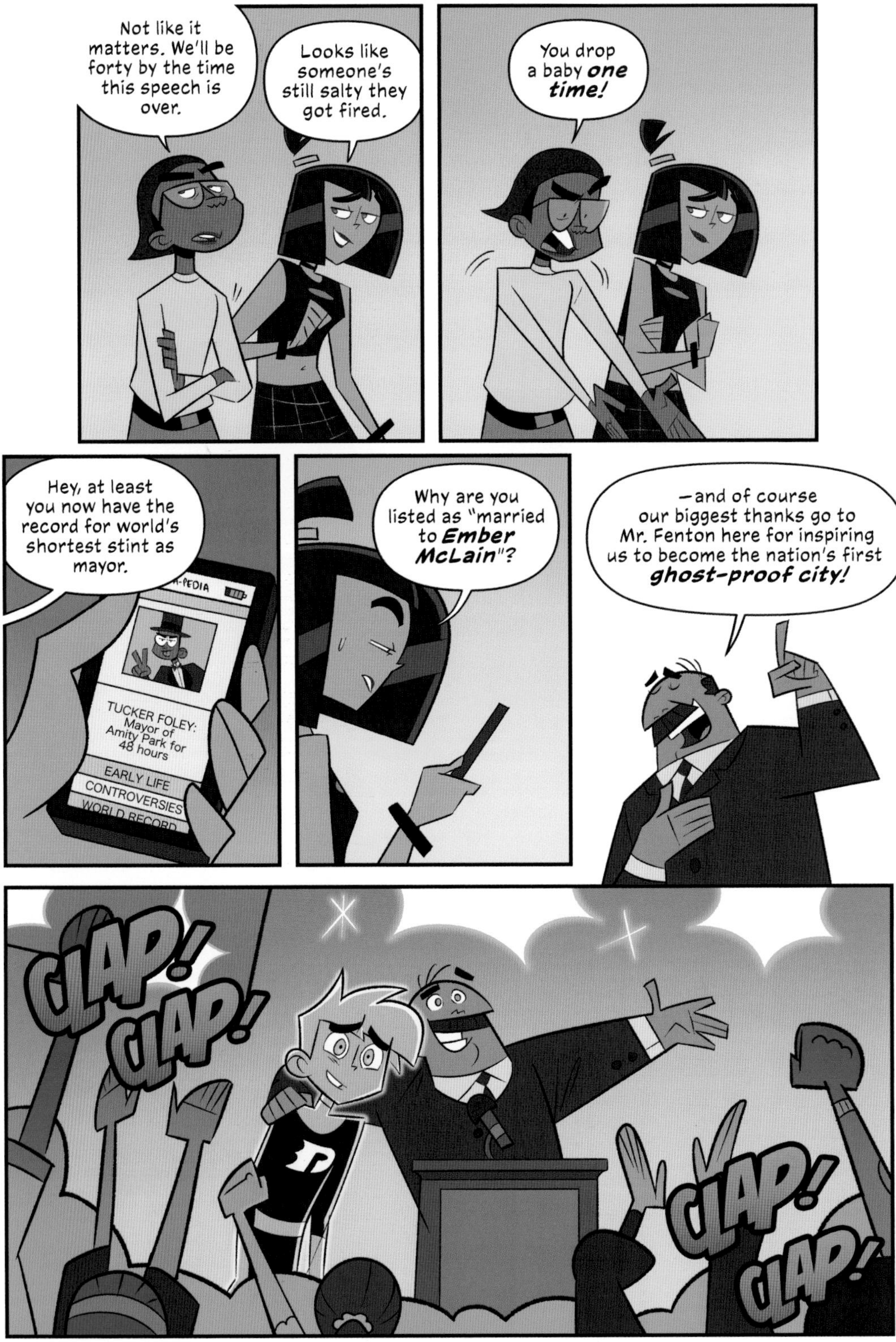
Not like it matters. We'll be forty by the time this speech is over.
Looks like someone's still salty they got fired.
You drop a baby **one time!**
Hey, at least you now have the record for world's shortest stint as mayor.
TUCKER FOLEY: Mayor of Amity Park for 48 hours
EARLY LIFE
CONTROVERSIES
Why are you listed as "married to **Ember McLain**"?
—and of course our biggest thanks go to Mr. Fenton here for inspiring us to become the nation's first **ghost-proof city!**
CLAP! CLAP!
CLAP! CLAP!

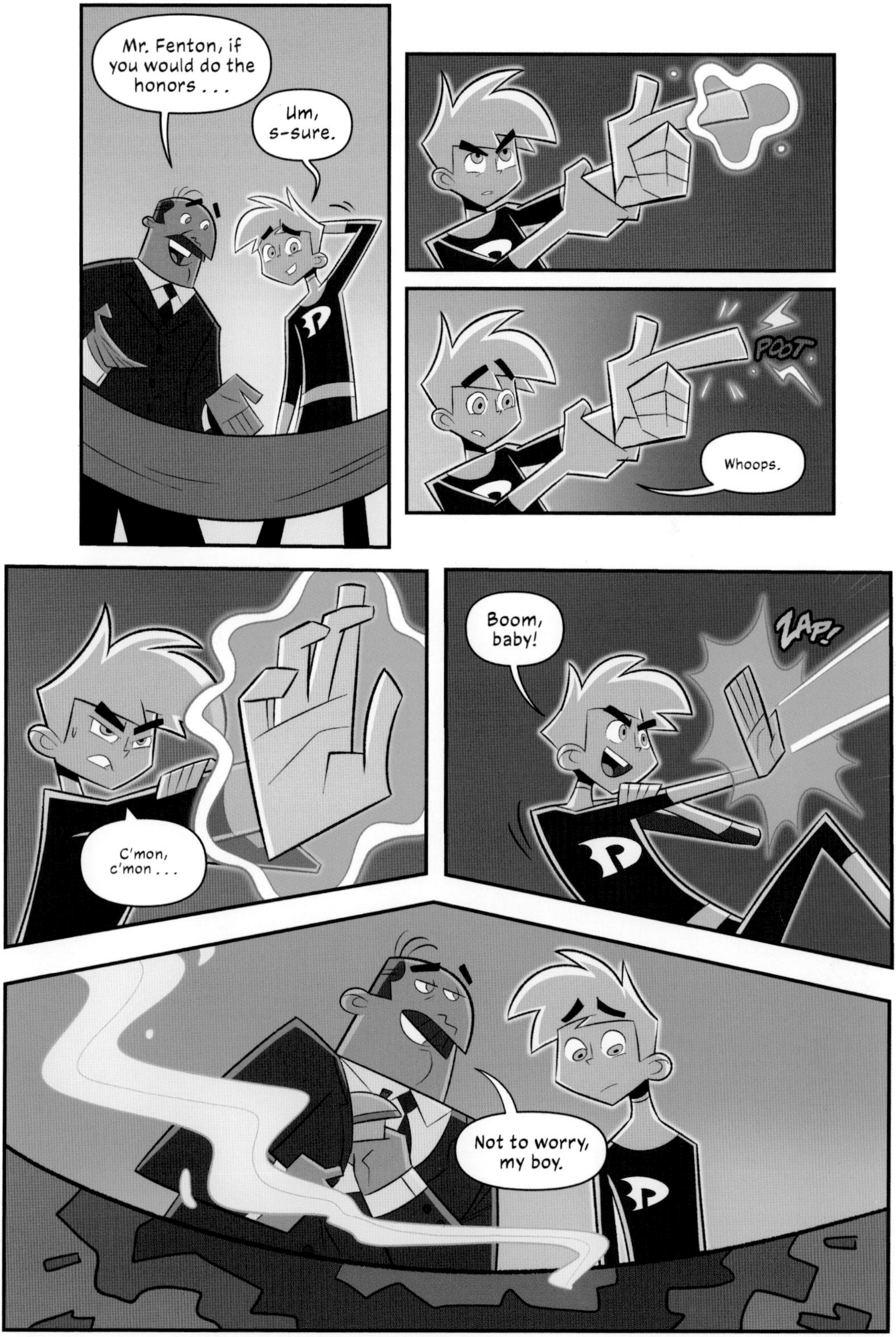

Mr. Fenton, if you would do the honors . . .
Um, s-sure.
POOT
Whoops.
C'mon, c'mon . . .
Boom, baby!
ZAP!
Not to worry, my boy.

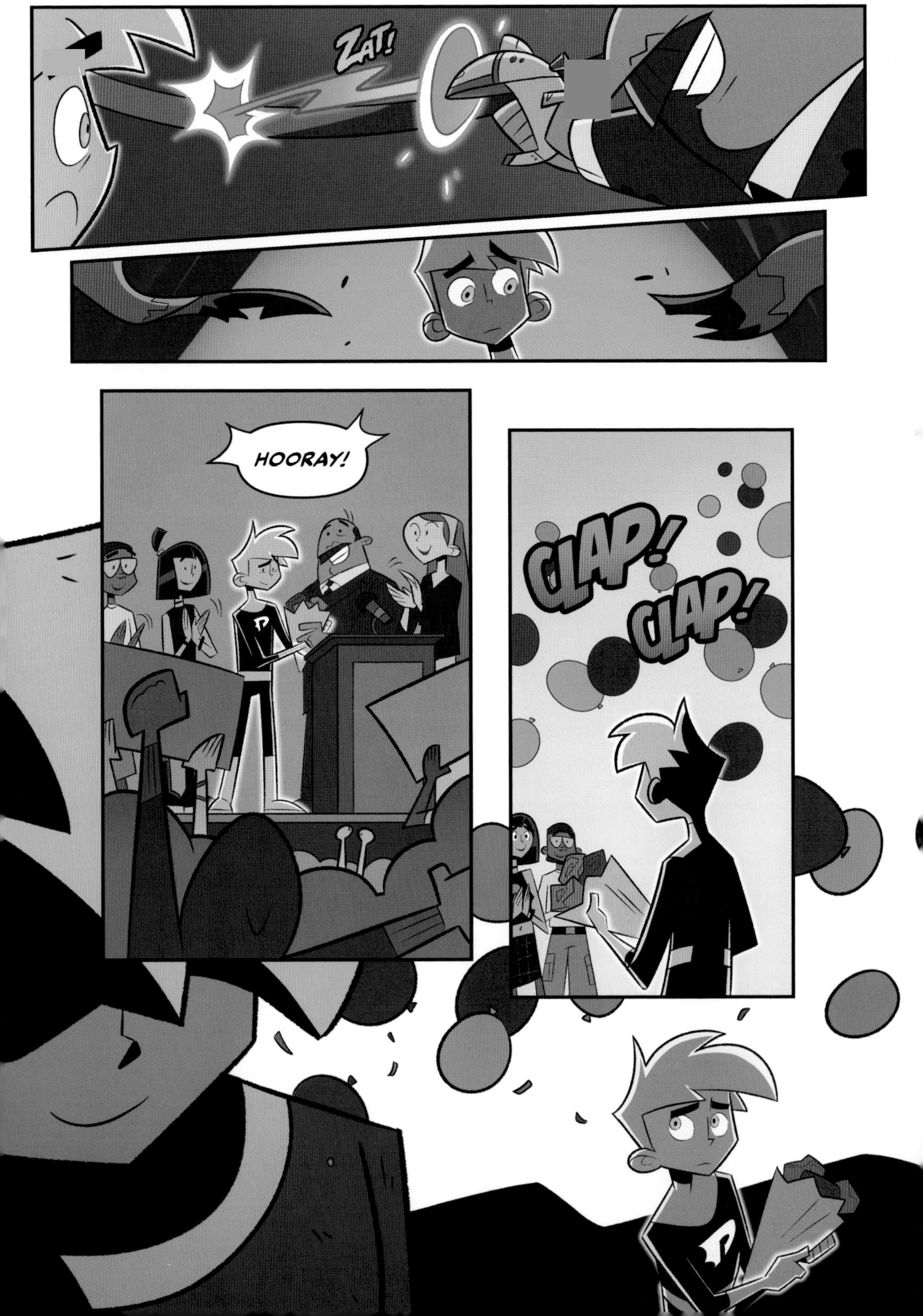
ZAT!
HOORAY!
CLAP!
CLAP!

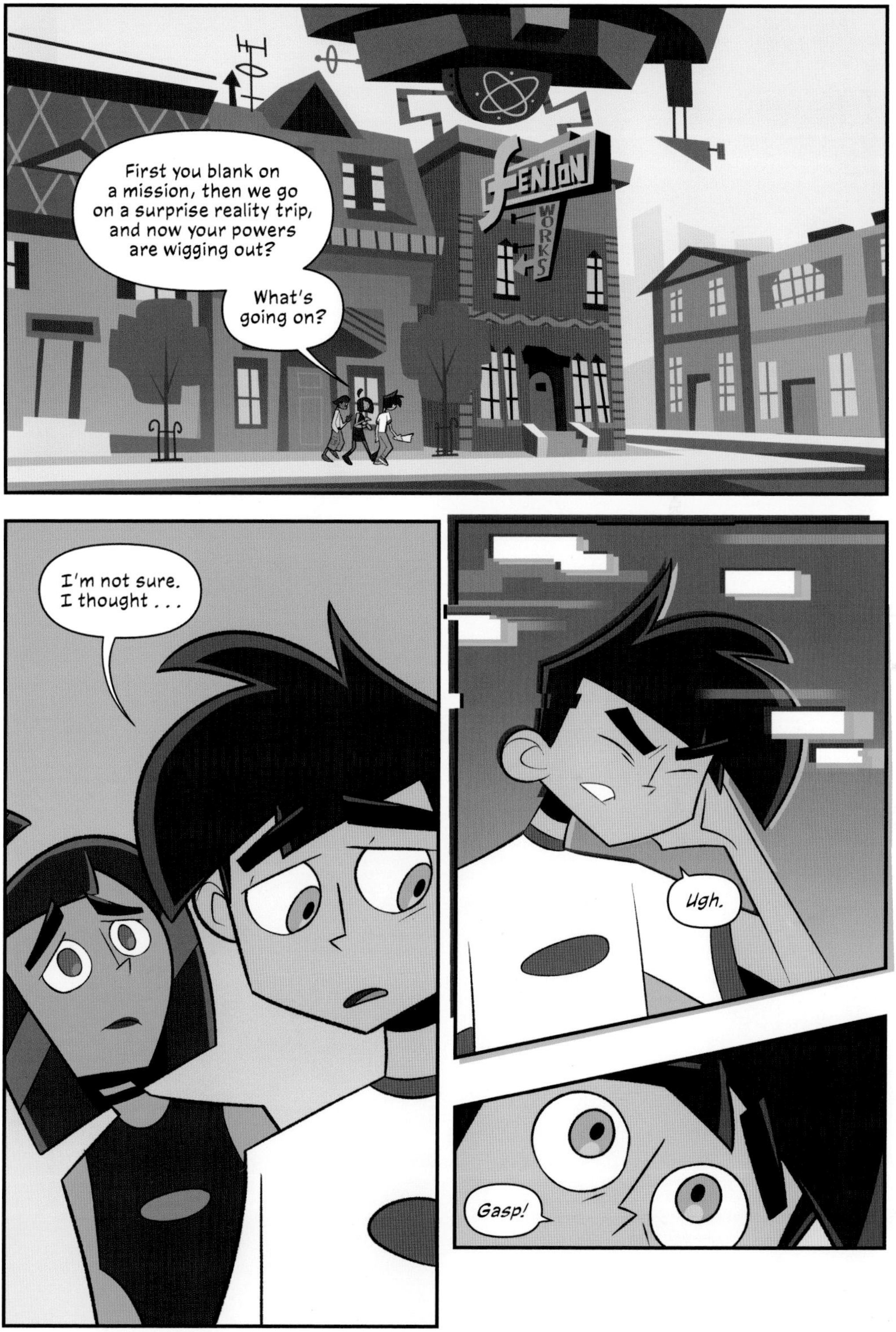

First you blank on a mission, then we go on a surprise reality trip, and now your powers are wigging out?
What's going on?
FENTON WORKS
I'm not sure. I thought . . .
Ugh.
Gasp!

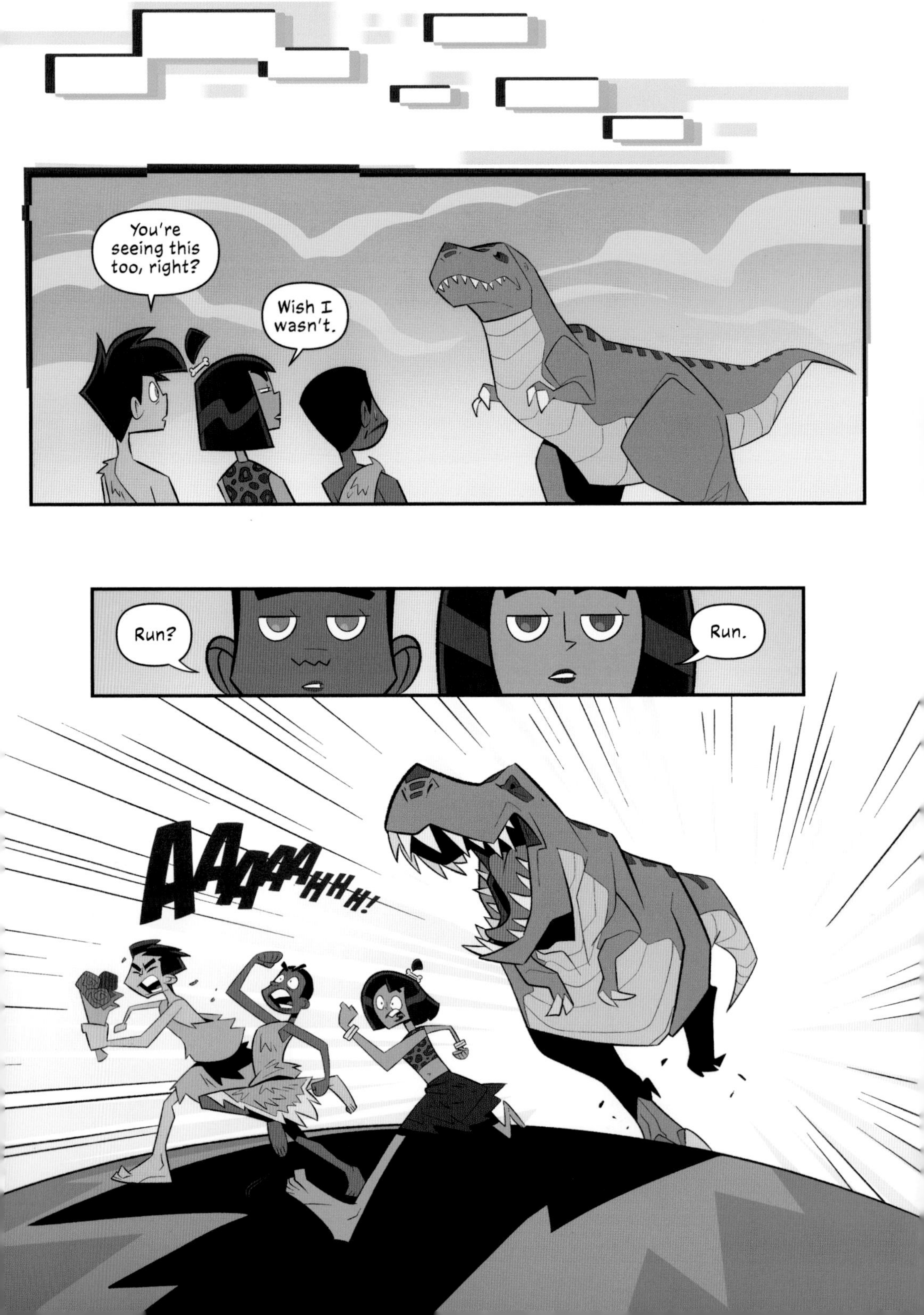
You're seeing this too, right?
Wish I wasn't.
Run?
Run.
AAAAAAHHHH!

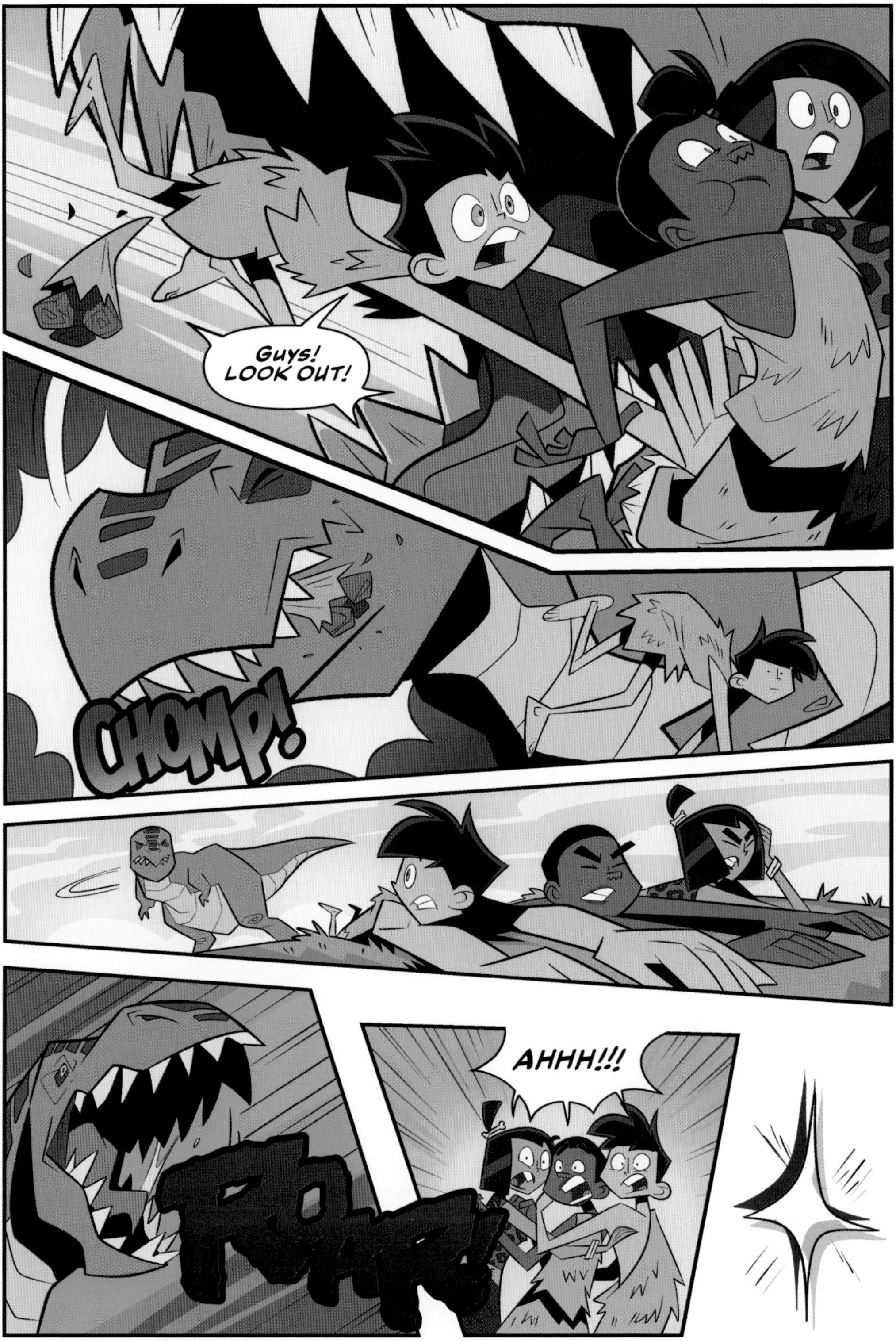
Guys!
LOOK OUT!
CHOMP!
AHHH!!!

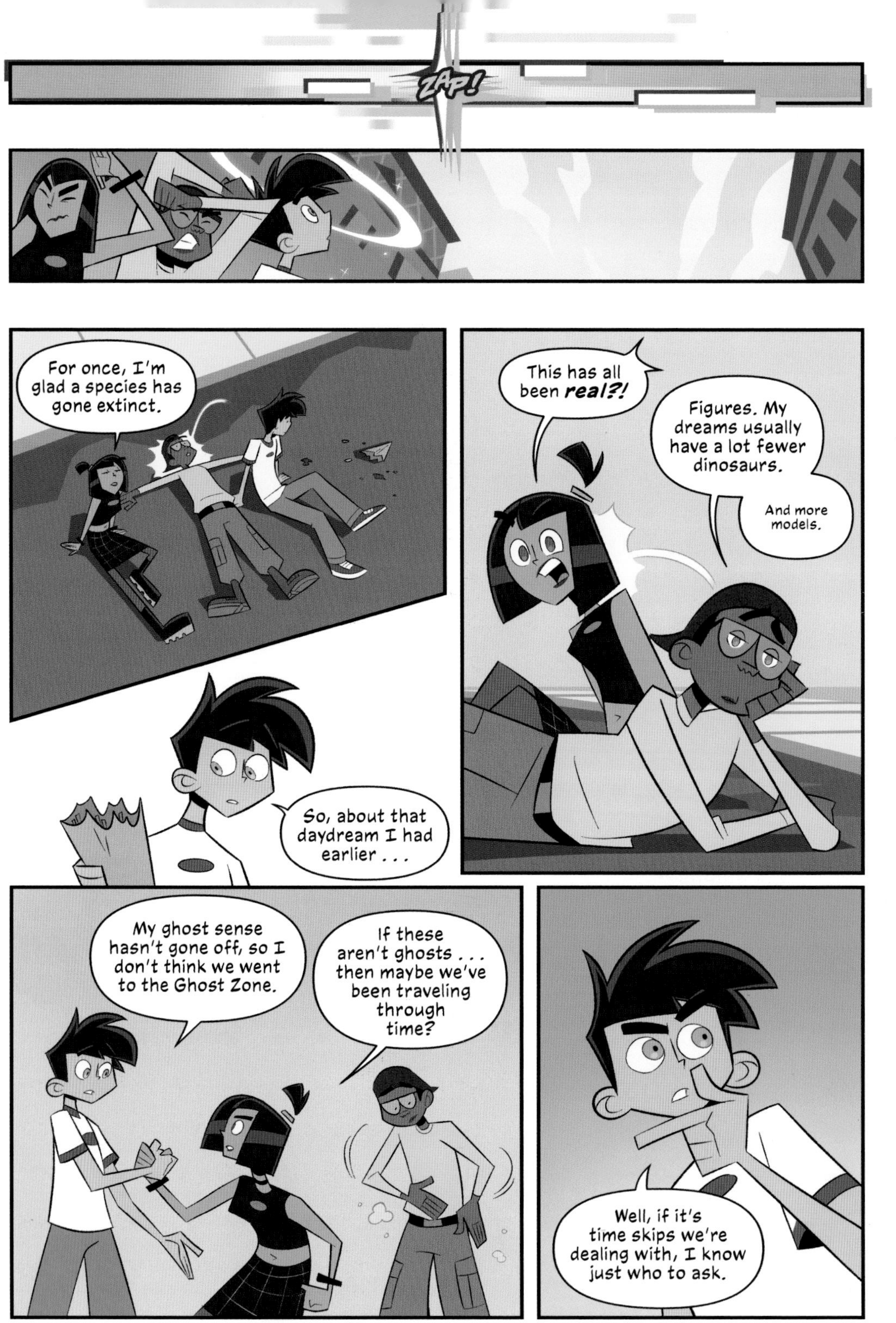

ZAP!
For once, I'm glad a species has gone extinct.
This has all been ***real?!***
Figures. My dreams usually have a lot fewer dinosaurs.
And more models.
So, about that daydream I had earlier . . .
My ghost sense hasn't gone off, so I don't think we went to the Ghost Zone.
If these aren't ghosts . . . then maybe we've been traveling through time?
Well, if it's time skips we're dealing with, I know just who to ask.

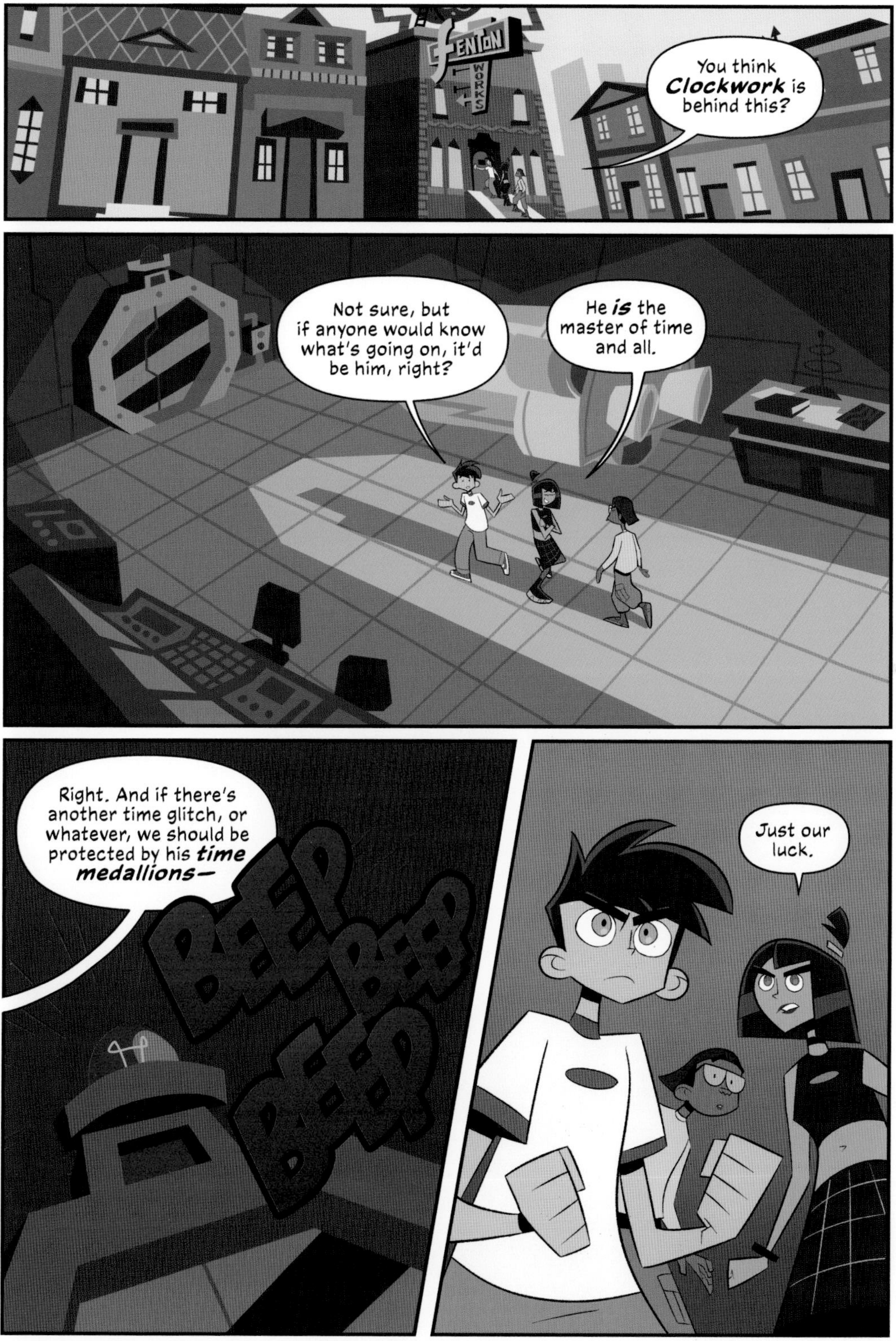
FENTON
WORKS
You think **Clockwork** is behind this?
Not sure, but if anyone would know what's going on, it'd be him, right?
He ***is*** the master of time and all.
Right. And if there's another time glitch, or whatever, we should be protected by his ***time medallions—***
BEEP
BEEP
BEEP
Just our luck.

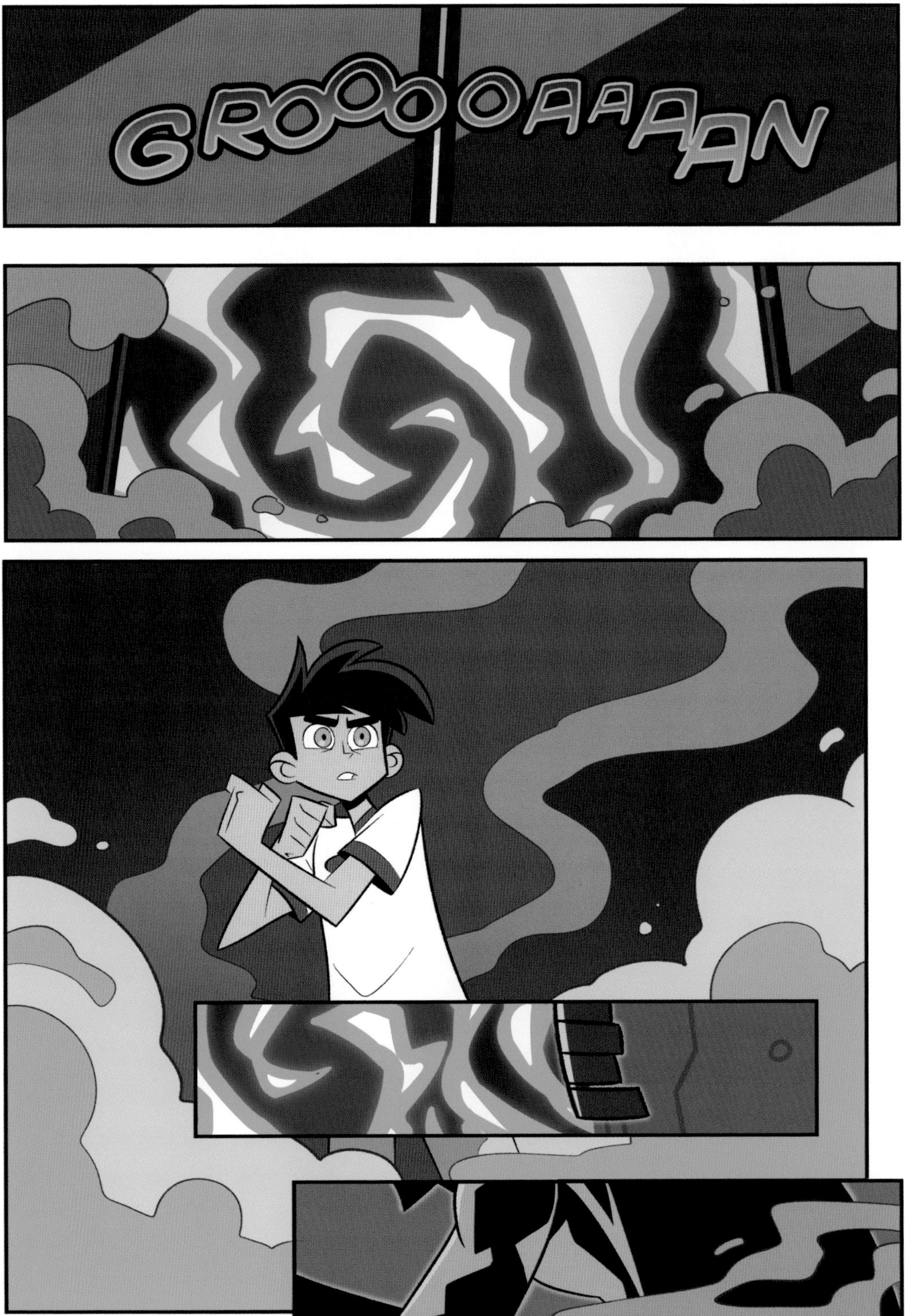
GROOOOAAAAAN

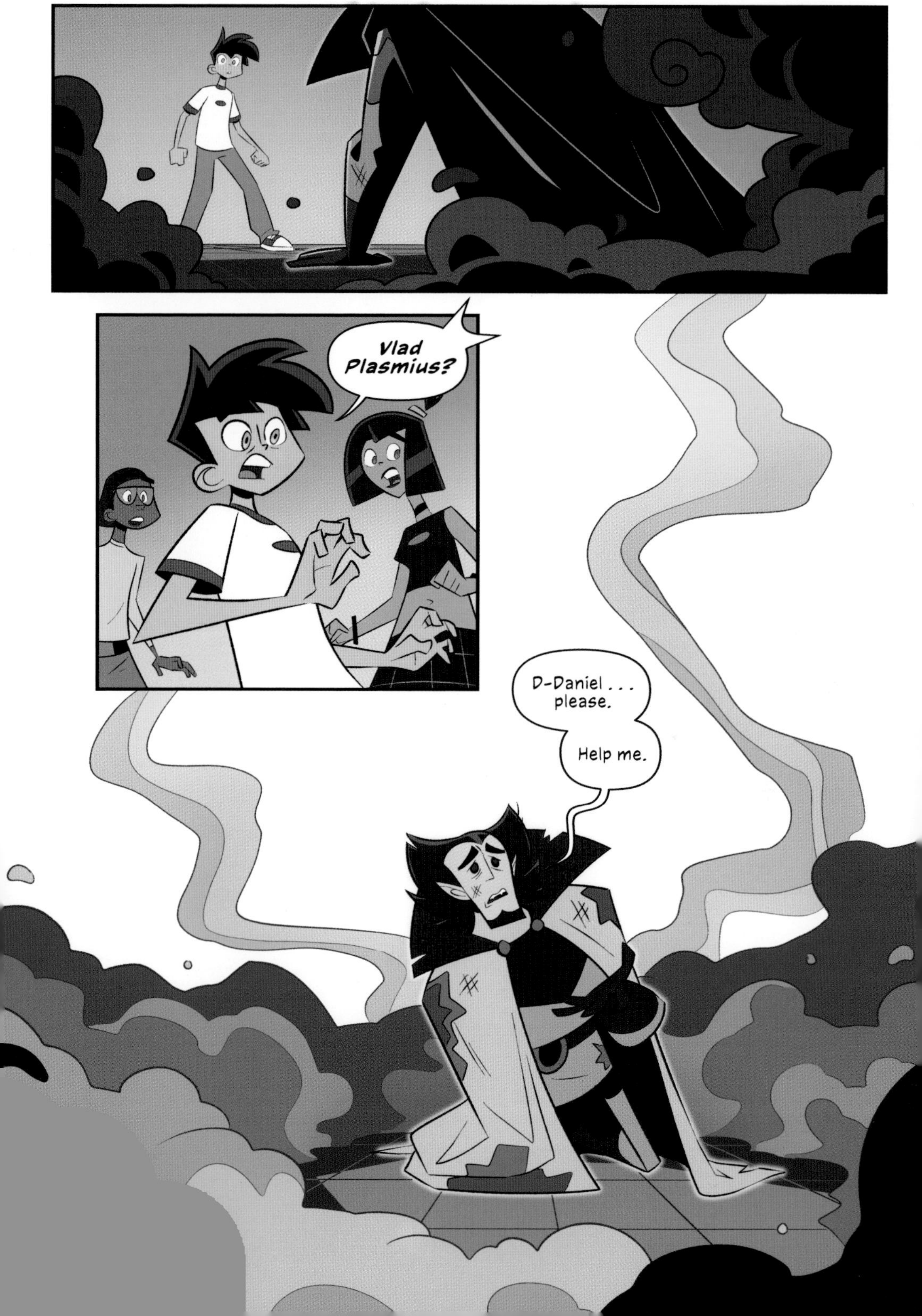
Vlad Plasmius?
D-Daniel . . . please.
Help me.

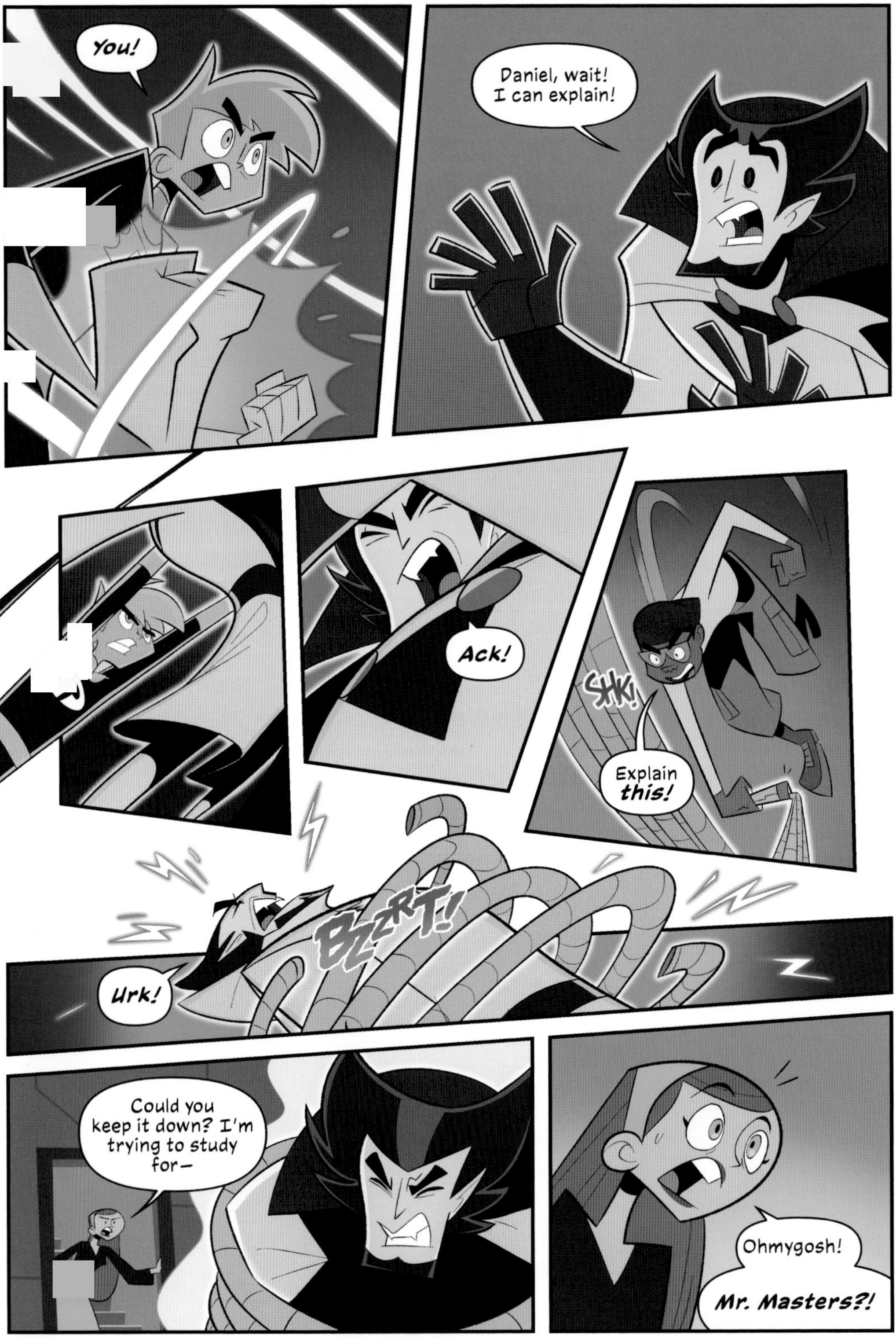
You!
Daniel, wait! I can explain!
Ack!
SHK!
Explain this!
BZZRT!
Urk!
Could you keep it down? I'm trying to study for—
Ohmygosh!
Mr. Masters?!

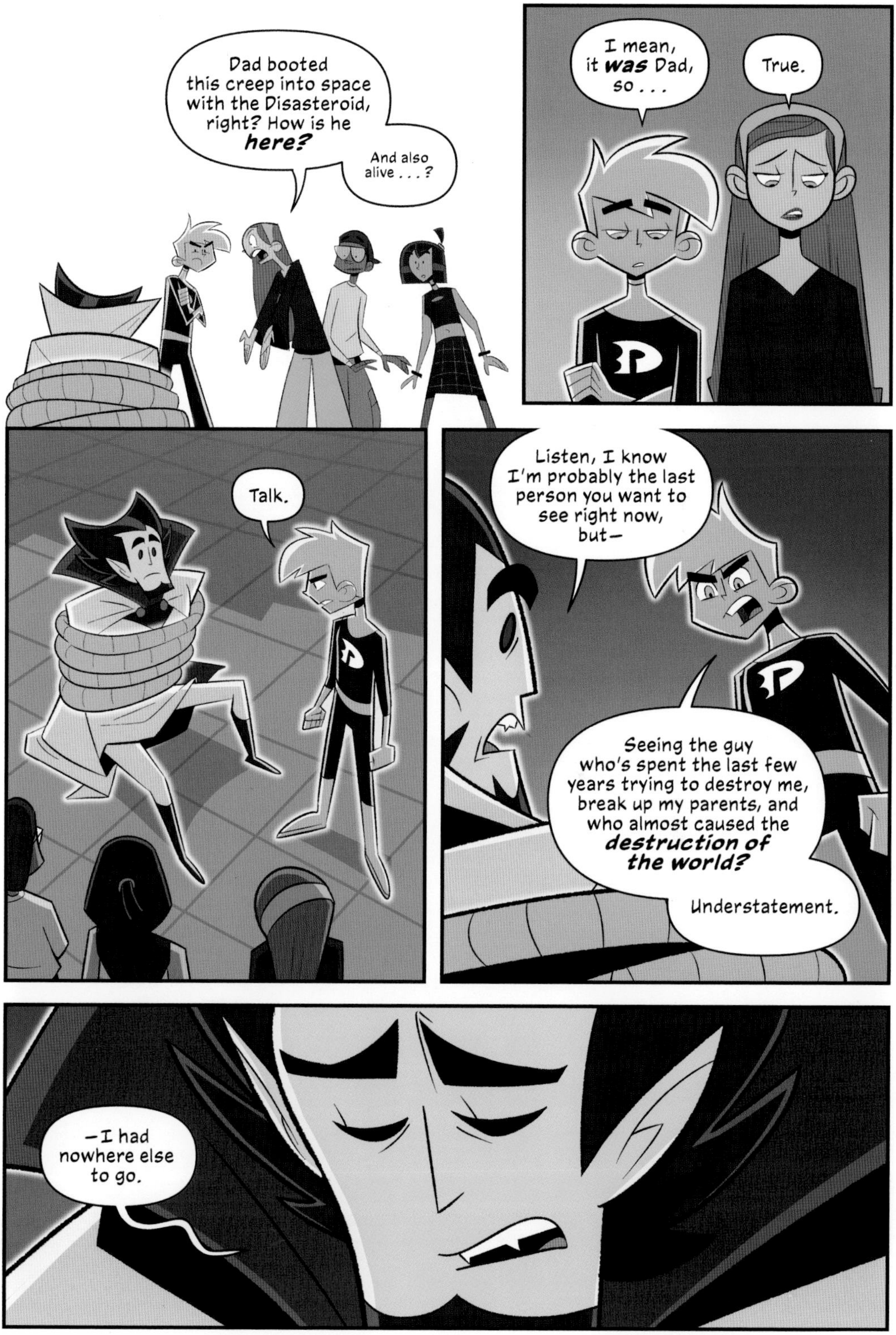
Dad booted this creep into space with the Disasteroid, right? How is he ***here?***
And also alive . . . ?
I mean, it ***was*** Dad, so . . .
True.
Talk.
Listen, I know I'm probably the last person you want to see right now, but—
Seeing the guy who's spent the last few years trying to destroy me, break up my parents, and who almost caused the ***destruction of the world?***
Understatement.
—I had nowhere else to go.

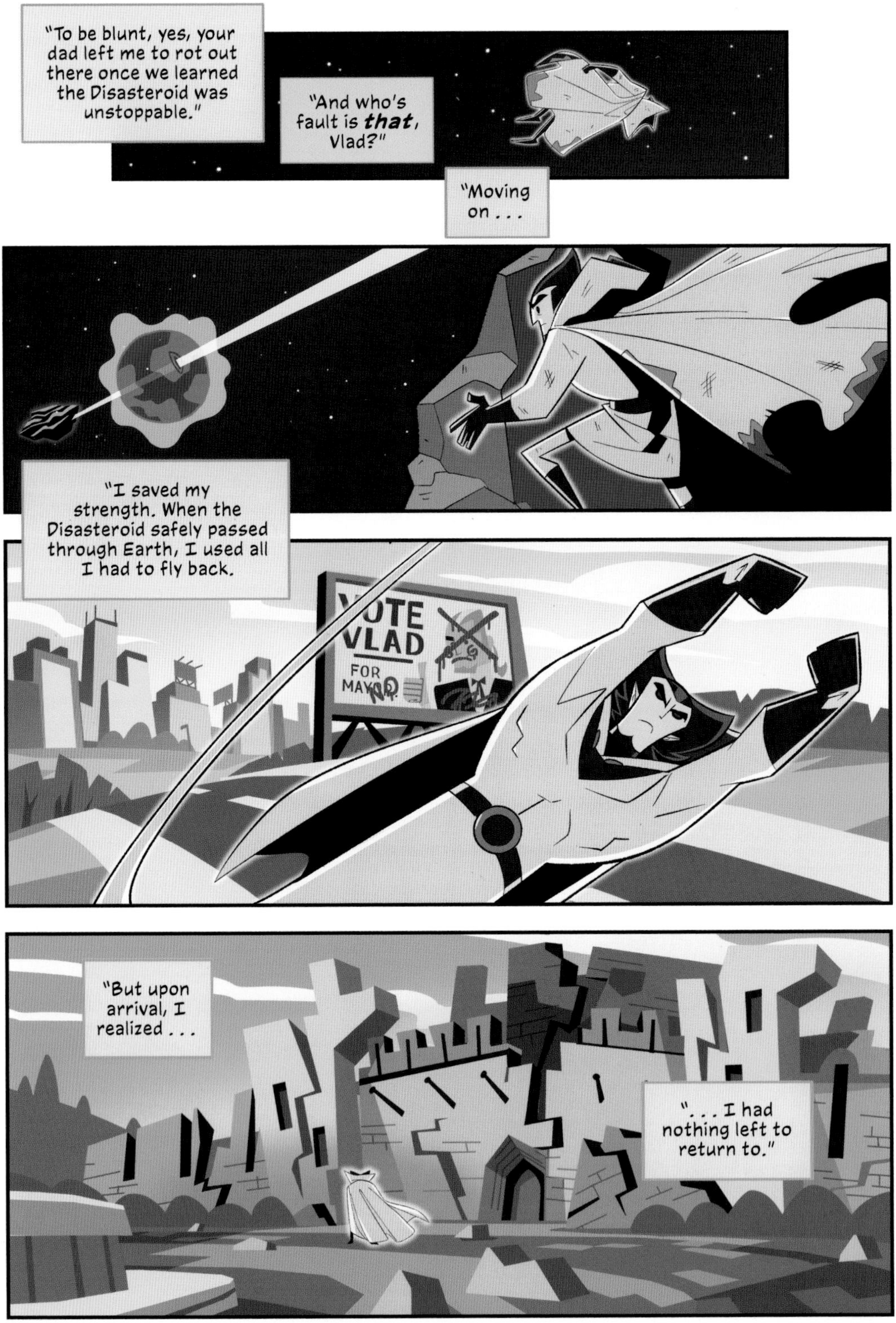
"To be blunt, yes, your dad left me to rot out there once we learned the Disasteroid was unstoppable."
"And who's fault is ***that***, Vlad?"
"Moving on . . .
"I saved my strength. When the Disasteroid safely passed through Earth, I used all I had to fly back.
VOTE
VLAD
FOR
"But upon arrival, I realized . . .
". . . I had nothing left to return to."

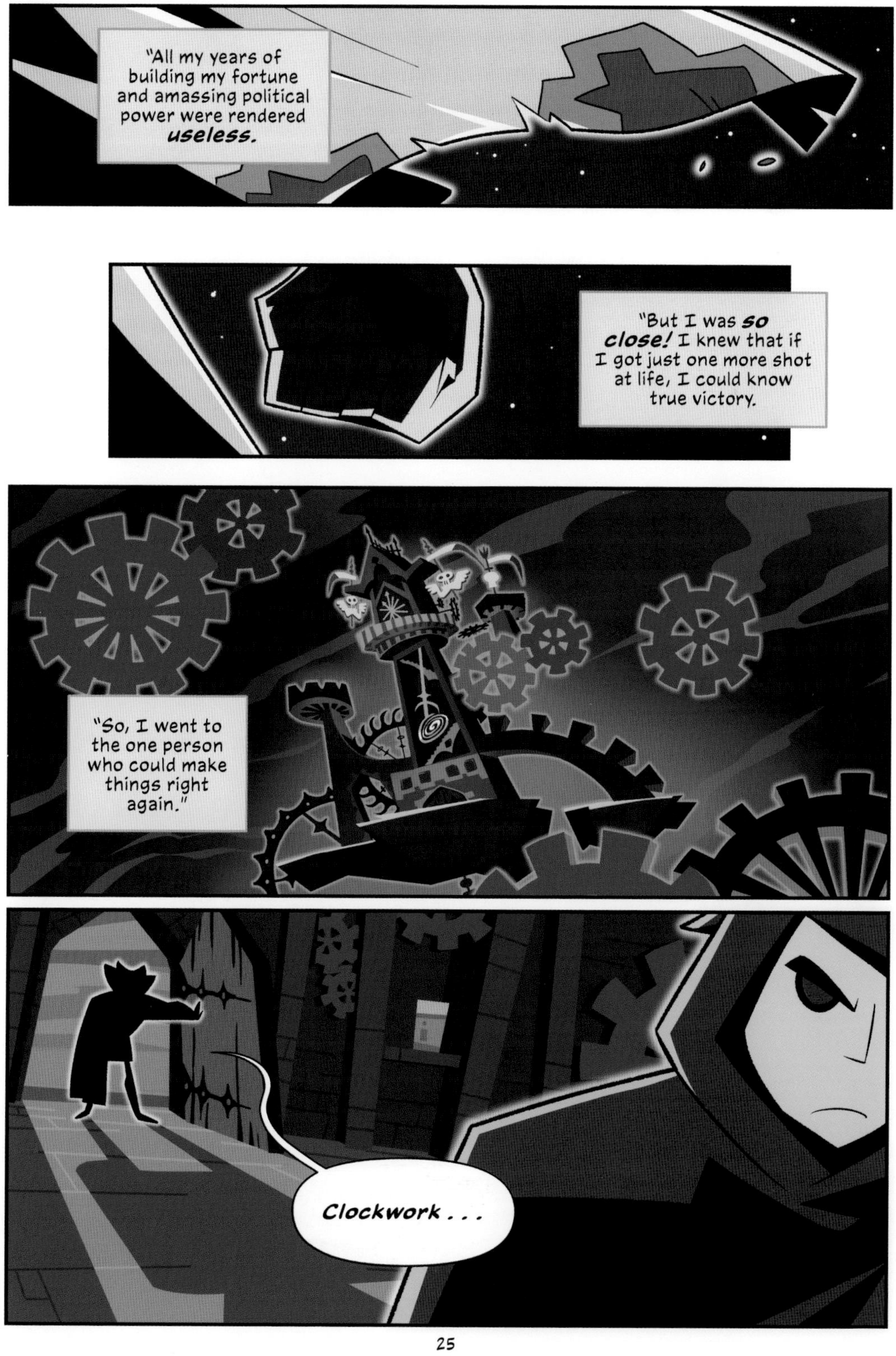
"All my years of building my fortune and amassing political power were rendered *useless.*
"But I was ***so close!*** I knew that if I got just one more shot at life, I could know true victory.
"So, I went to the one person who could make things right again."
Clockwork . . .

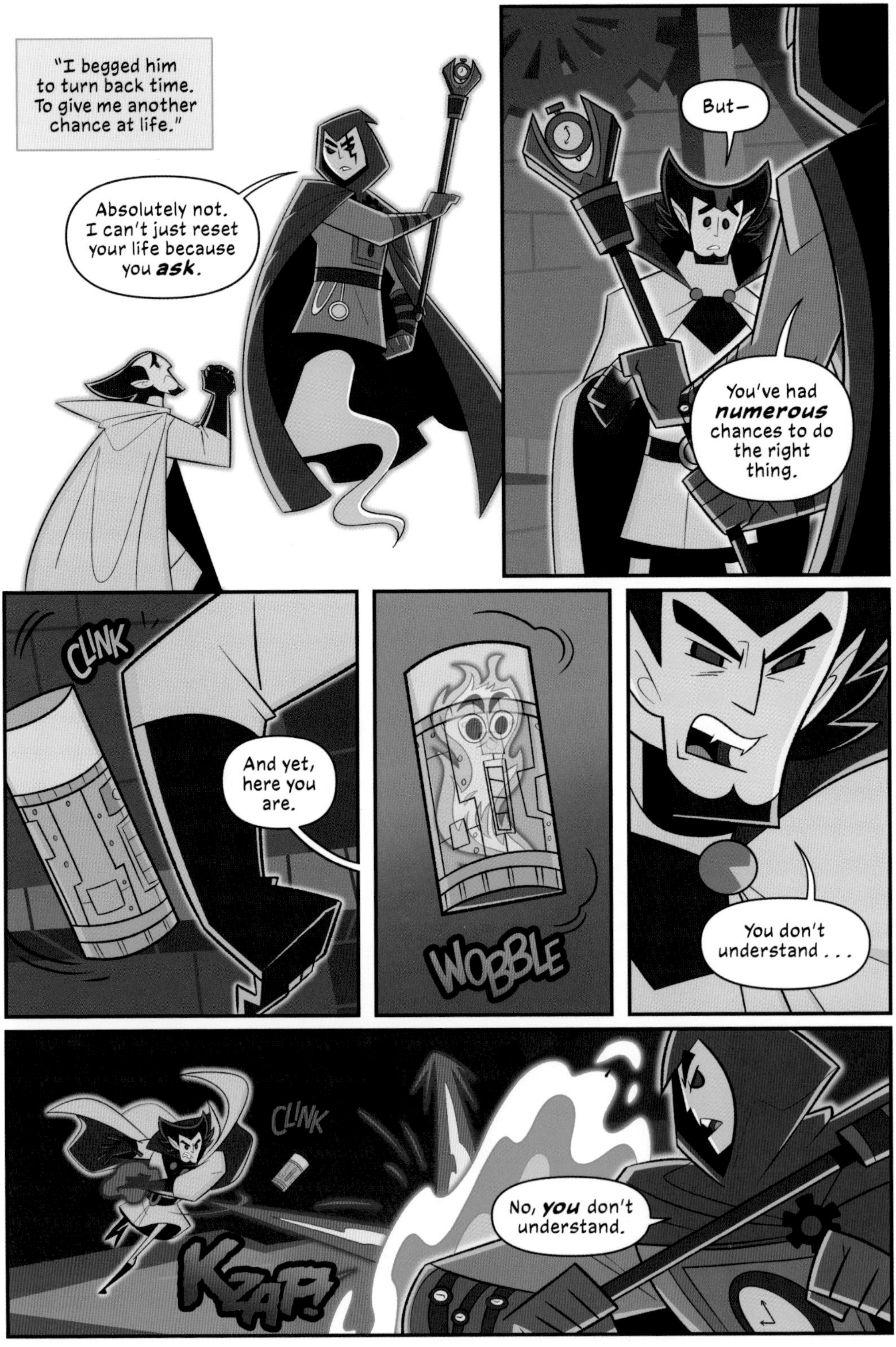

"I begged him to turn back time. To give me another chance at life."
Absolutely not. I can't just reset your life because you ***ask***.
But—
You've had ***numerous*** chances to do the right thing.
CLINK
And yet, here you are.
WOBBLE
You don't understand . . .
CLINK
KZAP!
No, ***you*** don't understand.

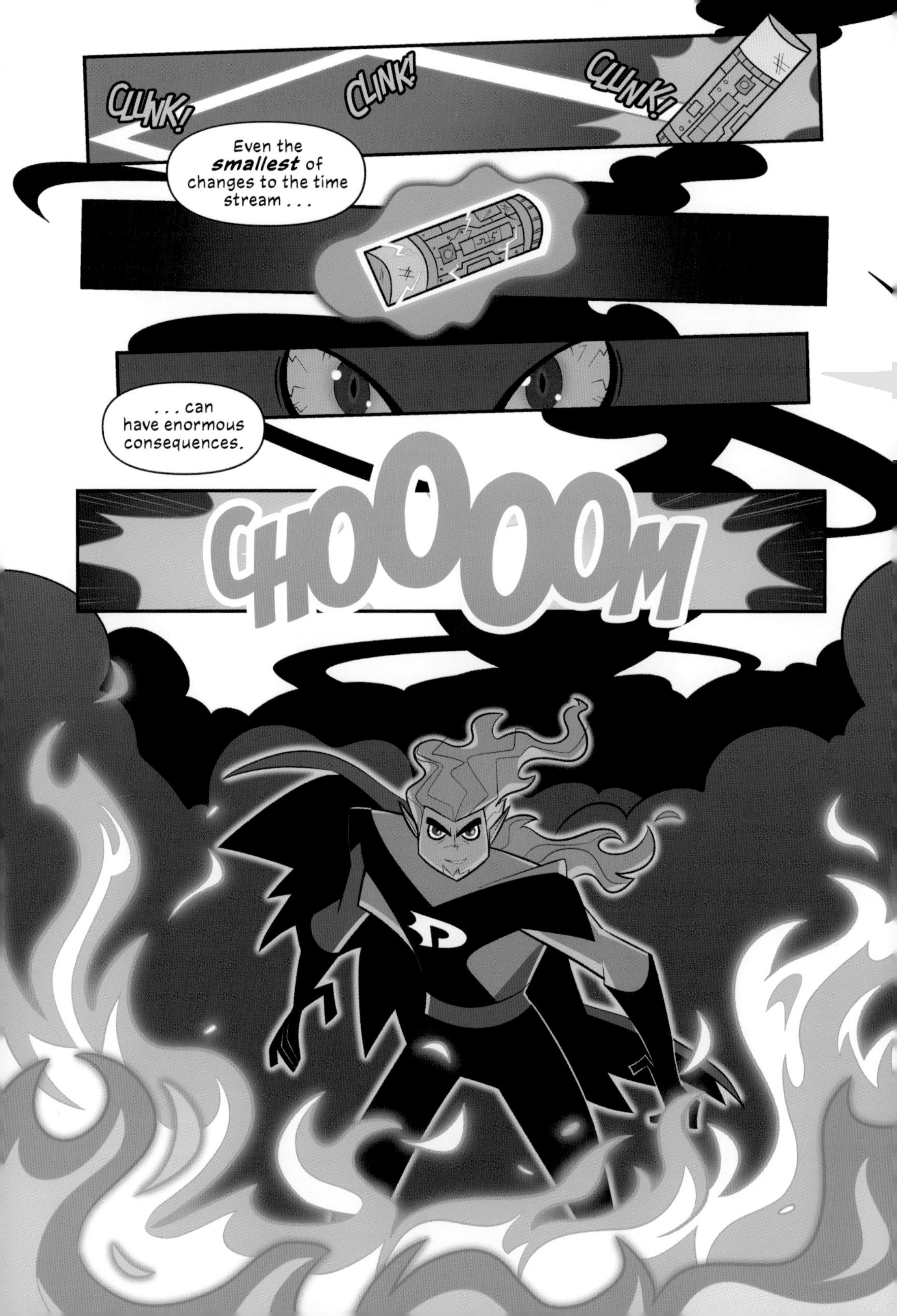
CLINK!
CLINK!
CLINK!
Even the ***smallest*** of changes to the time stream . . .
. . . can have enormous consequences.
CHOOOOM

FINALLY!

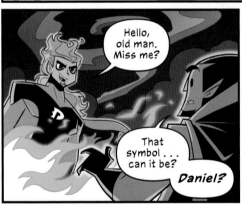

Hello, old man. Miss me?

That symbol... can it be?

Daniel?

Not anymore. I'm the combination of his ghost-self and yours. I'm *all phantom.*

At least, in my timeline I am.

Time OUT!

A timeline that will *never* happen.

A clone...?

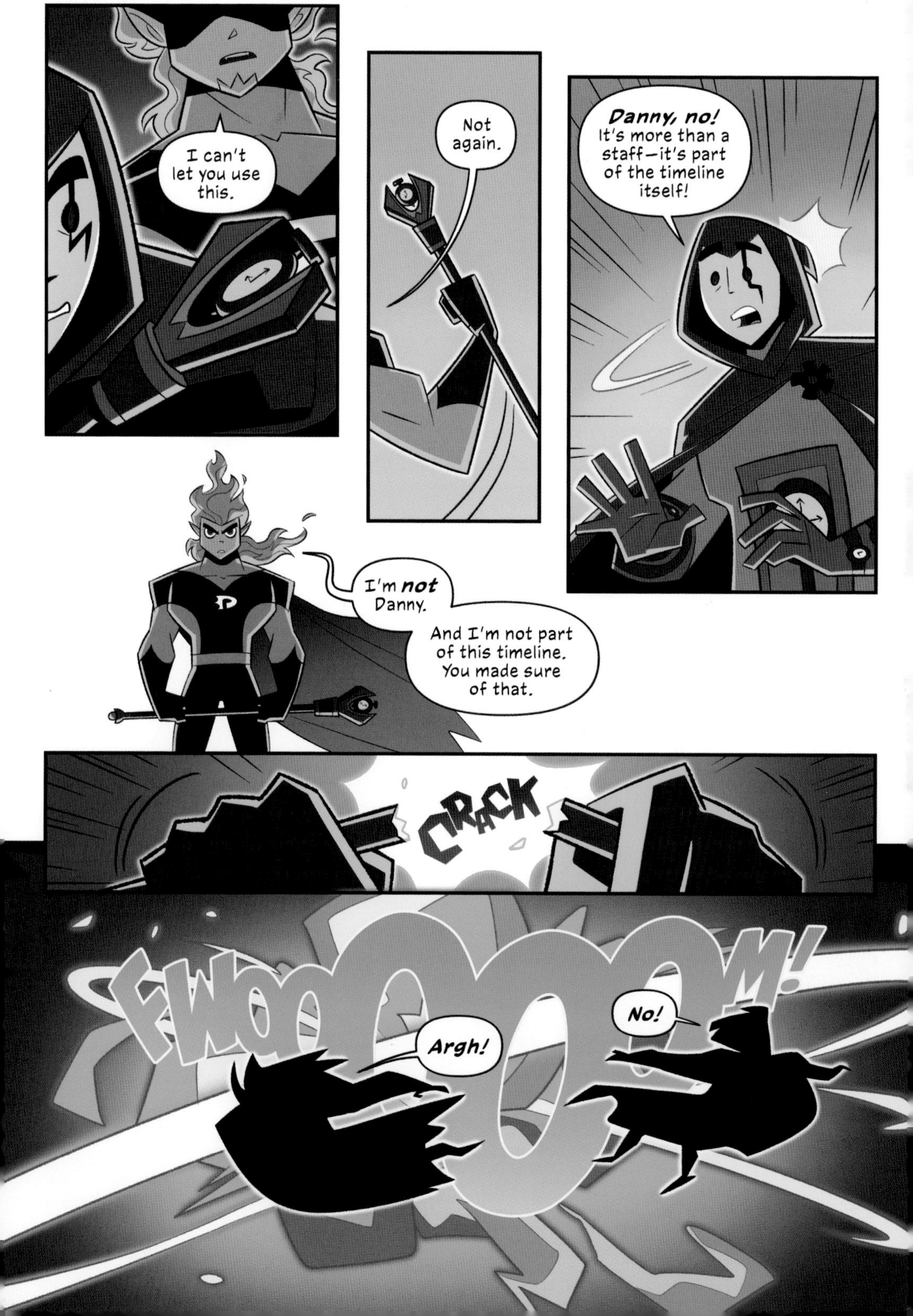

I can't let you use this.
Not again.
Danny, no! It's more than a staff—it's part of the timeline itself!
I'm not Danny.
And I'm not part of this timeline. You made sure of that.
CRACK
FWOOOOOM!
Argh!
No!

I'm afraid I can't let you threaten the timeline like this.

"Naturally, I put up a brave fight . . ."

Plasmius—

sigh . . .

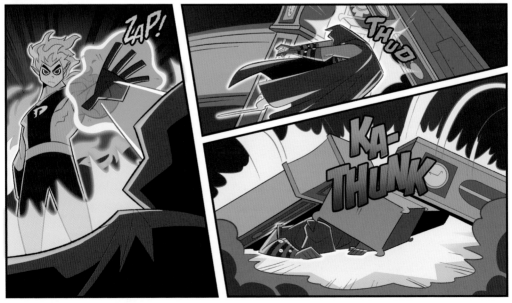

ZAP!

THUD

KA-THUNK

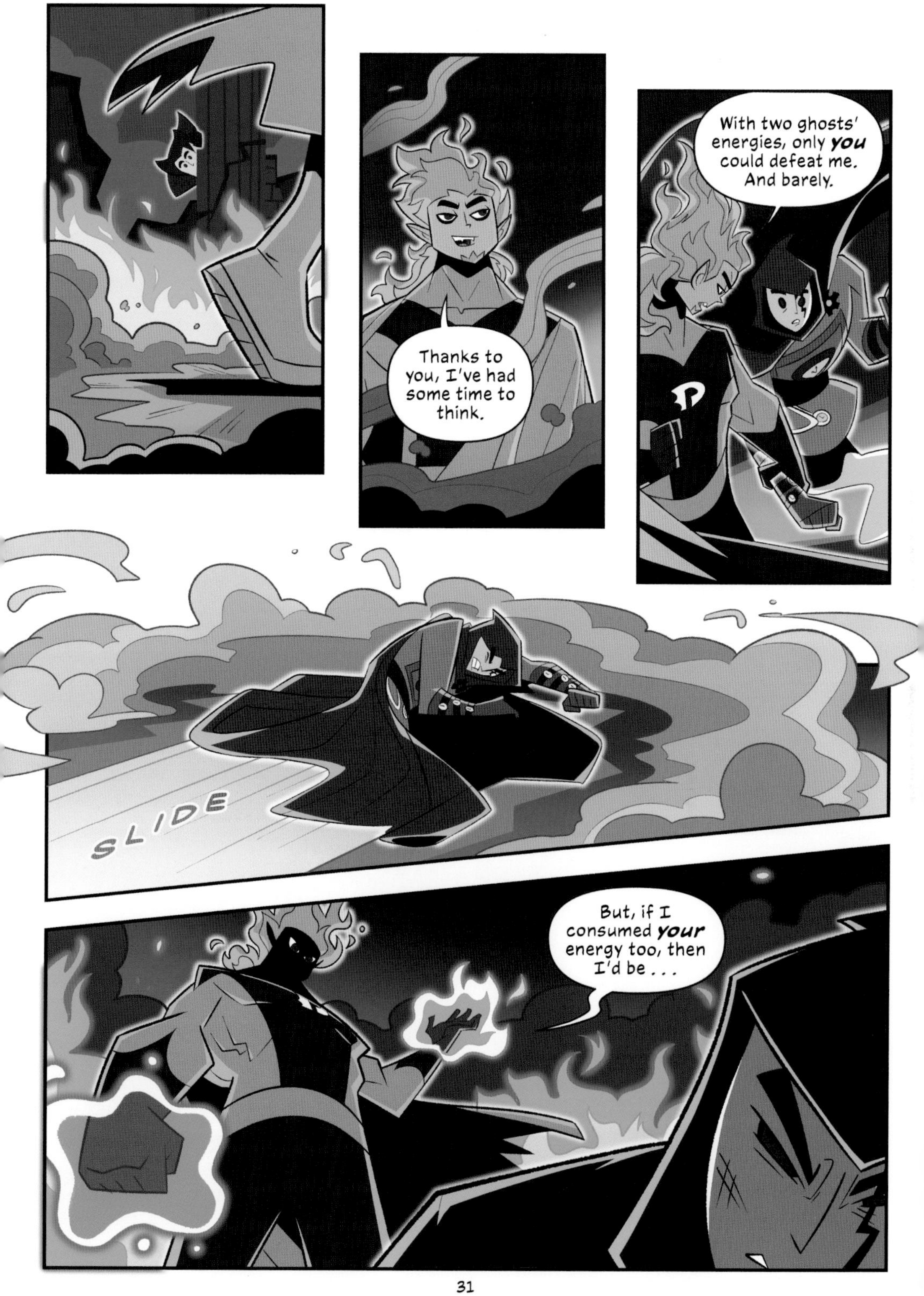
Thanks to you, I've had some time to think.
With two ghosts' energies, only ***you*** could defeat me. And barely.
SLIDE
But, if I consumed ***your*** energy too, then I'd be . . .

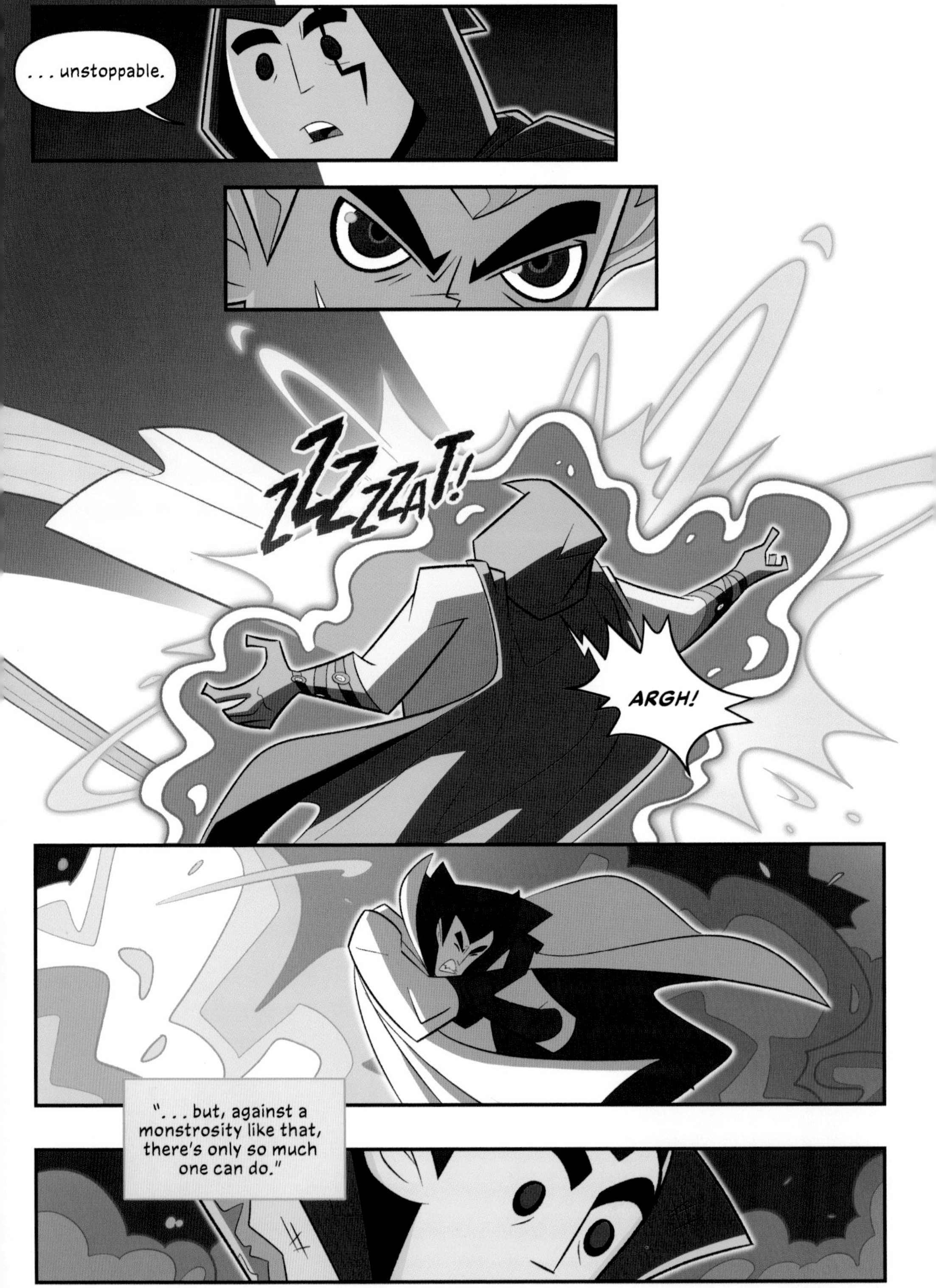

. . . unstoppable.
ZZZZZAT!
ARGH!
". . . but, against a monstrosity like that, there's only so much one can do."

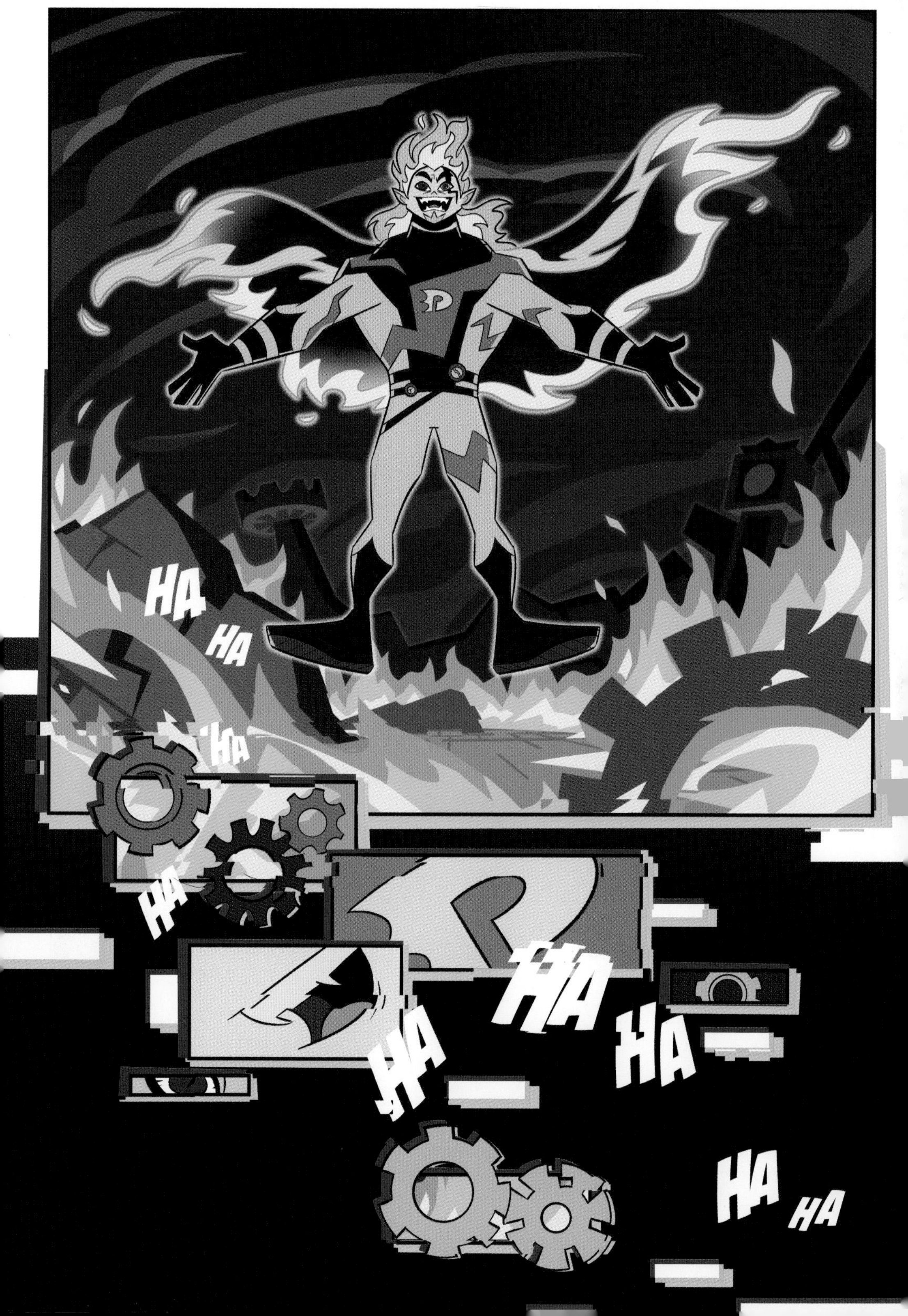
HA
HA
HA
HA
HA
HA
HA
HA
HA

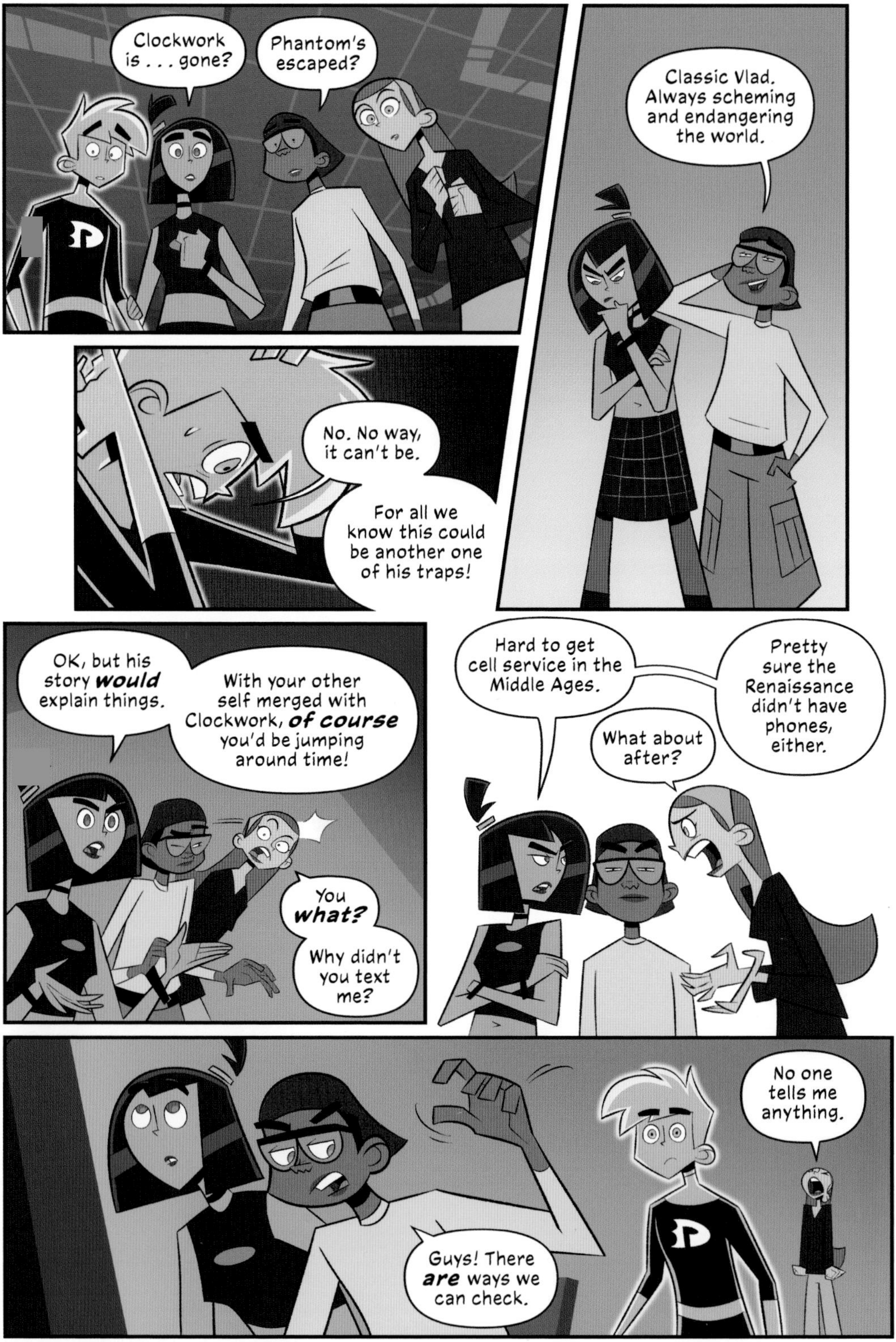
Clockwork is . . . gone?
Phantom's escaped?
Classic Vlad. Always scheming and endangering the world.
No. No way, it can't be.
For all we know this could be another one of his traps!
OK, but his story *would* explain things.
With your other self merged with Clockwork, *of course* you'd be jumping around time!
You *what?*
Why didn't you text me?
Hard to get cell service in the Middle Ages.
Pretty sure the Renaissance didn't have phones, either.
What about after?
No one tells me anything.
Guys! There *are* ways we can check.

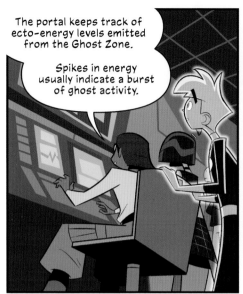

The portal keeps track of ecto-energy levels emitted from the Ghost Zone.

Spikes in energy usually indicate a burst of ghost activity.

And right now? We've got **atomic bomb-level** readings.

These energy levels are enough to tear a hole in the Ghost Zone itself!

If the situation's not stabilized, we're due for a **complete implosion** in less than twenty-four hours.

But if the Ghost Zone is destroyed, the human world goes, too!

I'm sorry, Daniel, but as you can see, our reality itself hangs in the balance.

Because of you!

Again!

Well, I wouldn't say it was **only** me . . .

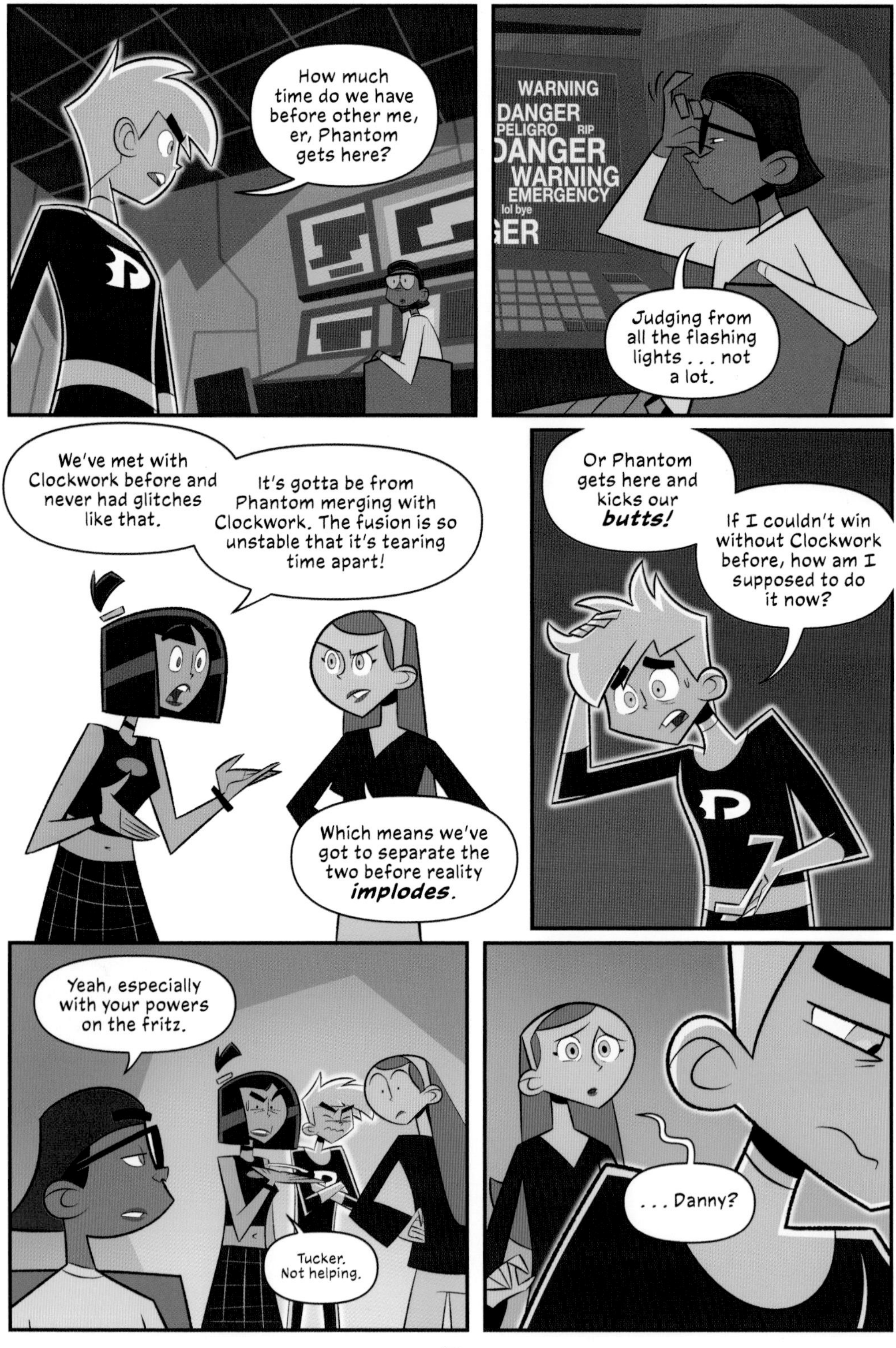
How much time do we have before other me, er, Phantom gets here?
WARNING
DANGER
PELIGRO
RIP
DANGER
WARNING
EMERGENCY
lol bye
GER
Judging from all the flashing lights . . . not a lot.
We've met with Clockwork before and never had glitches like that.
It's gotta be from Phantom merging with Clockwork. The fusion is so unstable that it's tearing time apart!
Which means we've got to separate the two before reality *implodes*.
Or Phantom gets here and kicks our *butts!*
If I couldn't win without Clockwork before, how am I supposed to do it now?
Yeah, especially with your powers on the fritz.
Tucker. Not helping.
. . . Danny?

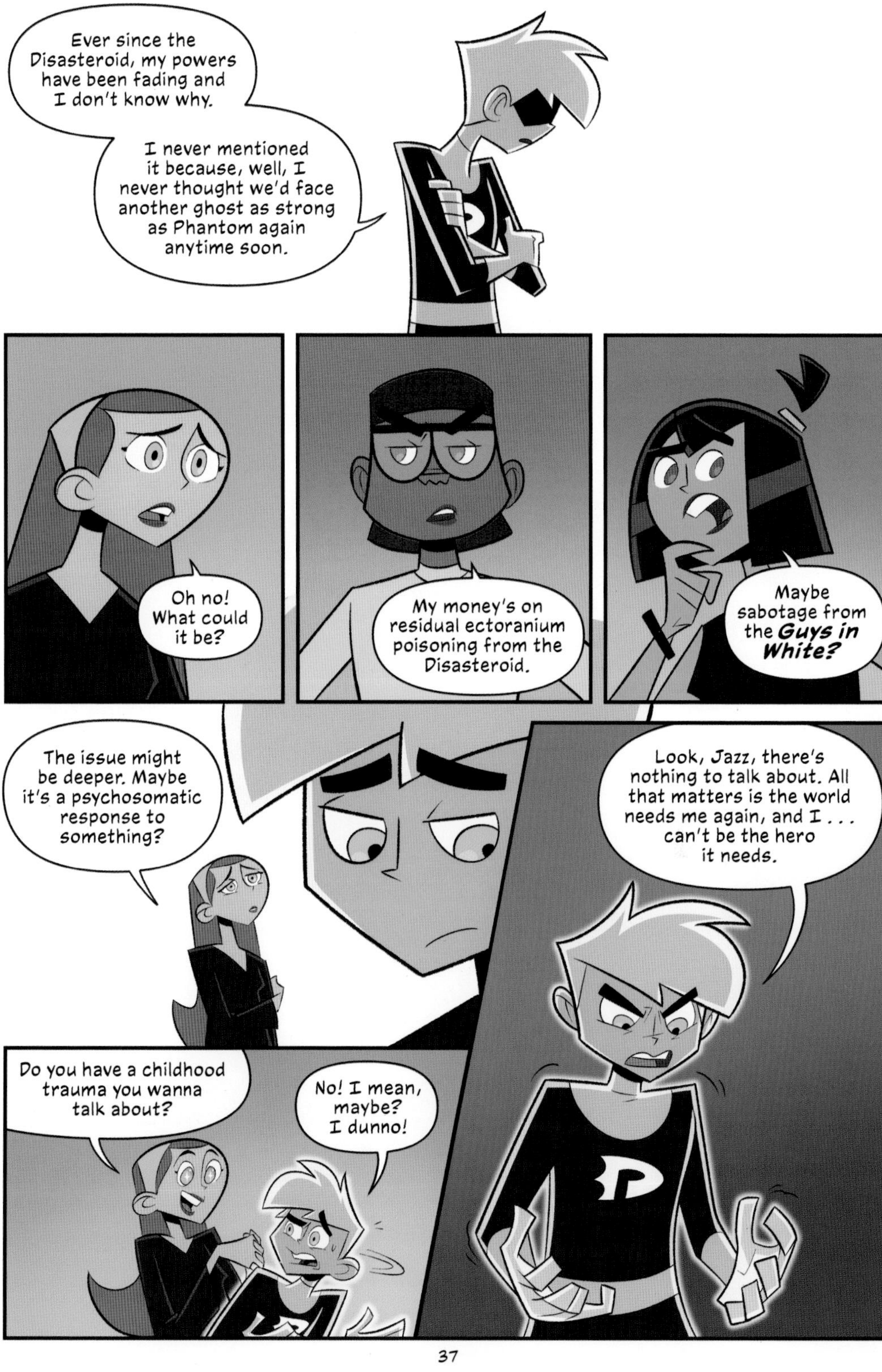
Ever since the Disasteroid, my powers have been fading and I don't know why.
I never mentioned it because, well, I never thought we'd face another ghost as strong as Phantom again anytime soon.
Oh no! What could it be?
My money's on residual ectoranium poisoning from the Disasteroid.
Maybe sabotage from the ***Guys in White?***
The issue might be deeper. Maybe it's a psychosomatic response to something?
Look, Jazz, there's nothing to talk about. All that matters is the world needs me again, and I . . . can't be the hero it needs.
Do you have a childhood trauma you wanna talk about?
No! I mean, maybe? I dunno!

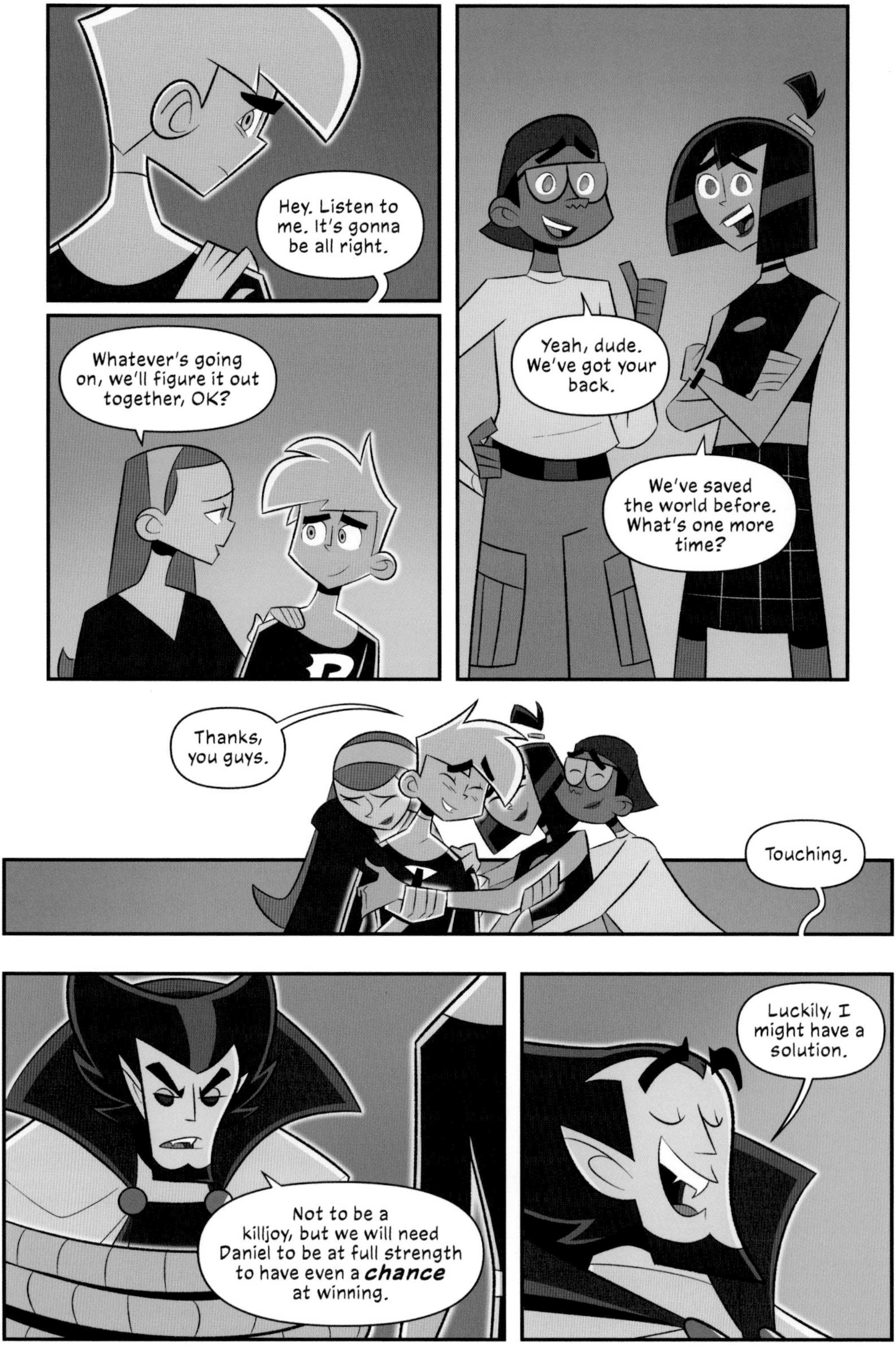
Hey. Listen to me. It's gonna be all right.
Whatever's going on, we'll figure it out together, OK?
Yeah, dude. We've got your back.
We've saved the world before. What's one more time?
Thanks, you guys.
Touching.
Not to be a killjoy, but we will need Daniel to be at full strength to have even a ***chance*** at winning.
Luckily, I might have a solution.

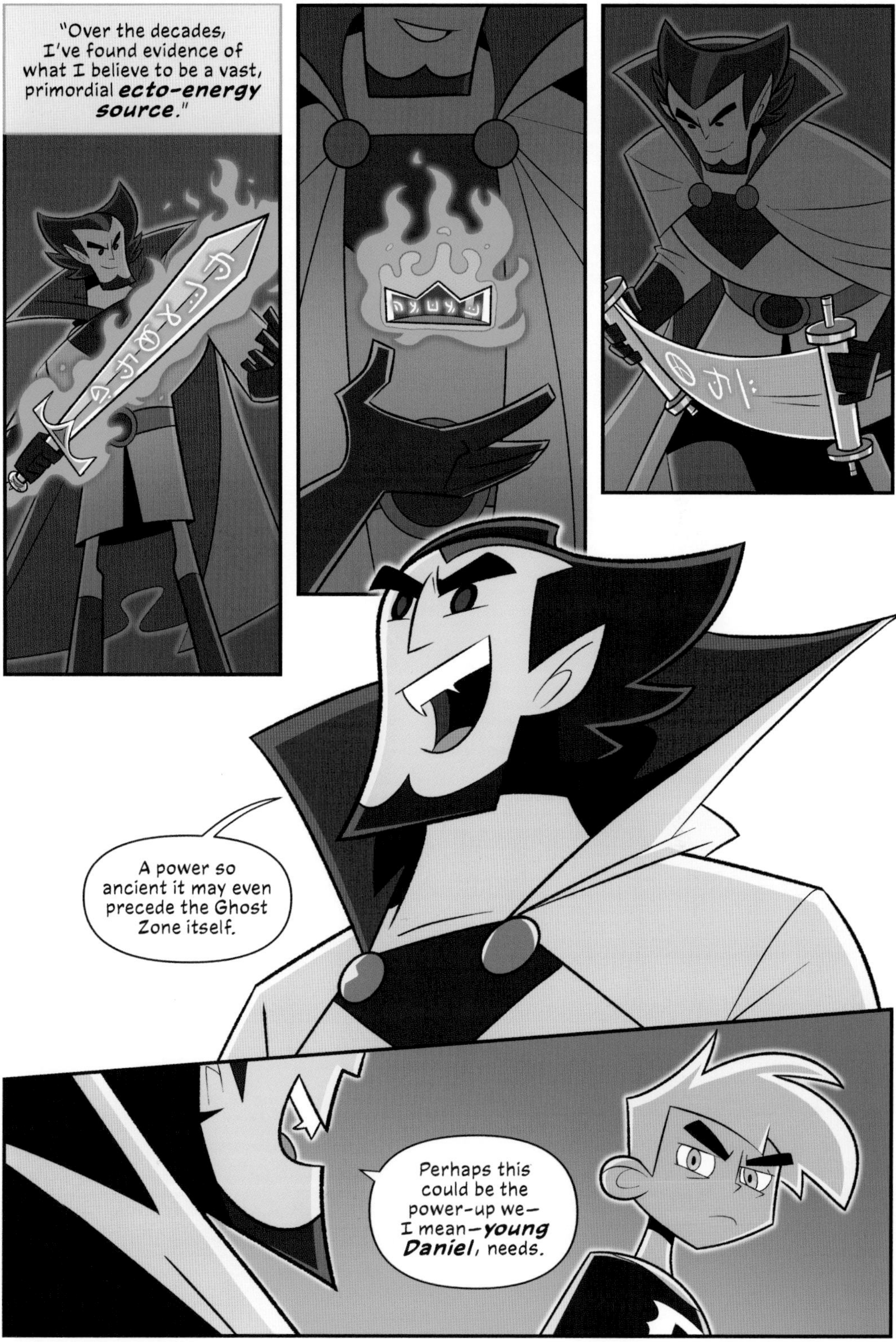
"Over the decades, I've found evidence of what I believe to be a vast, primordial ***ecto-energy source.***"
A power so ancient it may even precede the Ghost Zone itself.
Perhaps this could be the power-up we— I mean—***young Daniel***, needs.

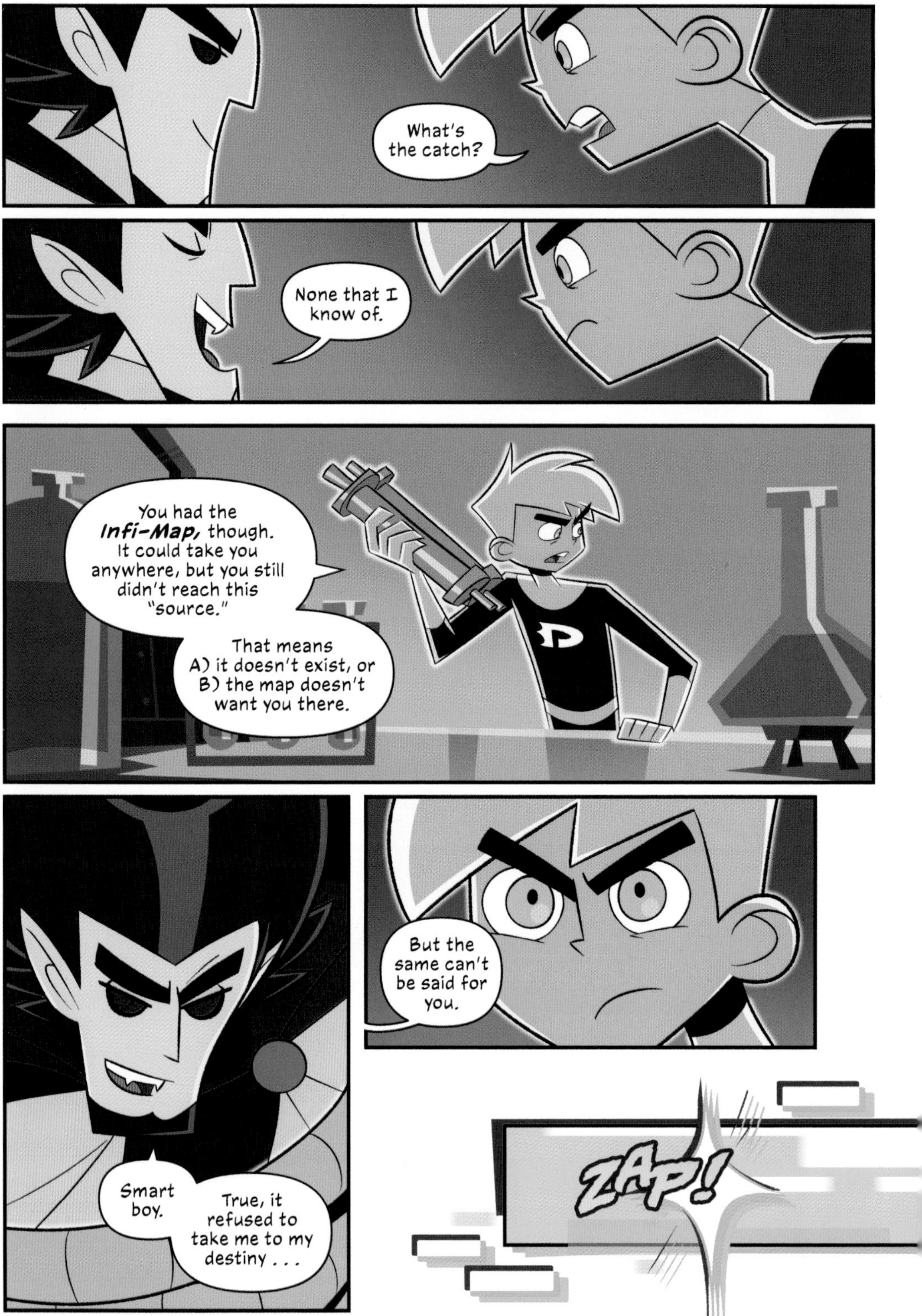
What's the catch?
None that I know of.
You had the *Infi-Map,* though. It could take you anywhere, but you still didn't reach this "source."
That means A) it doesn't exist, or B) the map doesn't want you there.
But the same can't be said for you.
Smart boy.
True, it refused to take me to my destiny . . .
ZAP!

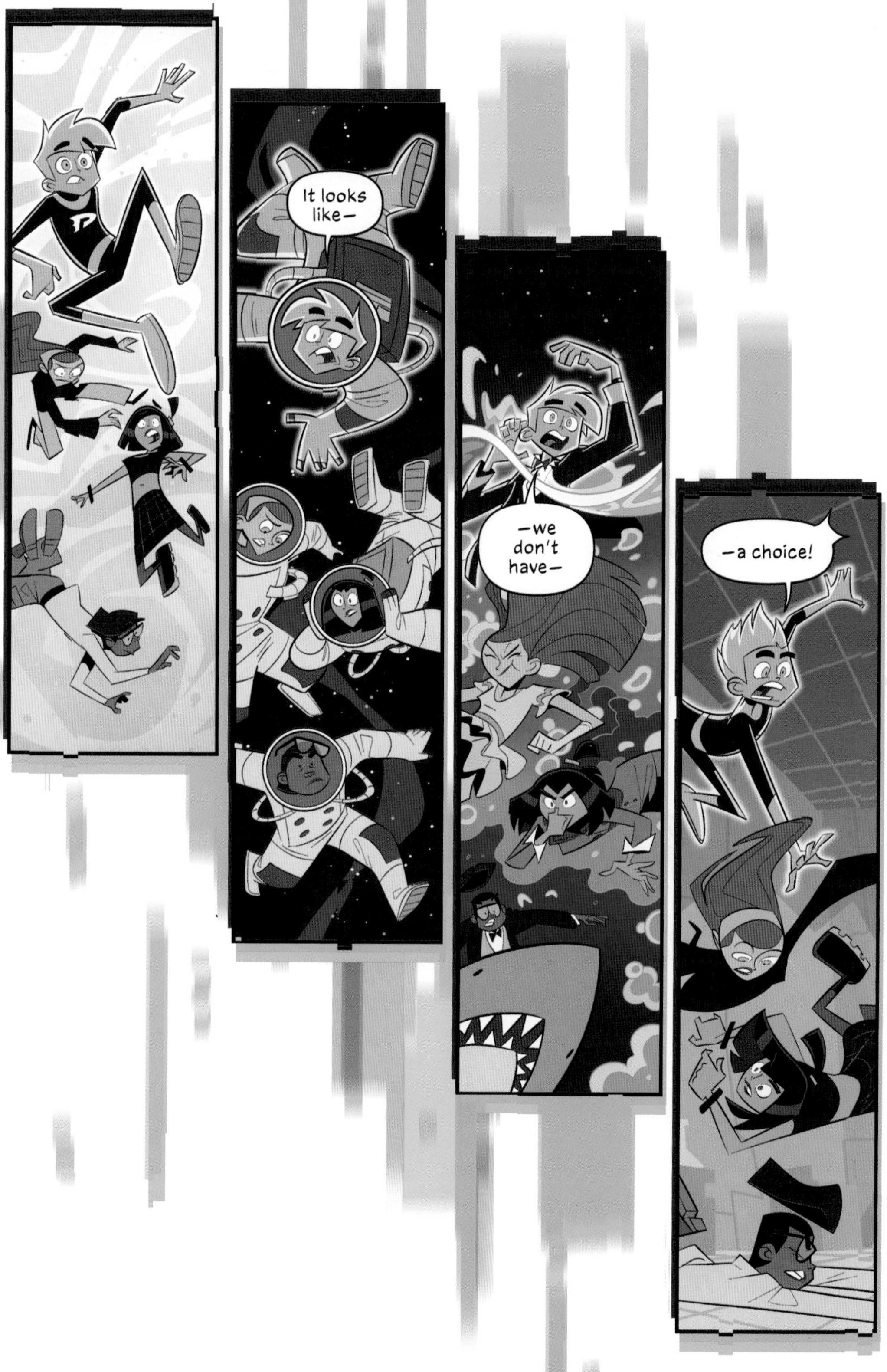

It looks like—
—we don't have—
—a choice!

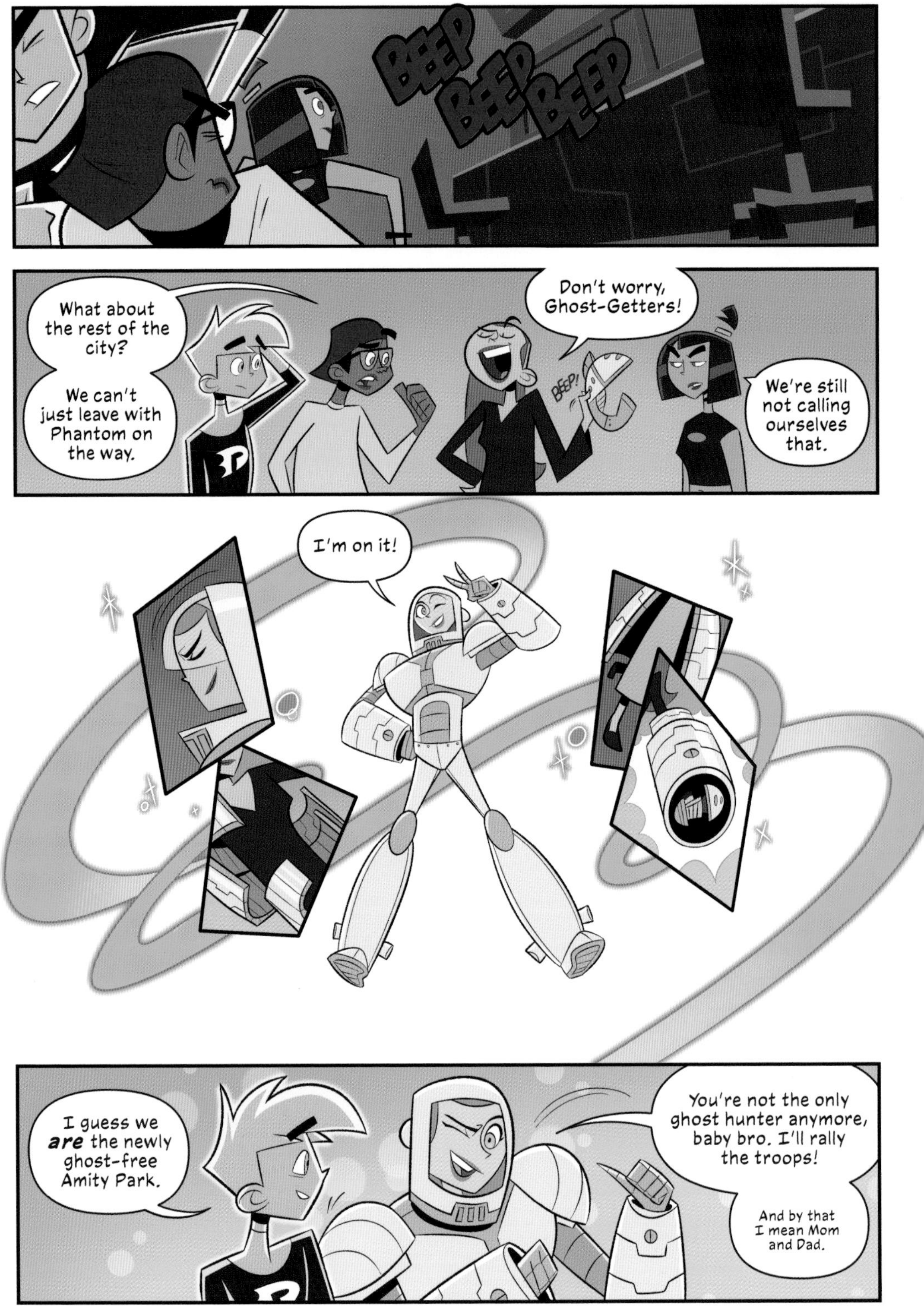
BEEP BEEP BEEP
What about the rest of the city?
We can't just leave with Phantom on the way.
Don't worry, Ghost-Getters!
BEEP!
We're still not calling ourselves that.
I'm on it!
I guess we *are* the newly ghost-free Amity Park.
You're not the only ghost hunter anymore, baby bro. I'll rally the troops!
And by that I mean Mom and Dad.

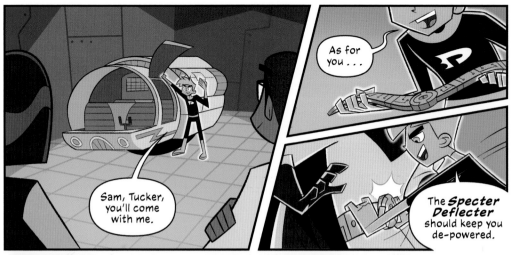

Sam, Tucker, you'll come with me.

As for you . . .

The **Specter Deflecter** should keep you de-powered.

Ack!

You're coming with us, so don't try anything.

Is this *really* necessary?

Necessary? No. Satisfying? Yes.

Tch. Teenagers . . .

Augh!

ZAP!

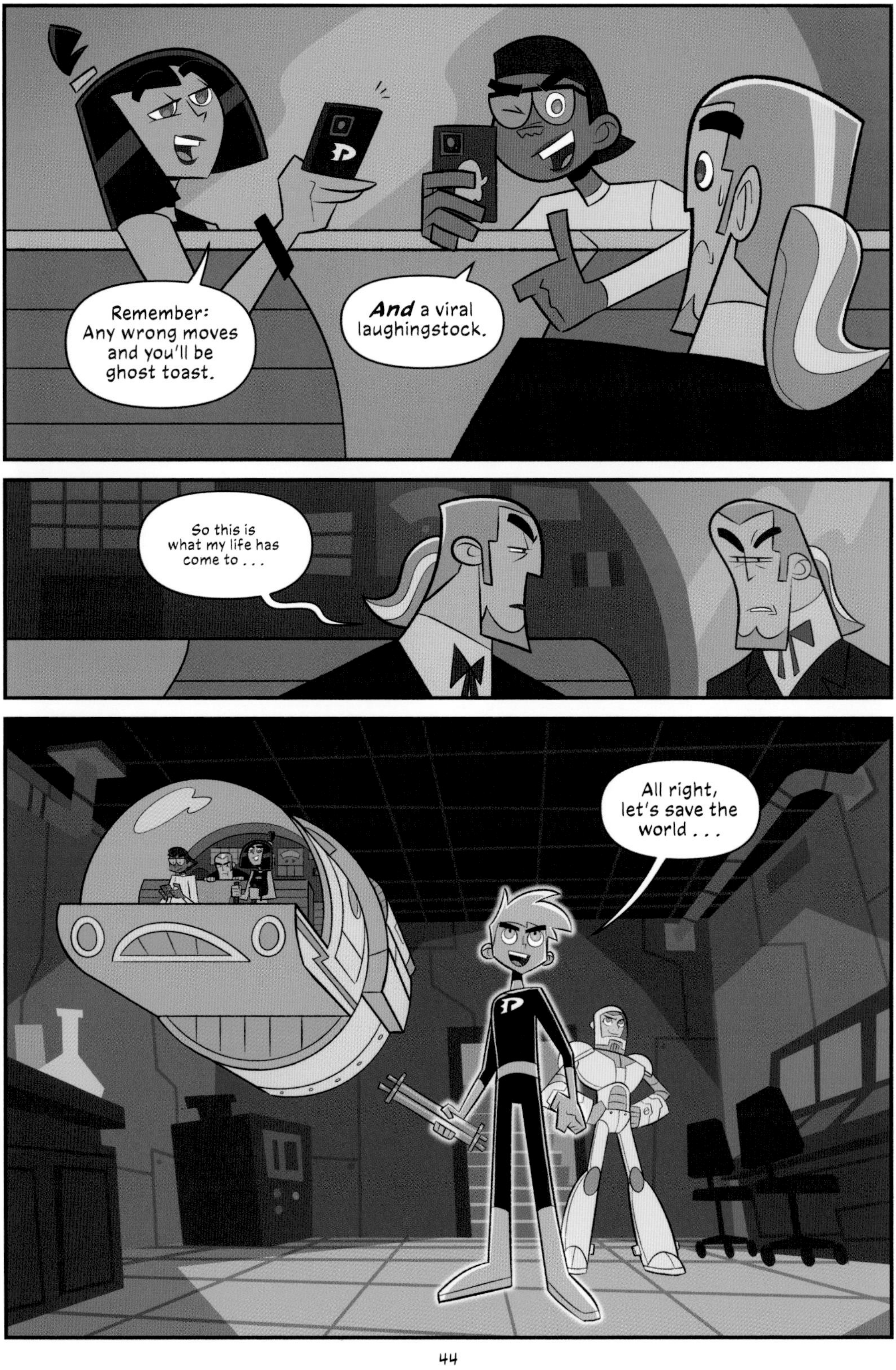

Remember: Any wrong moves and you'll be ghost toast.
And a viral laughingstock.
So this is what my life has come to . . .
All right, let's save the world . . .

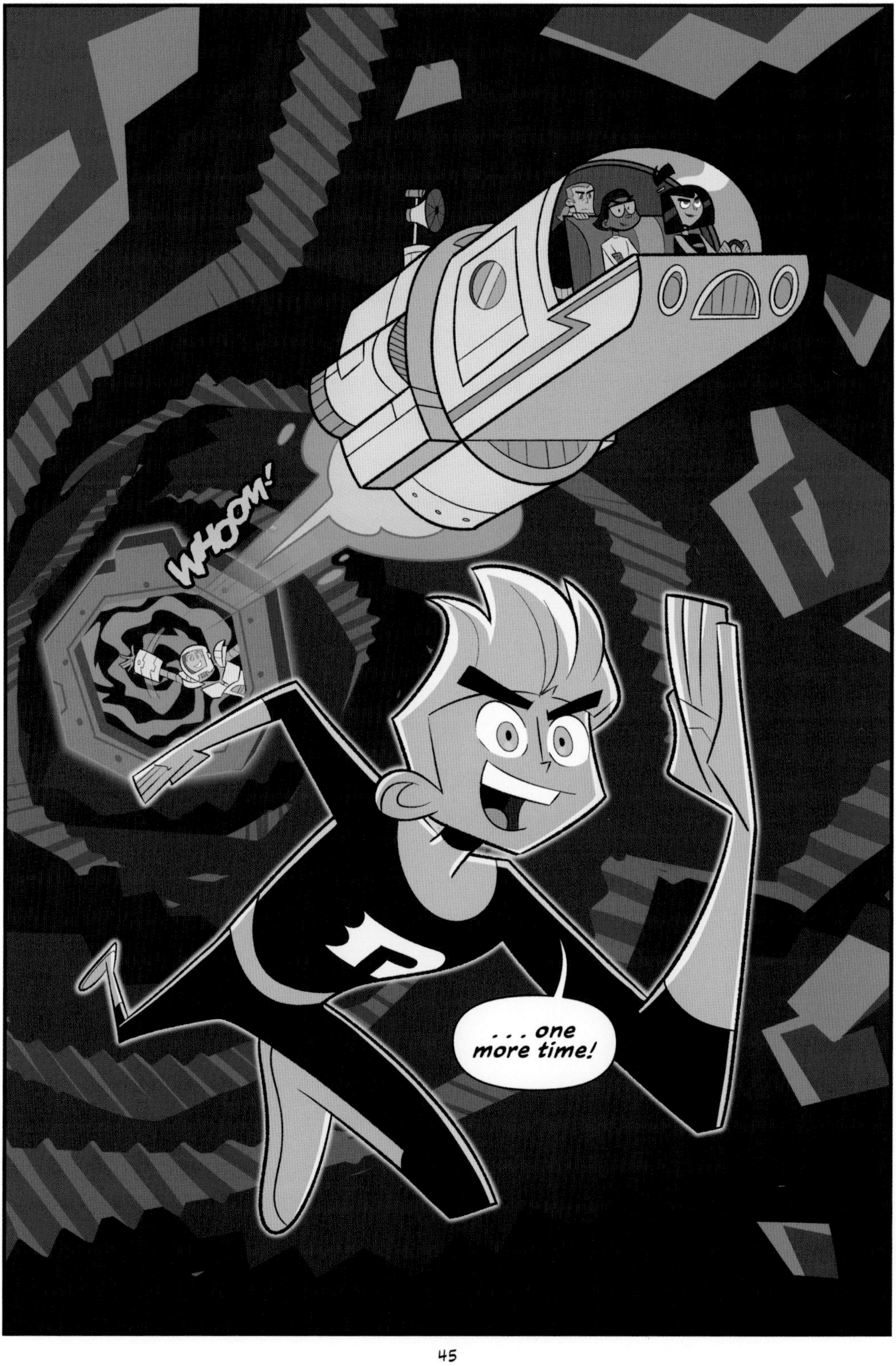
WHOOM!
. . . one more time!

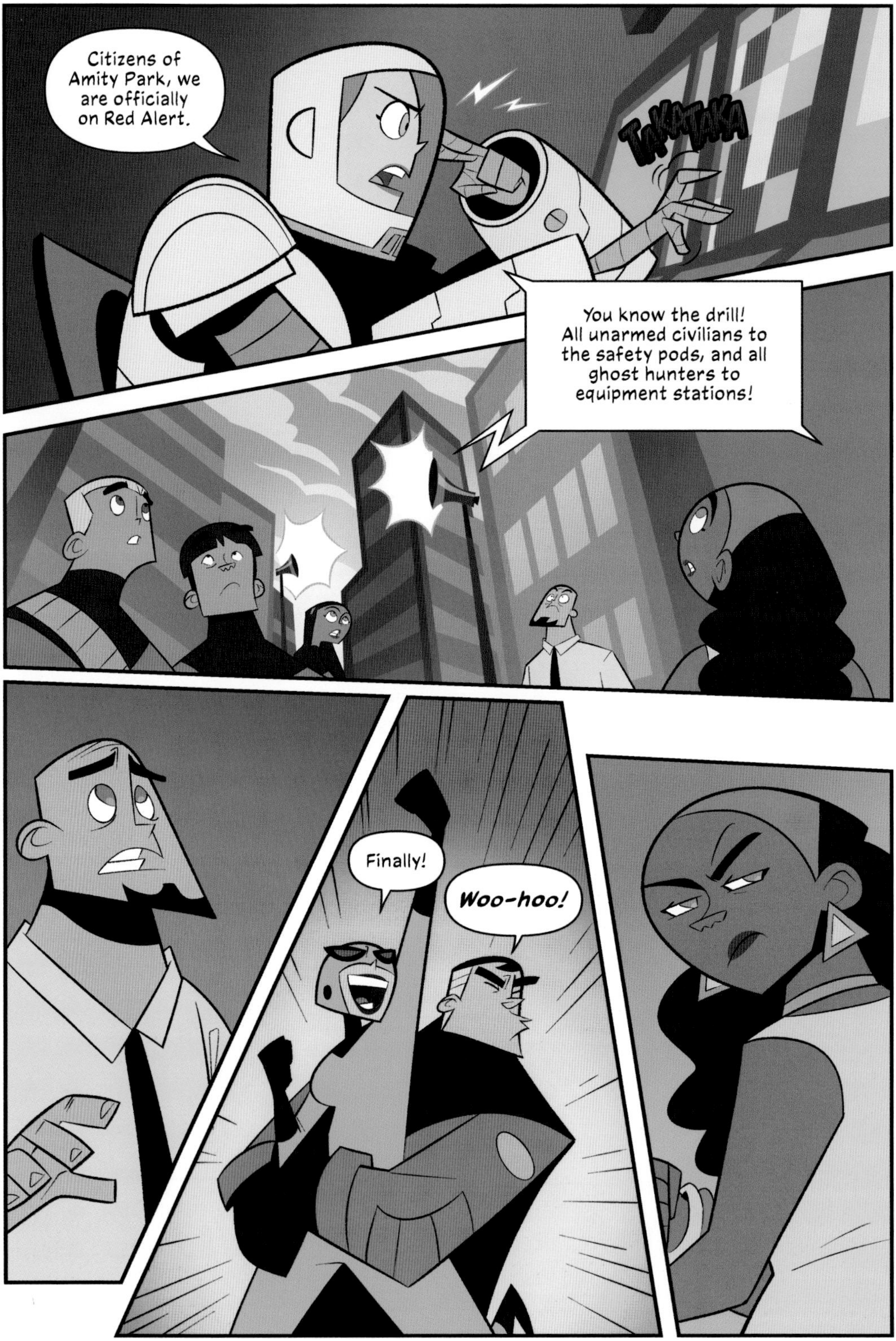

Citizens of Amity Park, we are officially on Red Alert.
TAKATAKA
You know the drill! All unarmed civilians to the safety pods, and all ghost hunters to equipment stations!
Finally!
Woo-hoo!

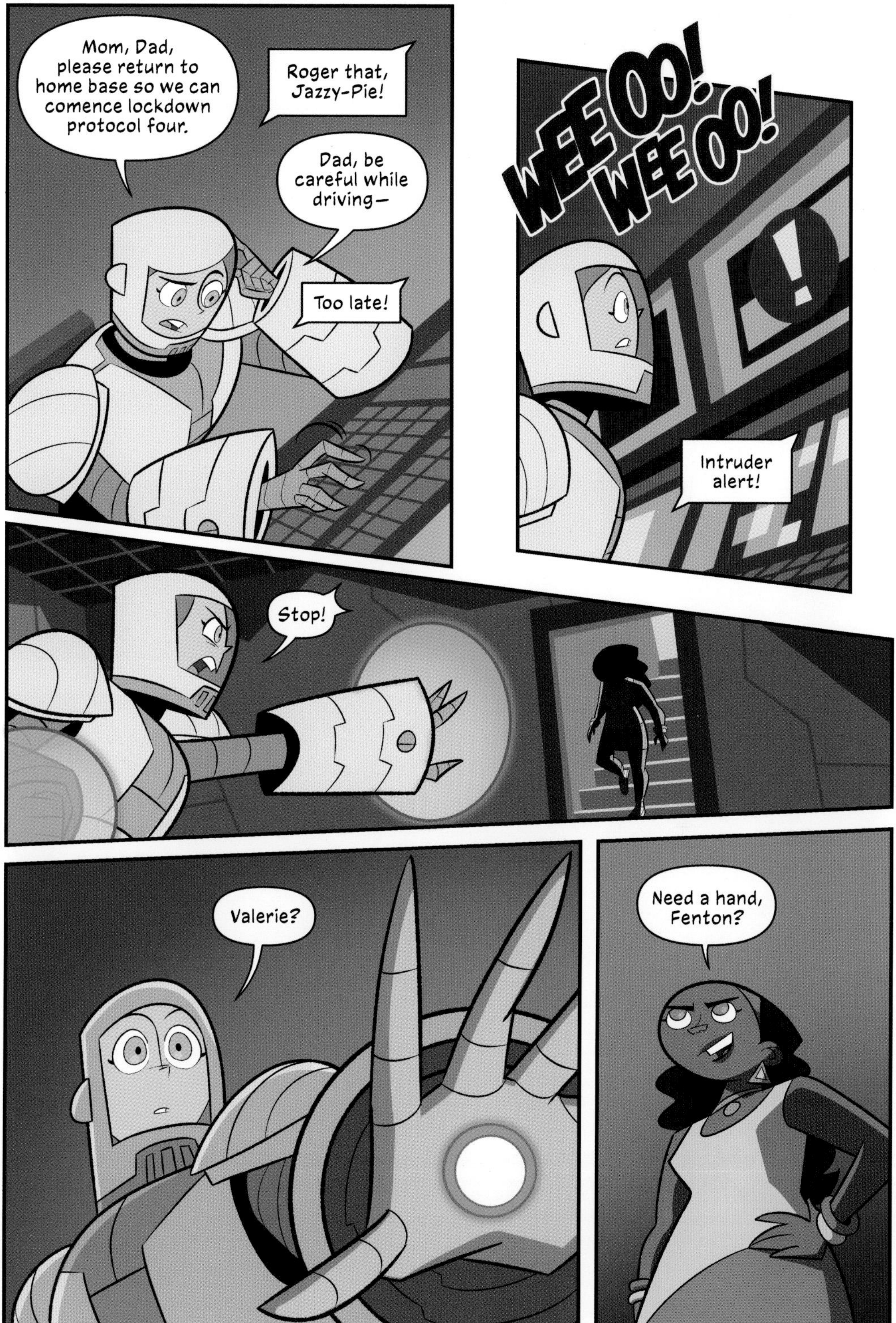

Mom, Dad, please return to home base so we can comence lockdown protocol four.
Roger that, Jazzy-Pie!
Dad, be careful while driving—
Too late!
WEE OO! WEE OO!
Intruder alert!
Stop!
Valerie?
Need a hand, Fenton?

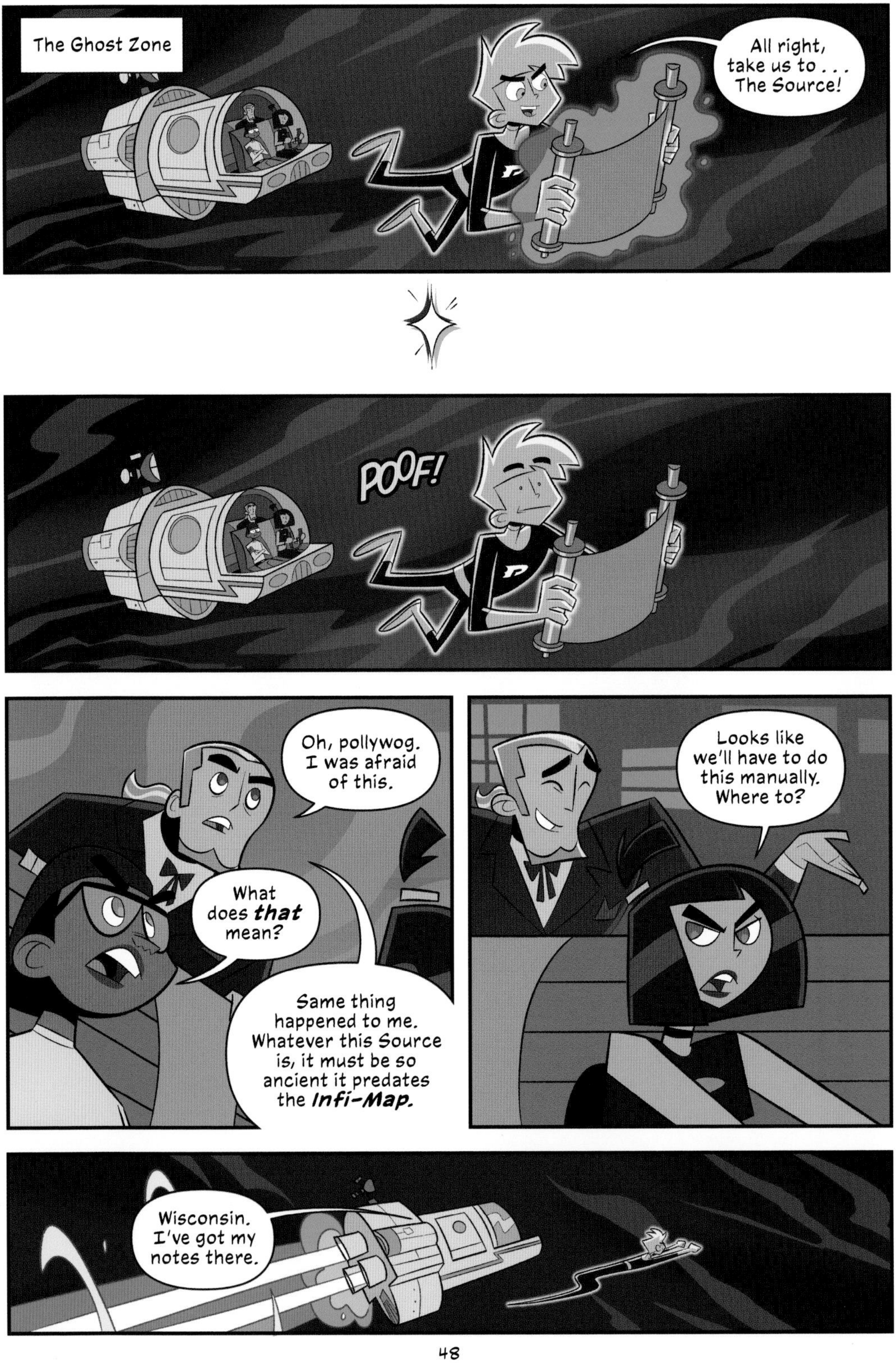
The Ghost Zone
All right, take us to . . . The Source!
POOF!
Oh, pollywog. I was afraid of this.
What does **that** mean?
Same thing happened to me. Whatever this Source is, it must be so ancient it predates the ***Infi-Map.***
Looks like we'll have to do this manually. Where to?
Wisconsin. I've got my notes there.

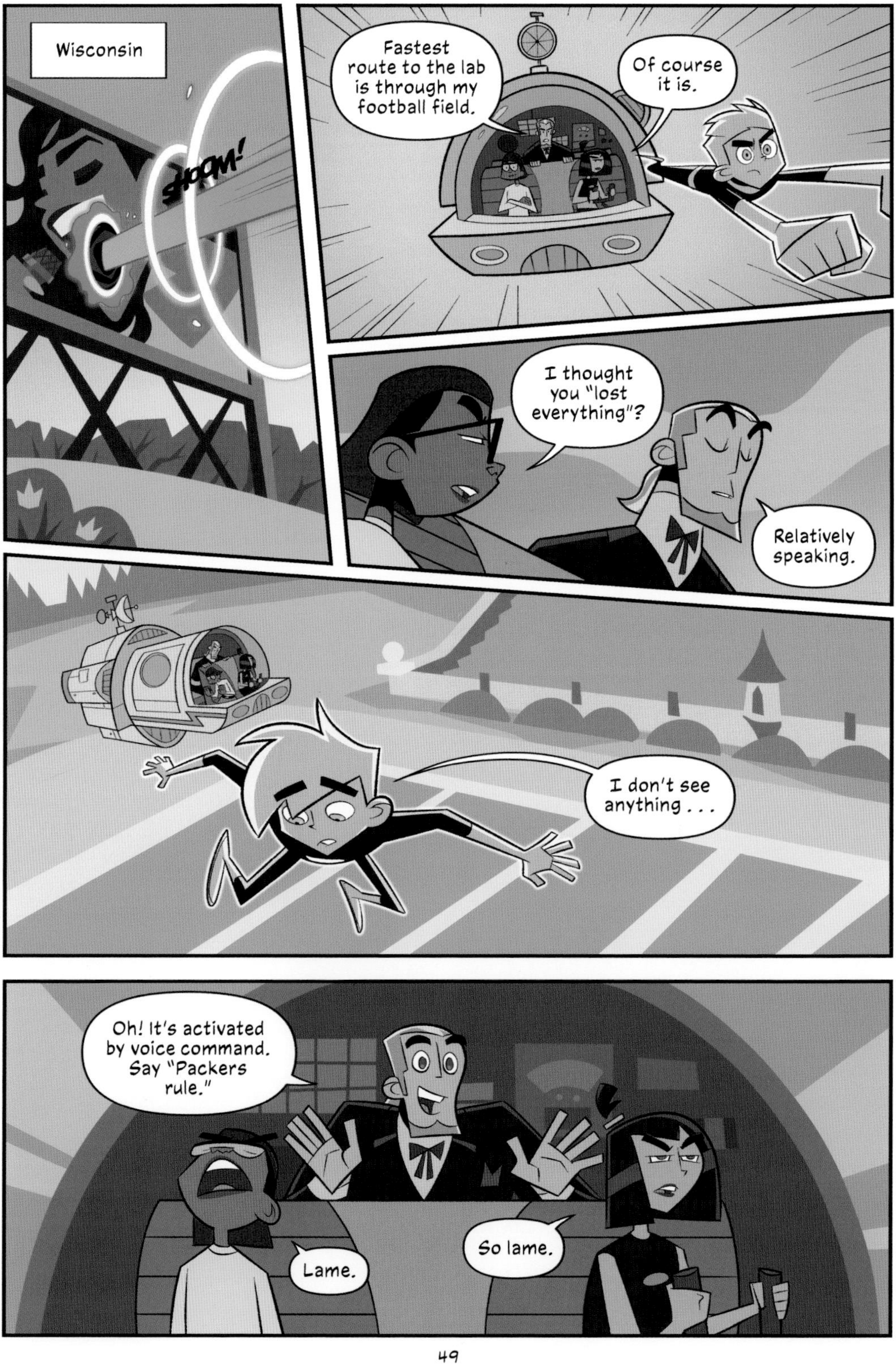

Wisconsin
SHOOM!
Fastest route to the lab is through my football field.
Of course it is.
I thought you "lost everything"?
Relatively speaking.
I don't see anything . . .
Oh! It's activated by voice command. Say "Packers rule."
Lame.
So lame.

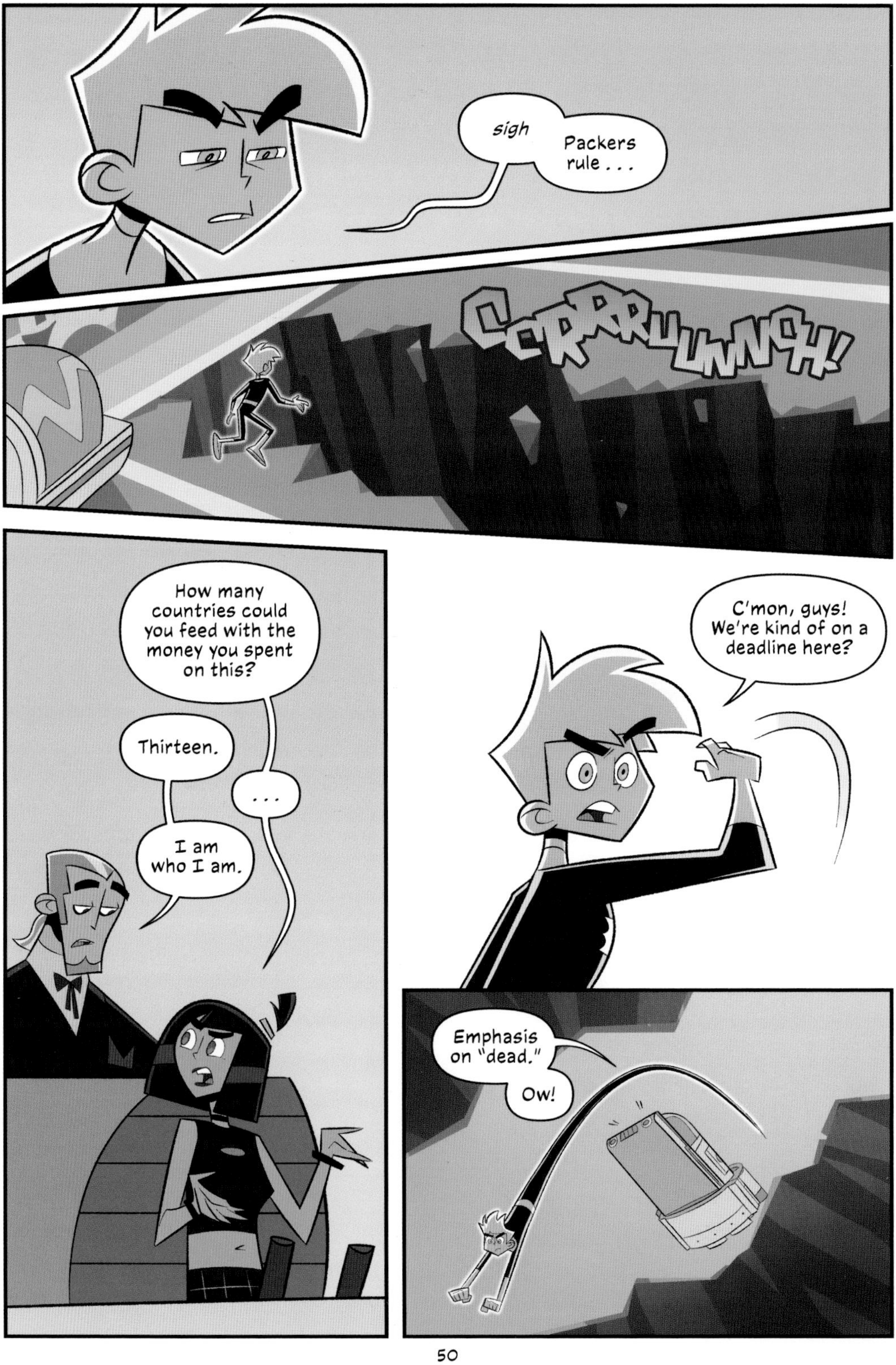

sigh
Packers rule . . .
C-CRRRUUNNCH!
How many countries could you feed with the money you spent on this?
Thirteen.
. . .
I am who I am.
C'mon, guys! We're kind of on a deadline here?
Emphasis on "dead."
Ow!

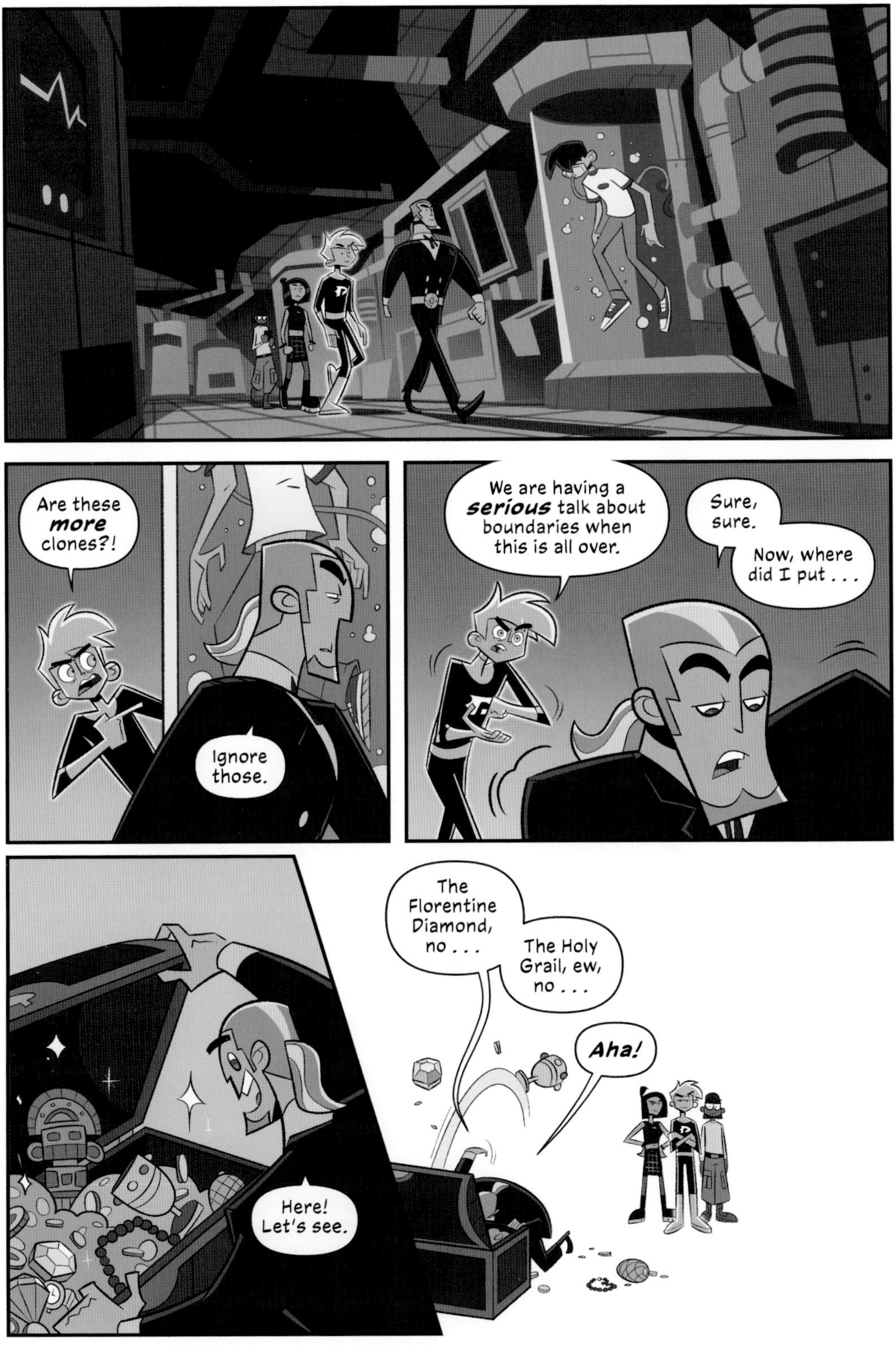

Are these *more* clones?!
Ignore those.
We are having a *serious* talk about boundaries when this is all over.
Sure, sure.
Now, where did I put . . .
Here! Let's see.
The Florentine Diamond, no . . .
The Holy Grail, ew, no . . .
Aha!

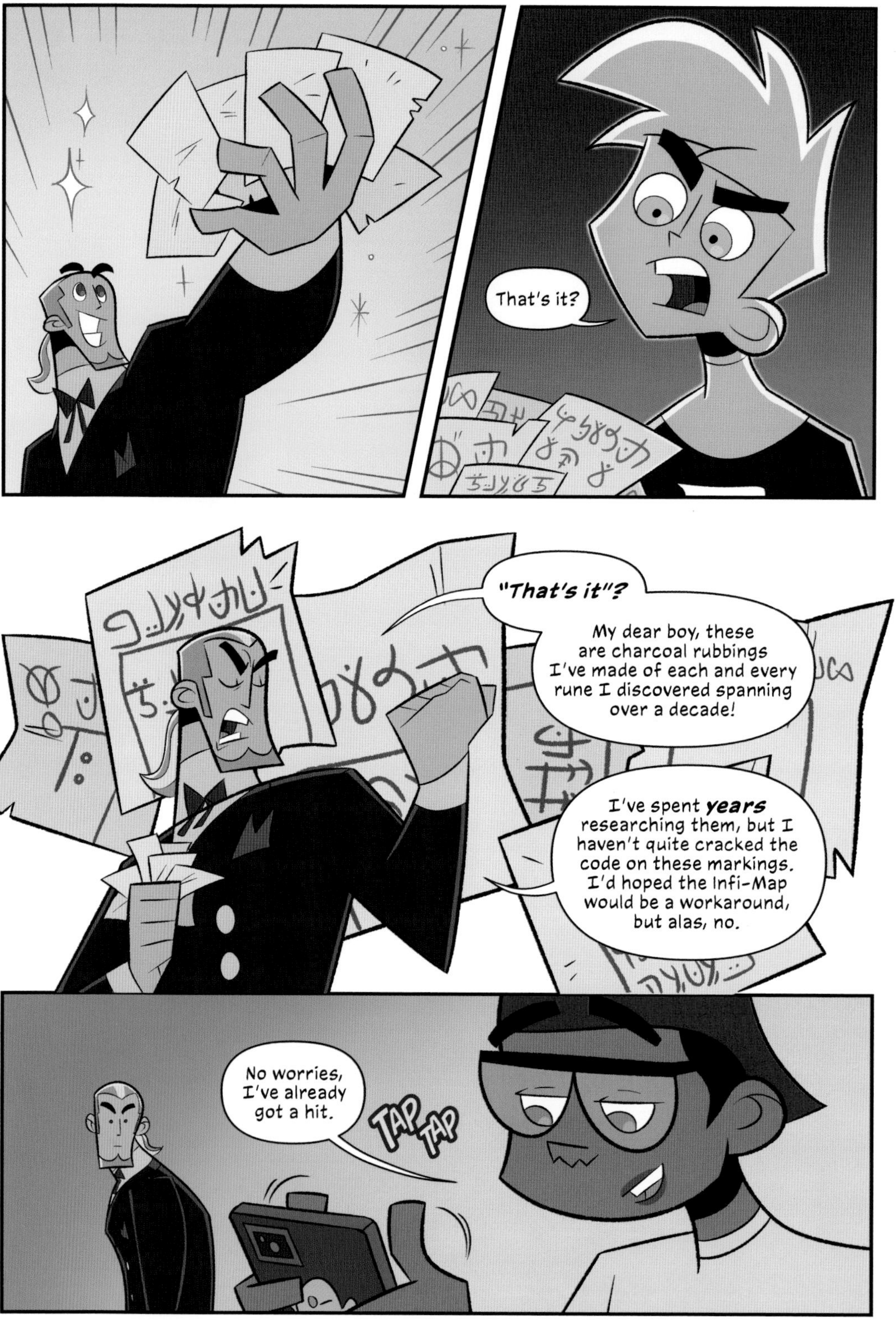
That's it?
"That's it"?
My dear boy, these are charcoal rubbings I've made of each and every rune I discovered spanning over a decade!
I've spent years researching them, but I haven't quite cracked the code on these markings. I'd hoped the Infi-Map would be a workaround, but alas, no.
No worries, I've already got a hit.
TAP TAP

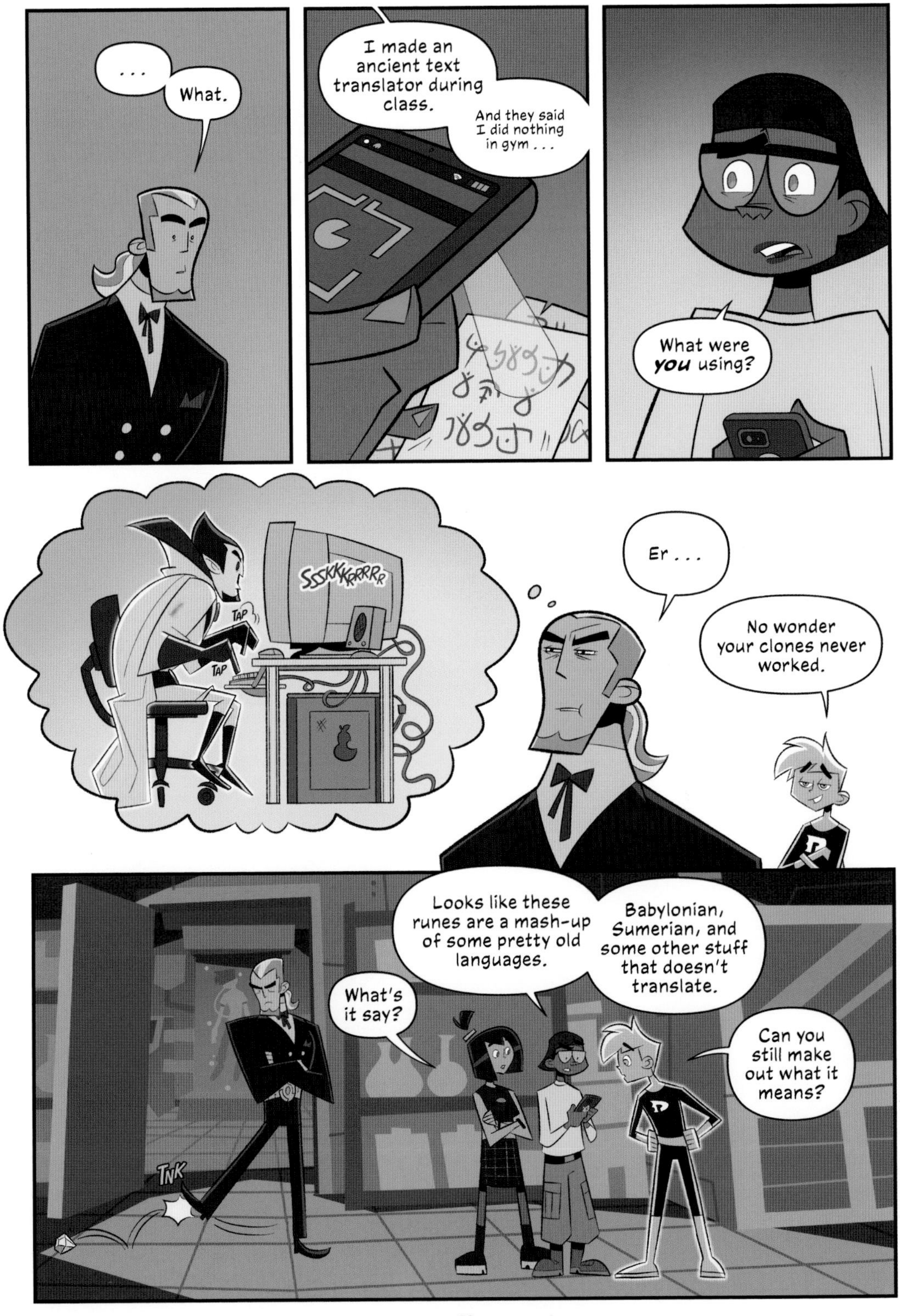
. . .
What.
I made an ancient text translator during class.
And they said I did nothing in gym . . .
What were *you* using?
SSSKKKRRRRR
TAP
TAP
Er . . .
No wonder your clones never worked.
What's it say?
Looks like these runes are a mash-up of some pretty old languages.
Babylonian, Sumerian, and some other stuff that doesn't translate.
Can you still make out what it means?
TNK

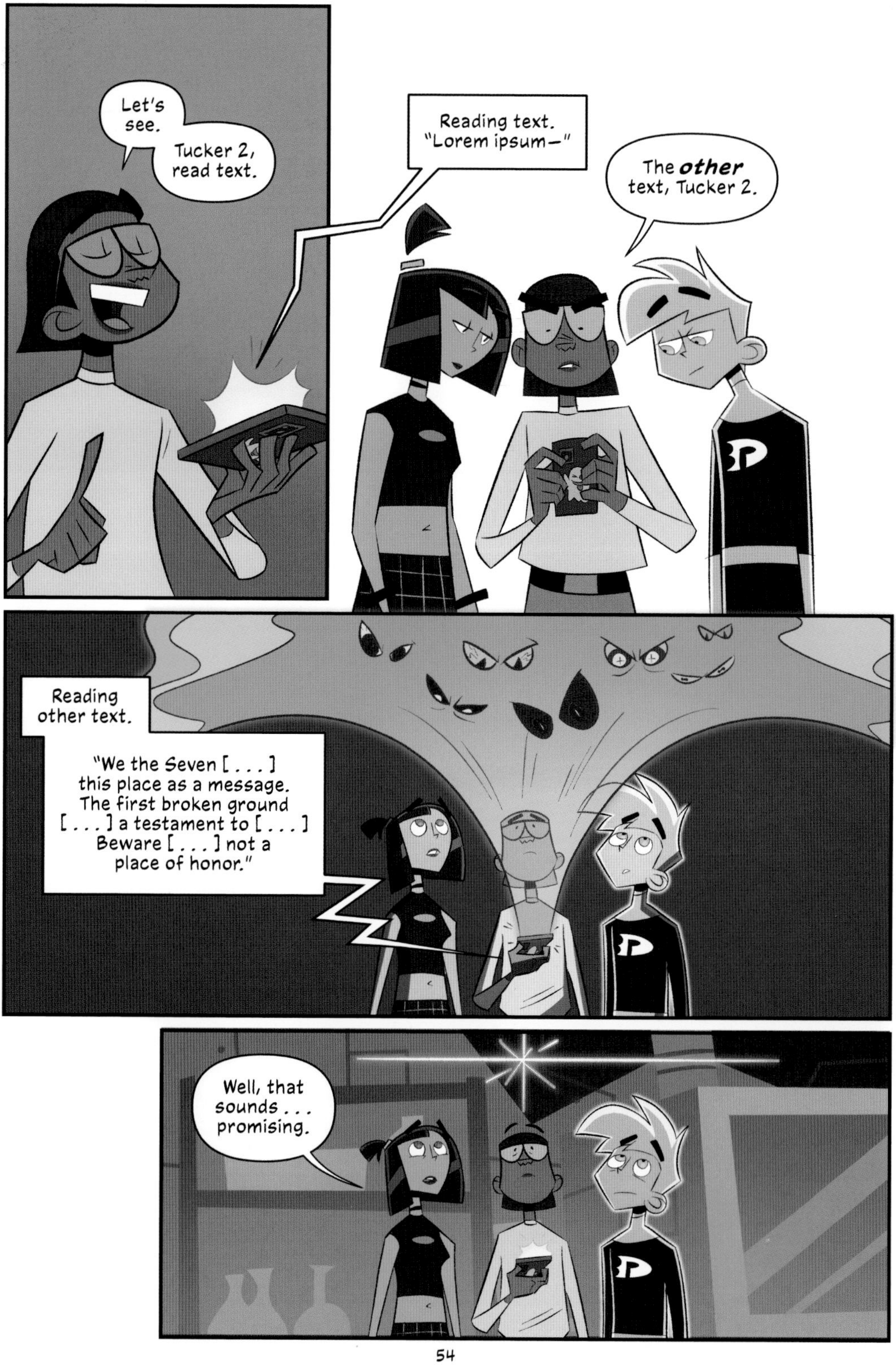

Let's see.
Tucker 2, read text.
Reading text. "Lorem ipsum—"
The *other* text, Tucker 2.
Reading other text.
"We the Seven [. . .] this place as a message. The first broken ground [. . .] a testament to [. . .] Beware [. . .] not a place of honor."
Well, that sounds . . . promising.

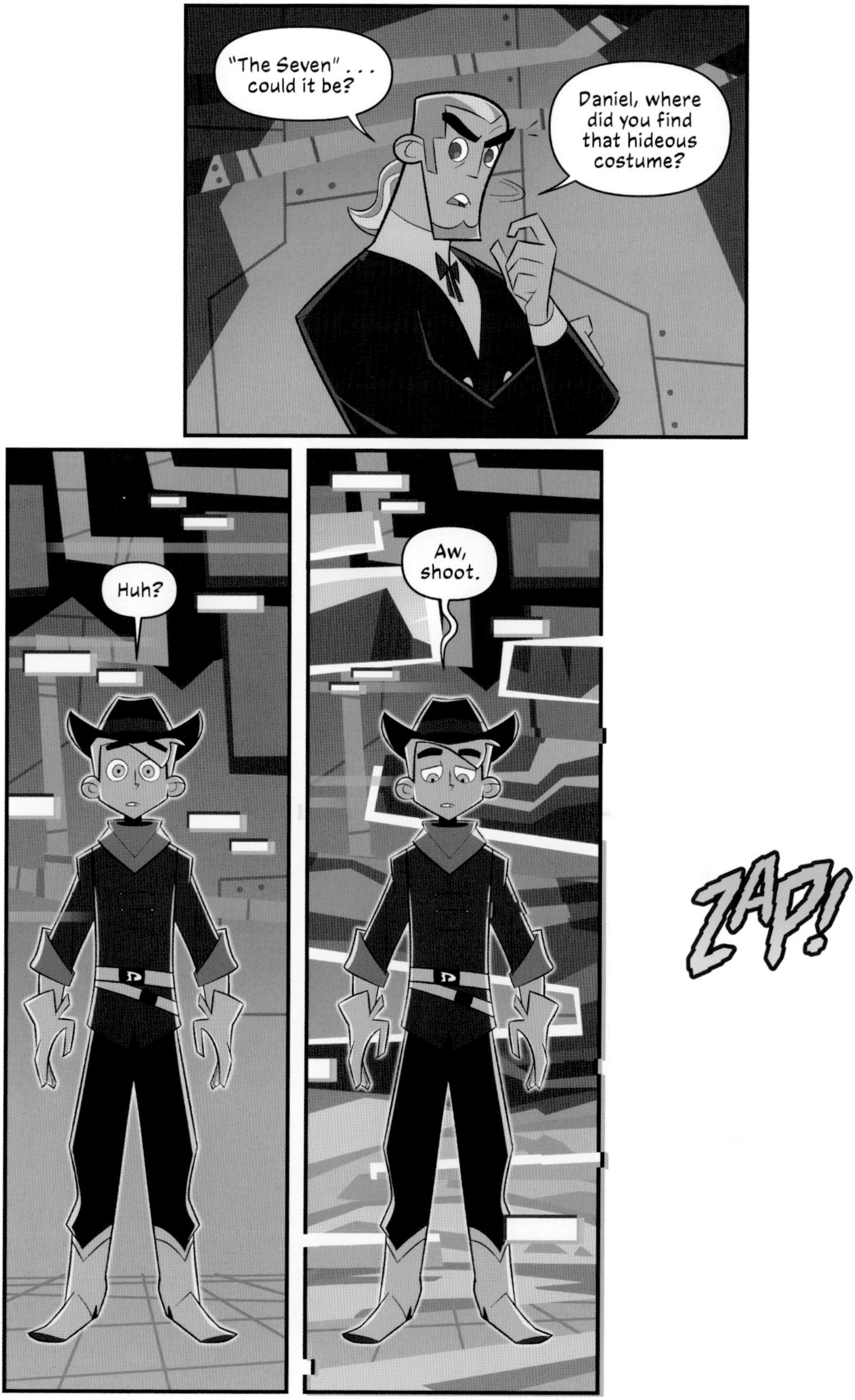
"The Seven" . . . could it be?
Daniel, where did you find that hideous costume?
Huh?
Aw, shoot.
ZAP!

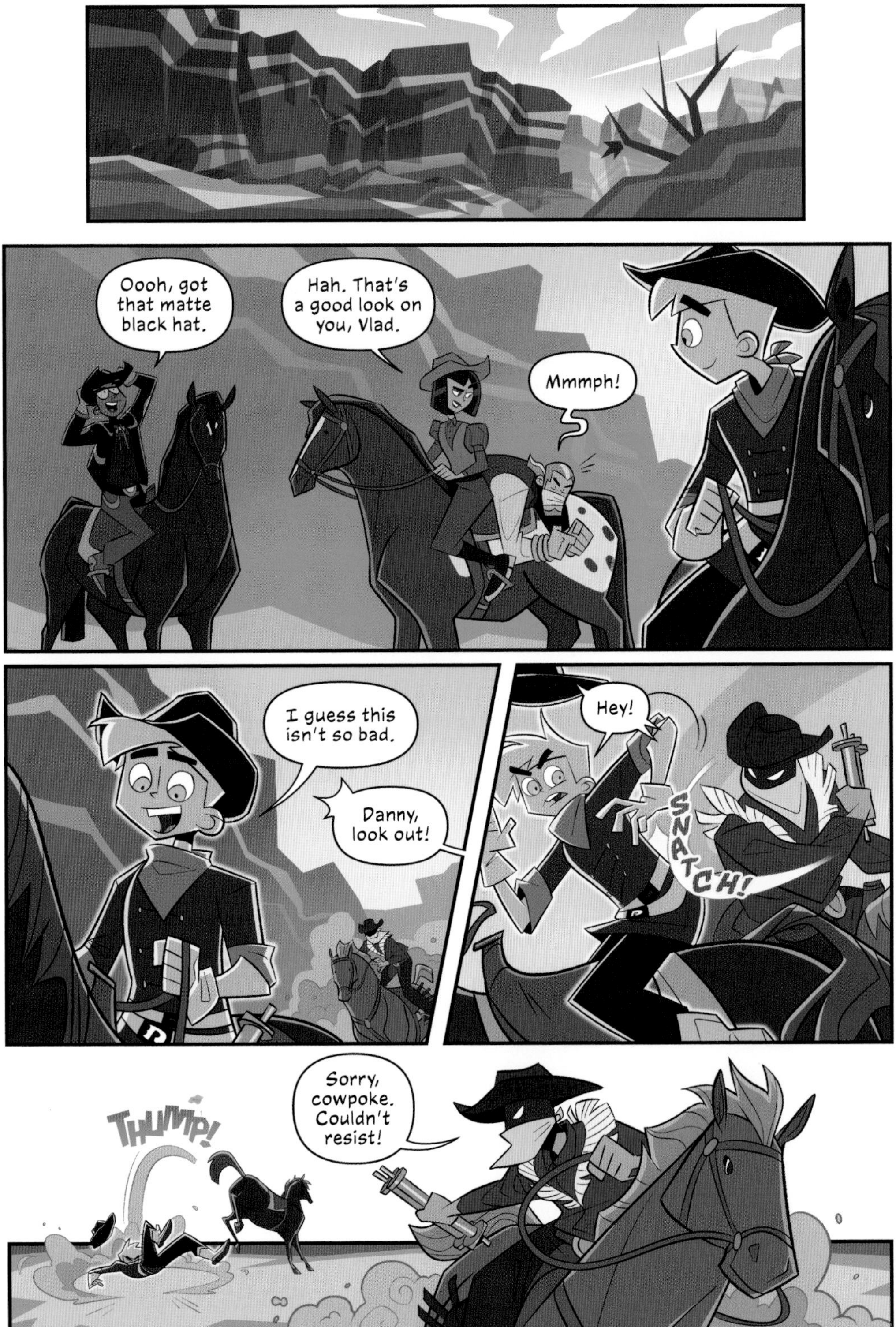
Oooh, got that matte black hat.
Hah. That's a good look on you, Vlad.
Mmmph!
I guess this isn't so bad.
Danny, look out!
Hey!
SNATCH!
Sorry, cowpoke. Couldn't resist!
THUMP!

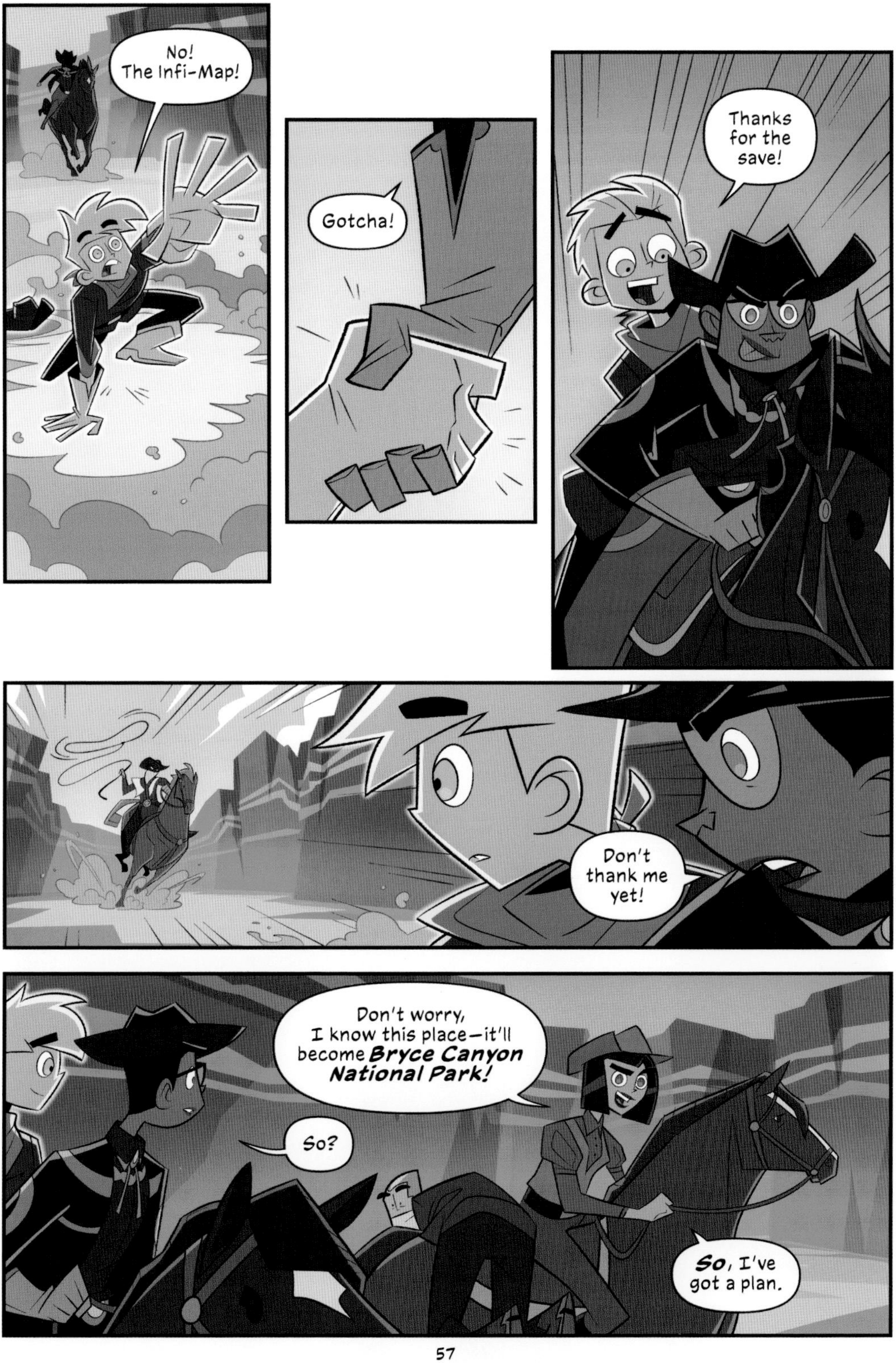
No! The Infi-Map!
Gotcha!
Thanks for the save!
Don't thank me yet!
Don't worry, I know this place—it'll become **Bryce Canyon National Park!**
So?
So, I've got a plan.

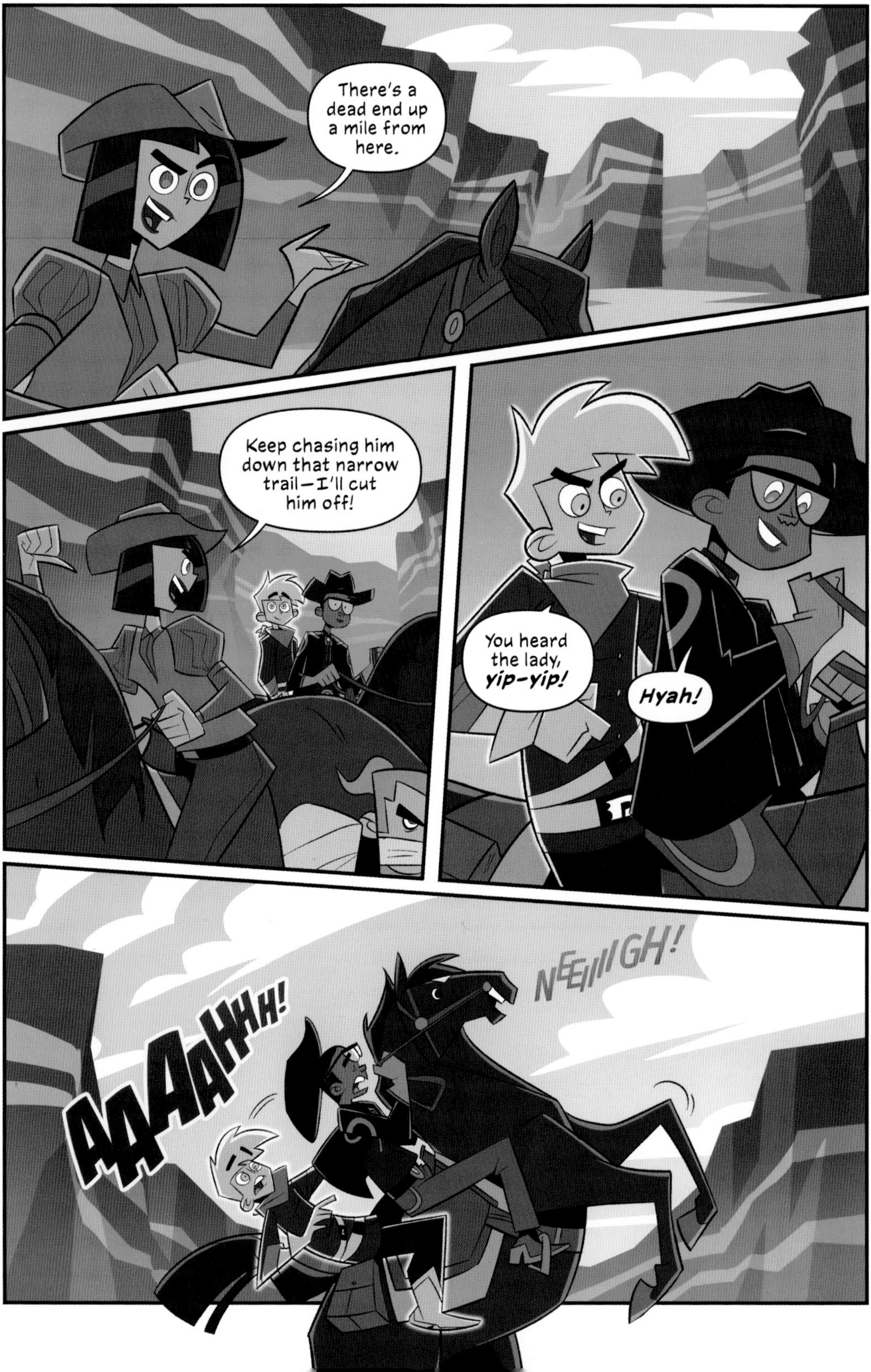
There's a dead end up a mile from here.
Keep chasing him down that narrow trail—I'll cut him off!
You heard the lady, ***yip-yip!***
Hyah!
NEEIIIIGH!
AAAAAHHH!

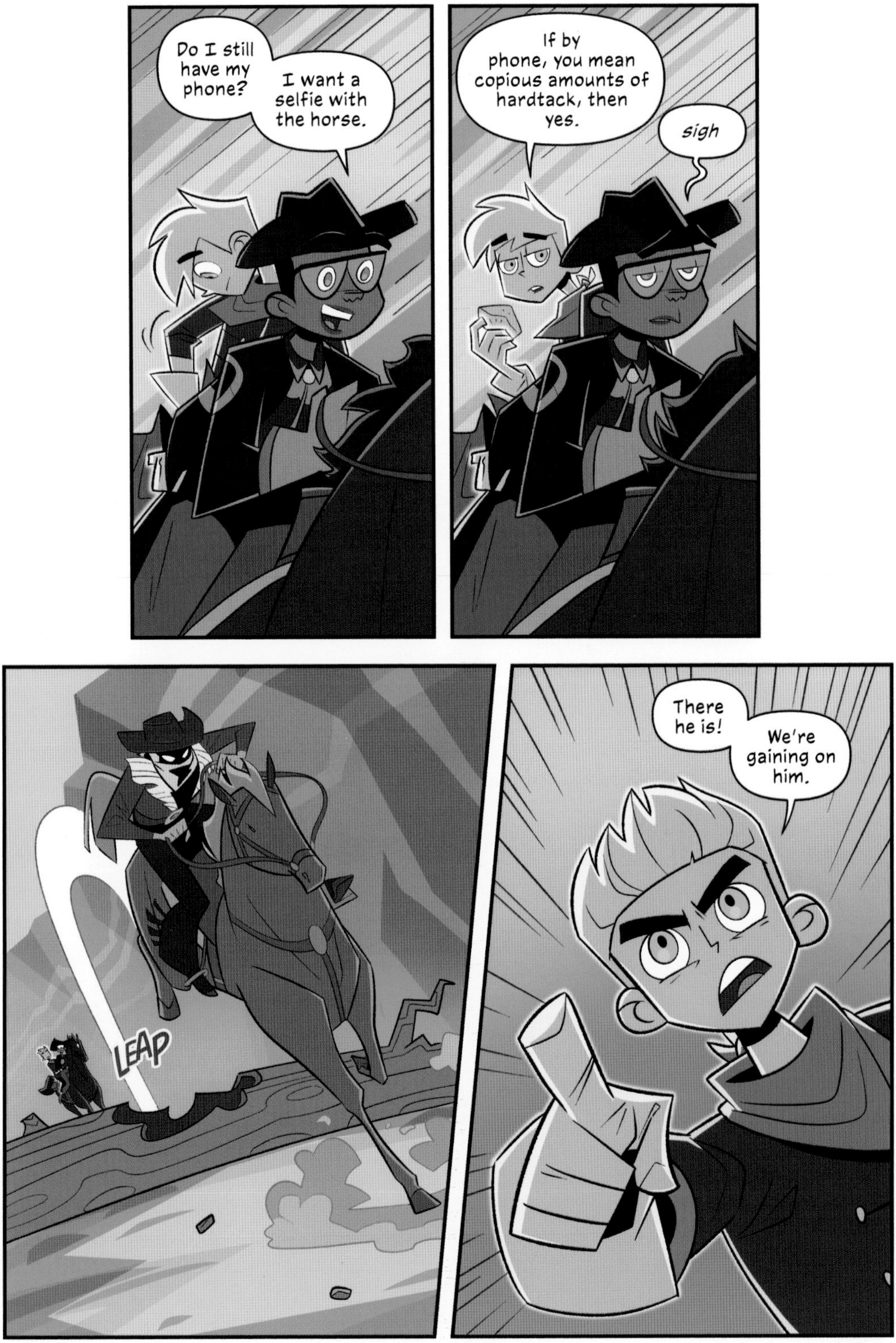
Do I still have my phone?
I want a selfie with the horse.
If by phone, you mean copious amounts of hardtack, then yes.
sigh
LEAP
There he is!
We're gaining on him.

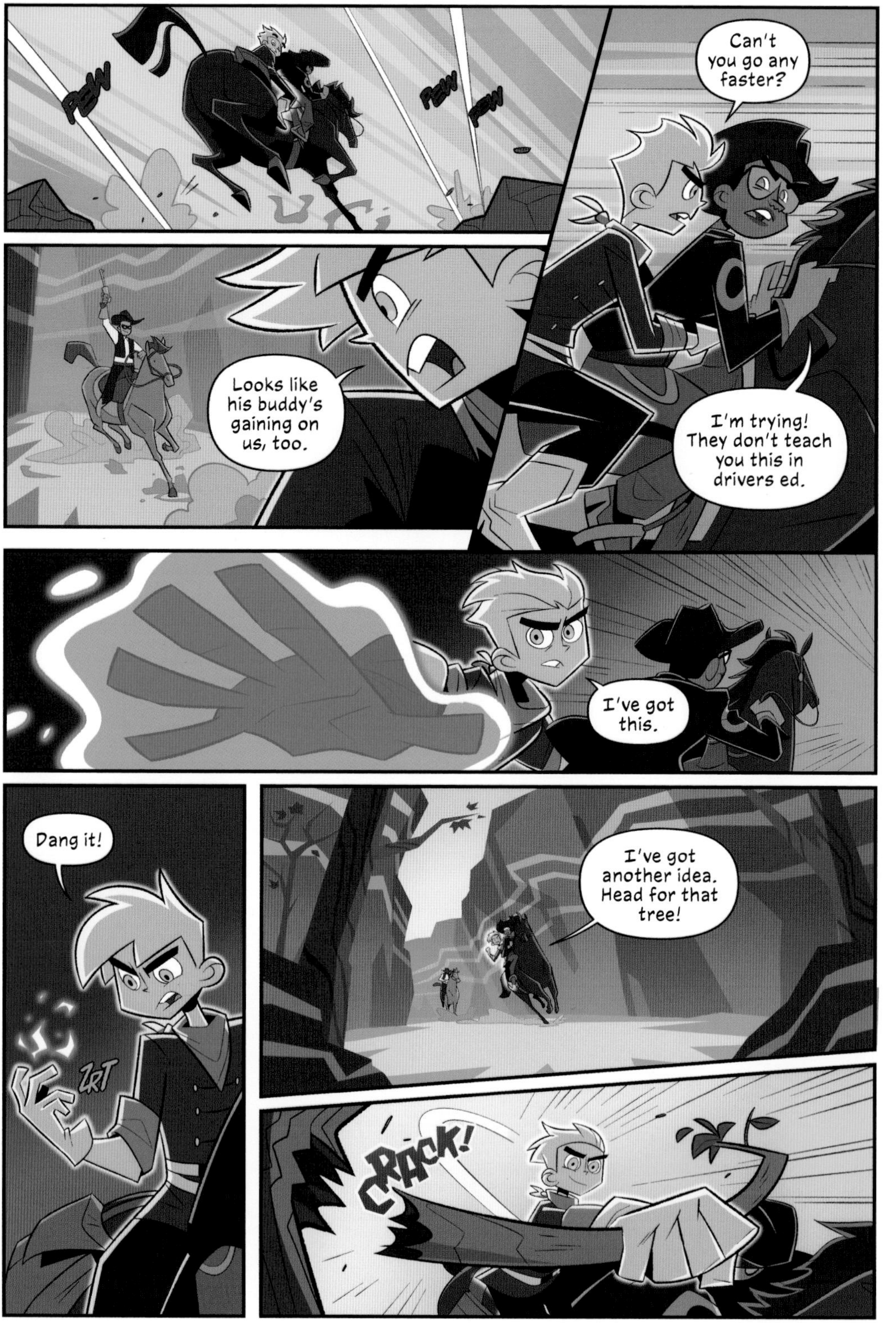
PEW
PEW
PEW
Can't you go any faster?
Looks like his buddy's gaining on us, too.
I'm trying! They don't teach you this in drivers ed.
I've got this.
Dang it!
ZRT
I've got another idea. Head for that tree!
CRACK!

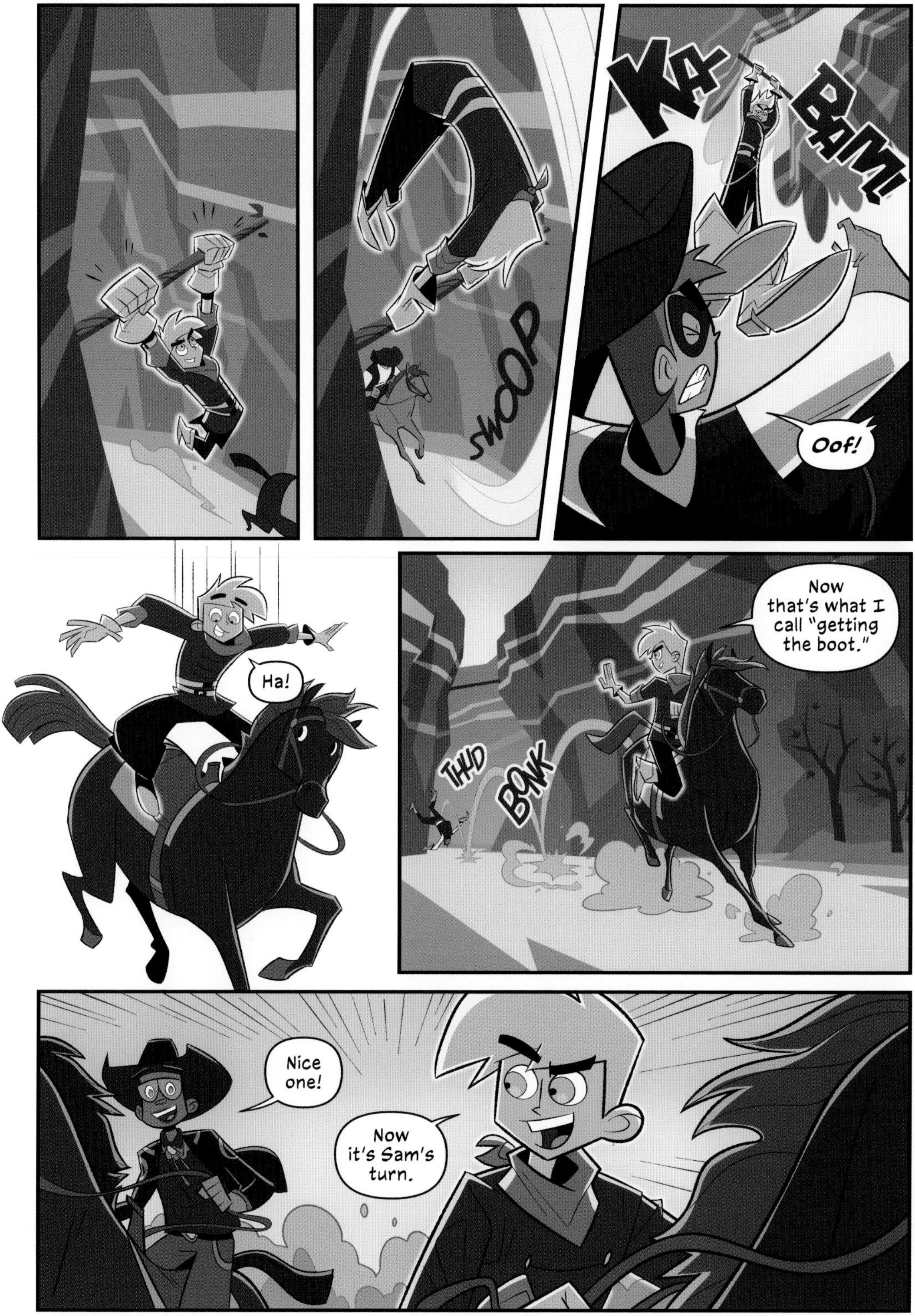
SWOOP
KA-BAM!
Oof!
Ha!
THUD
BONK
Now that's what I call "getting the boot."
Nice one!
Now it's Sam's turn.

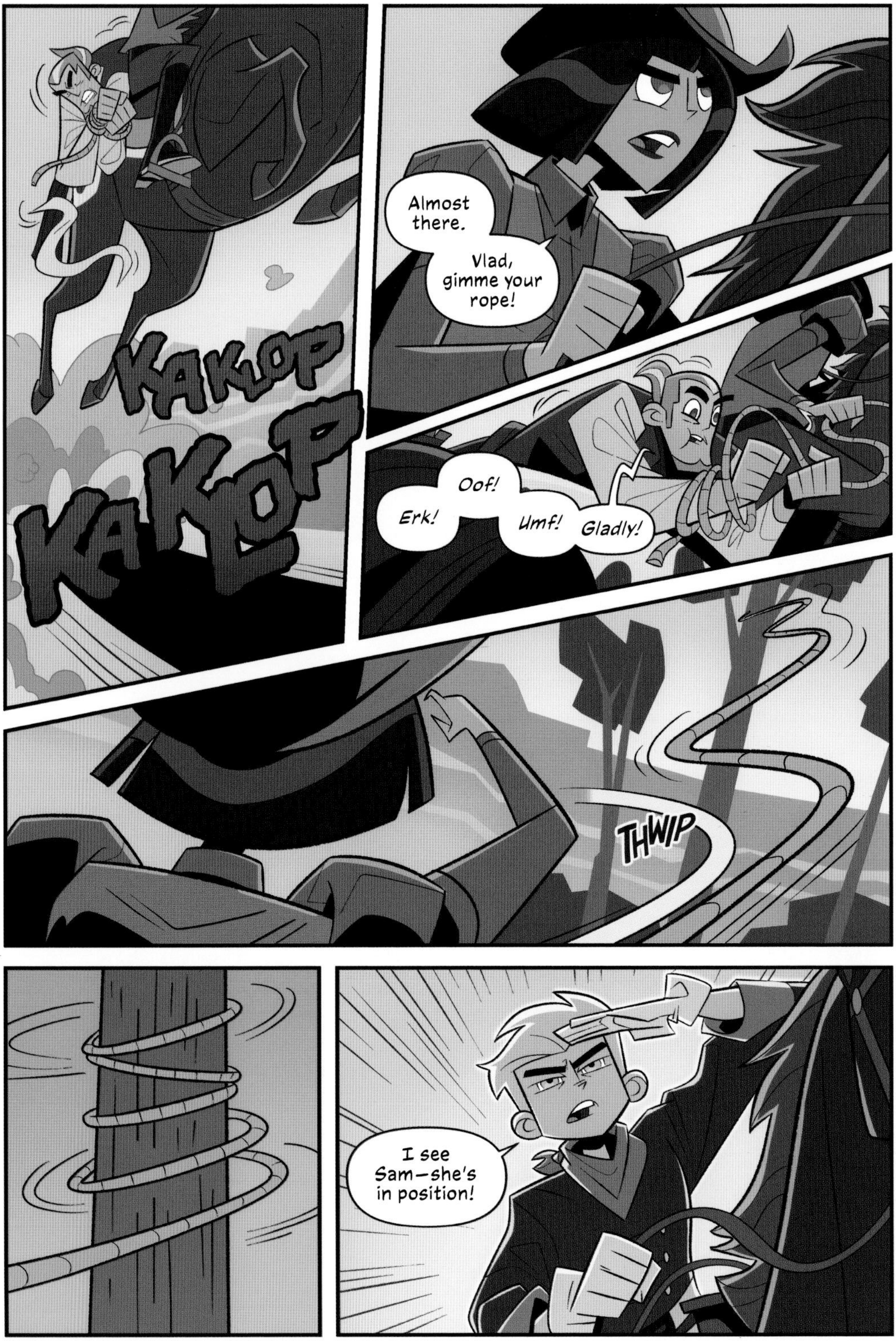
KAKLOP
KAKLOP
Almost there.
Vlad, gimme your rope!
Erk!
Oof!
Umf!
Gladly!
THWIP
I see Sam—she's in position!

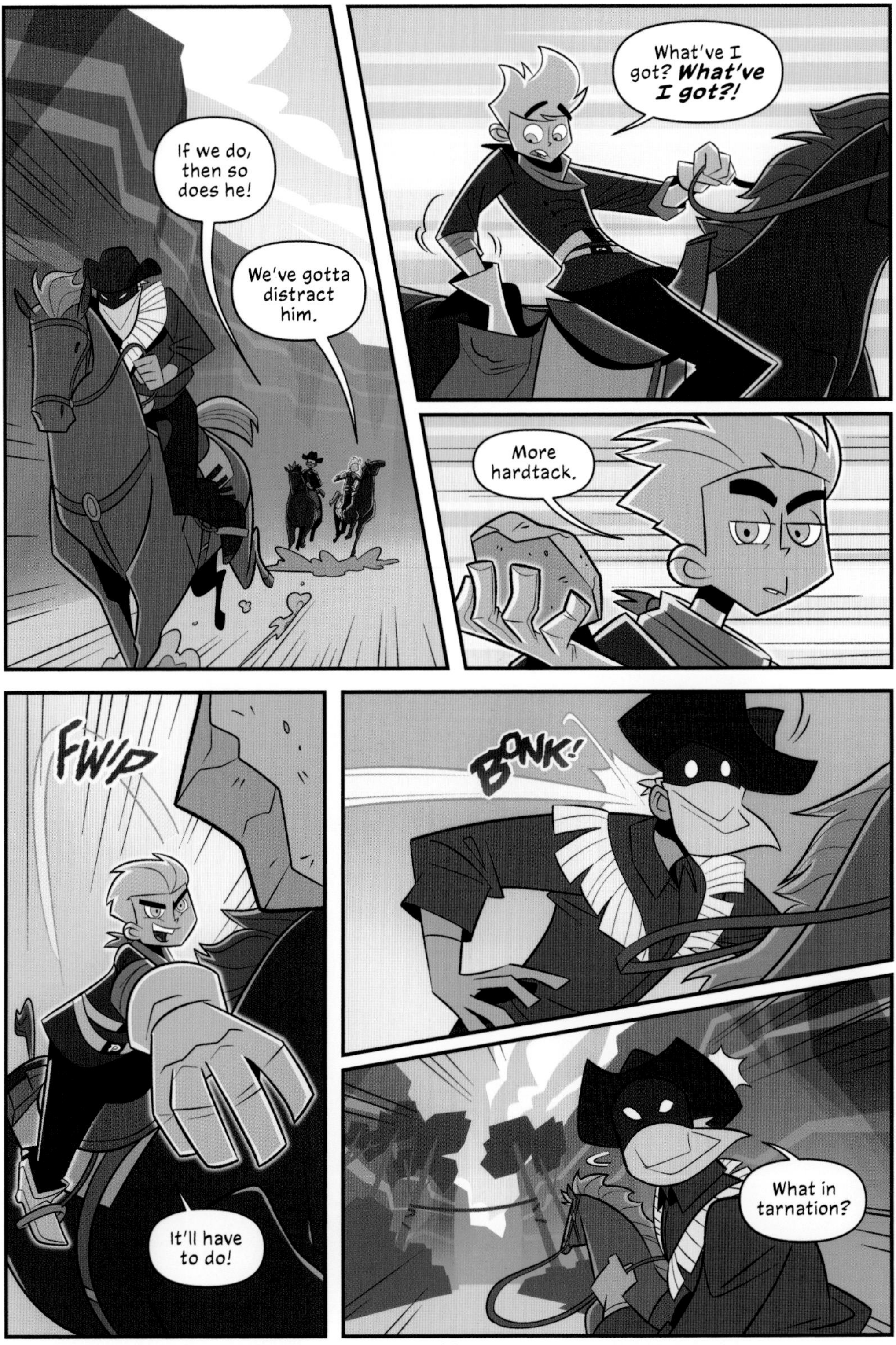

If we do, then so does he!
We've gotta distract him.
What've I got? What've I got?!
More hardtack.
FWIP
It'll have to do!
BONK!
What in tarnation?

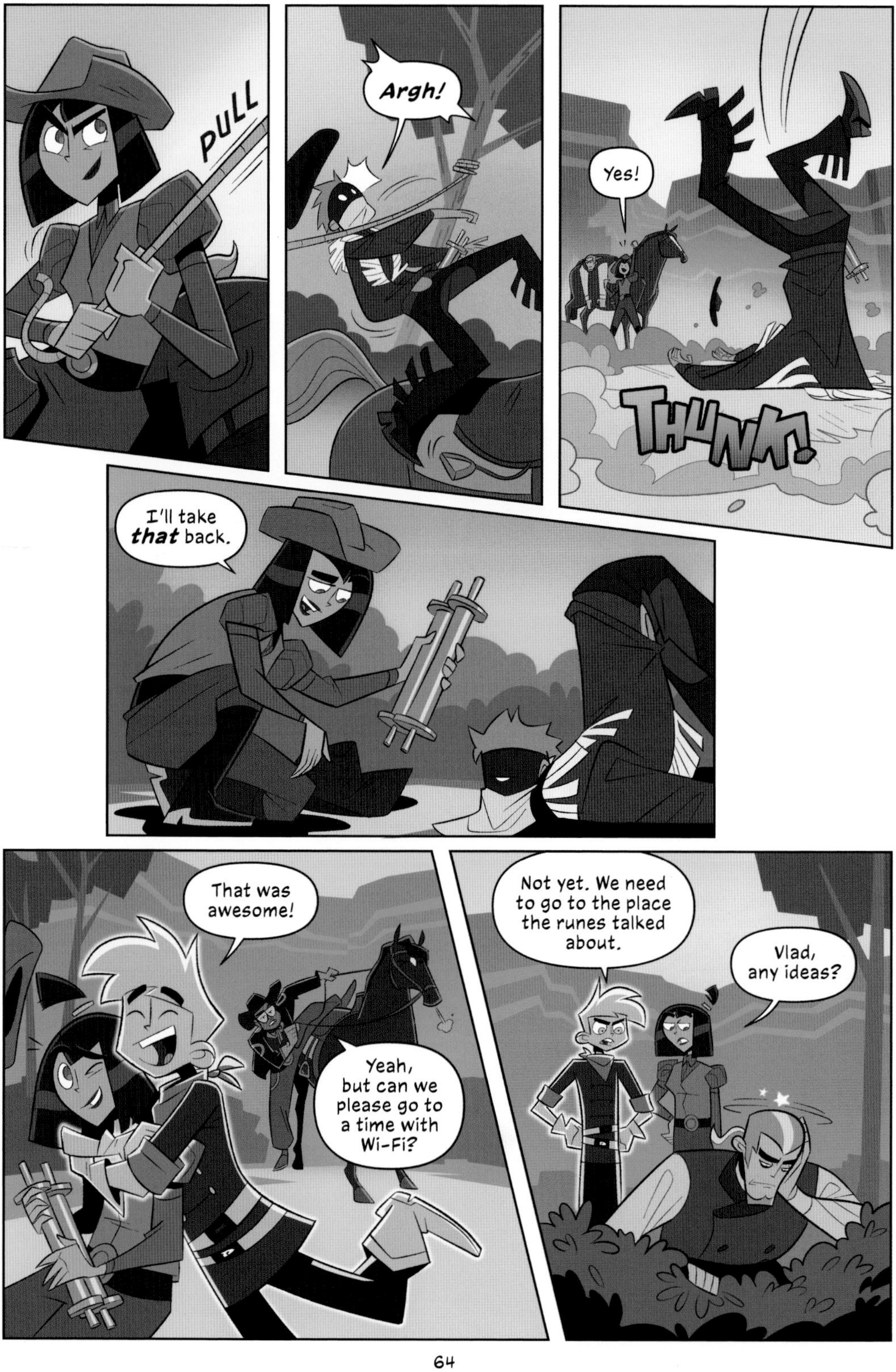
PULL
Argh!
Yes!
THUNK!
I'll take **that** back.
That was awesome!
Yeah, but can we please go to a time with Wi-Fi?
Not yet. We need to go to the place the runes talked about.
Vlad, any ideas?

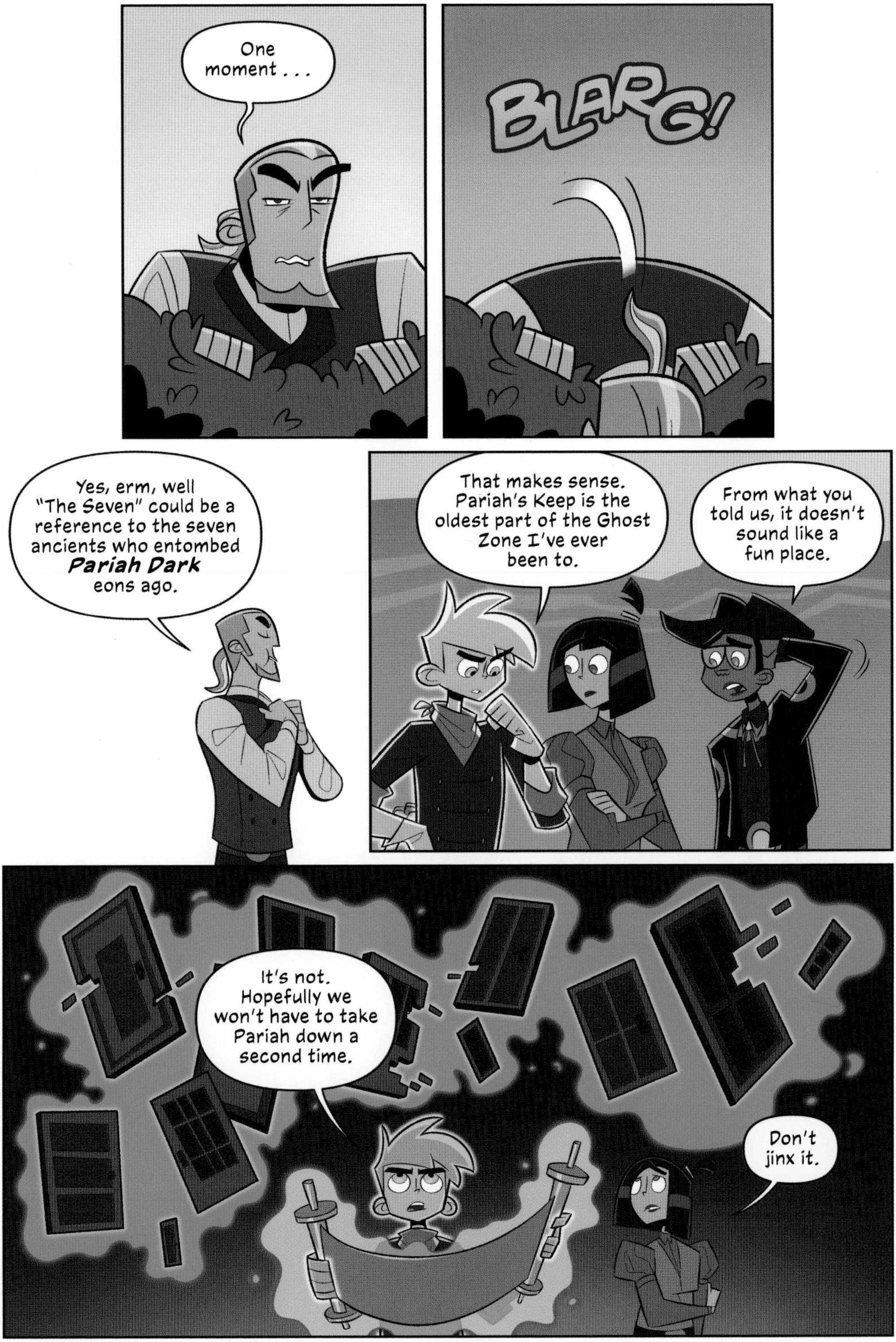
One moment . . .
BLARG!
Yes, erm, well "The Seven" could be a reference to the seven ancients who entombed ***Pariah Dark*** eons ago.
That makes sense. Pariah's Keep is the oldest part of the Ghost Zone I've ever been to.
From what you told us, it doesn't sound like a fun place.
It's not. Hopefully we won't have to take Pariah down a second time.
Don't jinx it.

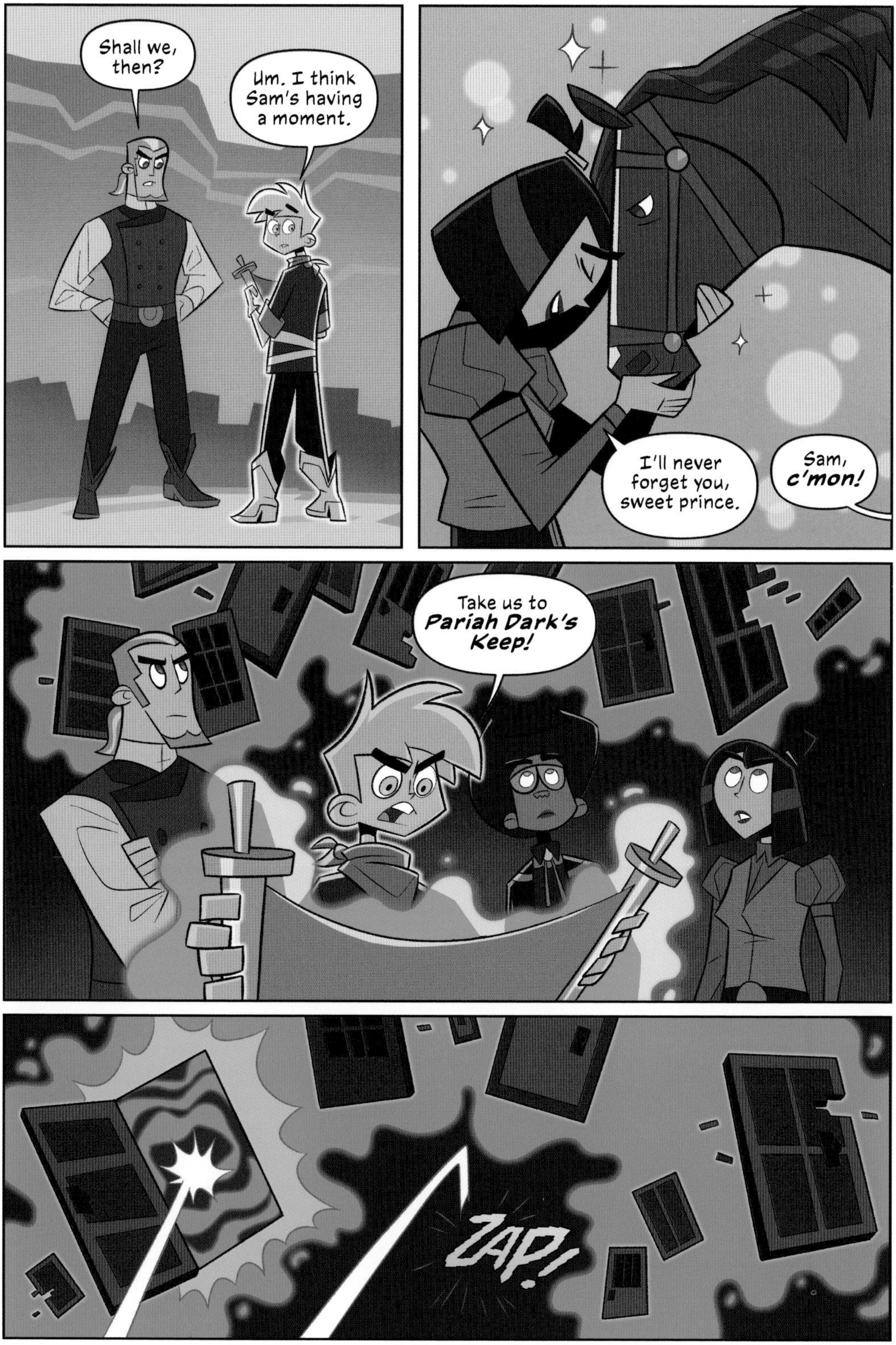
Shall we, then?
Um. I think Sam's having a moment.
I'll never forget you, sweet prince.
Sam, *c'mon!*
Take us to *Pariah Dark's Keep!*
ZAP!

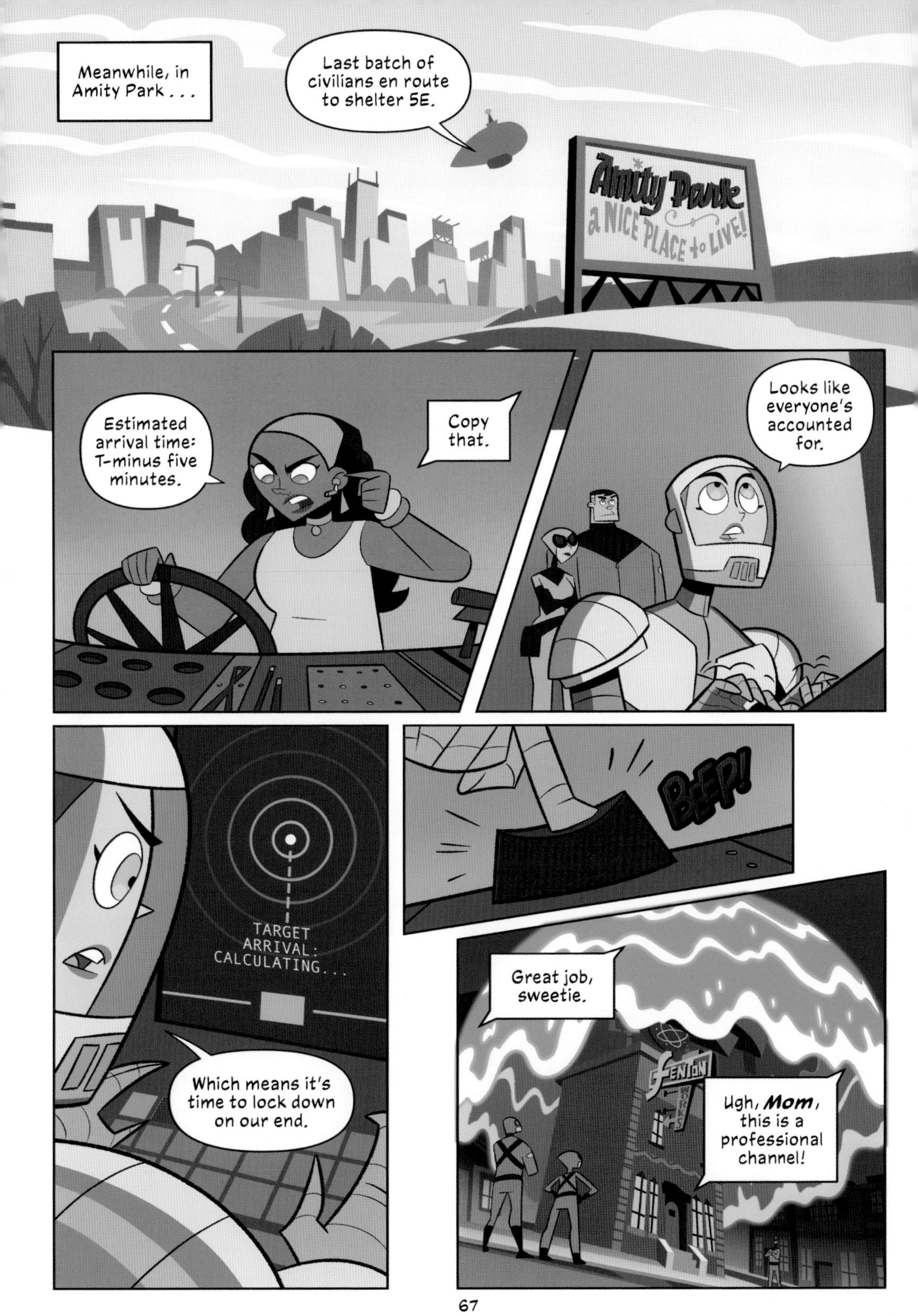
Meanwhile, in Amity Park . . .
Last batch of civilians en route to shelter 5E.
Amity Park
a NICE PLACE to LIVE!
Estimated arrival time: T-minus five minutes.
Copy that.
Looks like everyone's accounted for.
TARGET ARRIVAL: CALCULATING . . .
Which means it's time to lock down on our end.
BEEP!
Great job, sweetie.
FENTON WORKS
Ugh, **Mom**, this is a professional channel!

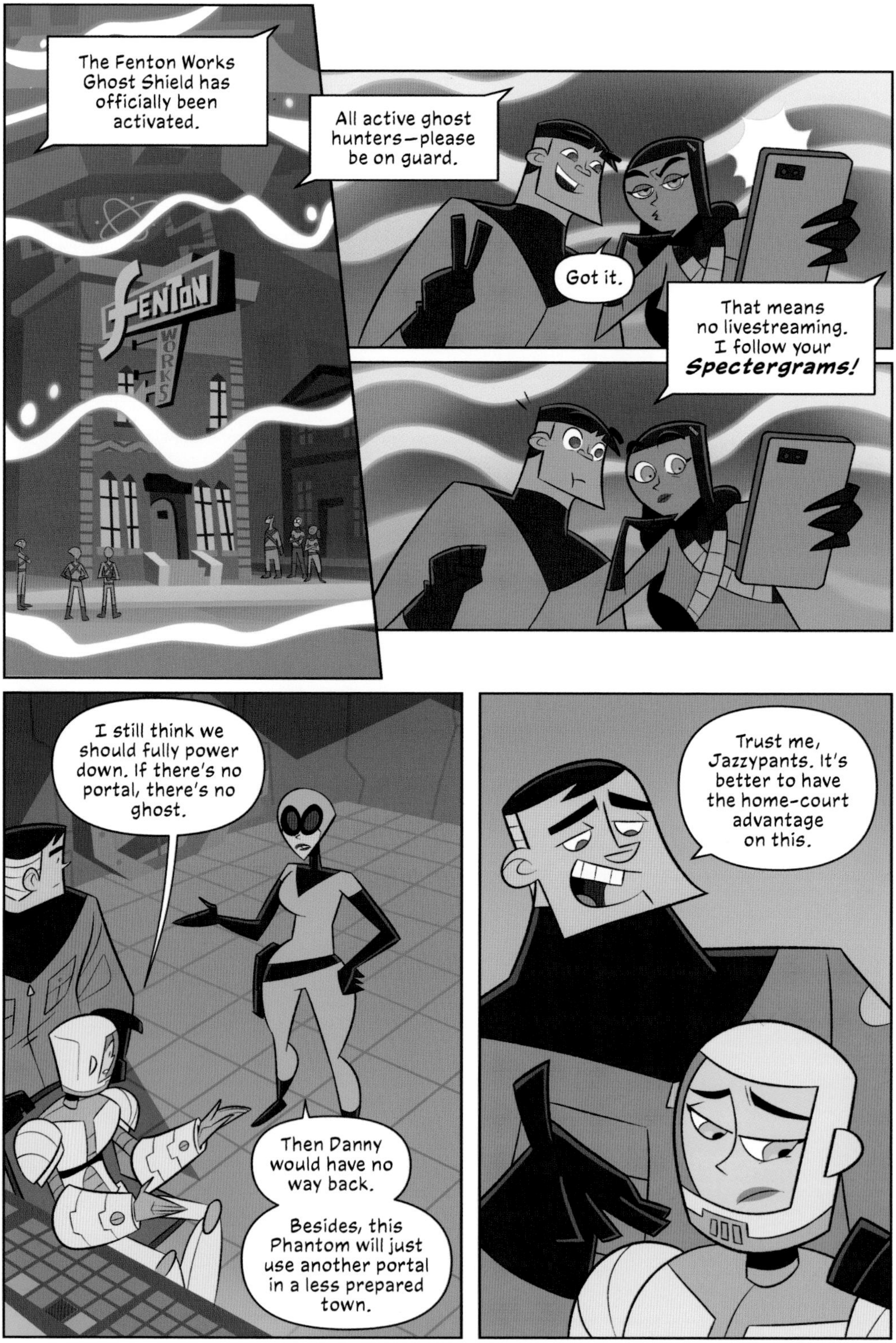
The Fenton Works Ghost Shield has officially been activated.
All active ghost hunters—please be on guard.
FENTON WORKS
Got it.
That means no livestreaming. I follow your *Spectergrams!*
I still think we should fully power down. If there's no portal, there's no ghost.
Then Danny would have no way back.
Besides, this Phantom will just use another portal in a less prepared town.
Trust me, Jazzypants. It's better to have the home-court advantage on this.

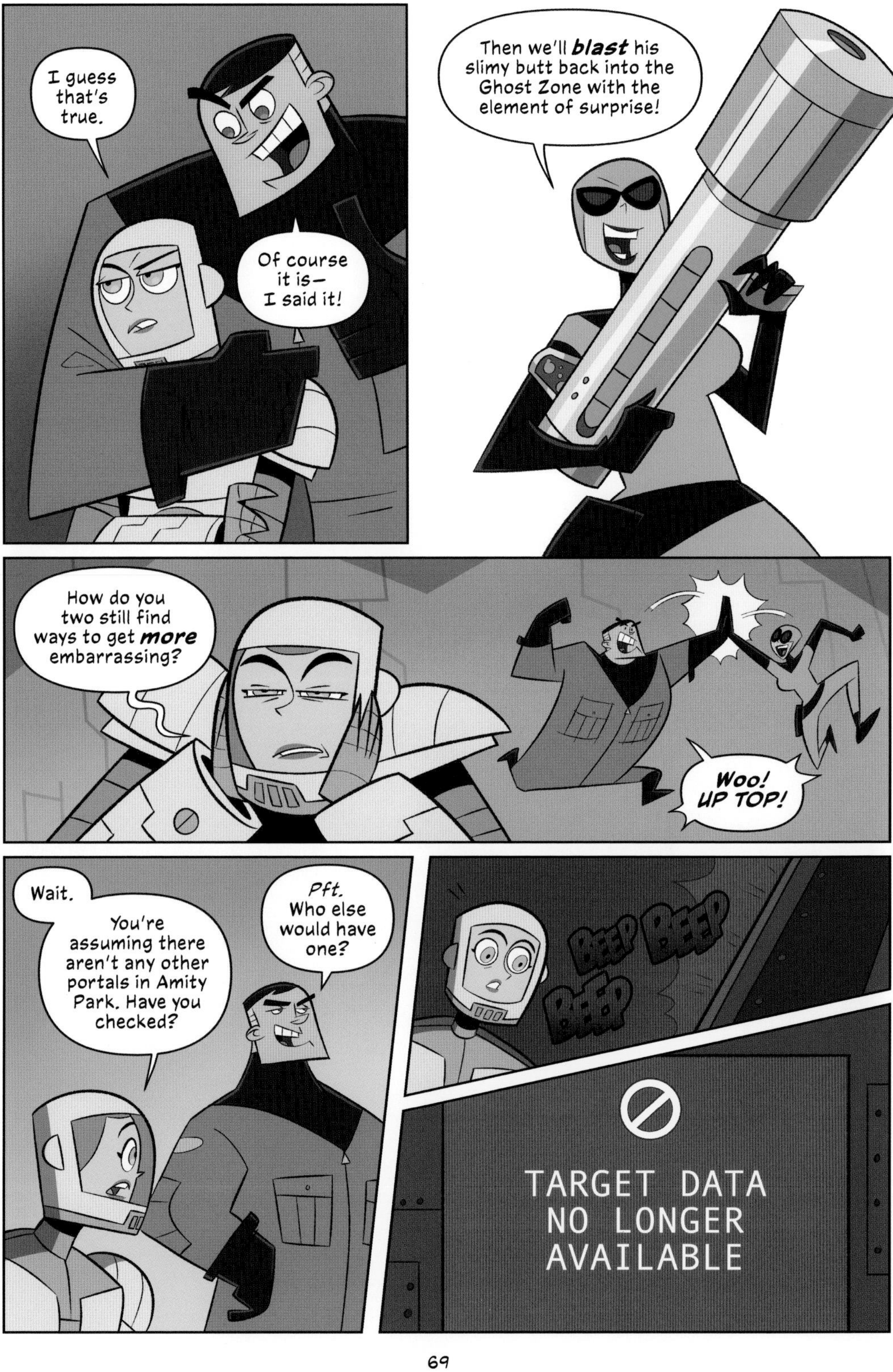
I guess that's true.
Of course it is— I said it!
Then we'll *blast* his slimy butt back into the Ghost Zone with the element of surprise!
How do you two still find ways to get *more* embarrassing?
Woo! UP TOP!
Wait.
You're assuming there aren't any other portals in Amity Park. Have you checked?
Pft. Who else would have one?
BEEP BEEP BEEP
TARGET DATA NO LONGER AVAILABLE

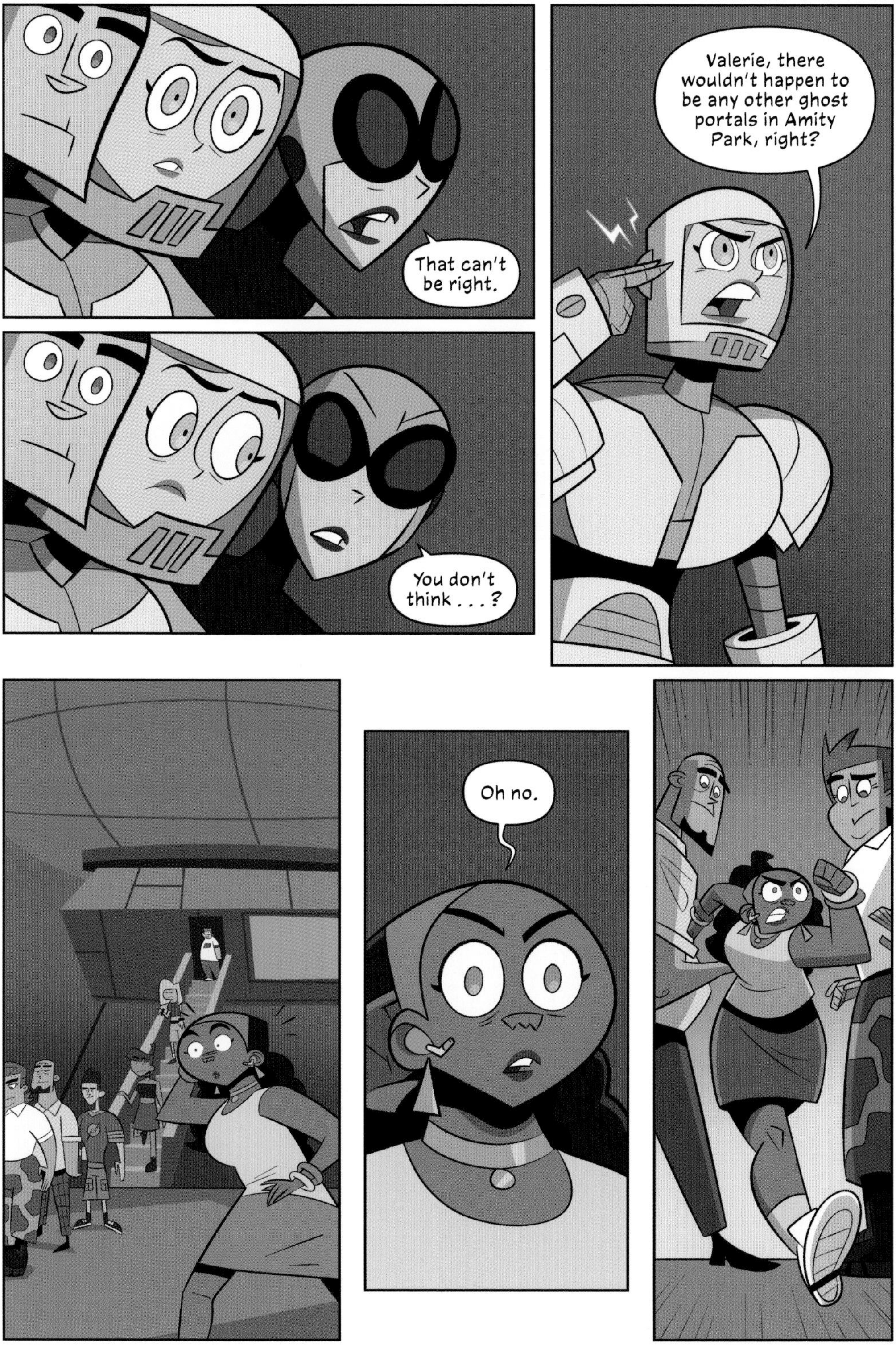
That can't be right.
You don't think . . . ?
Valerie, there wouldn't happen to be any other ghost portals in Amity Park, right?
Oh no.

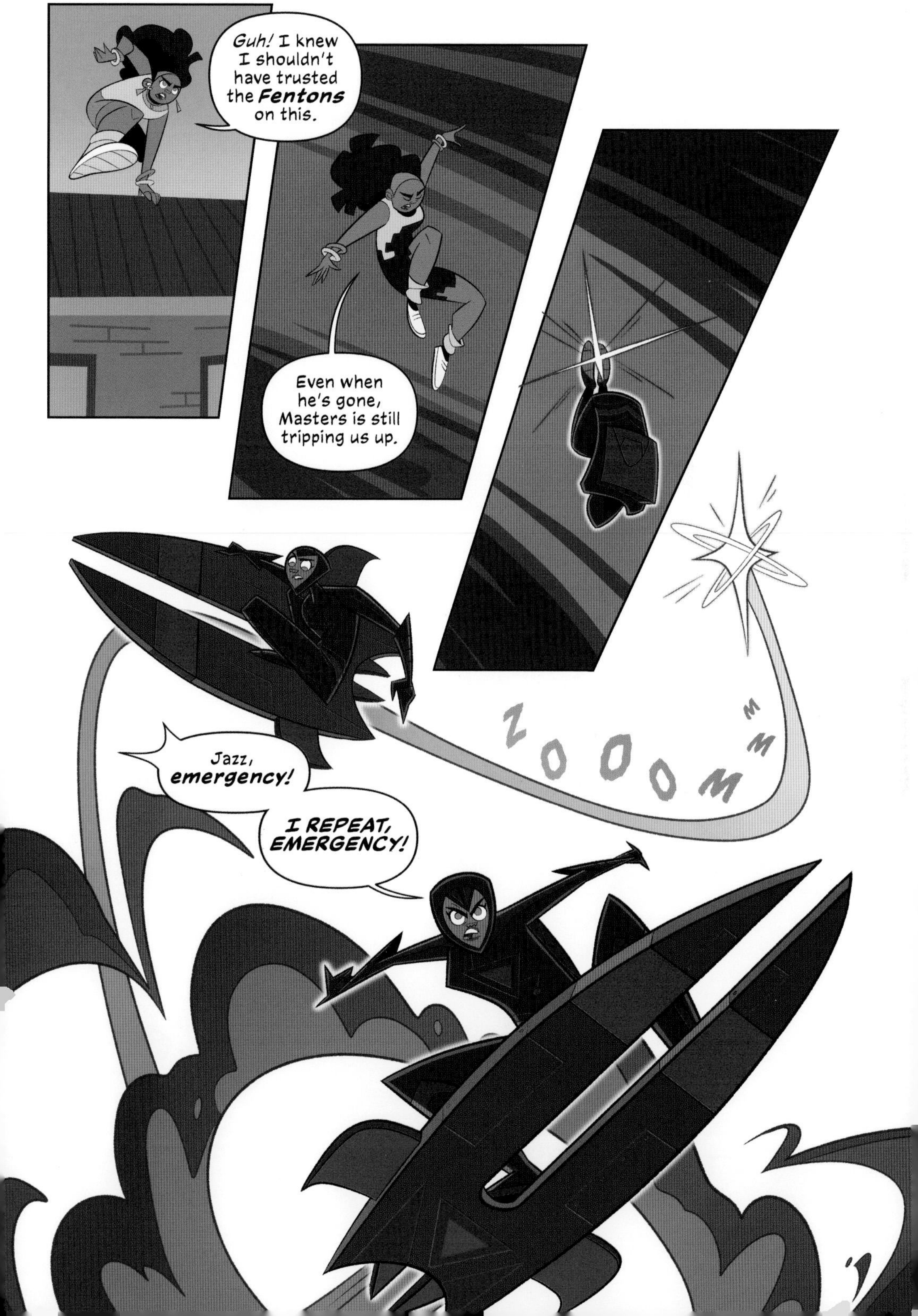
Guh! I knew I shouldn't have trusted the ***Fentons*** on this.
Even when he's gone, Masters is still tripping us up.
ZOOOMMMM
Jazz, ***emergency!***
I REPEAT, EMERGENCY!

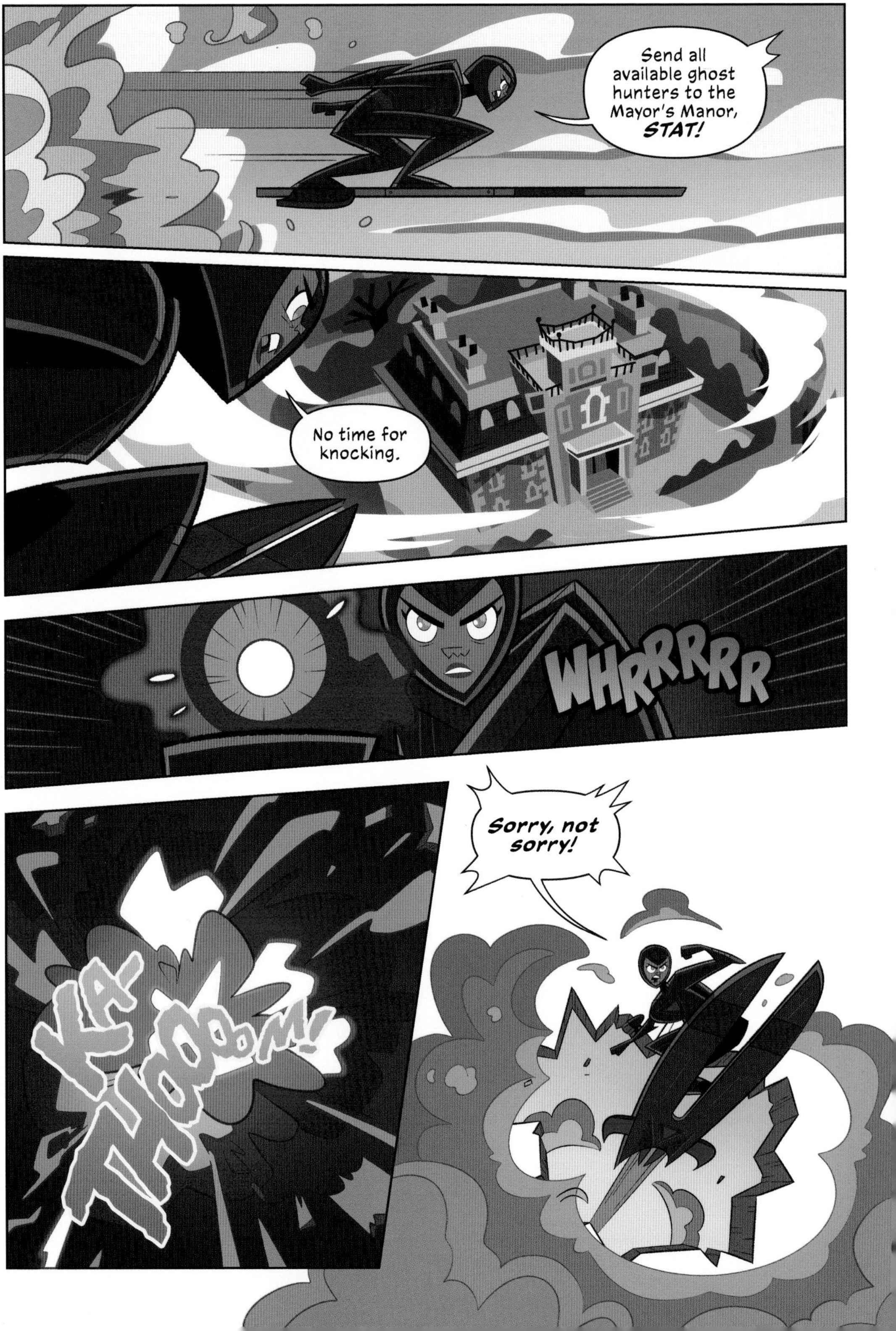

Send all available ghost hunters to the Mayor's Manor, ***STAT!***
No time for knocking.
WHRRRRR
Sorry, not sorry!
KA-THOOOM!

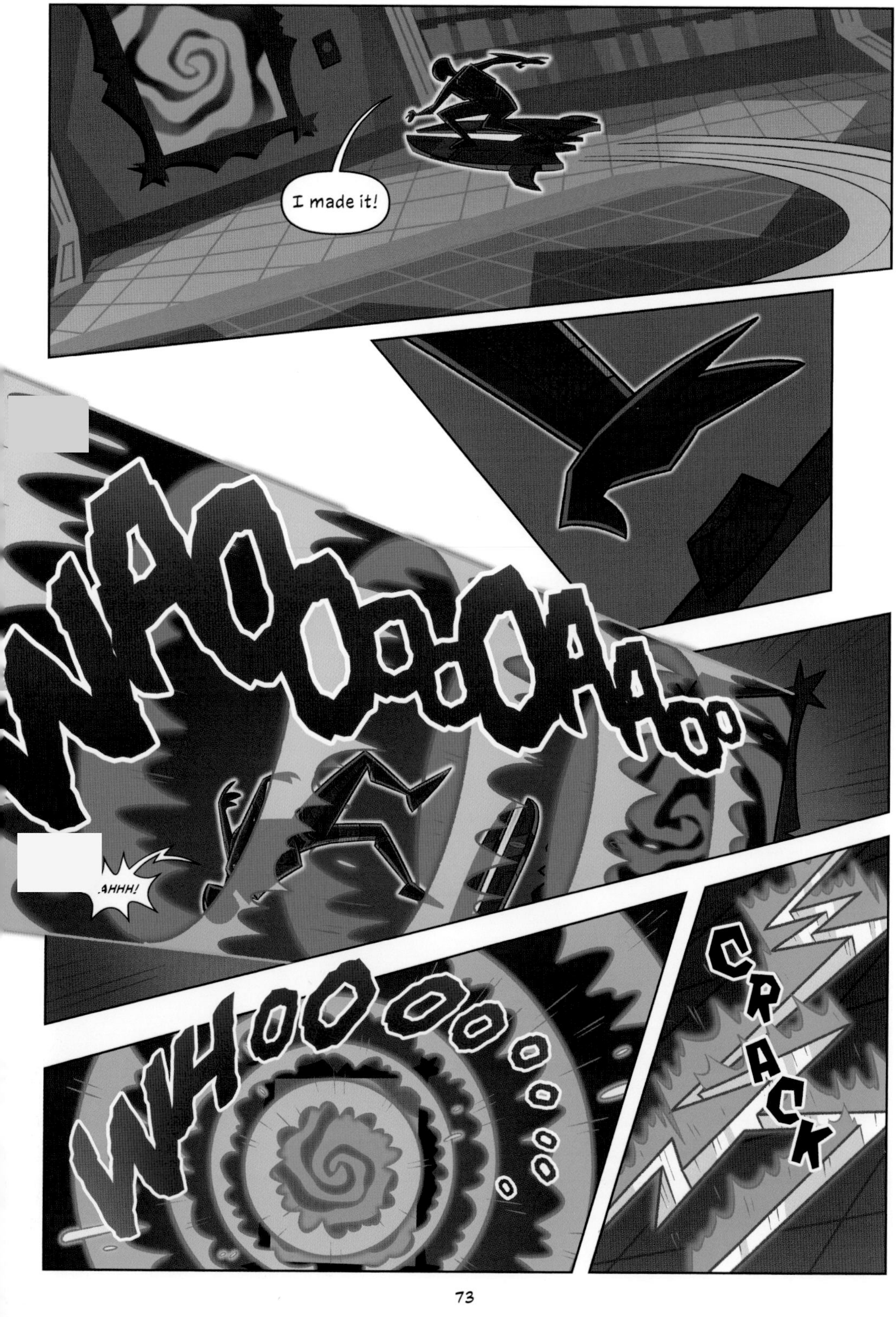
I made it!
WAOOOOAAoo
AHHH!
WHOOOOOOoooo...
CRACK

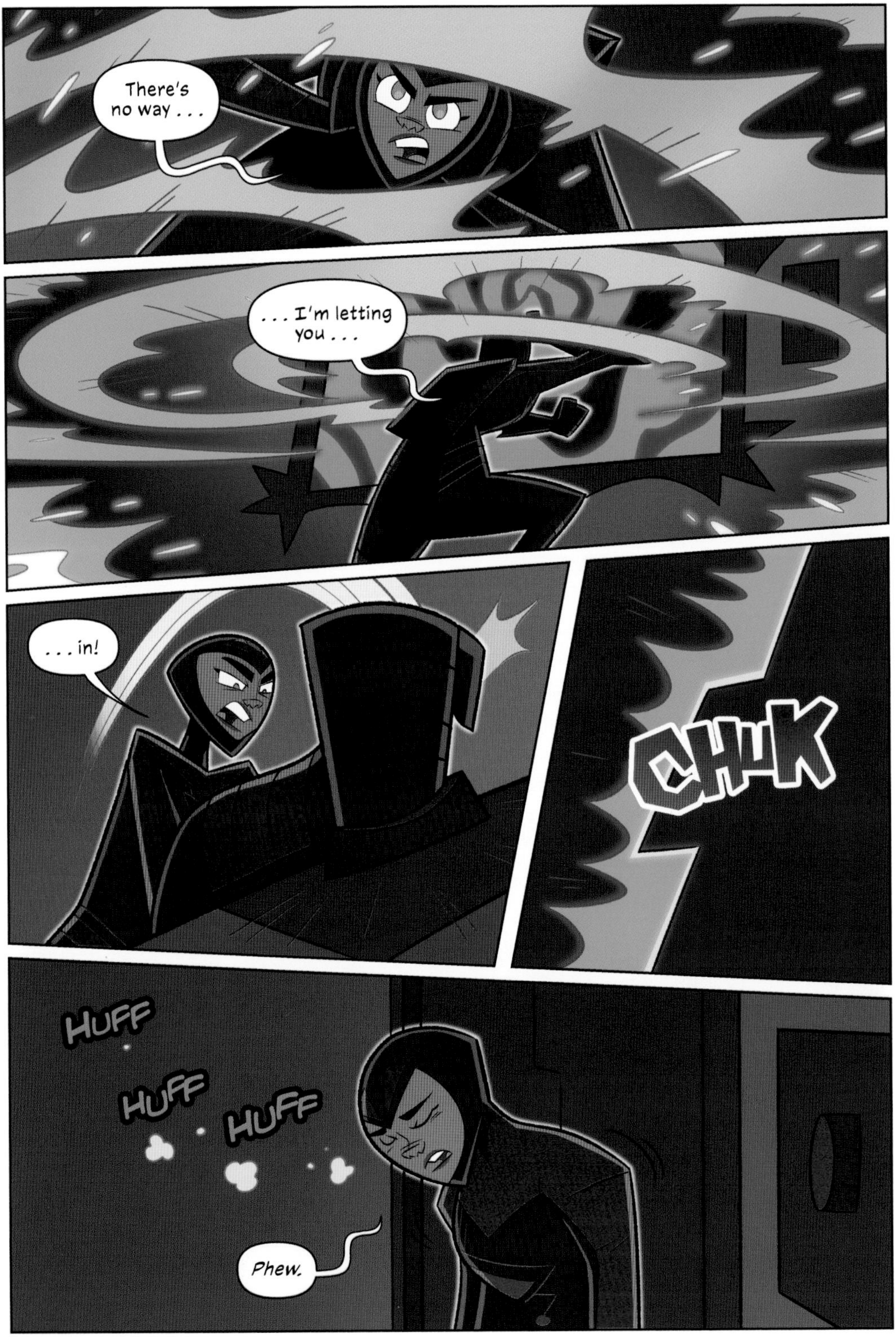
There's no way . . .
. . . I'm letting you . . .
. . . in!
CHUK
HUFF
HUFF
HUFF
Phew.

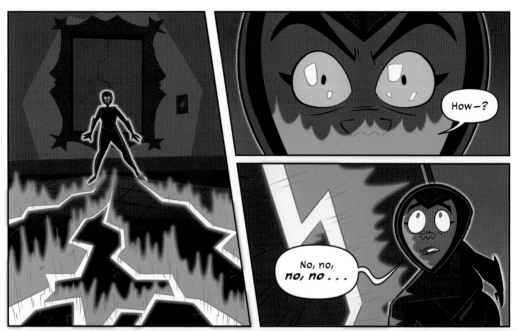

How—?

No, no, *no, no . . .*

THUD!

AHH!

BAM

BAM

BOOOOm!

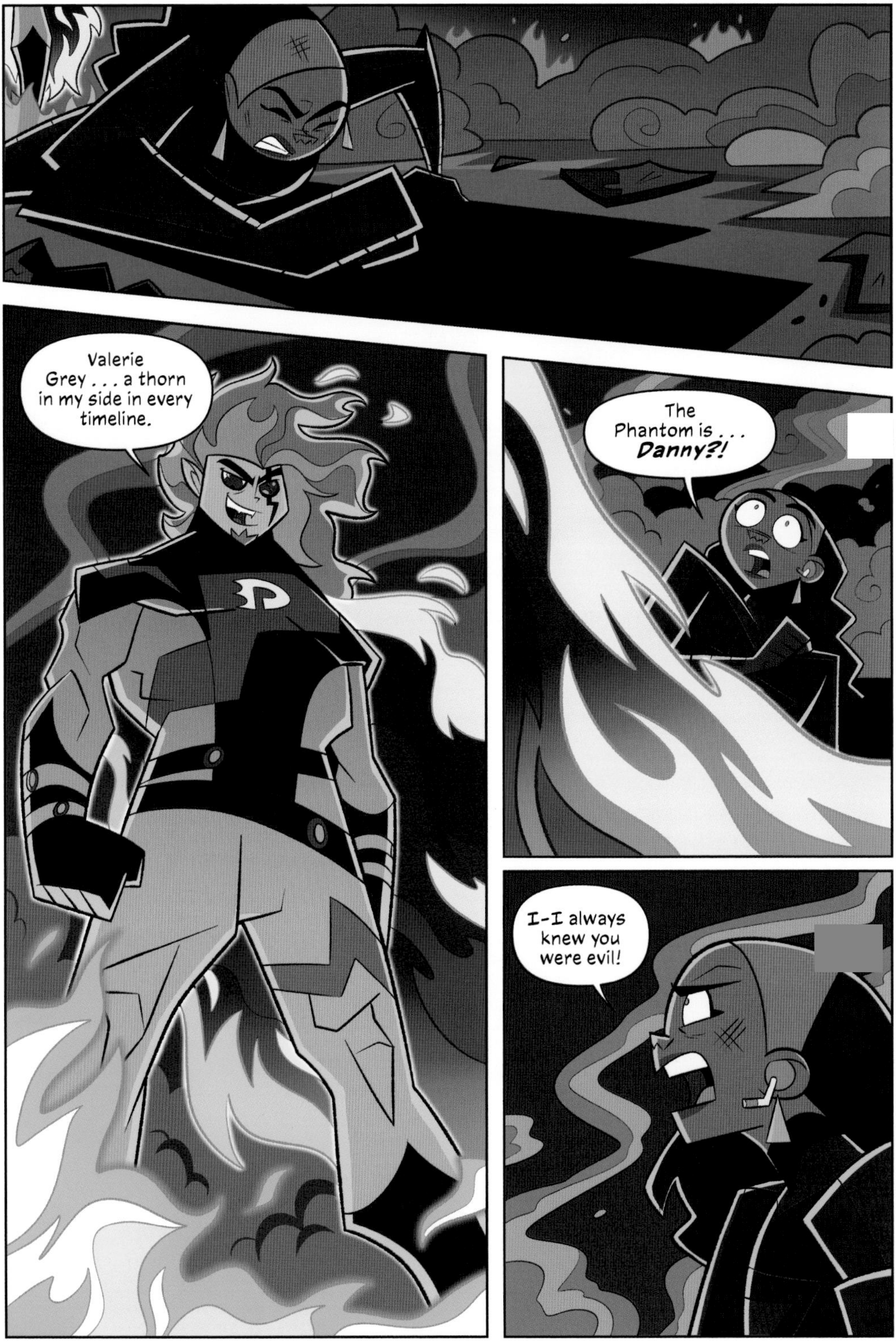
Valerie Grey . . . a thorn in my side in every timeline.
The Phantom is . . . **Danny?!**
I-I always knew you were evil!

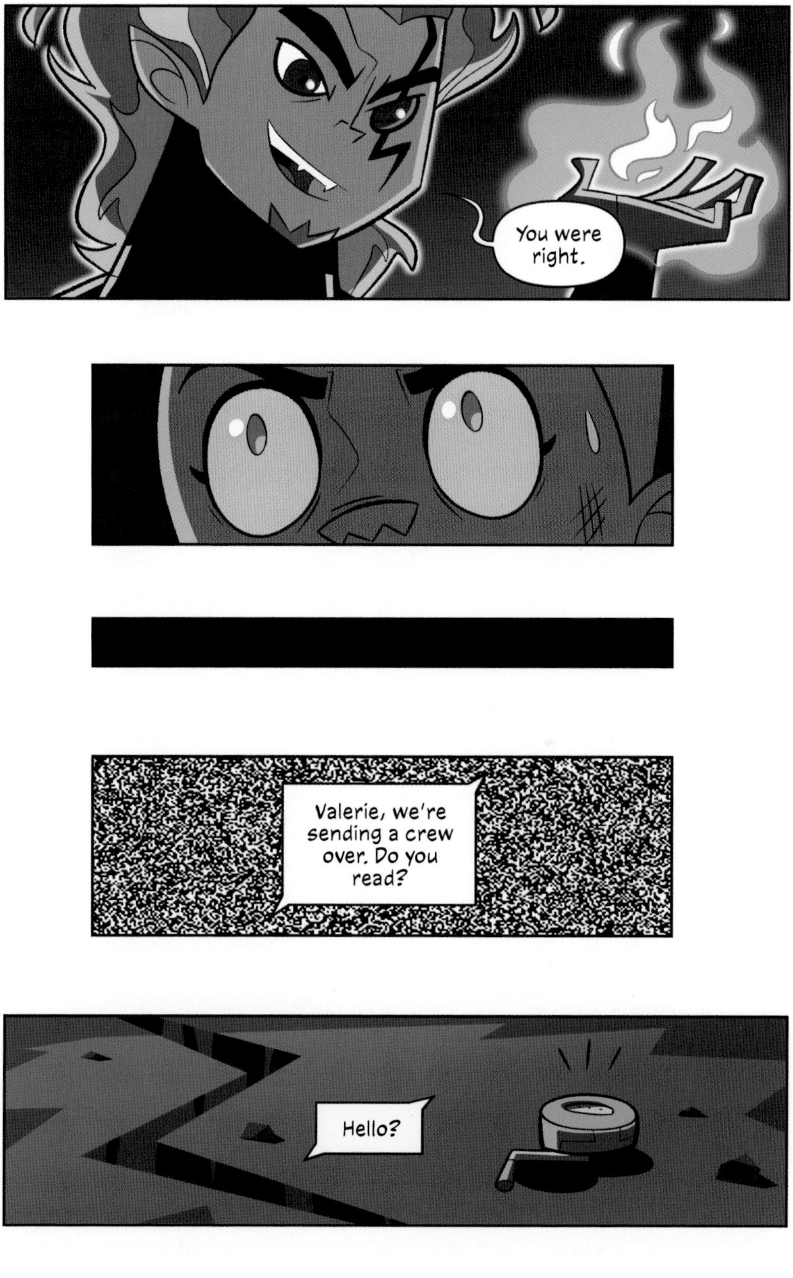
You were right.
Valerie, we're sending a crew over. Do you read?
Hello?

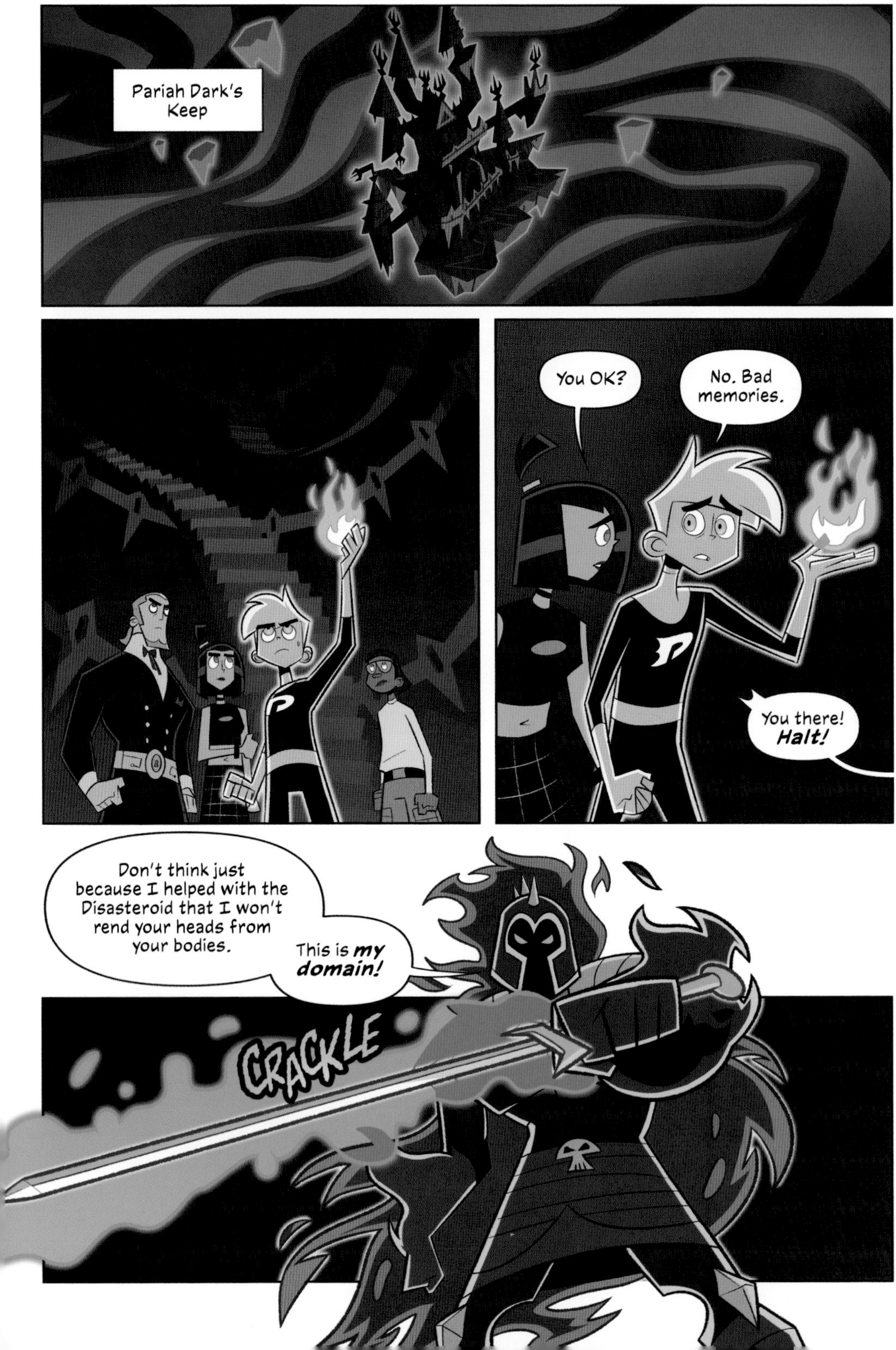
Pariah Dark's Keep
You OK?
No. Bad memories.
You there! Halt!
Don't think just because I helped with the Disasteroid that I won't rend your heads from your bodies.
This is my domain!
CRACKLE

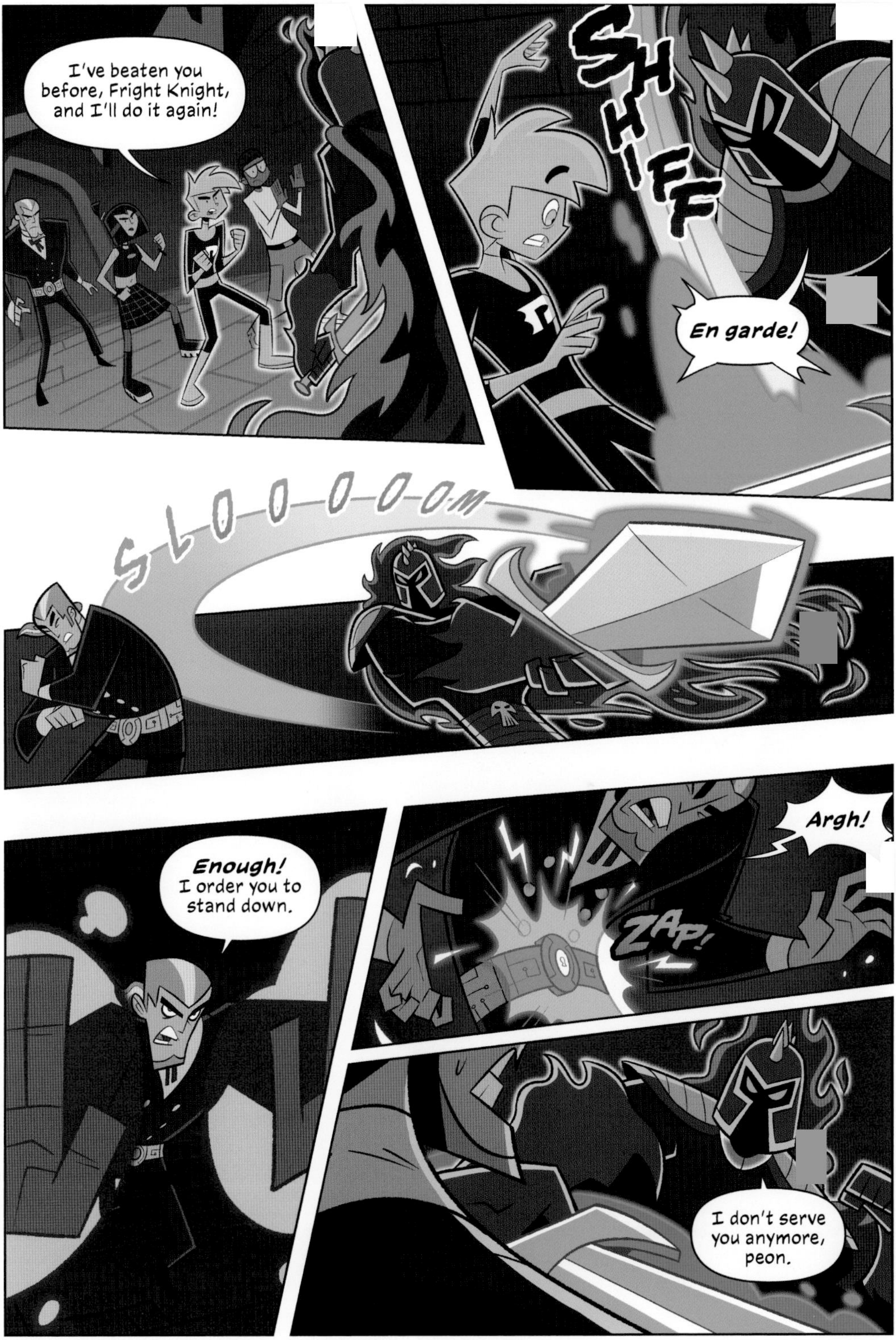

I've beaten you before, Fright Knight, and I'll do it again!
SHHIFF
En garde!
SLOOOOOOM
Enough! I order you to stand down.
Argh!
ZAP!
I don't serve you anymore, peon.

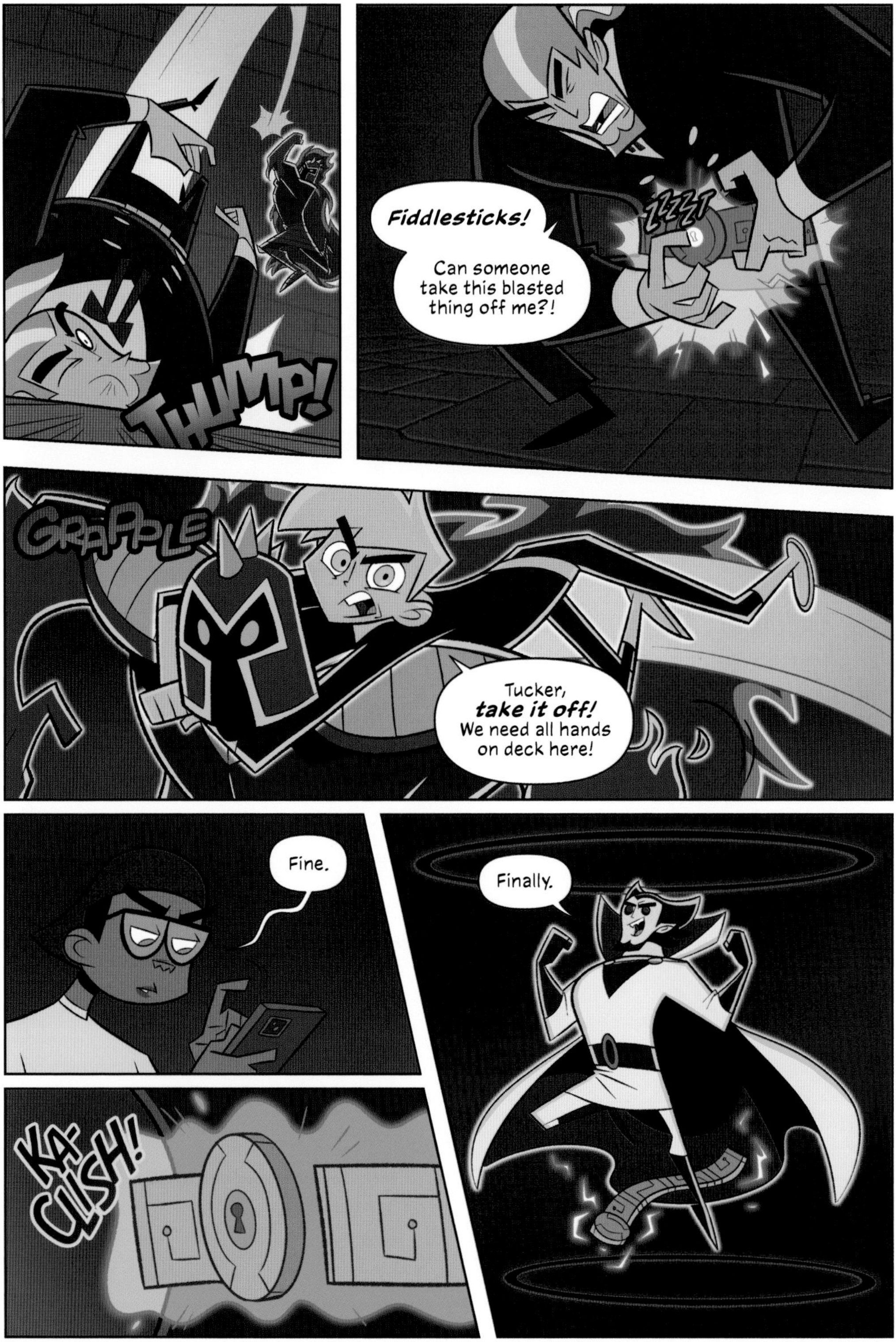
THUMP!
Fiddlesticks!
Can someone take this blasted thing off me?!
ZZZT
GRAPPLE
Tucker, ***take it off!*** We need all hands on deck here!
Fine.
Finally.
KA-CLISH!

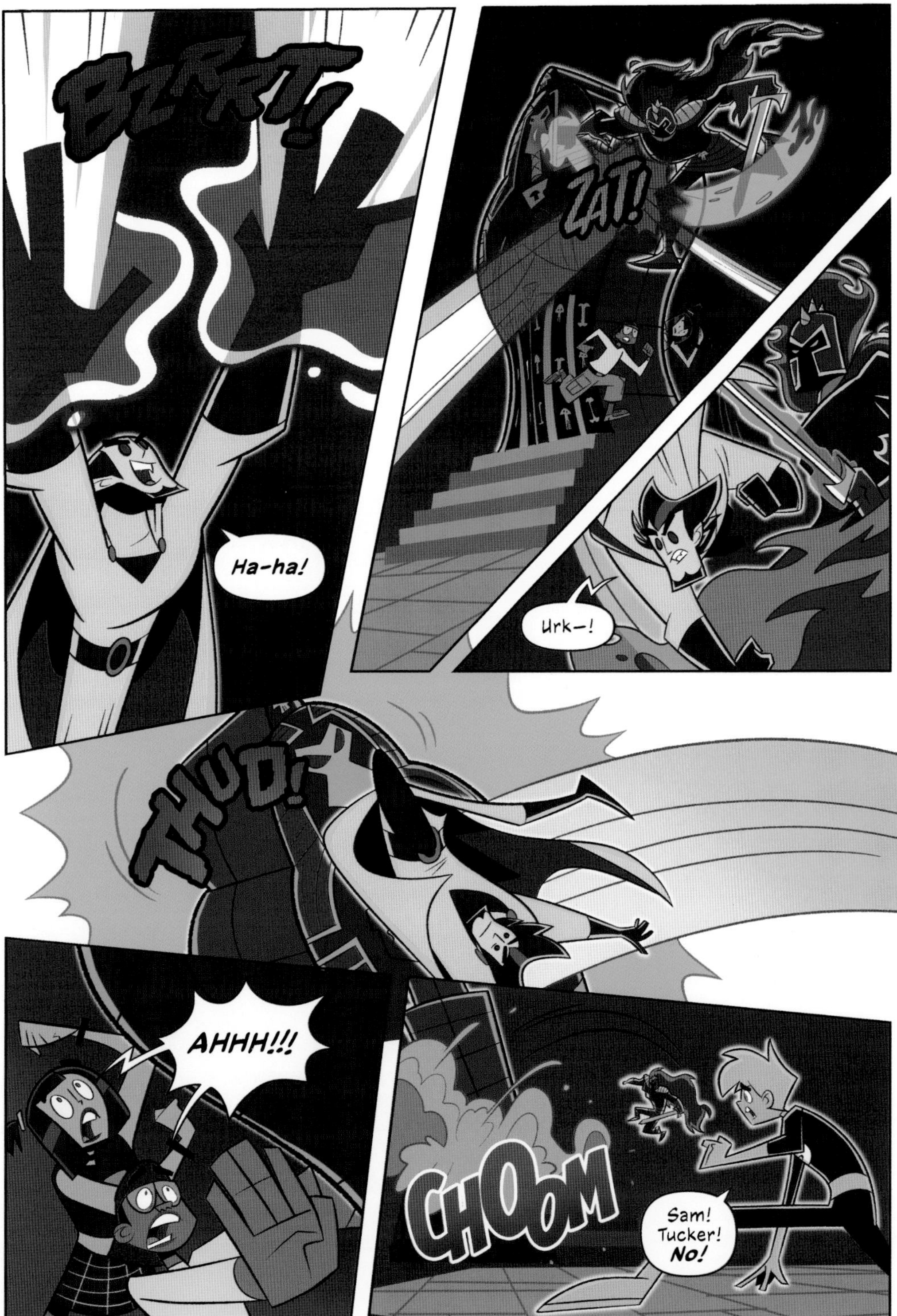
BZRRT!!
Ha-ha!
ZAT!
Urk–!
THUD!
AHHH!!!
CHOOM
Sam! Tucker! No!

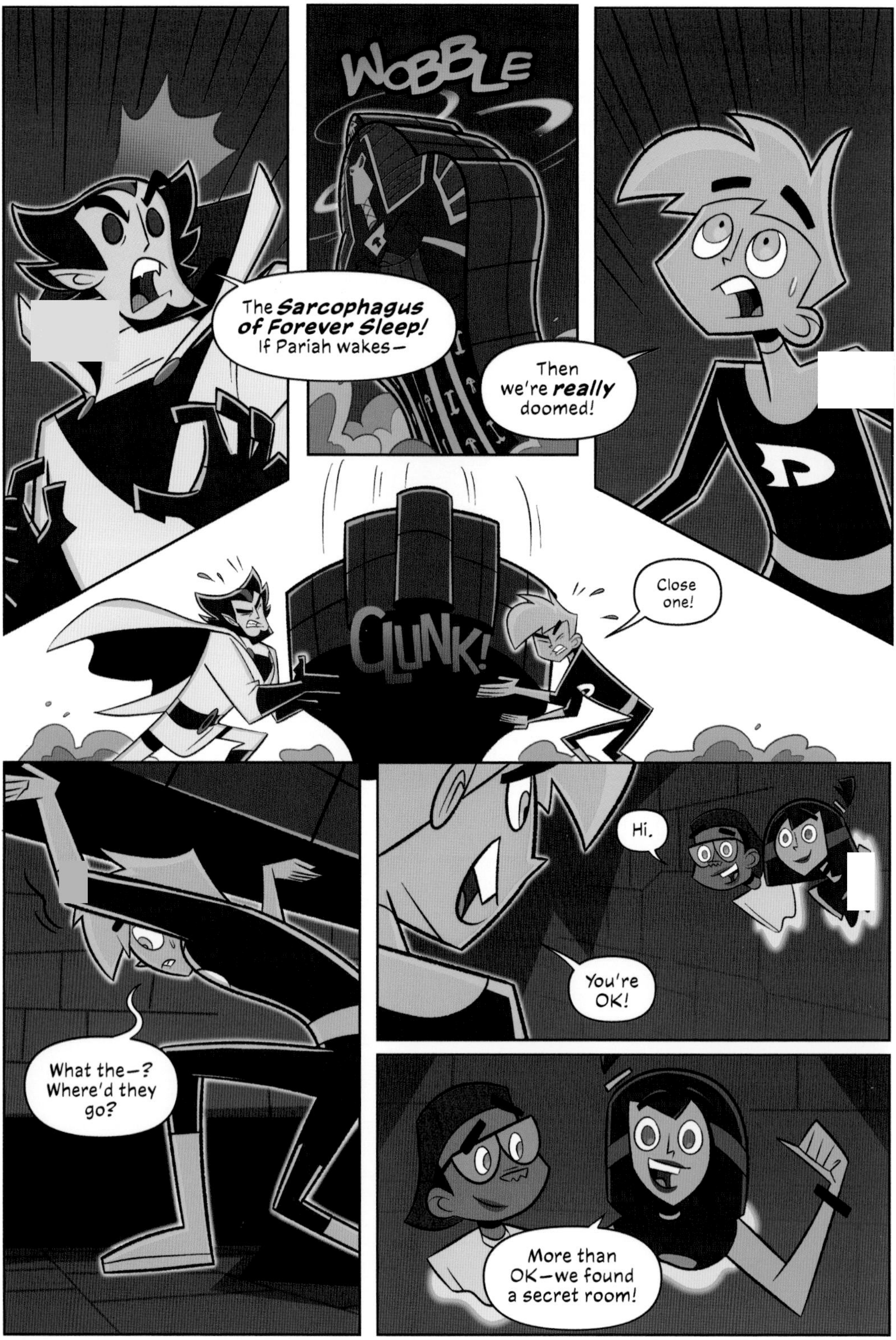

WOBBLE
The Sarcophagus of Forever Sleep! If Pariah wakes—
Then we're really doomed!
CLUNK!
Close one!
What the—? Where'd they go?
Hi.
You're OK!
More than OK—we found a secret room!

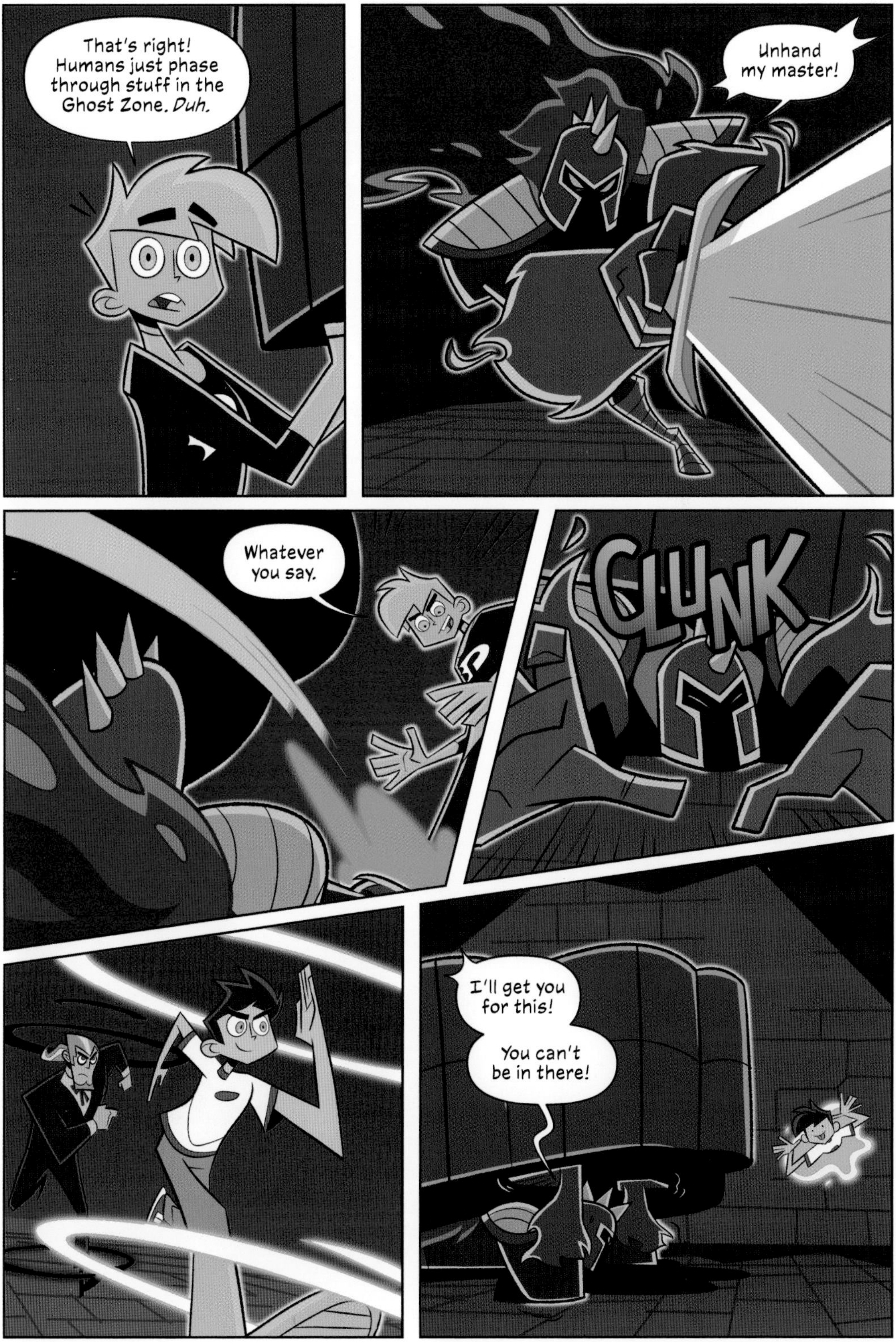
That's right! Humans just phase through stuff in the Ghost Zone. *Duh.*
Unhand my master!
Whatever you say.
CLUNK
I'll get you for this!
You can't be in there!

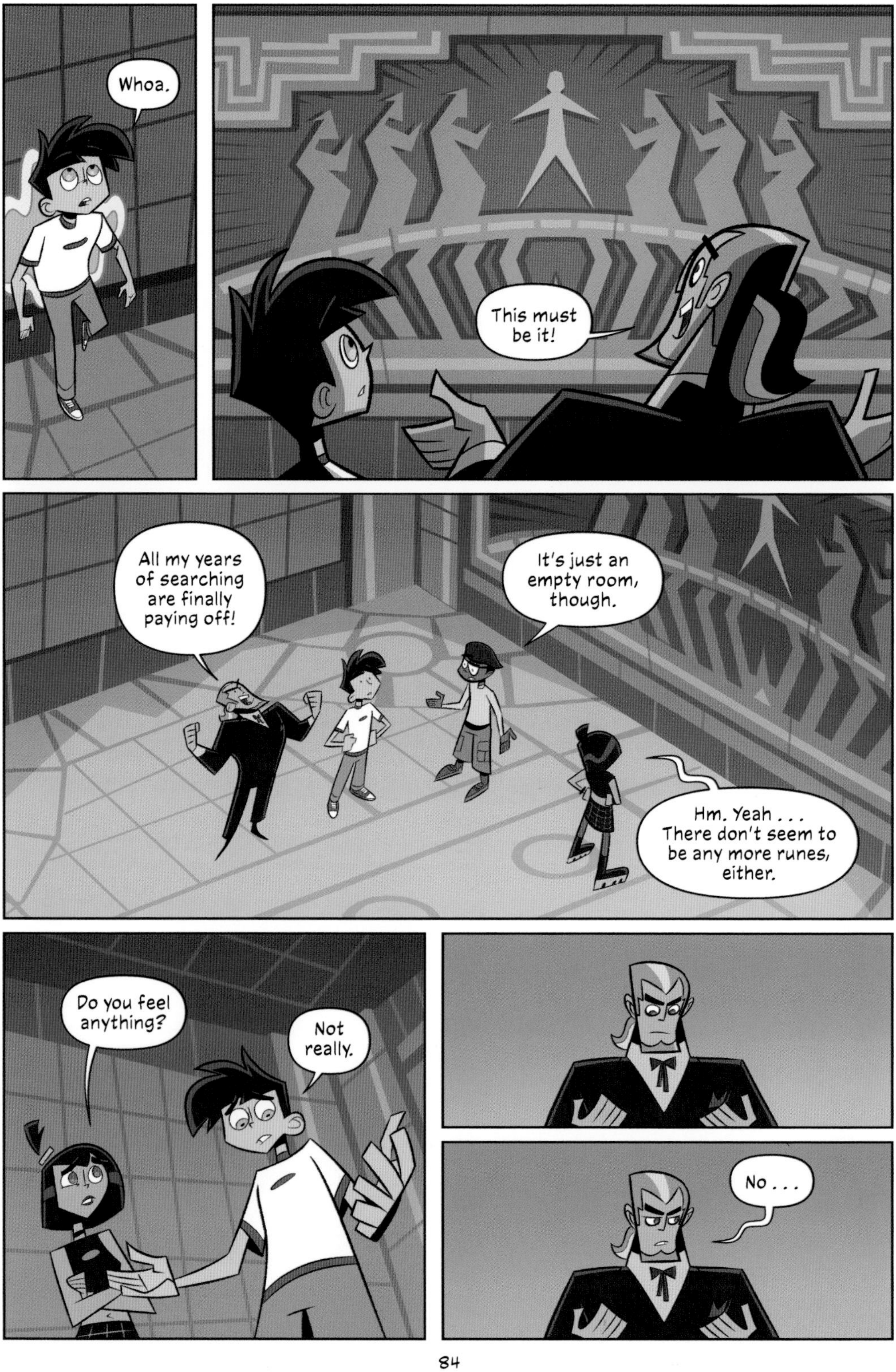

Whoa.
This must be it!
All my years of searching are finally paying off!
It's just an empty room, though.
Hm. Yeah . . . There don't seem to be any more runes, either.
Do you feel anything?
Not really.
No . . .

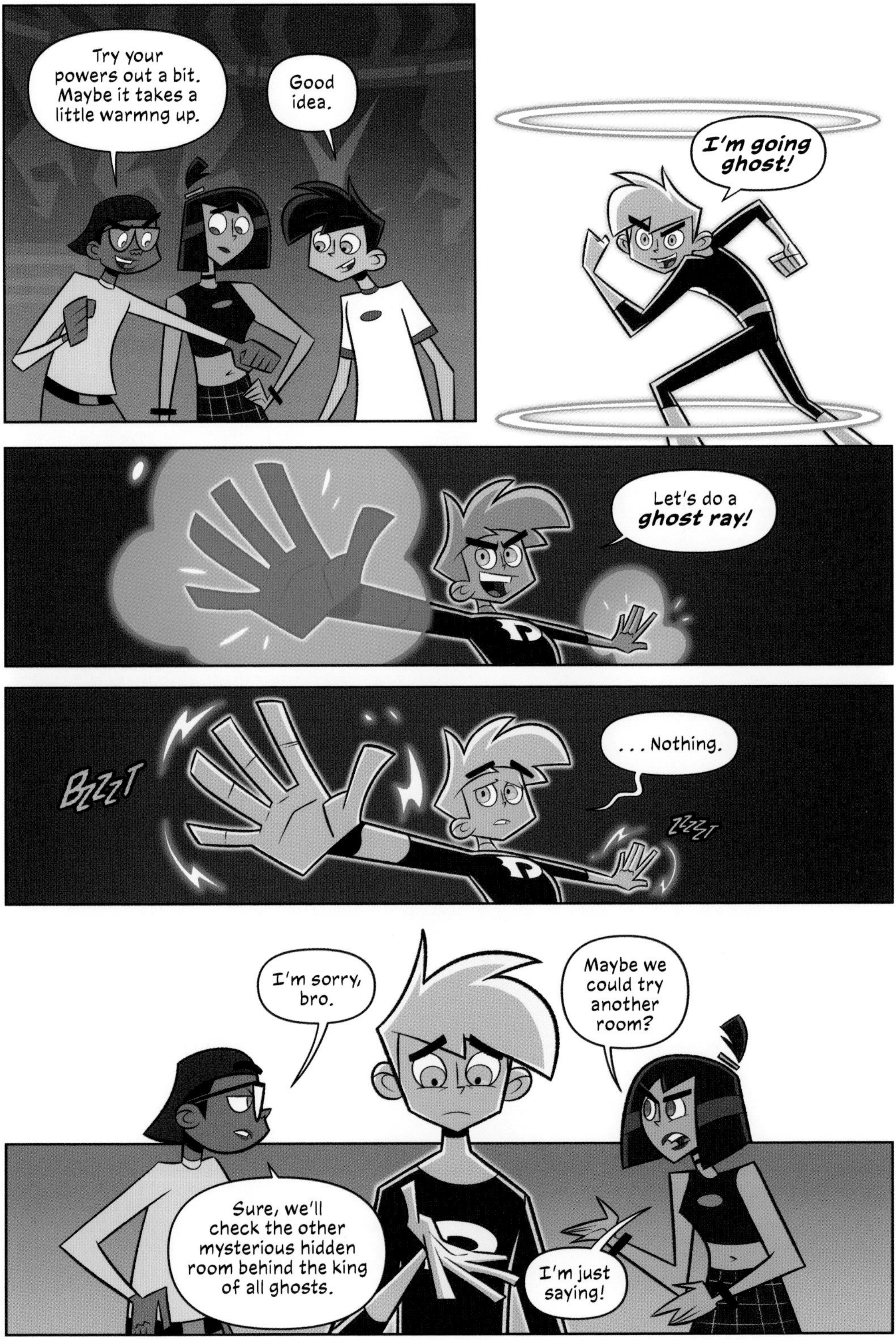
Try your powers out a bit. Maybe it takes a little warmng up.
Good idea.
I'm going ghost!
Let's do a ghost ray!
BZZZT
. . . Nothing.
ZZZZT
I'm sorry, bro.
Maybe we could try another room?
Sure, we'll check the other mysterious hidden room behind the king of all ghosts.
I'm just saying!

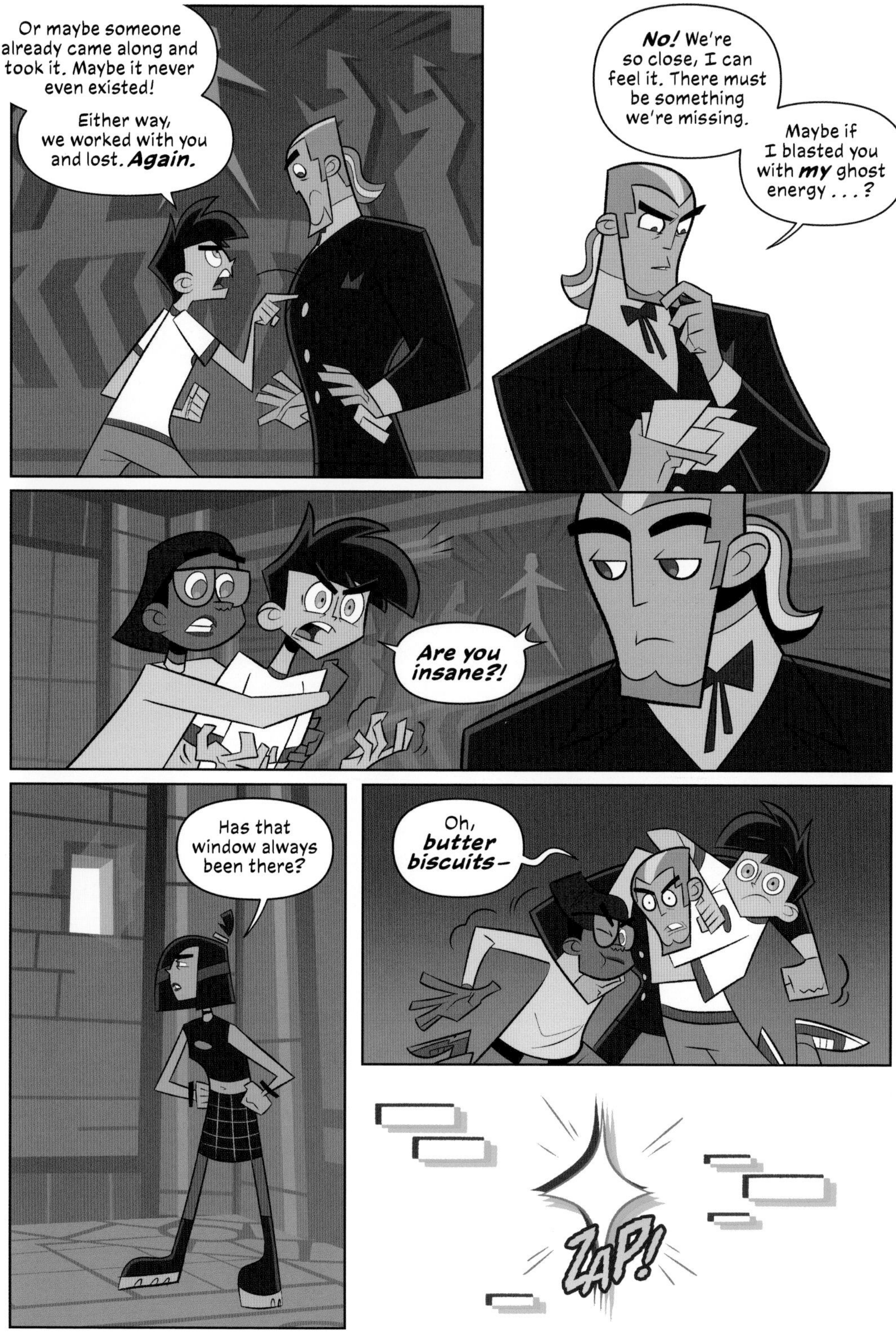
Or maybe someone already came along and took it. Maybe it never even existed!
Either way, we worked with you and lost. ***Again.***
No! We're so close, I can feel it. There must be something we're missing.
Maybe if I blasted you with ***my*** ghost energy . . . ?
Are you insane?!
Has that window always been there?
Oh, ***butter biscuits***–
ZAP!

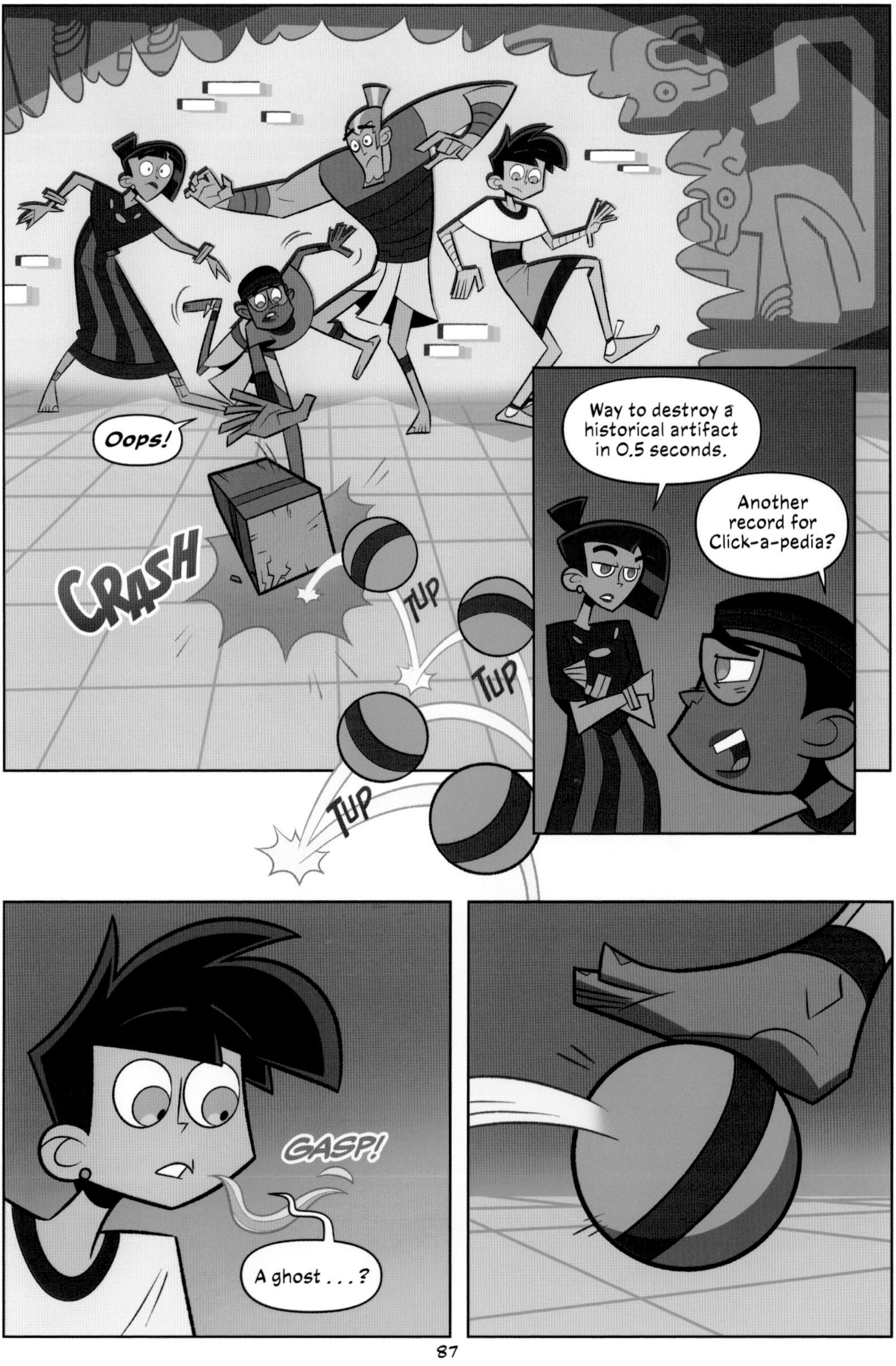
Oops!
CRASH
TUP
TUP
TUP
Way to destroy a historical artifact in 0.5 seconds.
Another record for Click-a-pedia?
GASP!
A ghost . . . ?

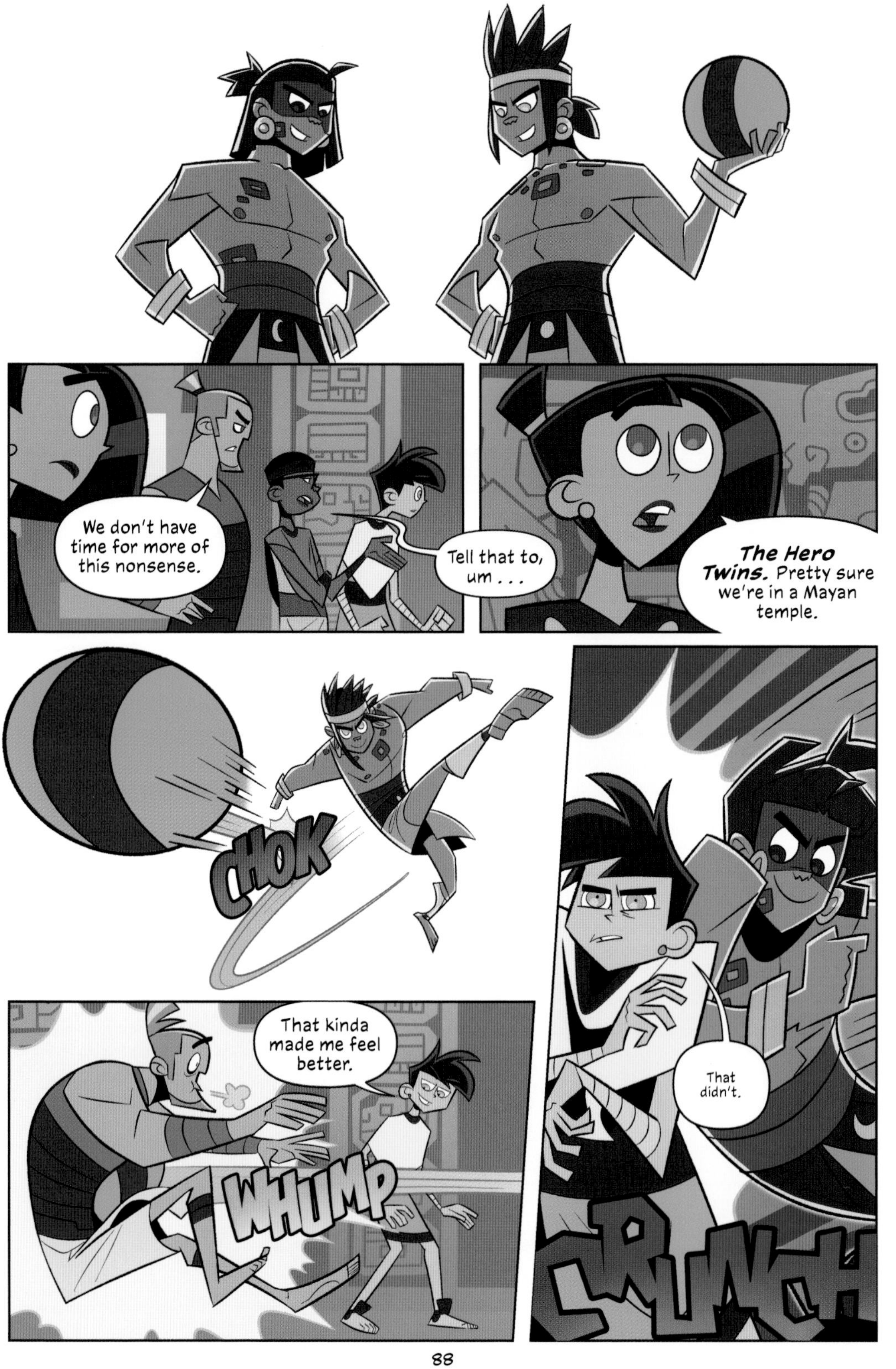
We don't have time for more of this nonsense.
Tell that to, um . . .
The Hero Twins. Pretty sure we're in a Mayan temple.
CHOK
That kinda made me feel better.
WHUMP
That didn't.
CRUNCH

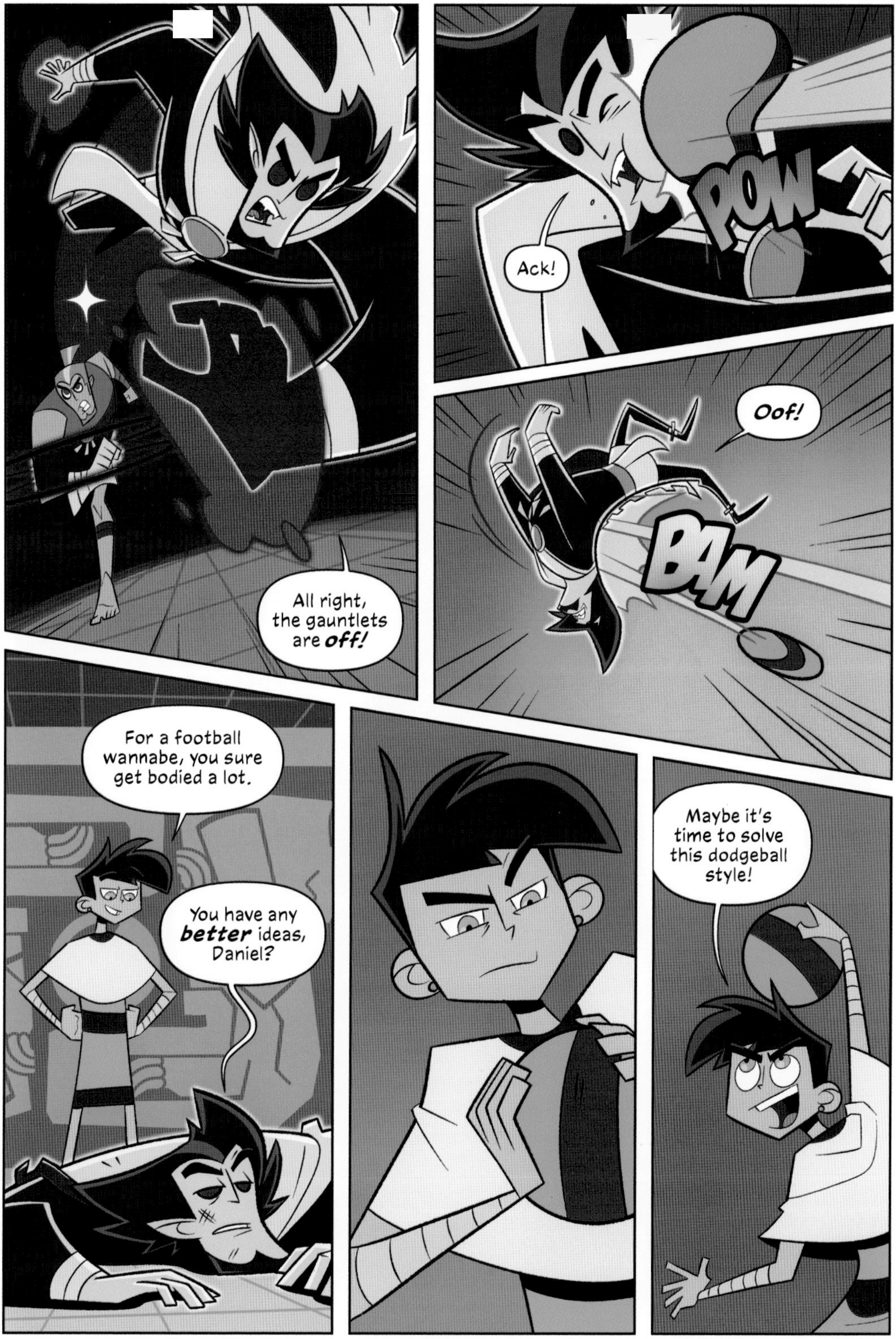
All right, the gauntlets are off!
POW
Ack!
Oof!
BAM
For a football wannabe, you sure get bodied a lot.
You have any better ideas, Daniel?
Maybe it's time to solve this dodgeball style!

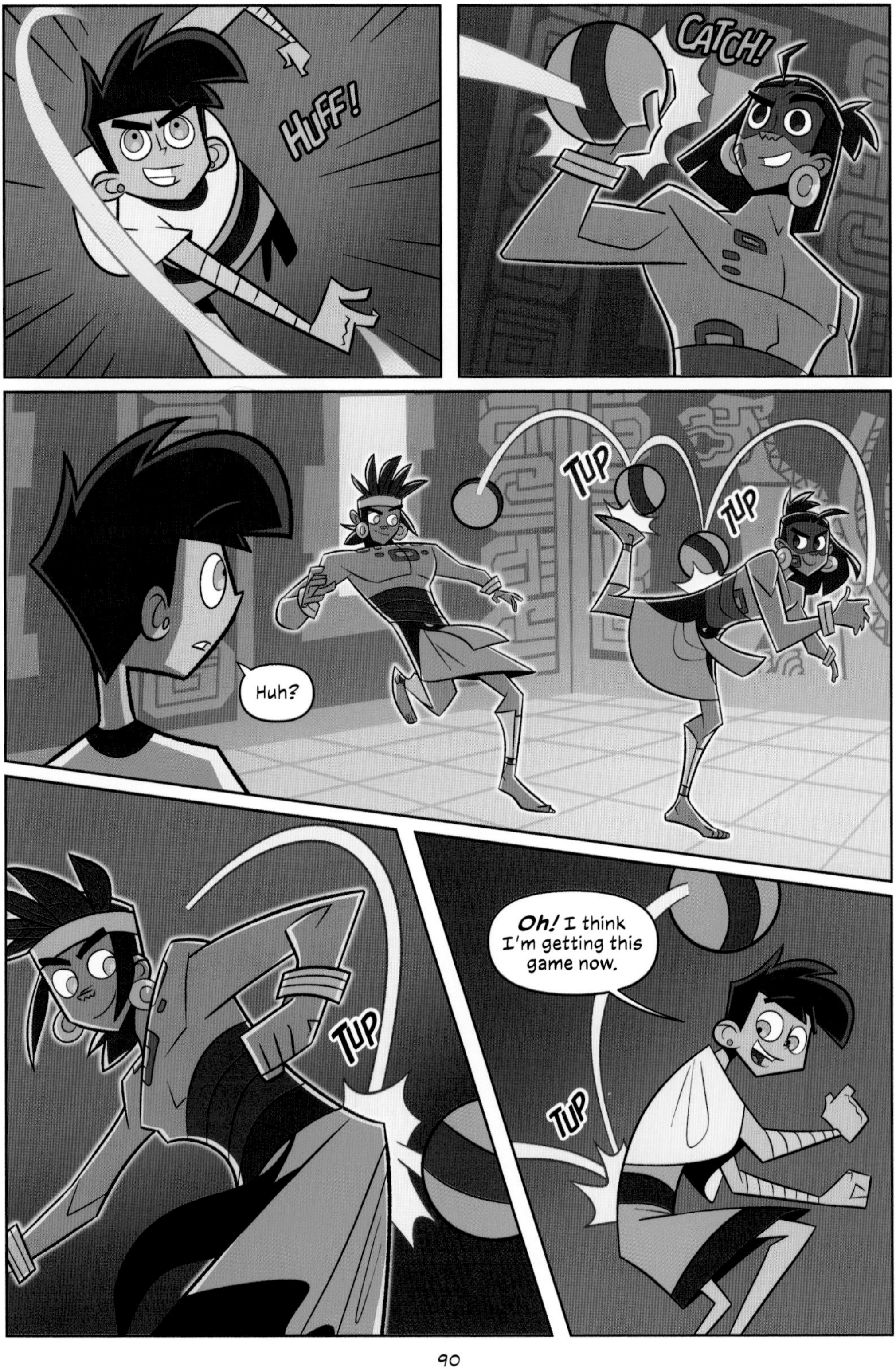
HUFF!
CATCH!
TUP
TUP
Huh?
TUP
Oh! I think I'm getting this game now.
TUP

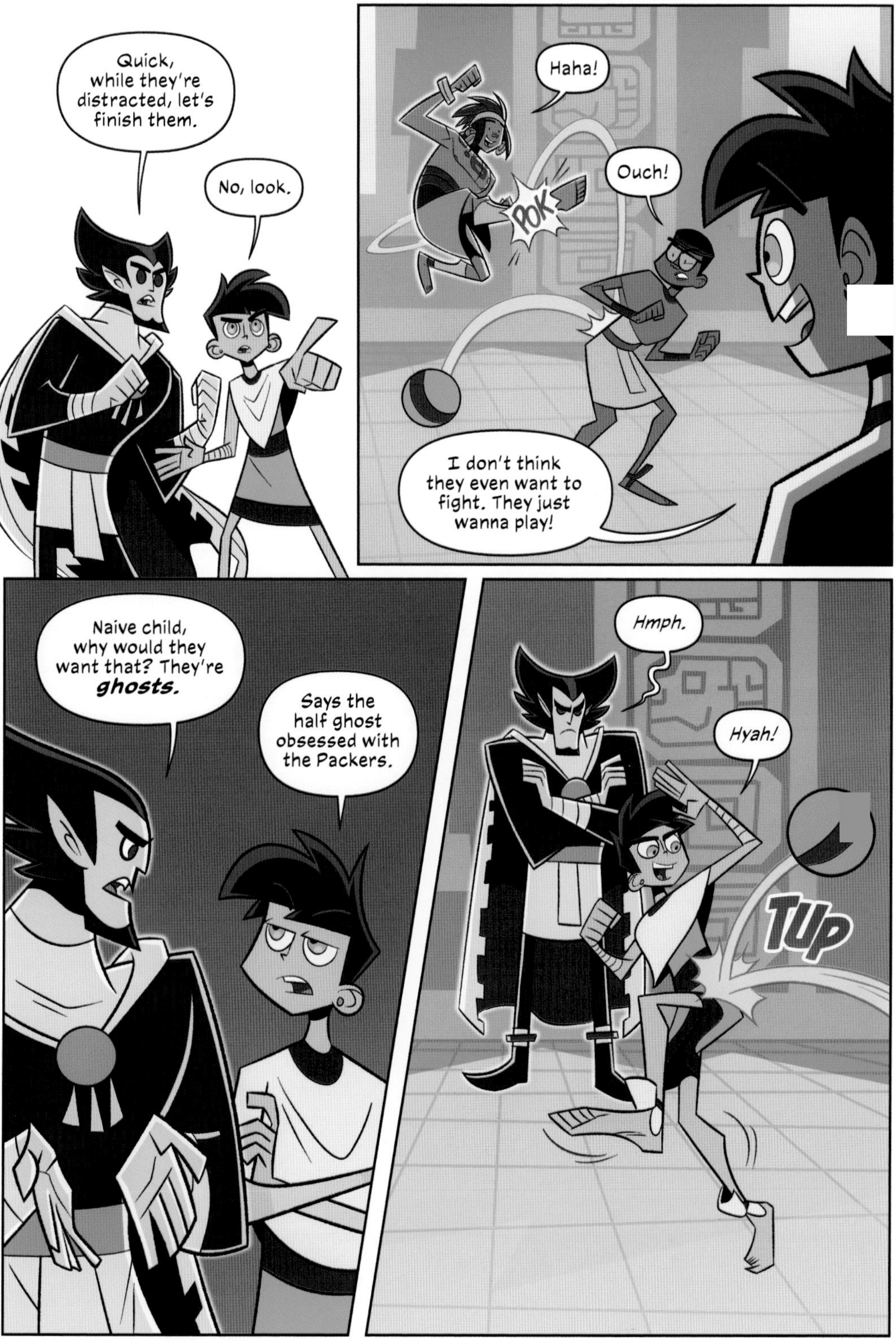
Quick, while they're distracted, let's finish them.
No, look.
Haha!
Ouch!
POK
I don't think they even want to fight. They just wanna play!
Naive child, why would they want that? They're *ghosts.*
Says the half ghost obsessed with the Packers.
Hmph.
Hyah!
TUP

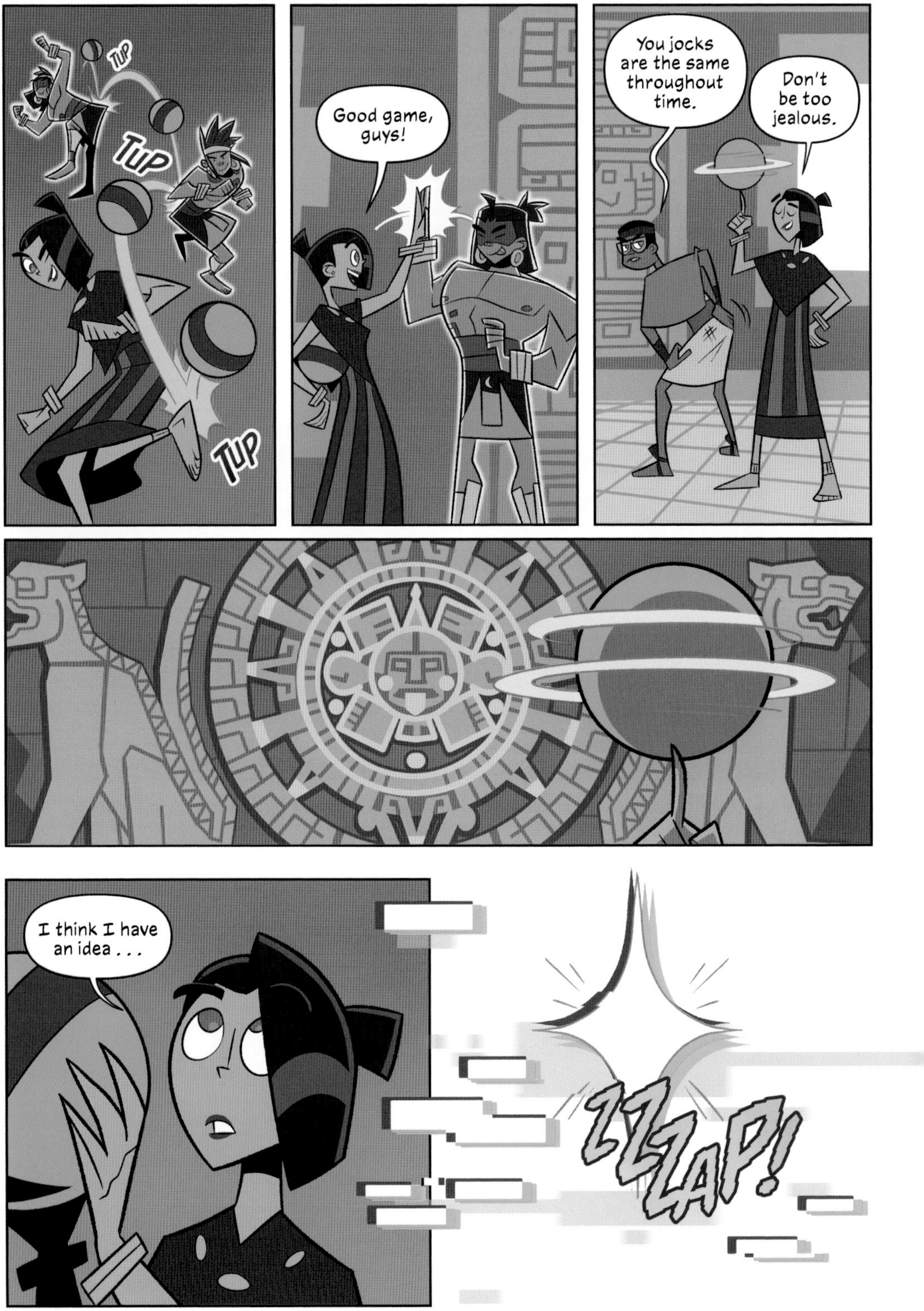
TUP
TUP
TUP
Good game, guys!
You jocks are the same throughout time.
Don't be too jealous.
I think I have an idea . . .
ZZZAP!

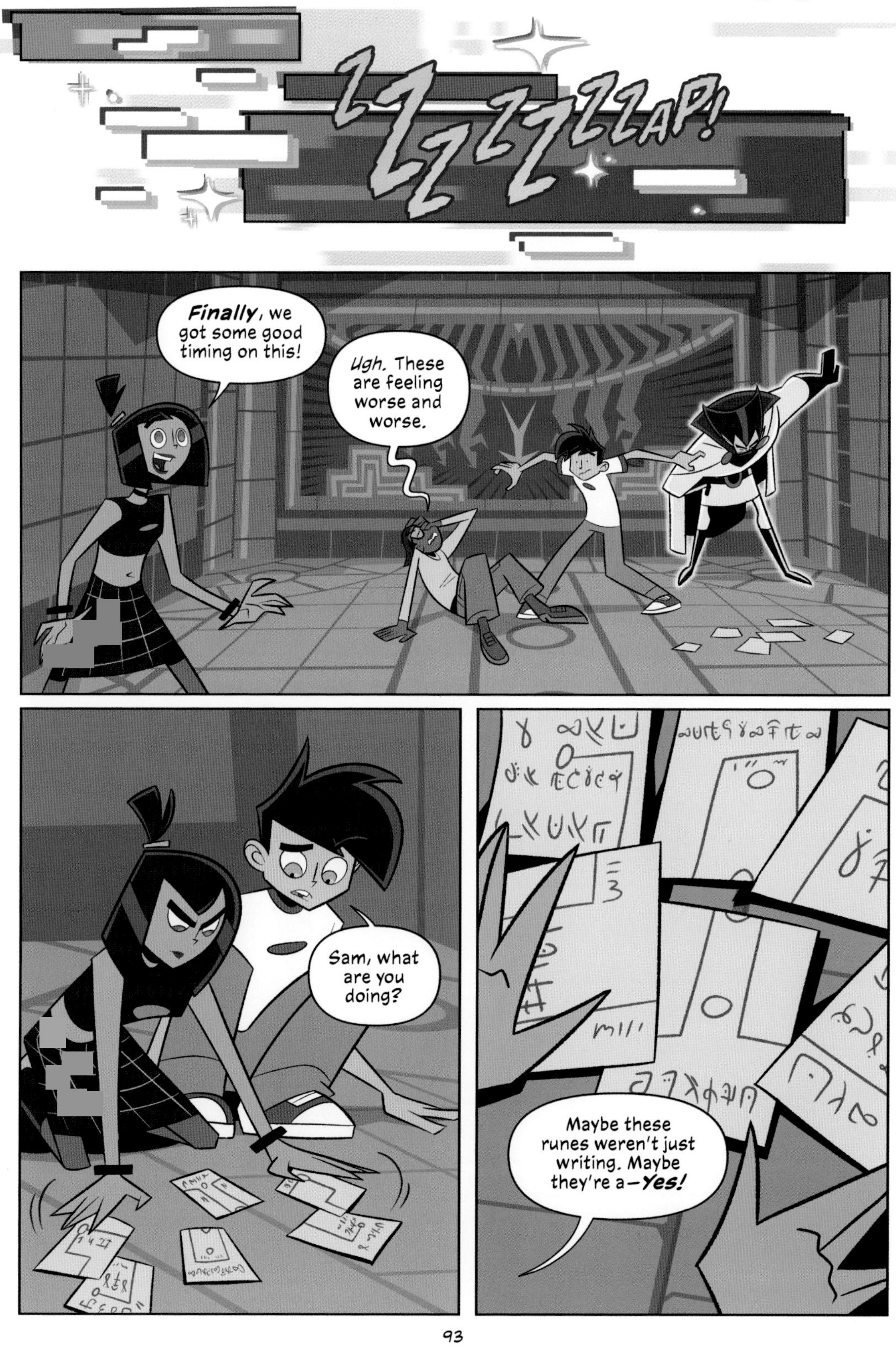
ZZZZZZZZAP!
Finally, we got some good timing on this!
Ugh. These are feeling worse and worse.
Sam, what are you doing?
Maybe these runes weren't just writing. Maybe they're a—***Yes!***

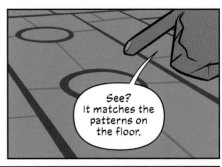

A map!

More like a cutaway diagram of the castle, by the looks of it.

See? It matches the patterns on the floor.

Nice one, Tuck!

It looks like there are seven spaces here. There should be matching ones on the floor.

On it!

CHOK

Guys! Check this out!

94

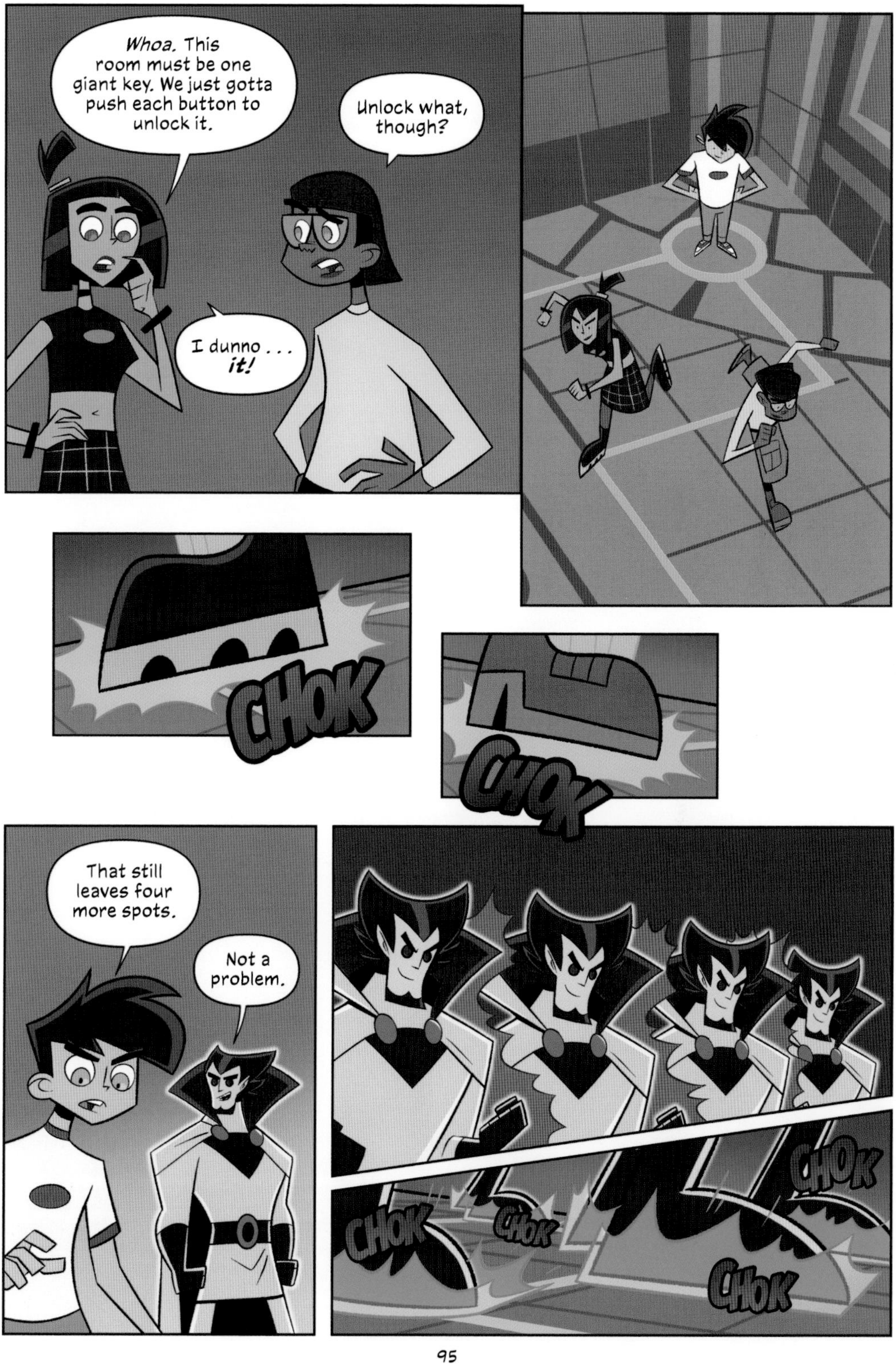
Whoa. This room must be one giant key. We just gotta push each button to unlock it.
Unlock what, though?
I dunno . . . it!
CHOK
CHOK
That still leaves four more spots.
Not a problem.
CHOK
CHOK
CHOK
CHOK

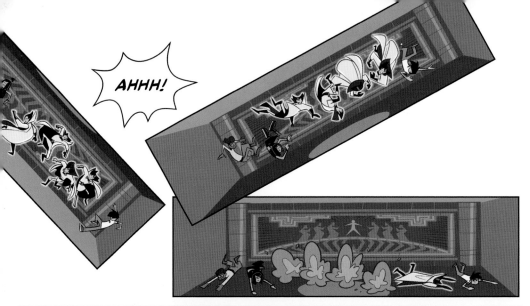

AHHH!

KrRrRt

Could it really be . . . ?

Heck!!! **Yeah!!!** Who's the best?!

BROOOO!!!!

DUDE!!!!!!

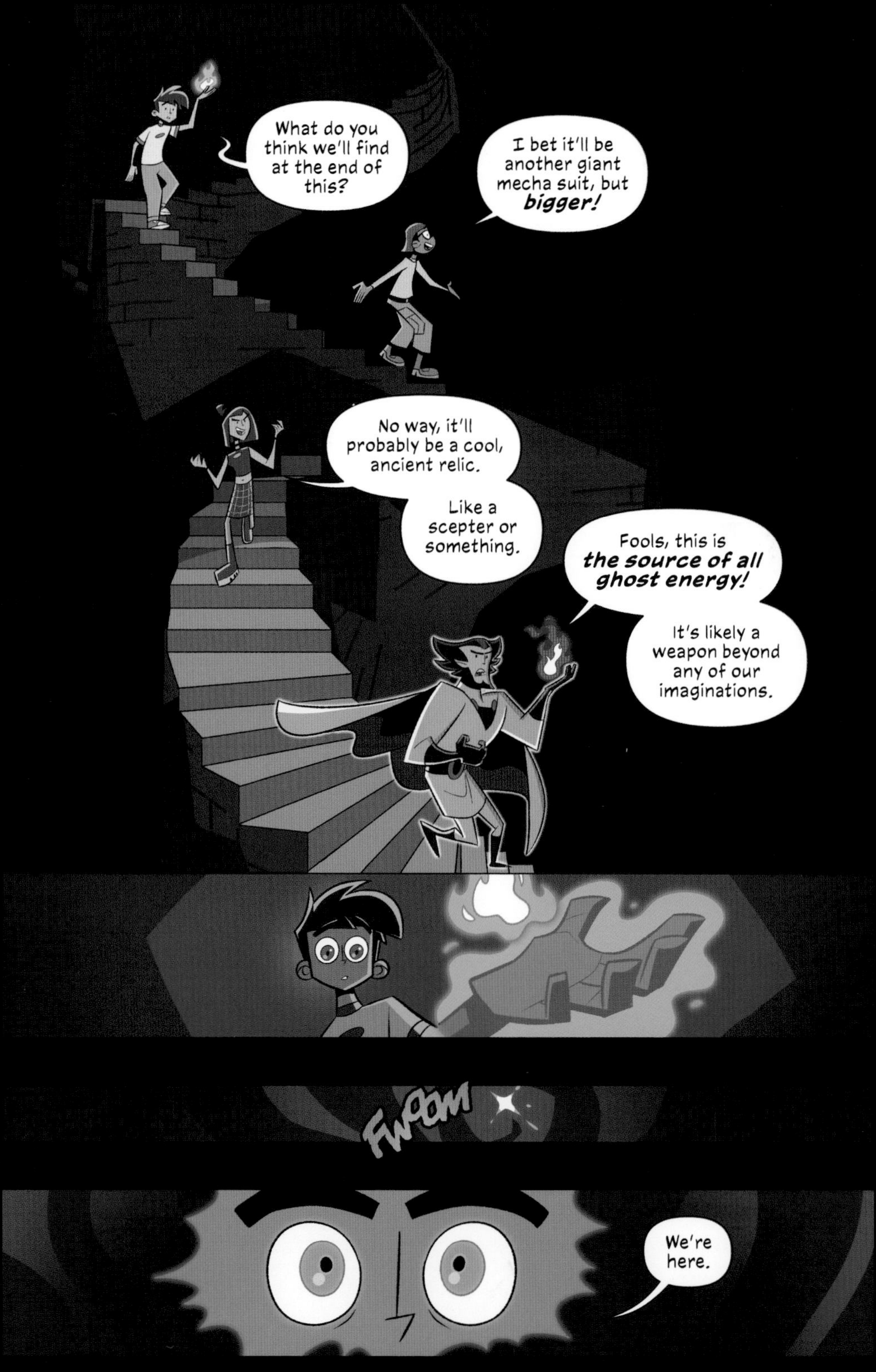
What do you think we'll find at the end of this?
I bet it'll be another giant mecha suit, but *bigger!*
No way, it'll probably be a cool, ancient relic.
Like a scepter or something.
Fools, this is *the source of all ghost energy!*
It's likely a weapon beyond any of our imaginations.
FWOOM
We're here.

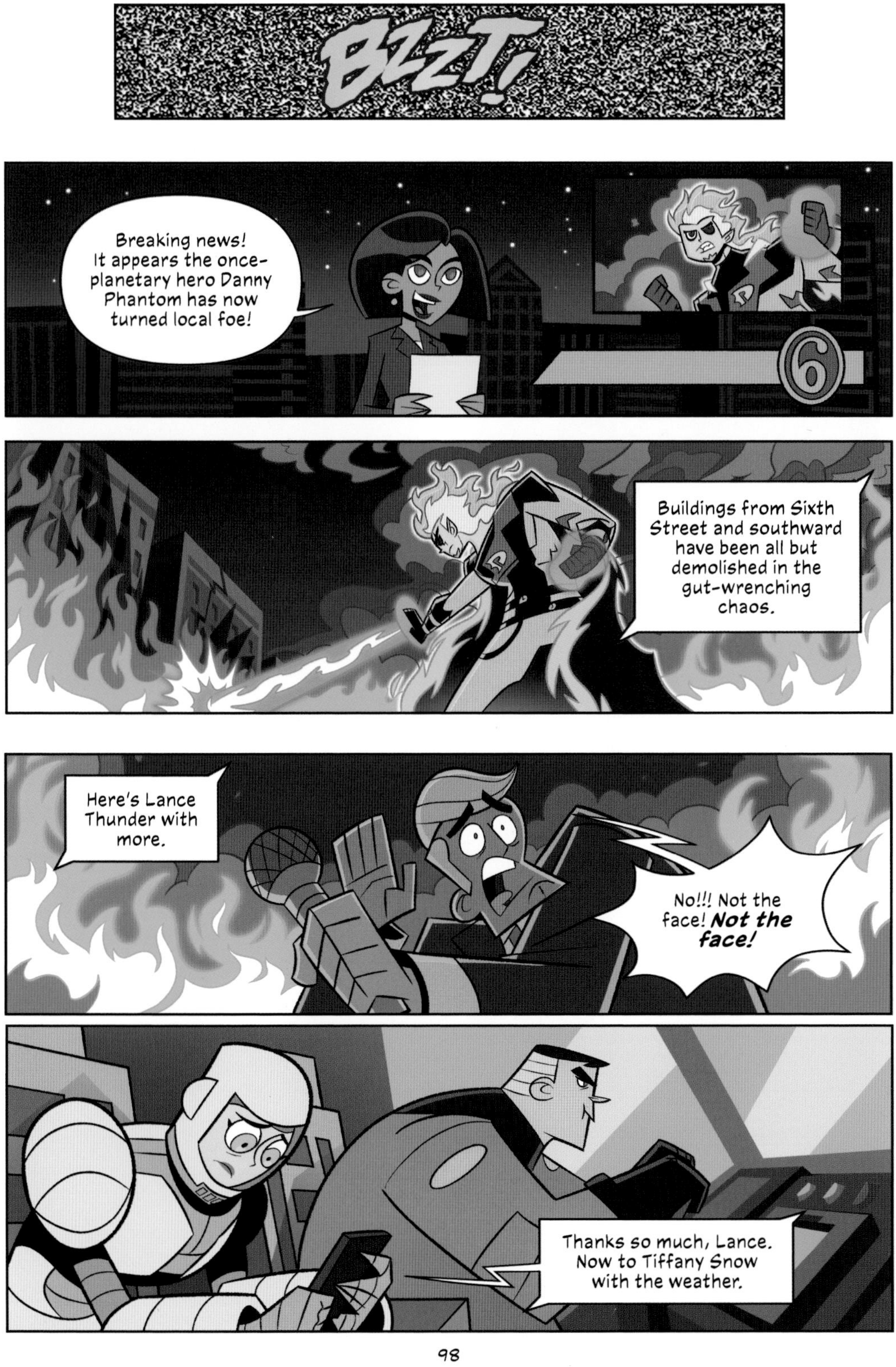
BZZT!
Breaking news! It appears the once-planetary hero Danny Phantom has now turned local foe!
6
Buildings from Sixth Street and southward have been all but demolished in the gut-wrenching chaos.
Here's Lance Thunder with more.
No!!! Not the face! ***Not the face!***
Thanks so much, Lance. Now to Tiffany Snow with the weather.

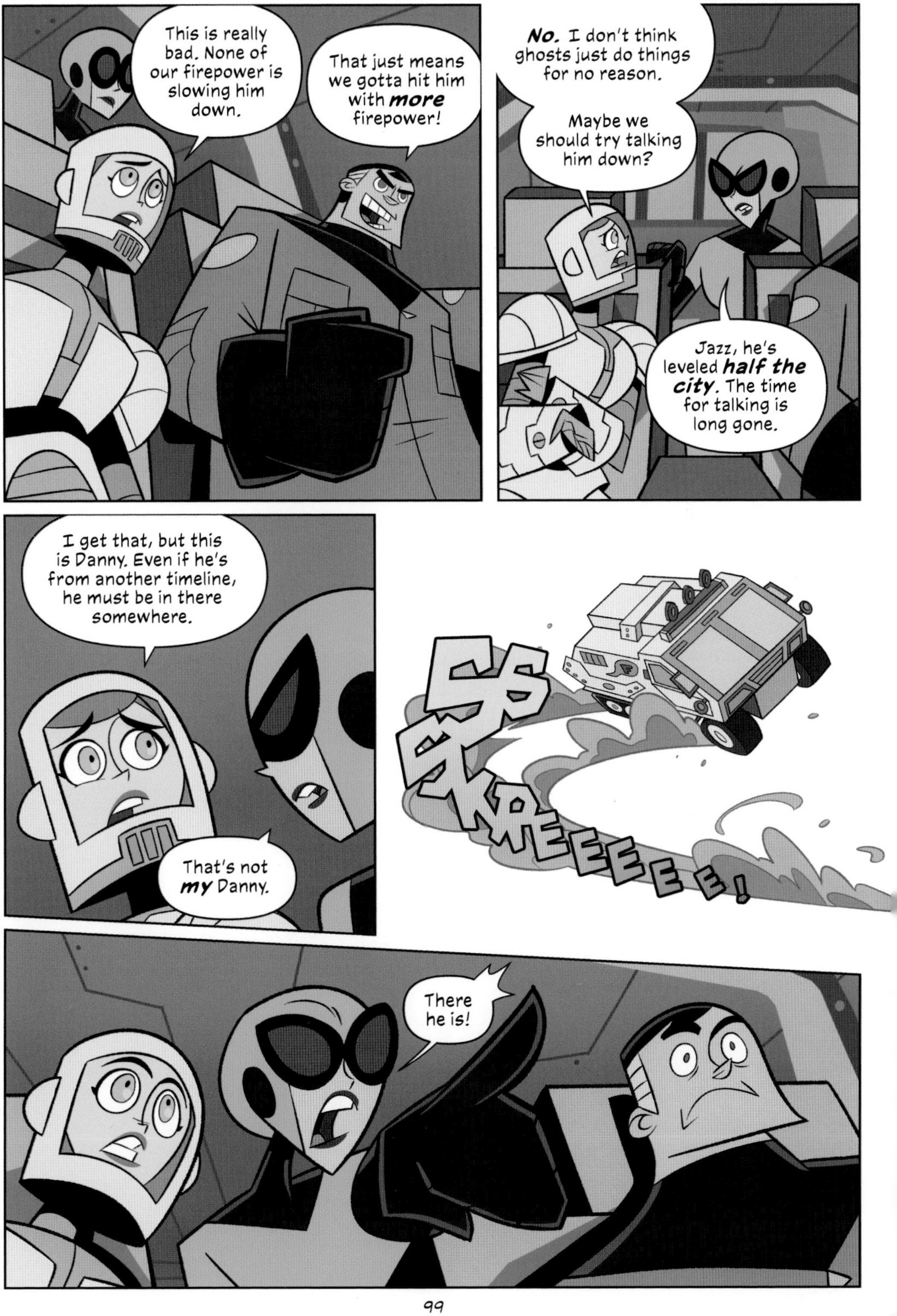
This is really bad. None of our firepower is slowing him down.
That just means we gotta hit him with ***more*** firepower!
No. I don't think ghosts just do things for no reason.
Maybe we should try talking him down?
Jazz, he's leveled ***half the city***. The time for talking is long gone.
I get that, but this is Danny. Even if he's from another timeline, he must be in there somewhere.
That's not ***my*** Danny.
SSKREEEEEE!
There he is!

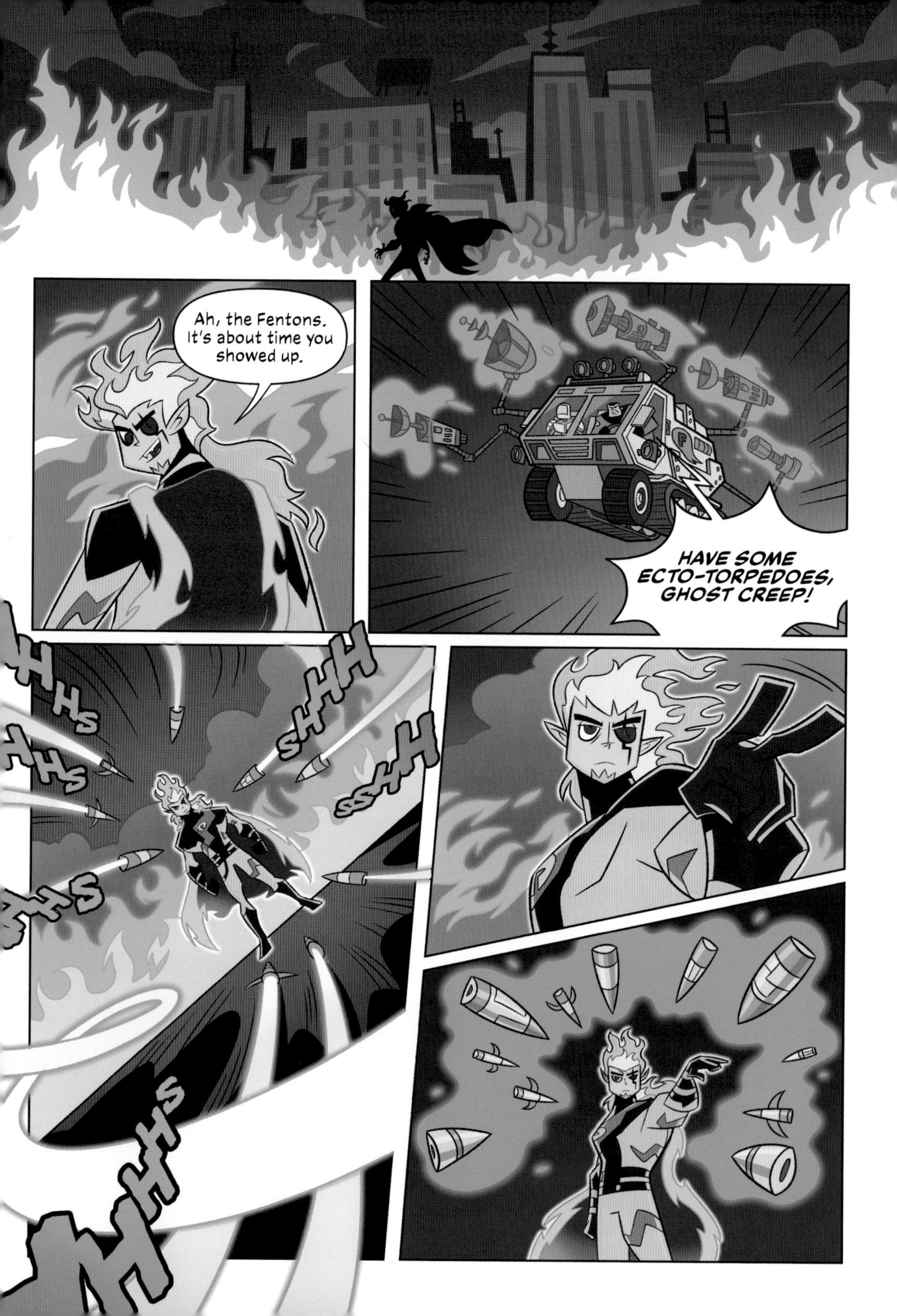

Ah, the Fentons. It's about time you showed up.
HAVE SOME ECTO-TORPEDOES, GHOST CREEP!
SHHH
SHHH
SHHH
SHHH
SHHH
SSHHH
SHHHH

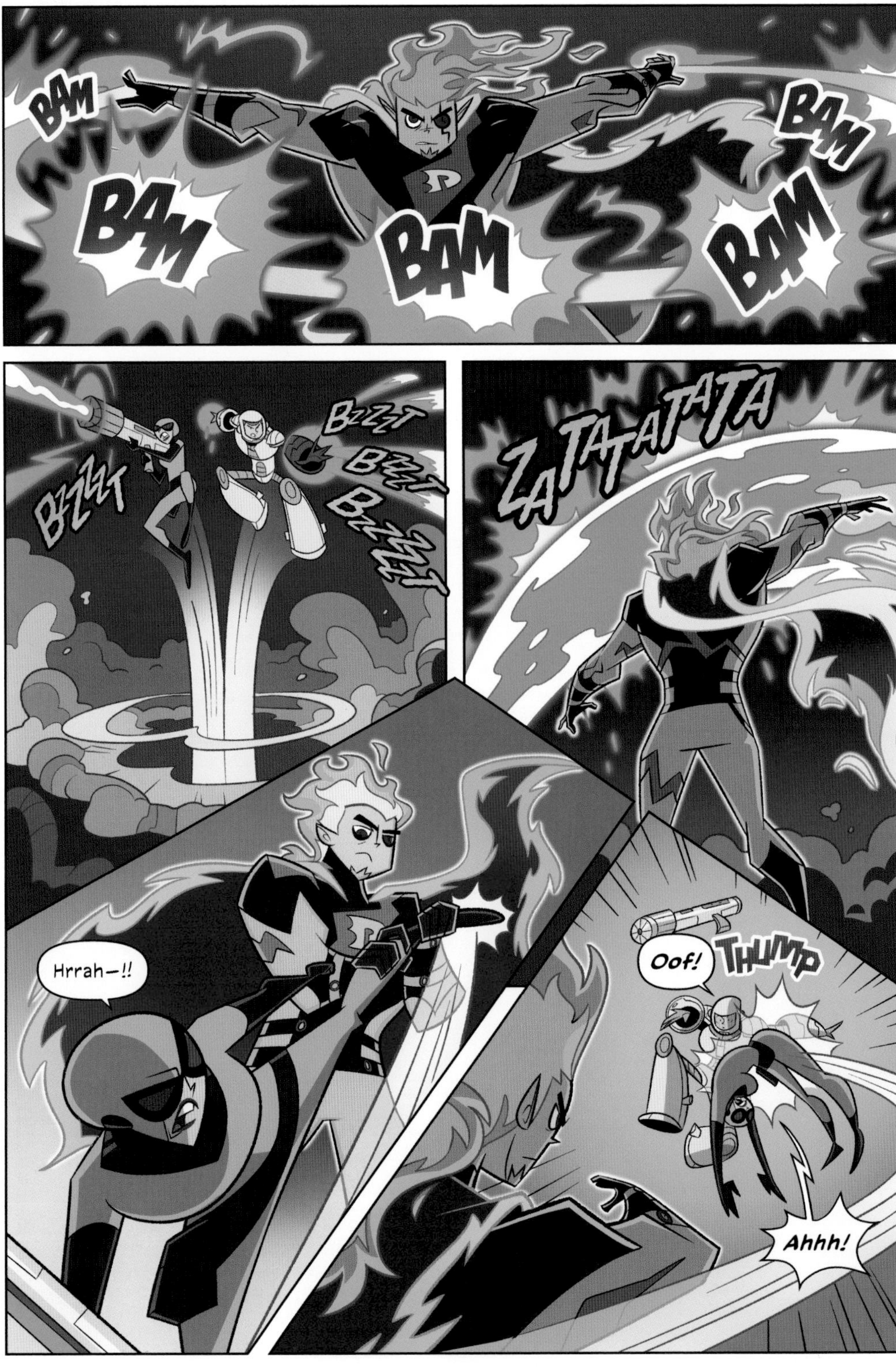
BAM
BAM
BAM
BAM
BAM
BZZZT
BZZT
BZZT
BZZZT
ZATATATATA
Hrrah—!!
Oof!
THUMP
Ahhh!

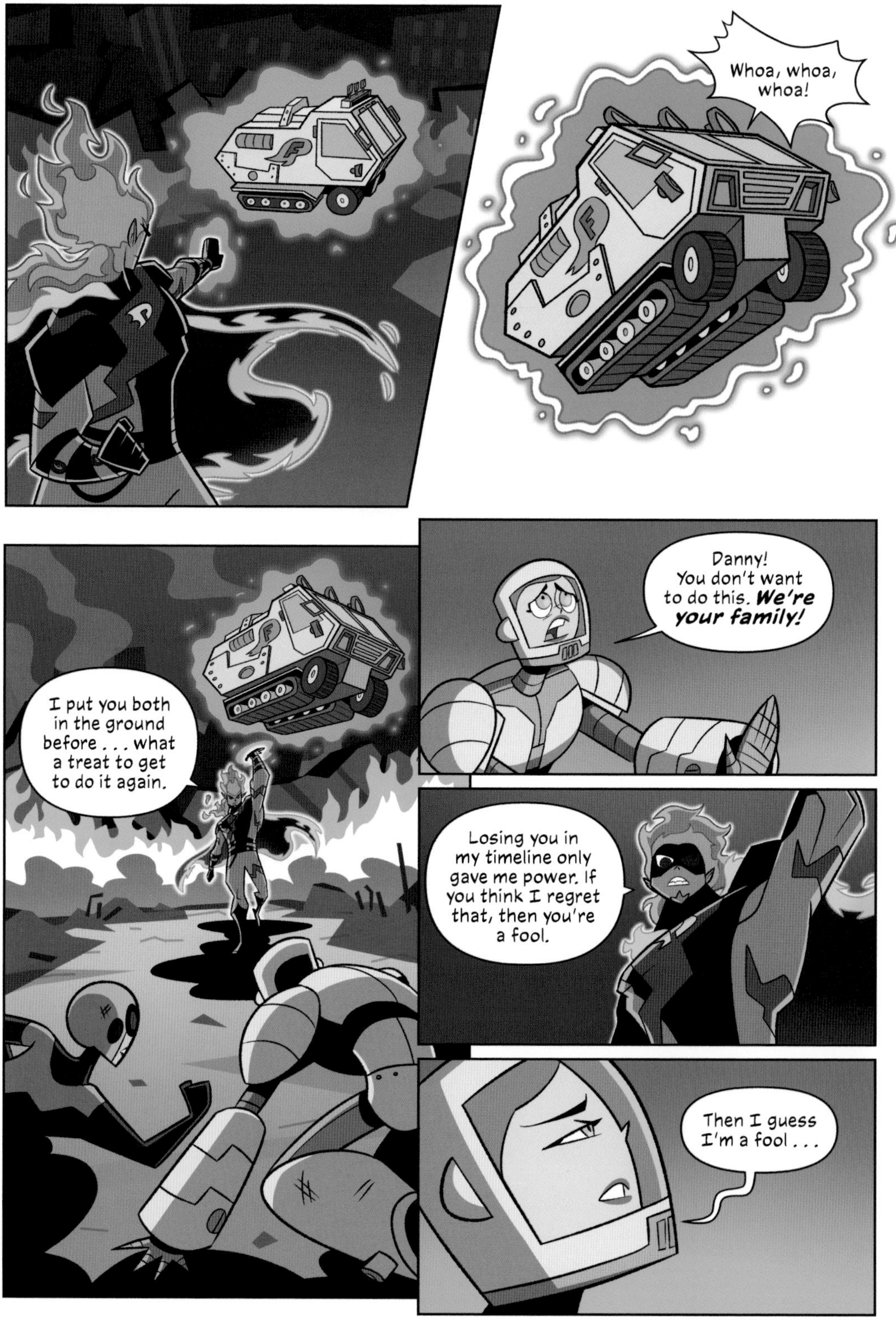
Whoa, whoa, whoa!
I put you both in the ground before . . . what a treat to get to do it again.
Danny! You don't want to do this. ***We're your family!***
Losing you in my timeline only gave me power. If you think I regret that, then you're a fool.
Then I guess I'm a fool . . .

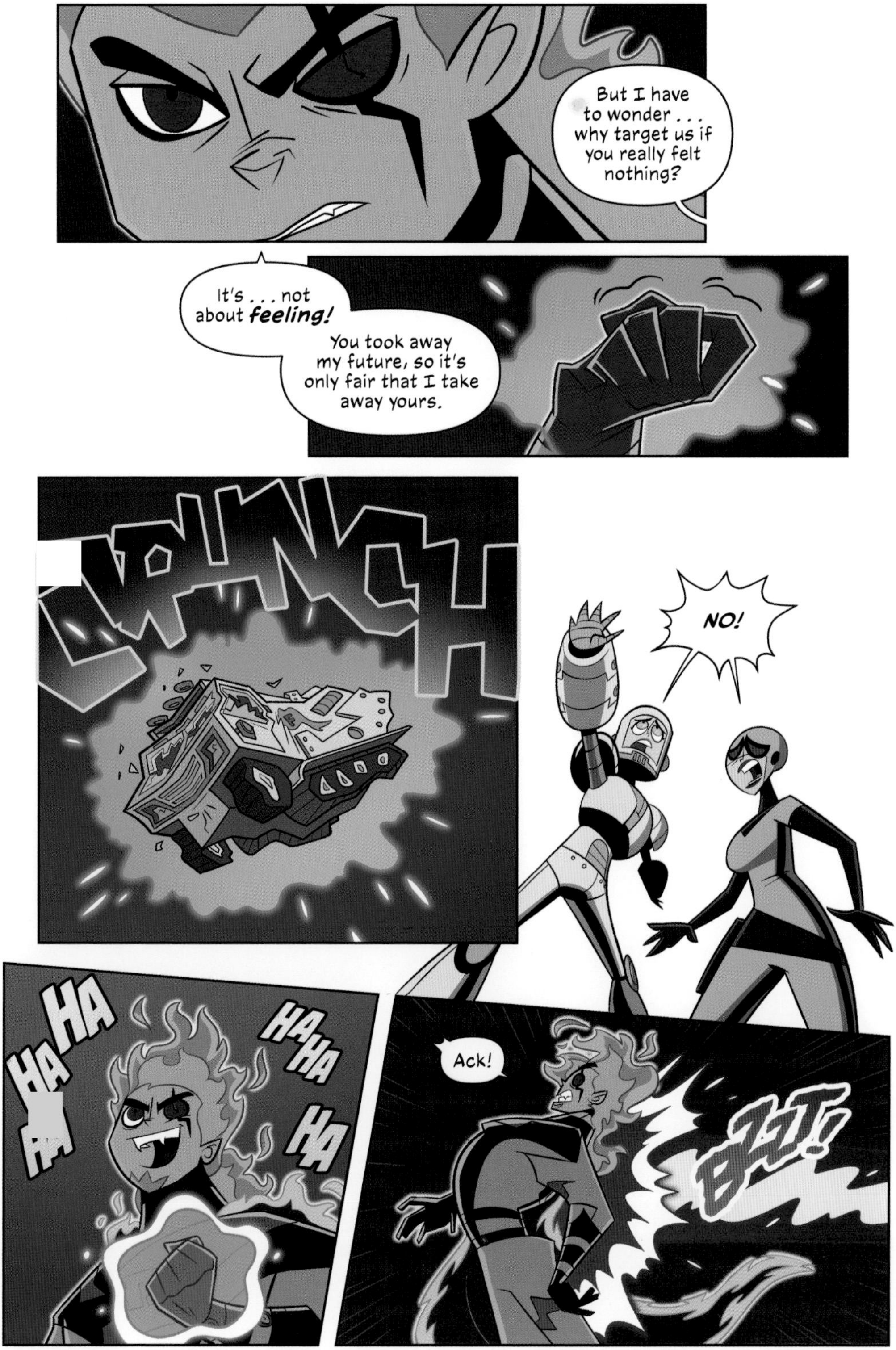
But I have to wonder . . . why target us if you really felt nothing?
It's . . . not about *feeling!*
You took away my future, so it's only fair that I take away yours.
NO!
HA HA
HA HA
HA
Ack!
BZZT!

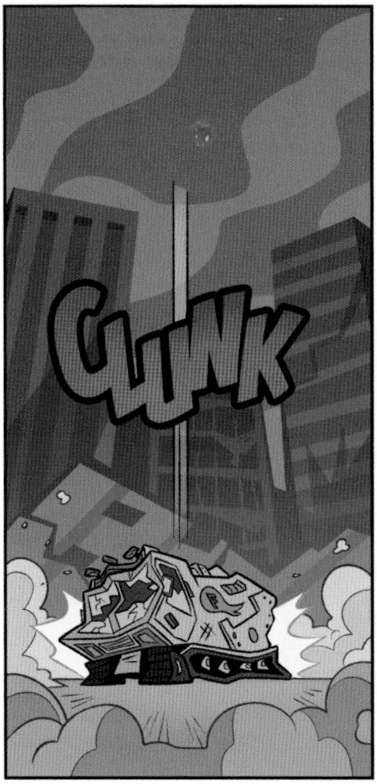
CLUNK

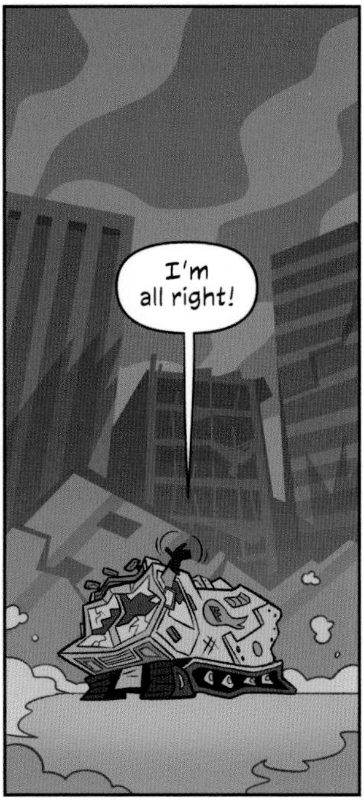
I'm all right!

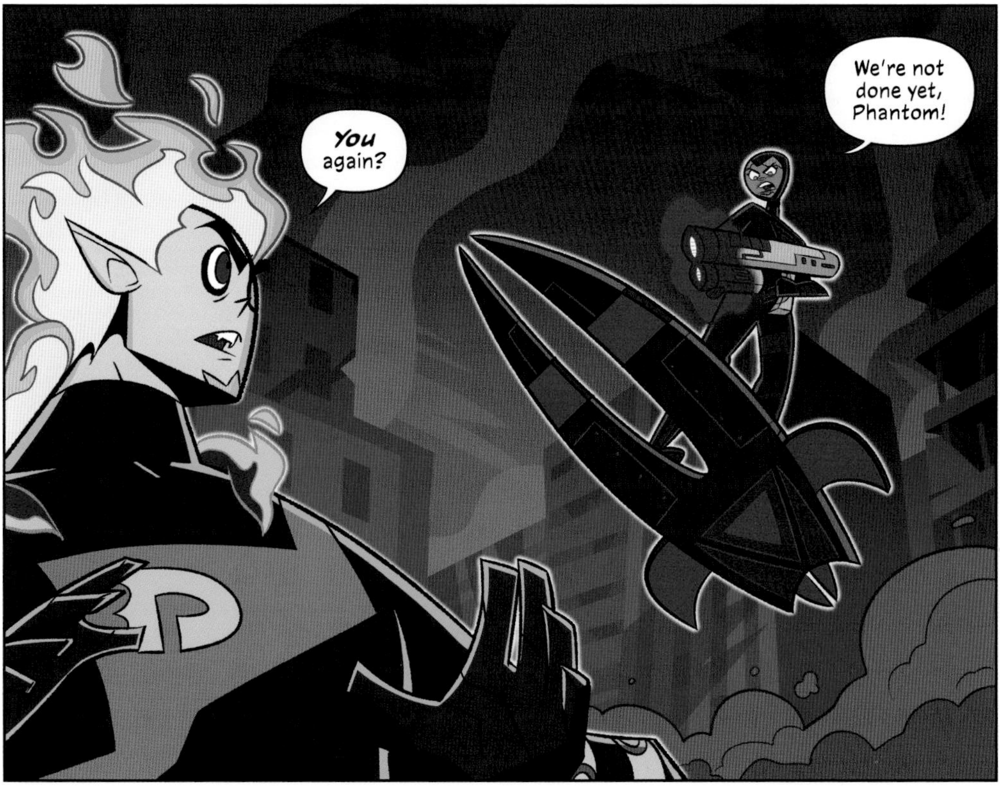
You again?
We're not done yet, Phantom!

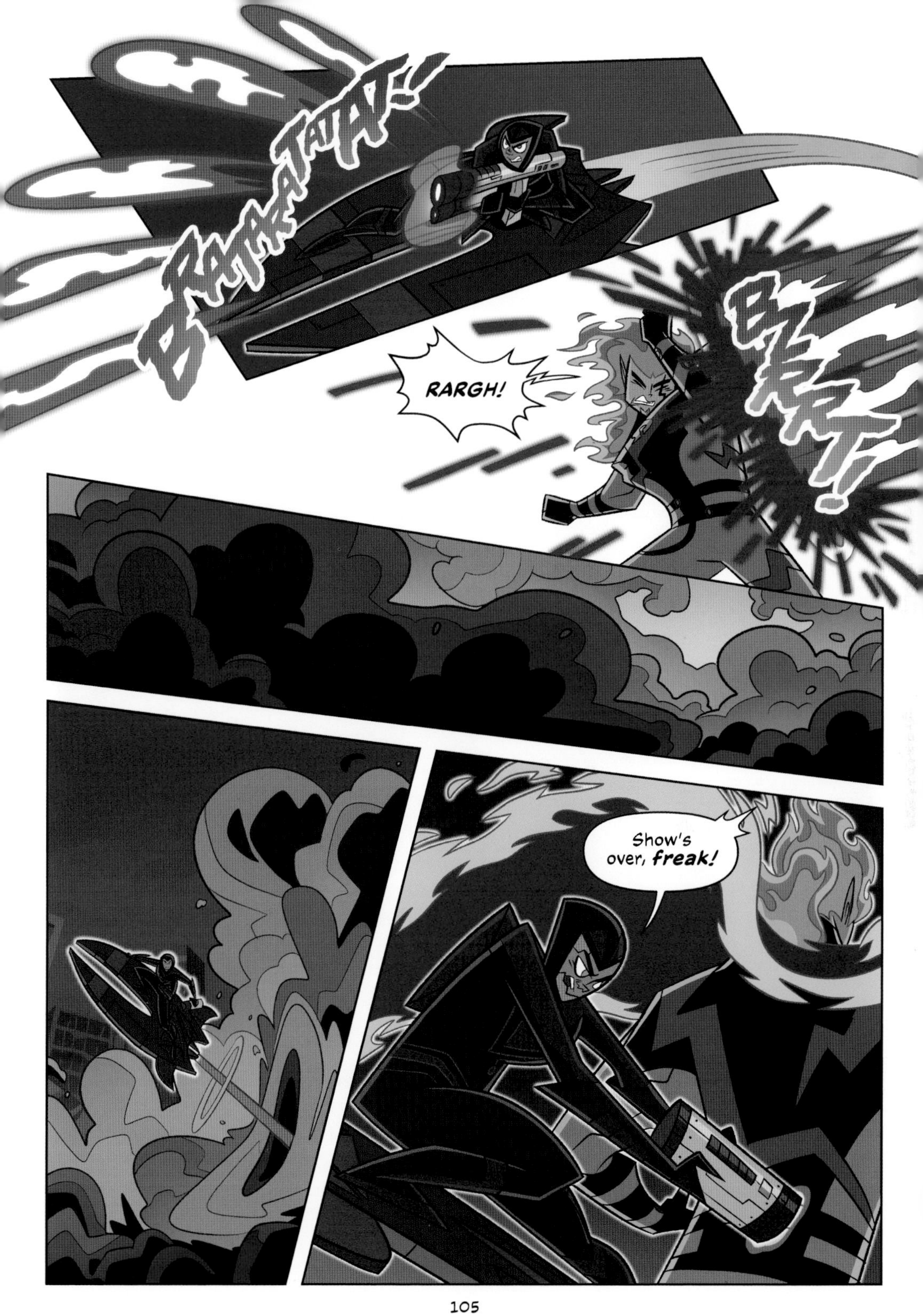
BRATATATAT!!
RARGH!
BZZRRT!
Show's over, freak!

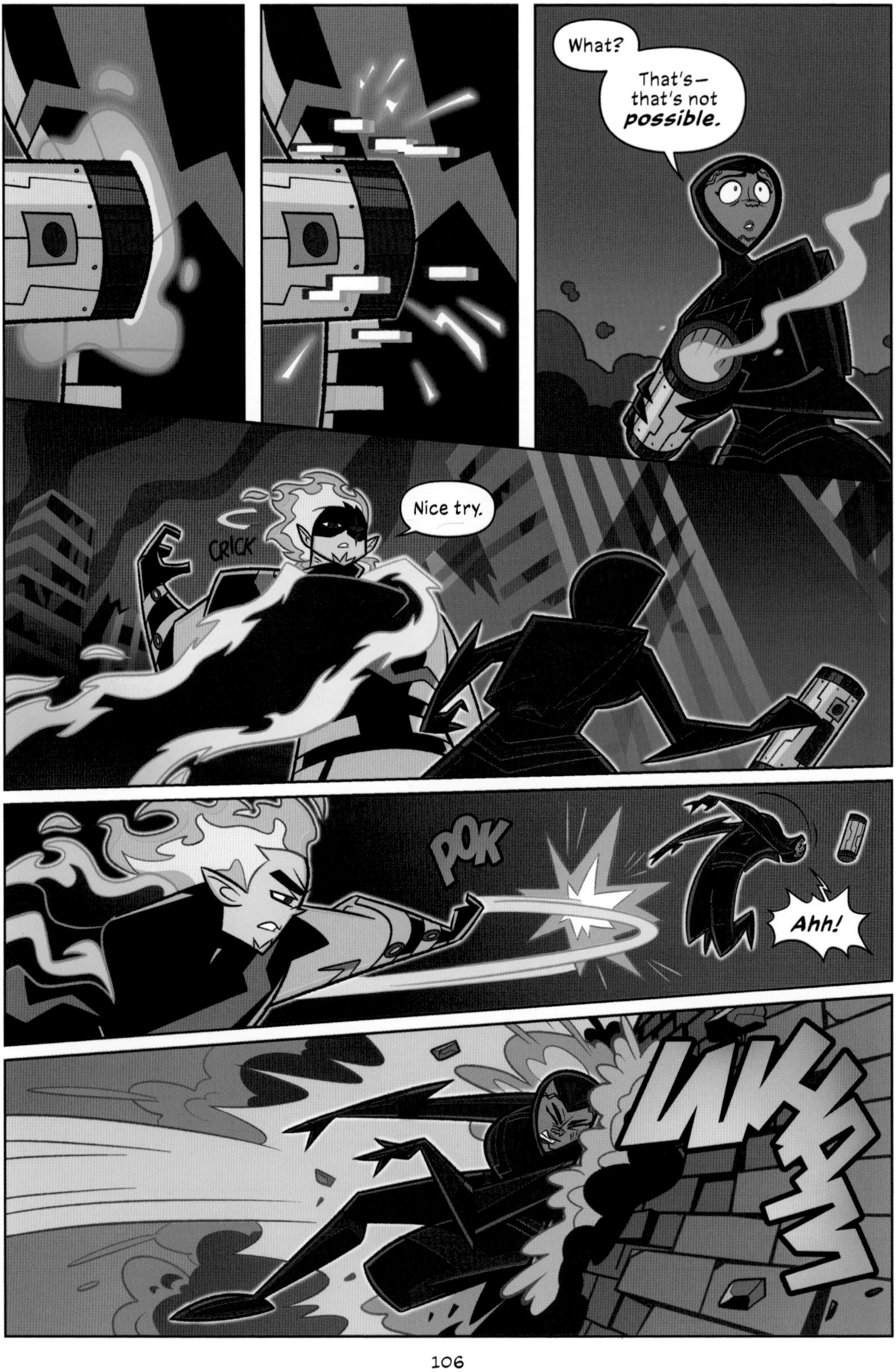
What?
That's—
that's not
possible.
Nice try.
CRICK
POK
Ahh!
WHAM

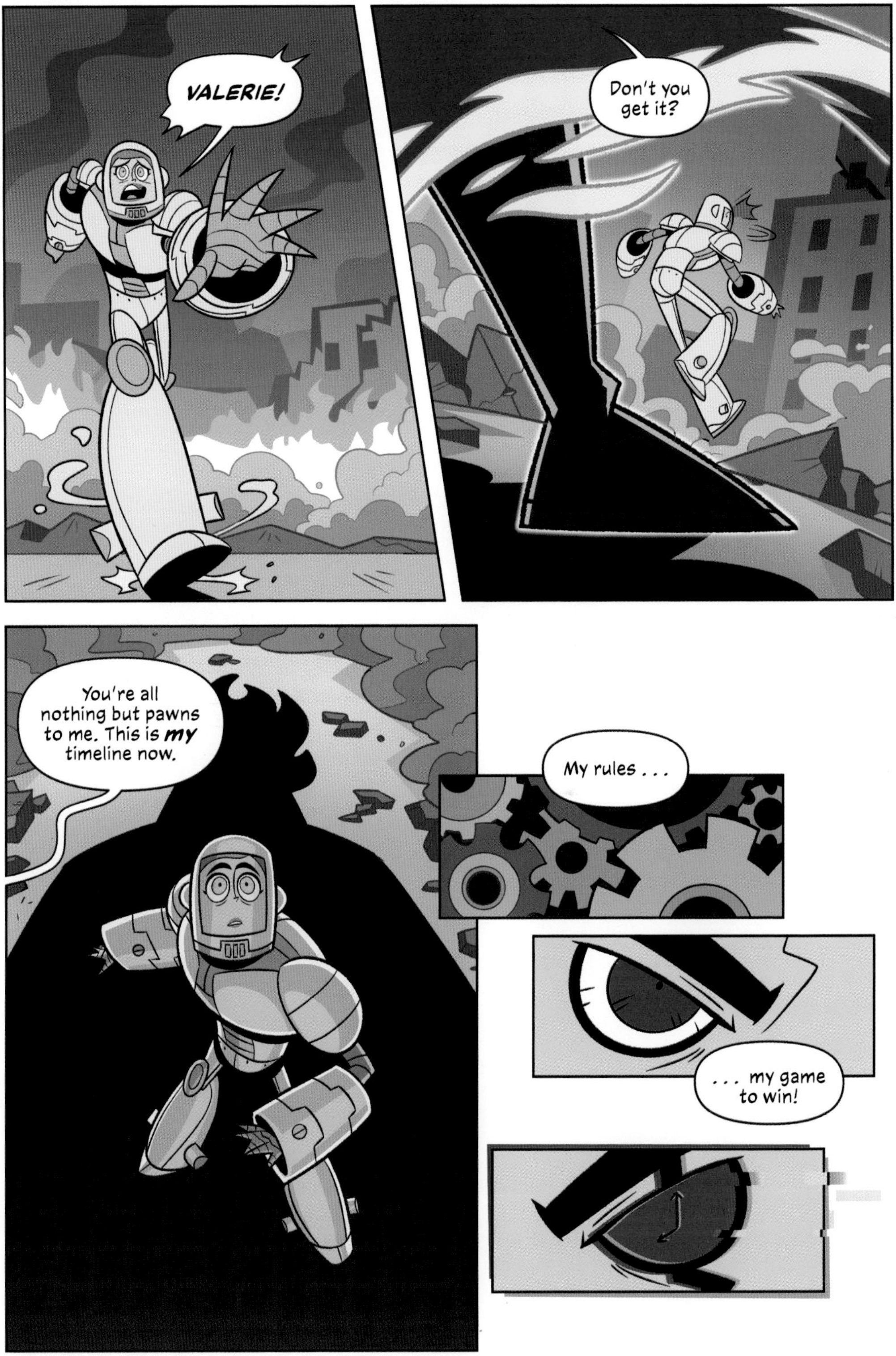
VALERIE!
Don't you get it?
You're all nothing but pawns to me. This is ***my*** timeline now.
My rules . . .
. . . my game to win!

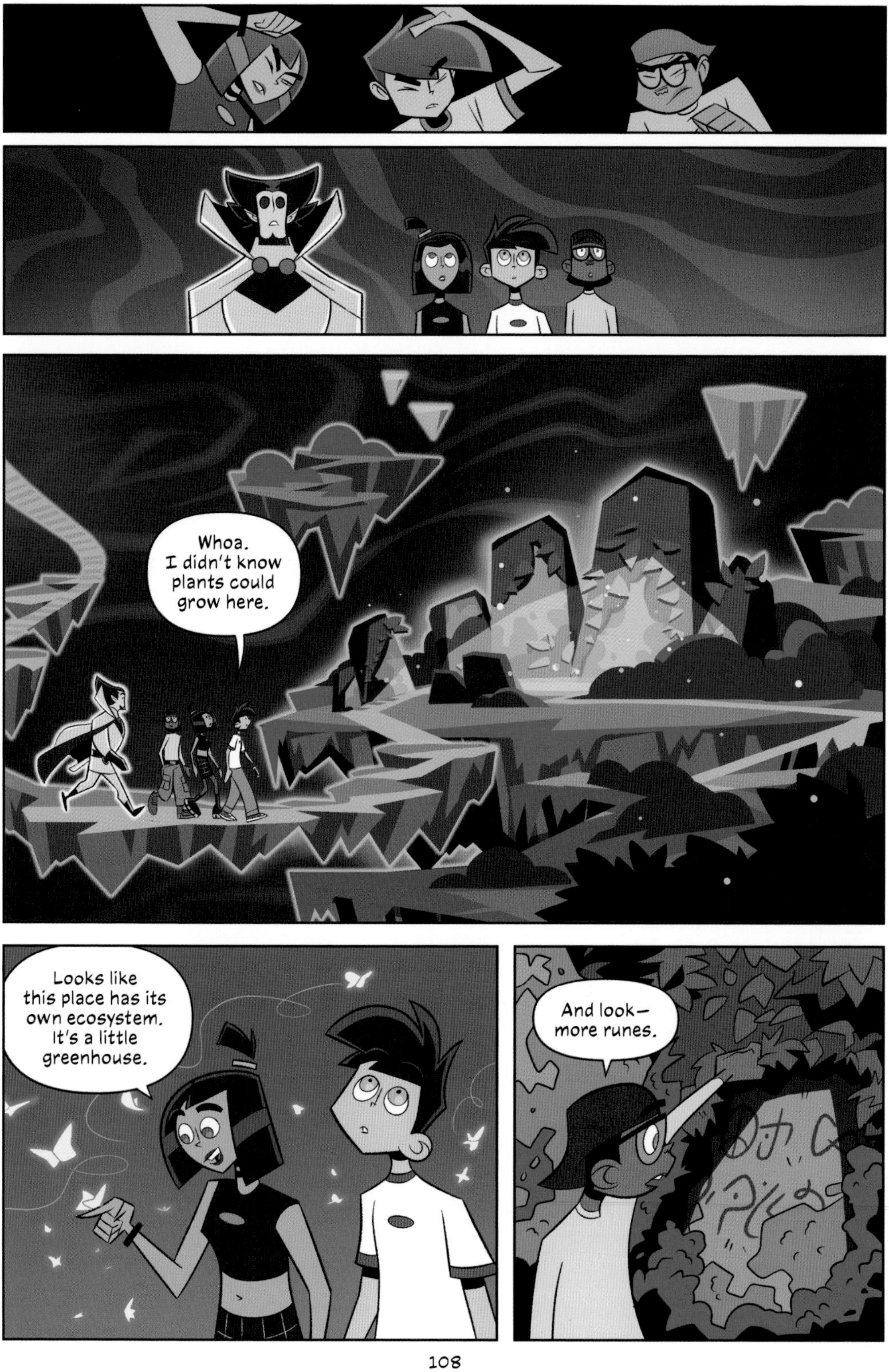
Whoa. I didn't know plants could grow here.
Looks like this place has its own ecosystem. It's a little greenhouse.
And look—more runes.

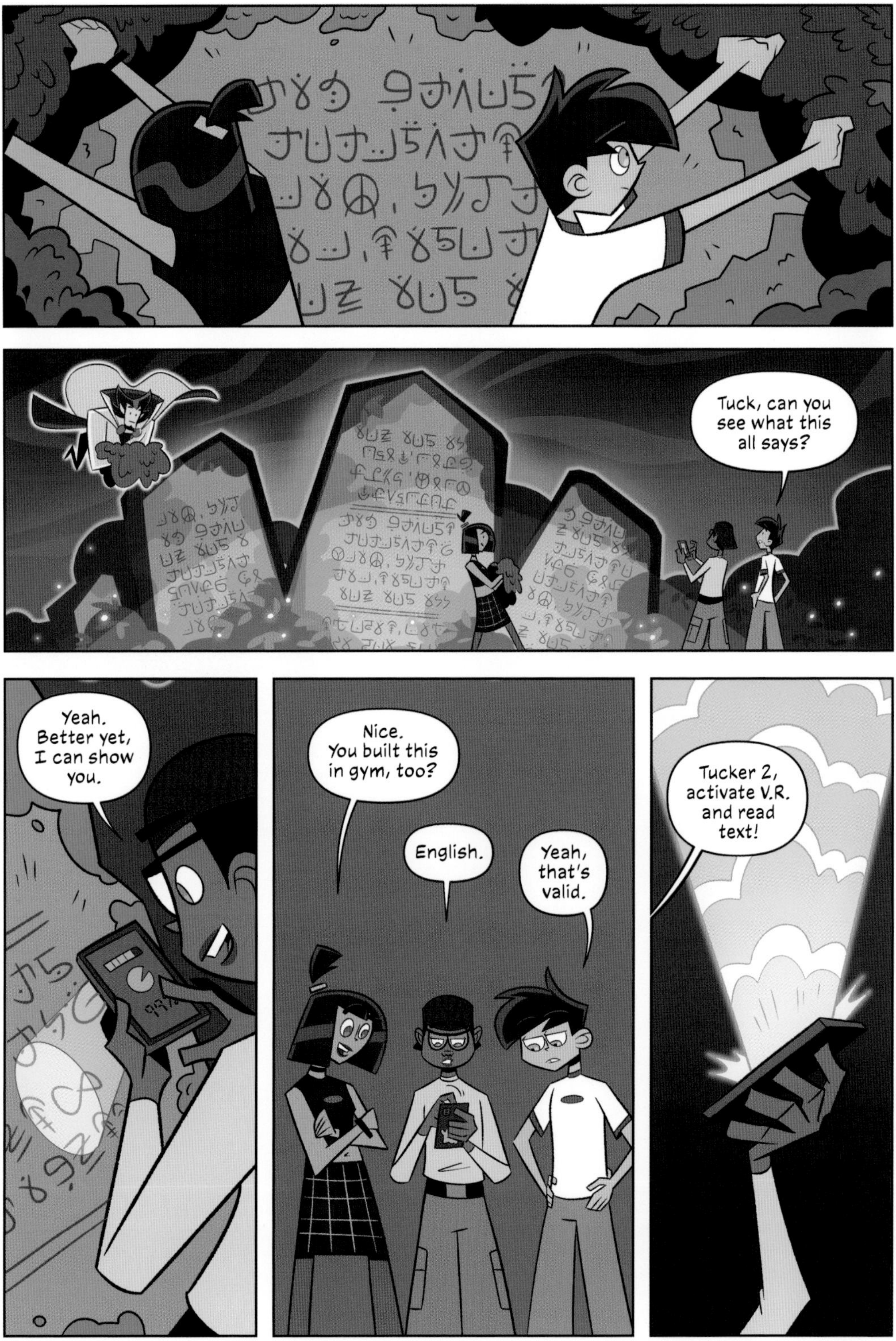
Tuck, can you see what this all says?
Yeah. Better yet, I can show you.
Nice. You built this in gym, too?
English.
Yeah, that's valid.
Tucker 2, activate V.R. and read text!

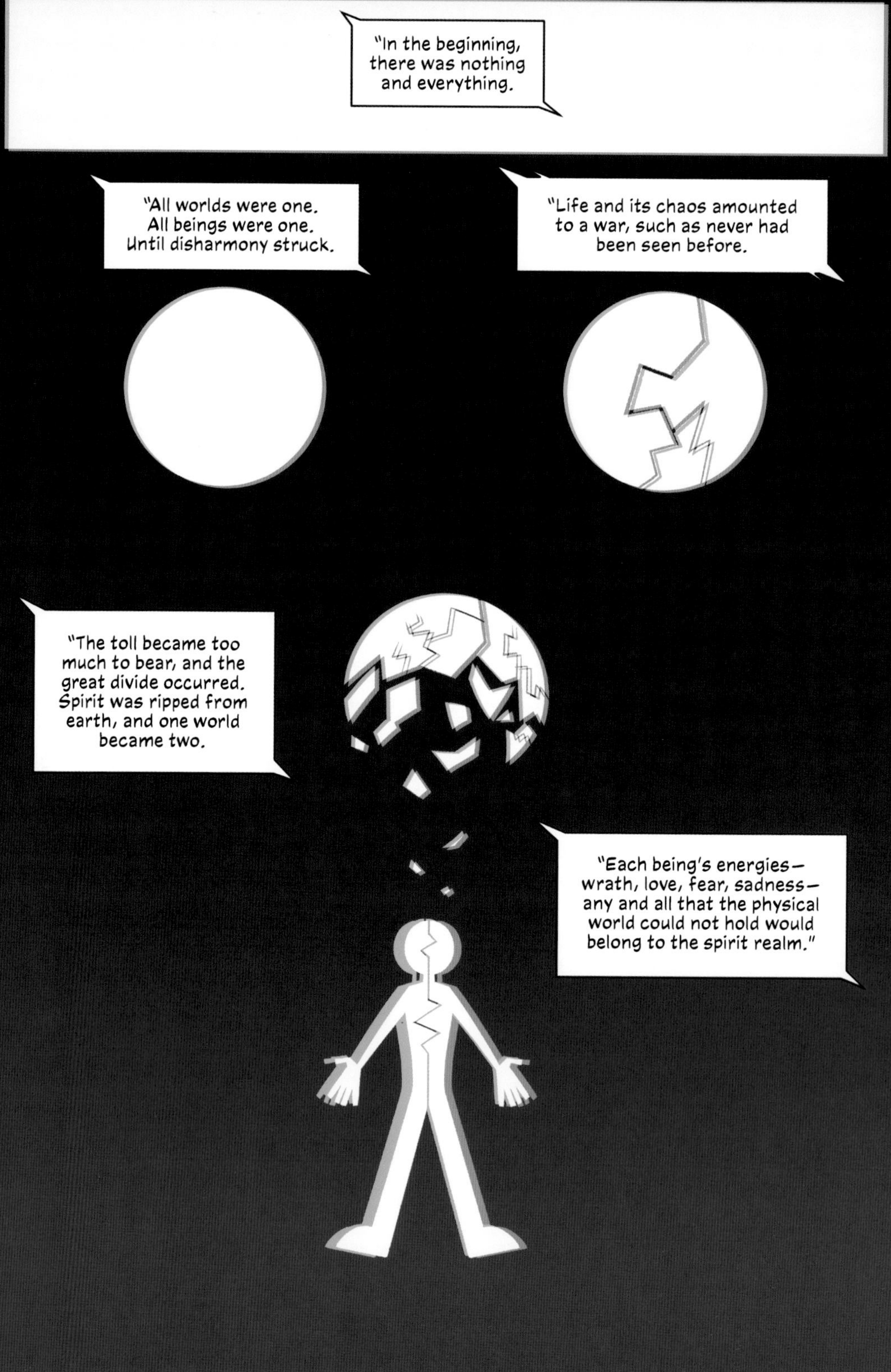
"In the beginning, there was nothing and everything.
"All worlds were one. All beings were one. Until disharmony struck.
"Life and its chaos amounted to a war, such as never had been seen before.
"The toll became too much to bear, and the great divide occurred. Spirit was ripped from earth, and one world became two.
"Each being's energies—wrath, love, fear, sadness—any and all that the physical world could not hold would belong to the spirit realm."

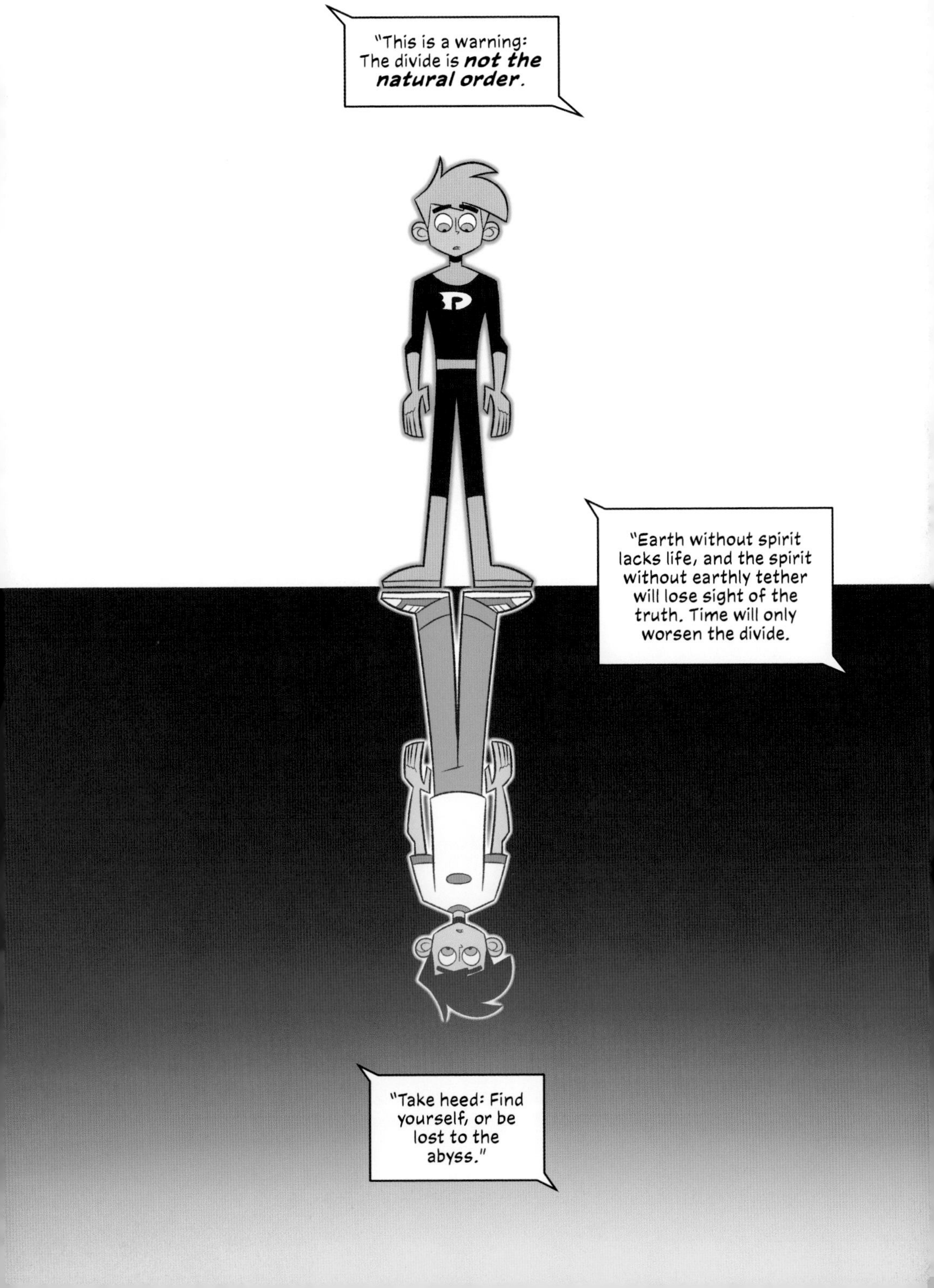
"This is a warning: The divide is ***not the natural order***.
"Earth without spirit lacks life, and the spirit without earthly tether will lose sight of the truth. Time will only worsen the divide.
"Take heed: Find yourself, or be lost to the abyss."

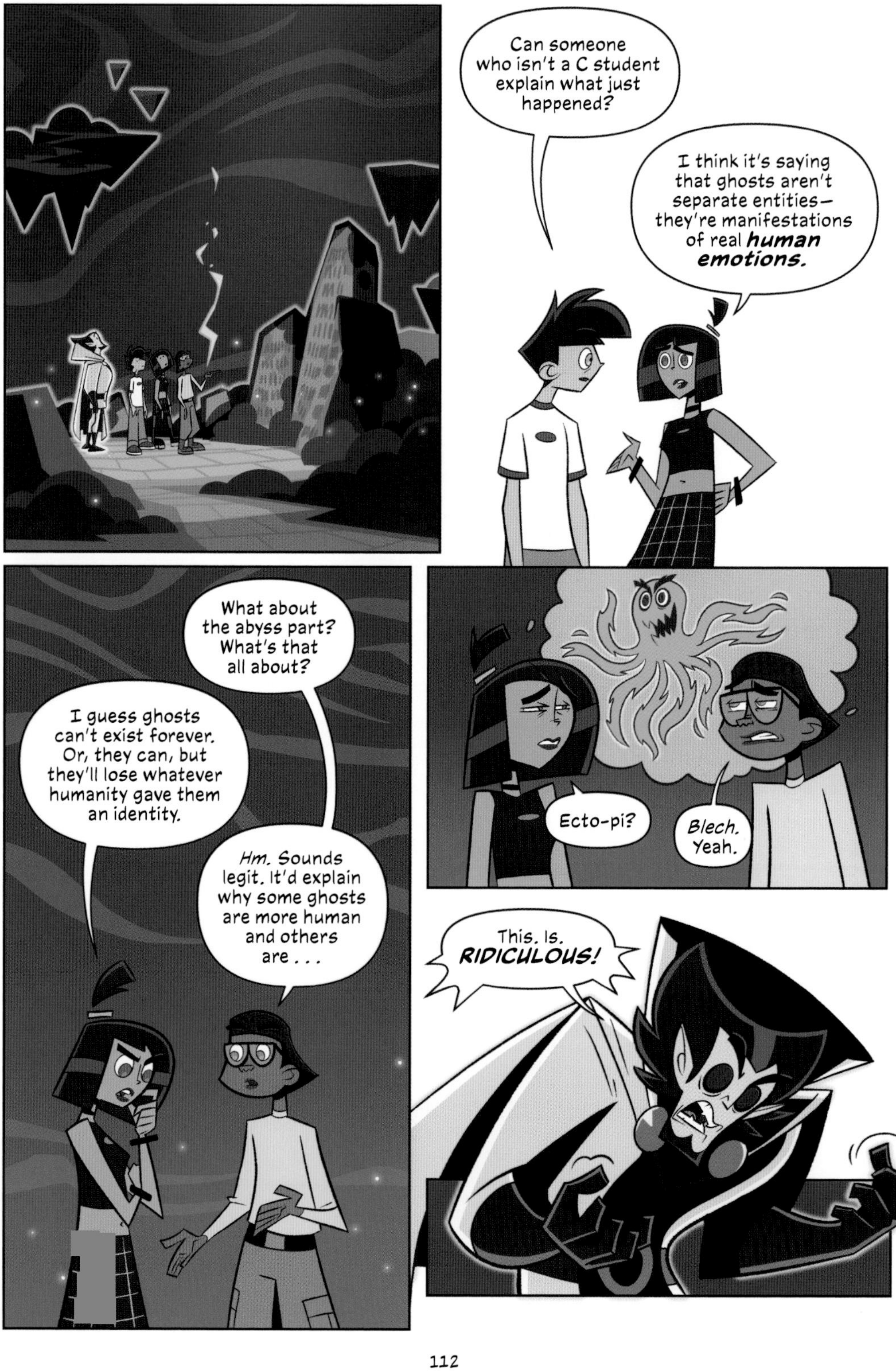

Can someone who isn't a C student explain what just happened?
I think it's saying that ghosts aren't separate entities—they're manifestations of real ***human emotions.***
What about the abyss part? What's that all about?
I guess ghosts can't exist forever. Or, they can, but they'll lose whatever humanity gave them an identity.
Hm. Sounds legit. It'd explain why some ghosts are more human and others are . . .
Ecto-pi?
Blech. Yeah.
This. Is. ***RIDICULOUS!***

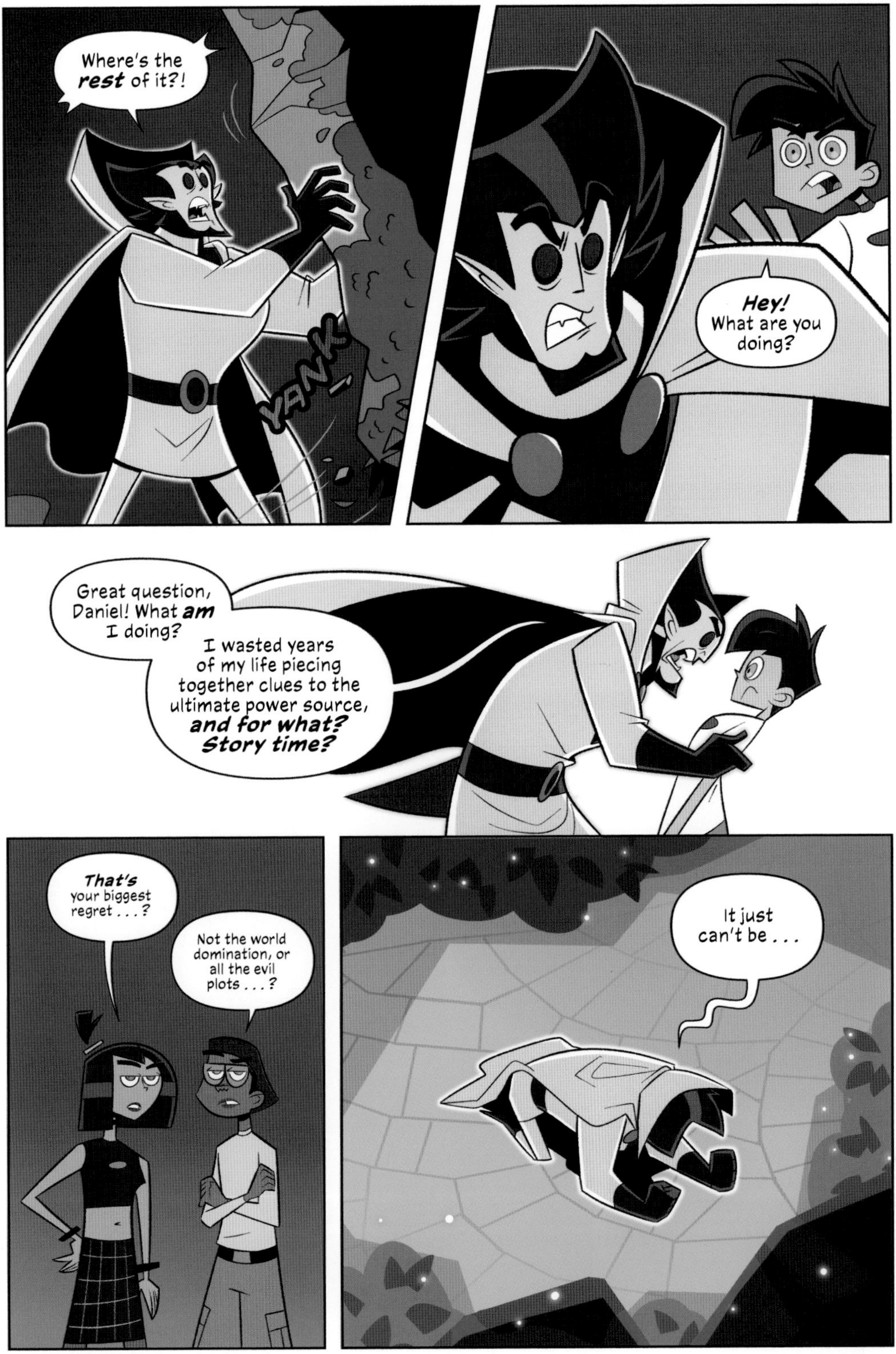
Where's the ***rest*** of it?!
YANK
Hey! What are you doing?
Great question, Daniel! What ***am*** I doing?
I wasted years of my life piecing together clues to the ultimate power source, ***and for what? Story time?***
That's your biggest regret . . . ?
Not the world domination, or all the evil plots . . . ?
It just can't be . . .

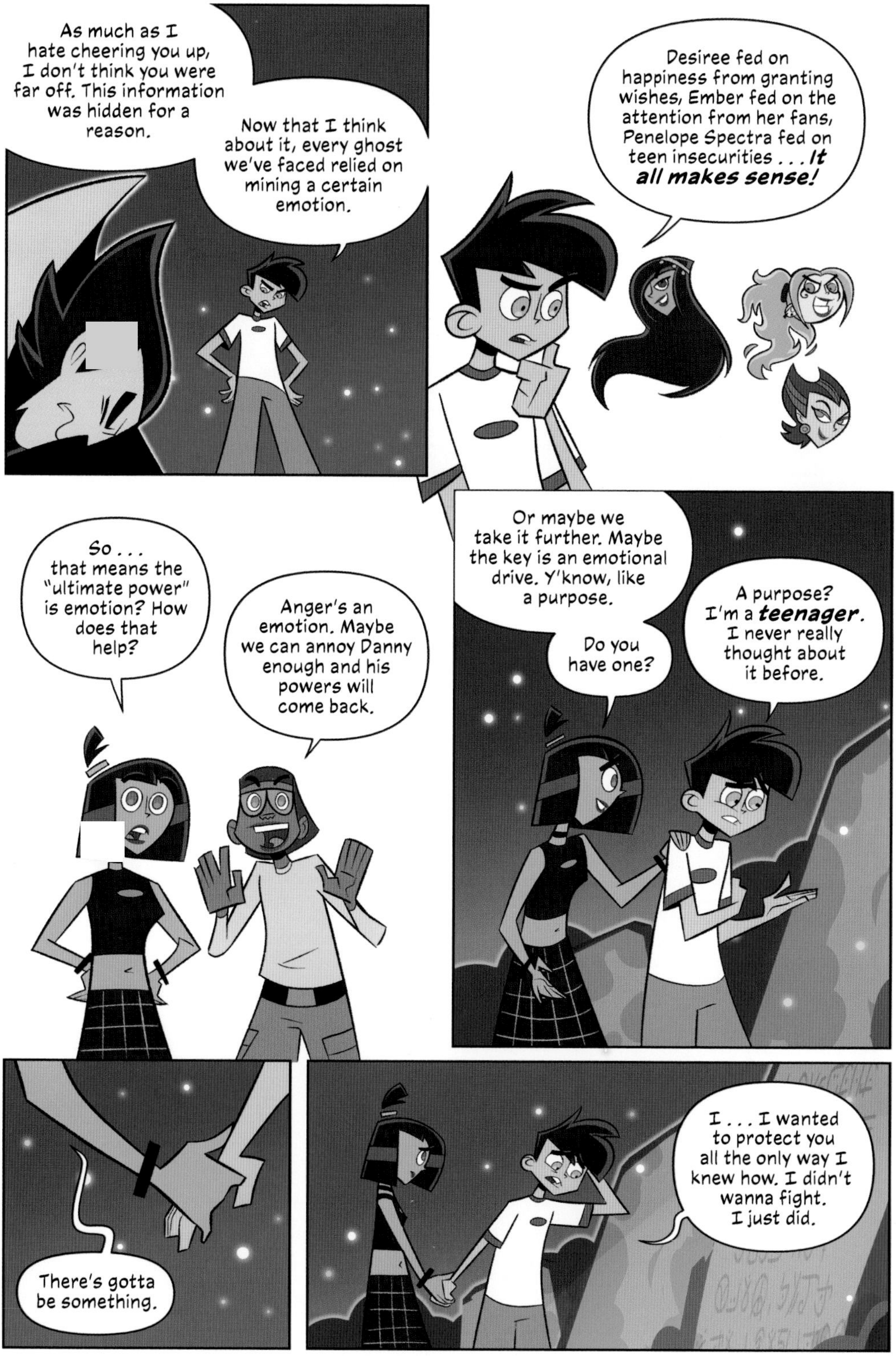
As much as I hate cheering you up, I don't think you were far off. This information was hidden for a reason.
Now that I think about it, every ghost we've faced relied on mining a certain emotion.
Desiree fed on happiness from granting wishes, Ember fed on the attention from her fans, Penelope Spectra fed on teen insecurities . . . ***It all makes sense!***
So . . . that means the "ultimate power" is emotion? How does that help?
Anger's an emotion. Maybe we can annoy Danny enough and his powers will come back.
Or maybe we take it further. Maybe the key is an emotional drive. Y'know, like a purpose.
Do you have one?
A purpose? I'm a ***teenager***. I never really thought about it before.
There's gotta be something.
I . . . I wanted to protect you all the only way I knew how. I didn't wanna fight. I just did.

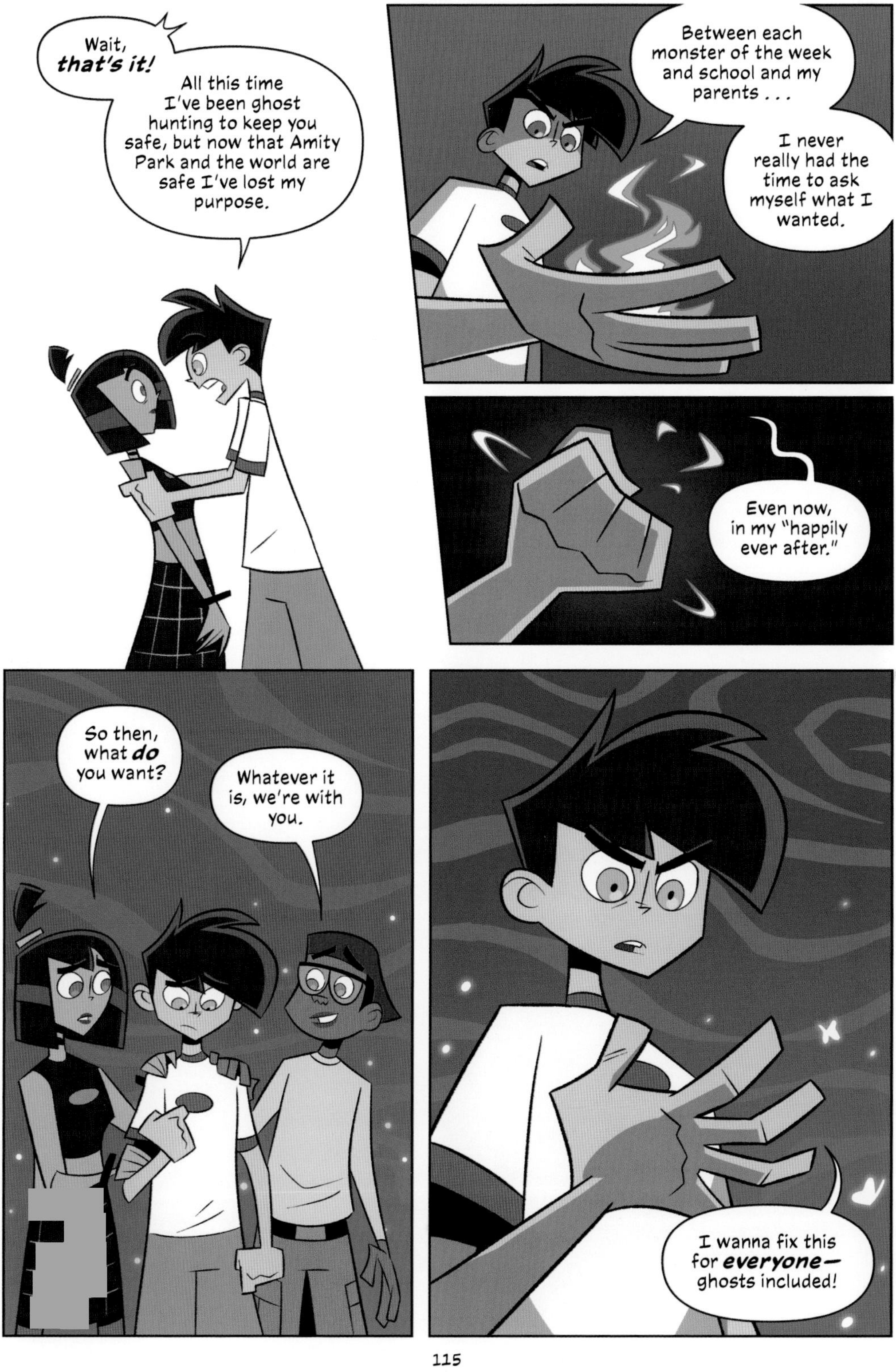
Wait, ***that's it!***
All this time I've been ghost hunting to keep you safe, but now that Amity Park and the world are safe I've lost my purpose.
Between each monster of the week and school and my parents . . .
I never really had the time to ask myself what I wanted.
Even now, in my "happily ever after."
So then, what ***do*** you want?
Whatever it is, we're with you.
I wanna fix this for ***everyone***—ghosts included!

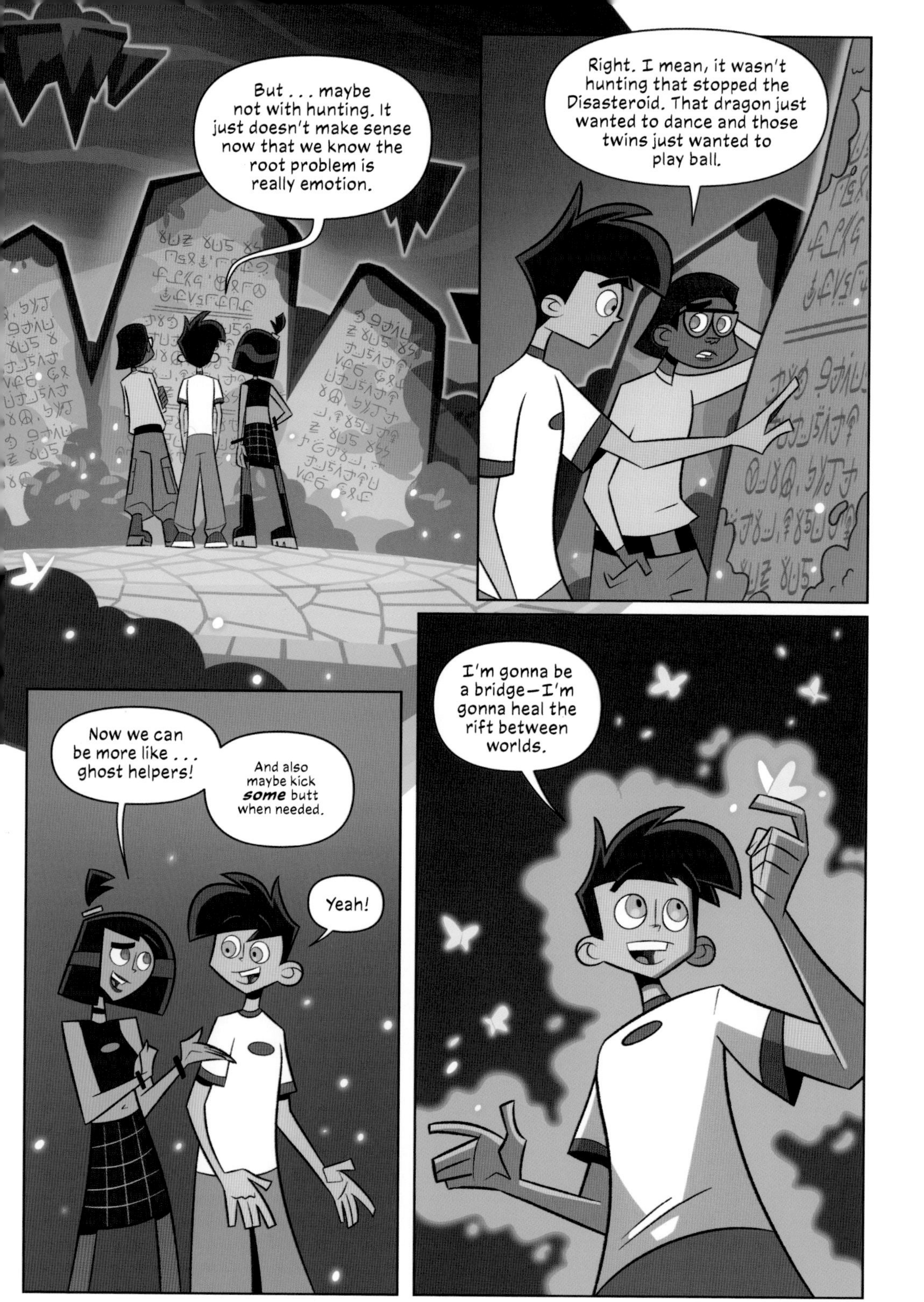
But . . . maybe not with hunting. It just doesn't make sense now that we know the root problem is really emotion.
Right. I mean, it wasn't hunting that stopped the Disasteroid. That dragon just wanted to dance and those twins just wanted to play ball.
Now we can be more like . . . ghost helpers!
And also maybe kick **some** butt when needed.
Yeah!
I'm gonna be a bridge—I'm gonna heal the rift between worlds.

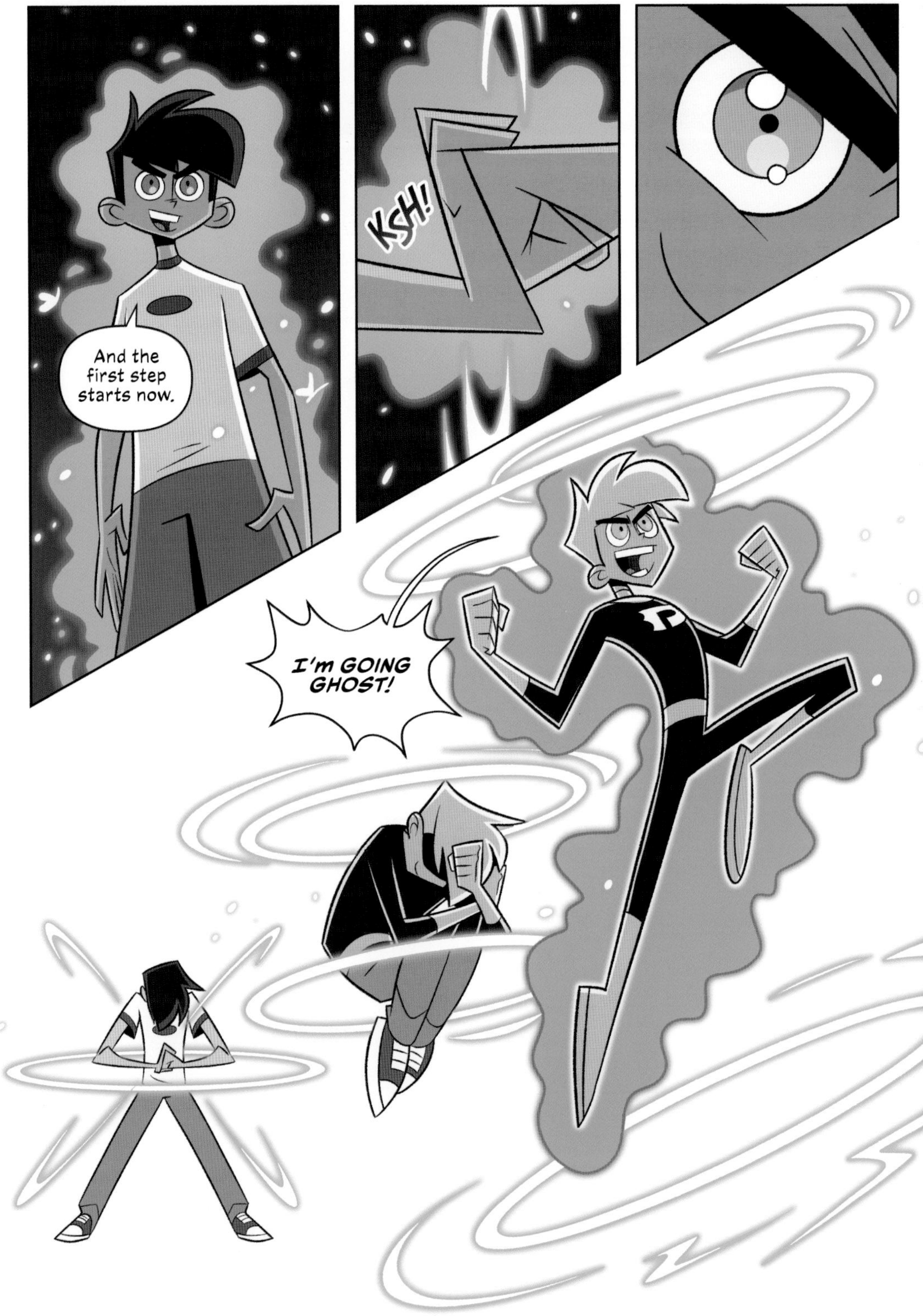
And the first step starts now.
KSH!
I'm GOING GHOST!

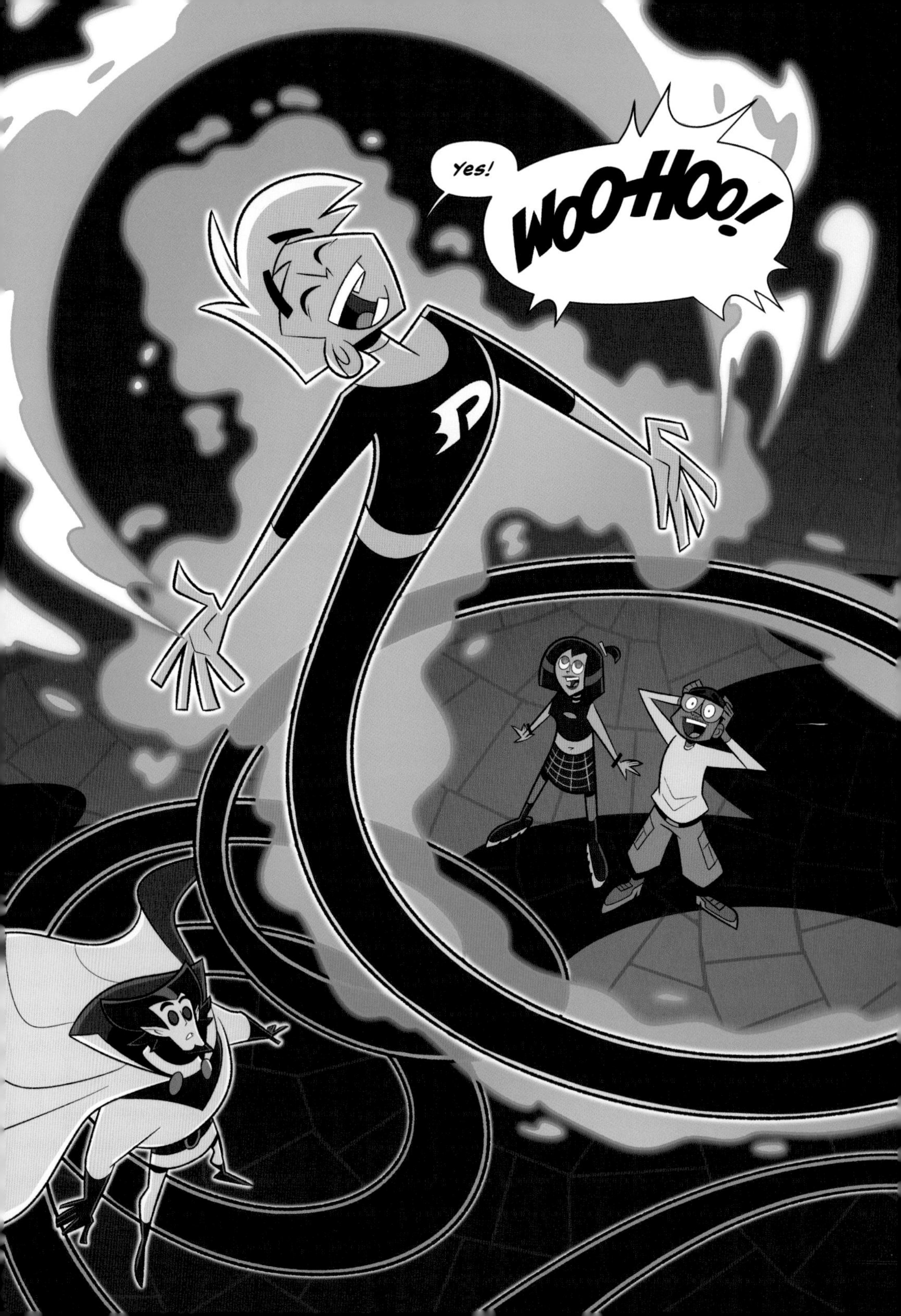
Yes!
WOO-HOO!

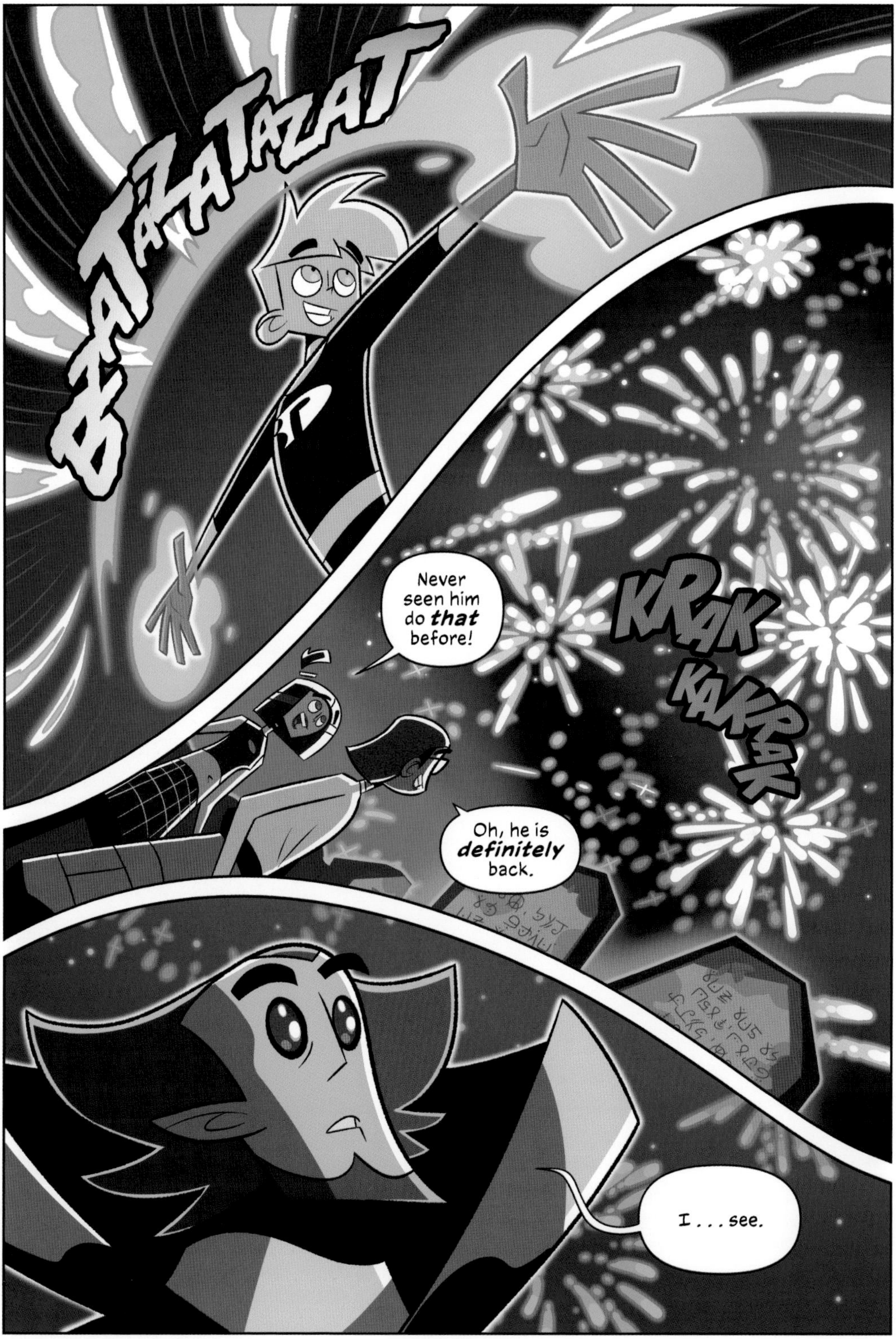
BZZATAZATAZAT
Never seen him do ***that*** before!
KRAK KAKRAK
Oh, he is ***definitely*** back.
I . . . see.

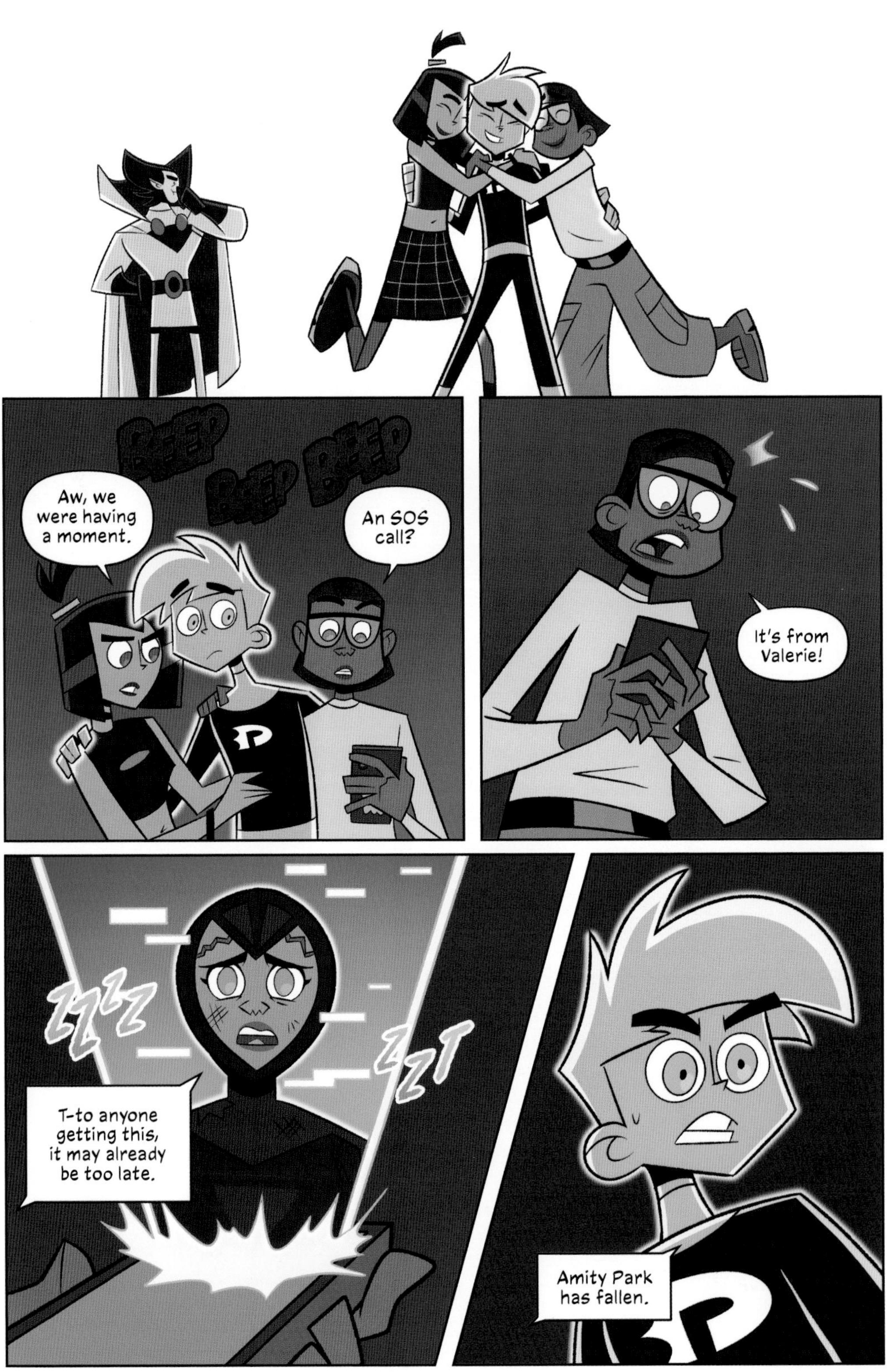
BEEP
BEEP BEEP
Aw, we were having a moment.
An SOS call?
It's from Valerie!
ZZZZ
ZZT
T-to anyone getting this, it may already be too late.
Amity Park has fallen.

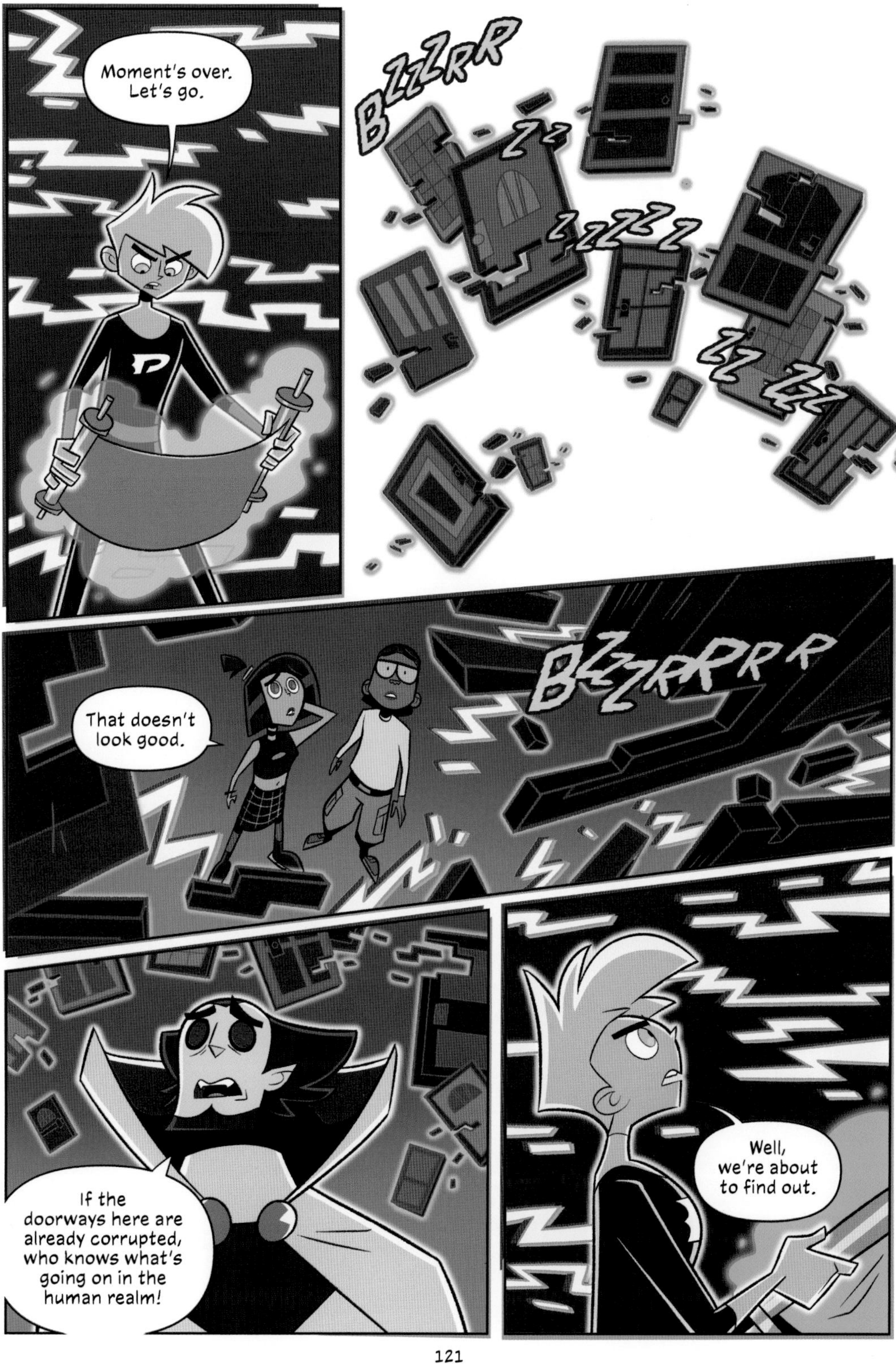
Moment's over. Let's go.
BZZZRR
Z Z
ZZZZZ
ZZ
ZZZ
BZZZRRRRR
That doesn't look good.
If the doorways here are already corrupted, who knows what's going on in the human realm!
Well, we're about to find out.

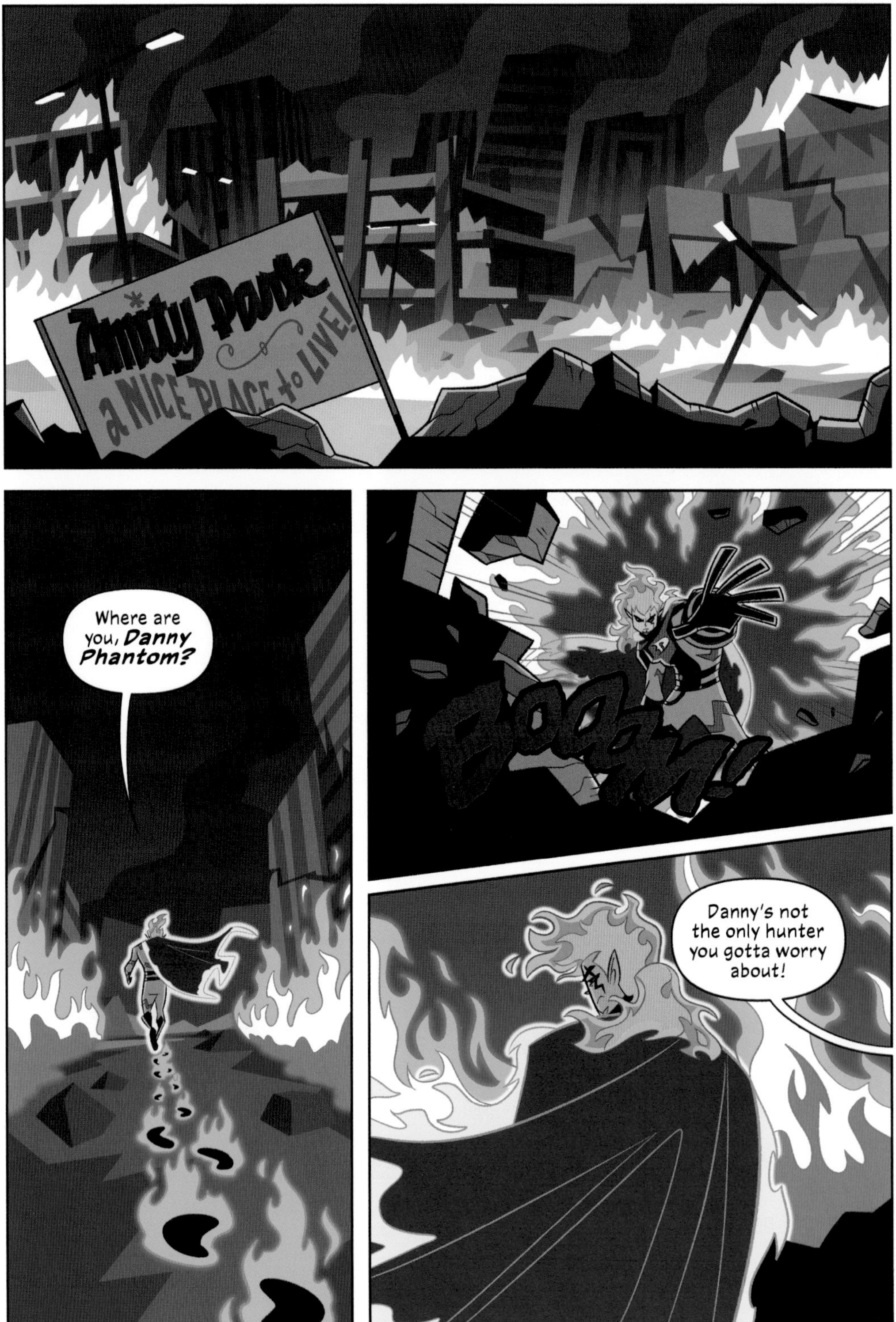
Amity Park
a NICE PLACE to LIVE!
Where are you, Danny Phantom?
BOOM!
Danny's not the only hunter you gotta worry about!

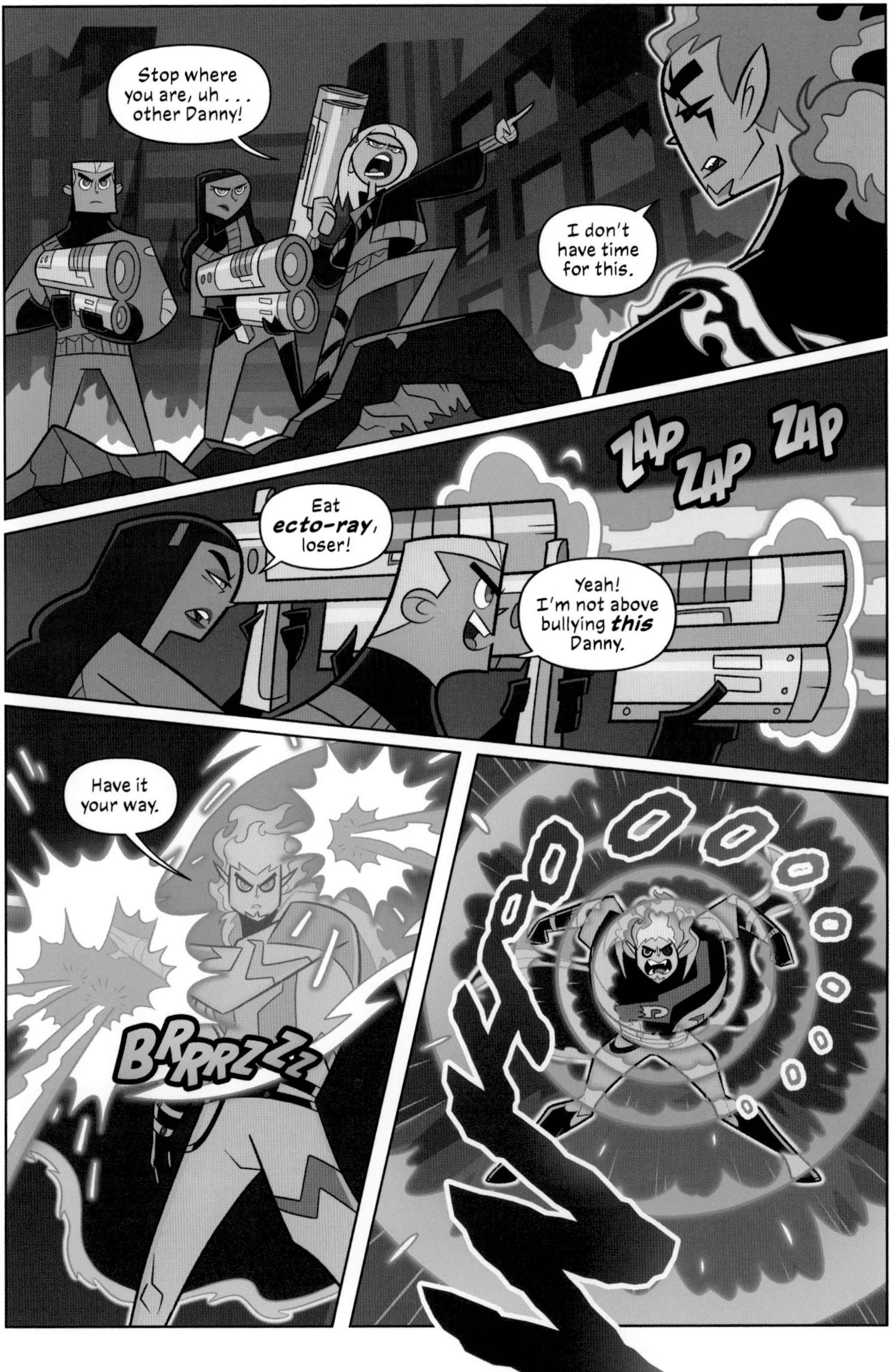

Stop where you are, uh . . . other Danny!
I don't have time for this.
ZAP ZAP ZAP
Eat *ecto-ray*, loser!
Yeah! I'm not above bullying *this* Danny.
Have it your way.
BRRRZZZ

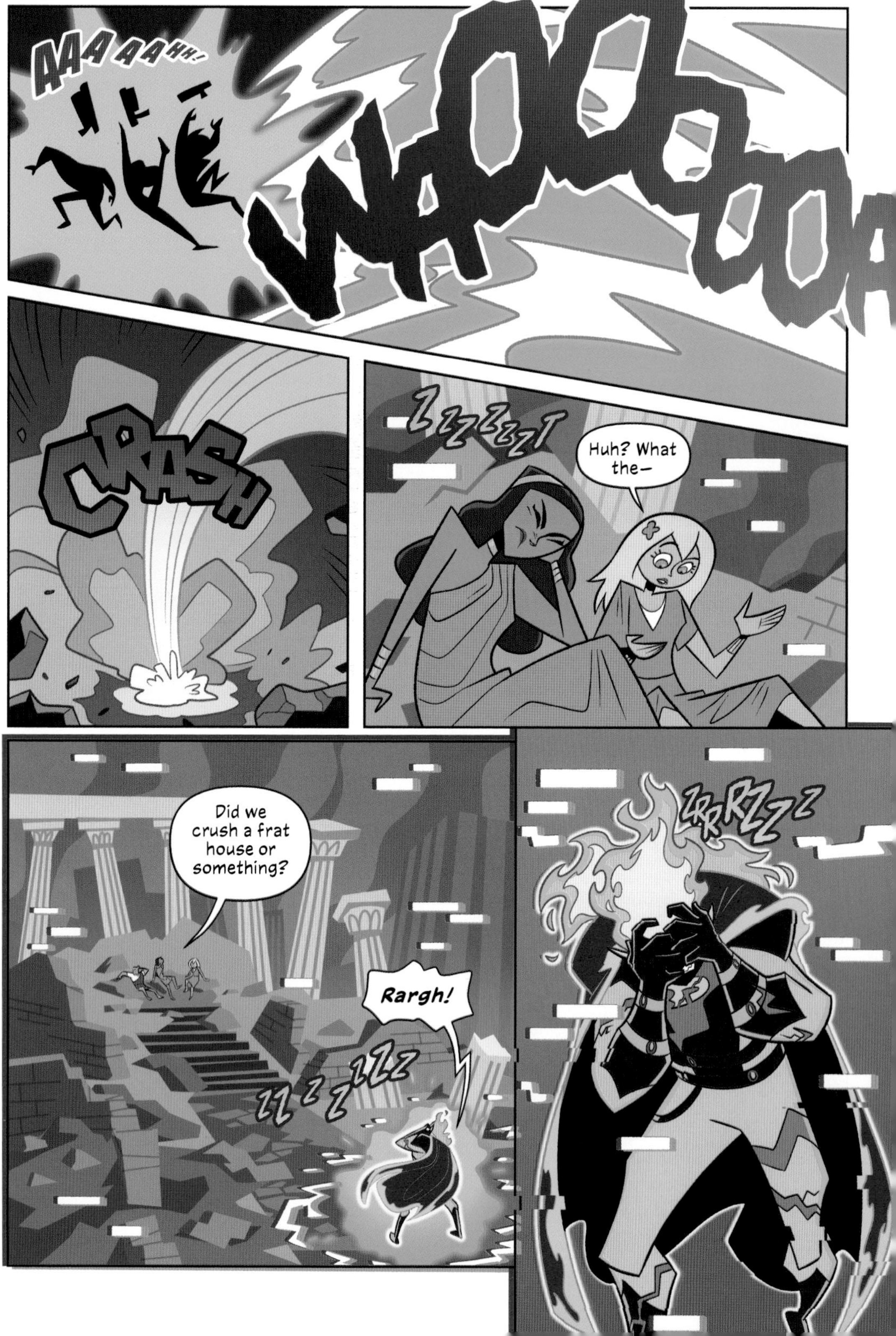
AAAAAHH!
VKAOOOOOOA
CRASH
ZZZZZZT
Huh? What the—
Did we crush a frat house or something?
Rargh!
ZZZZZZ
ZRRRZZZZ

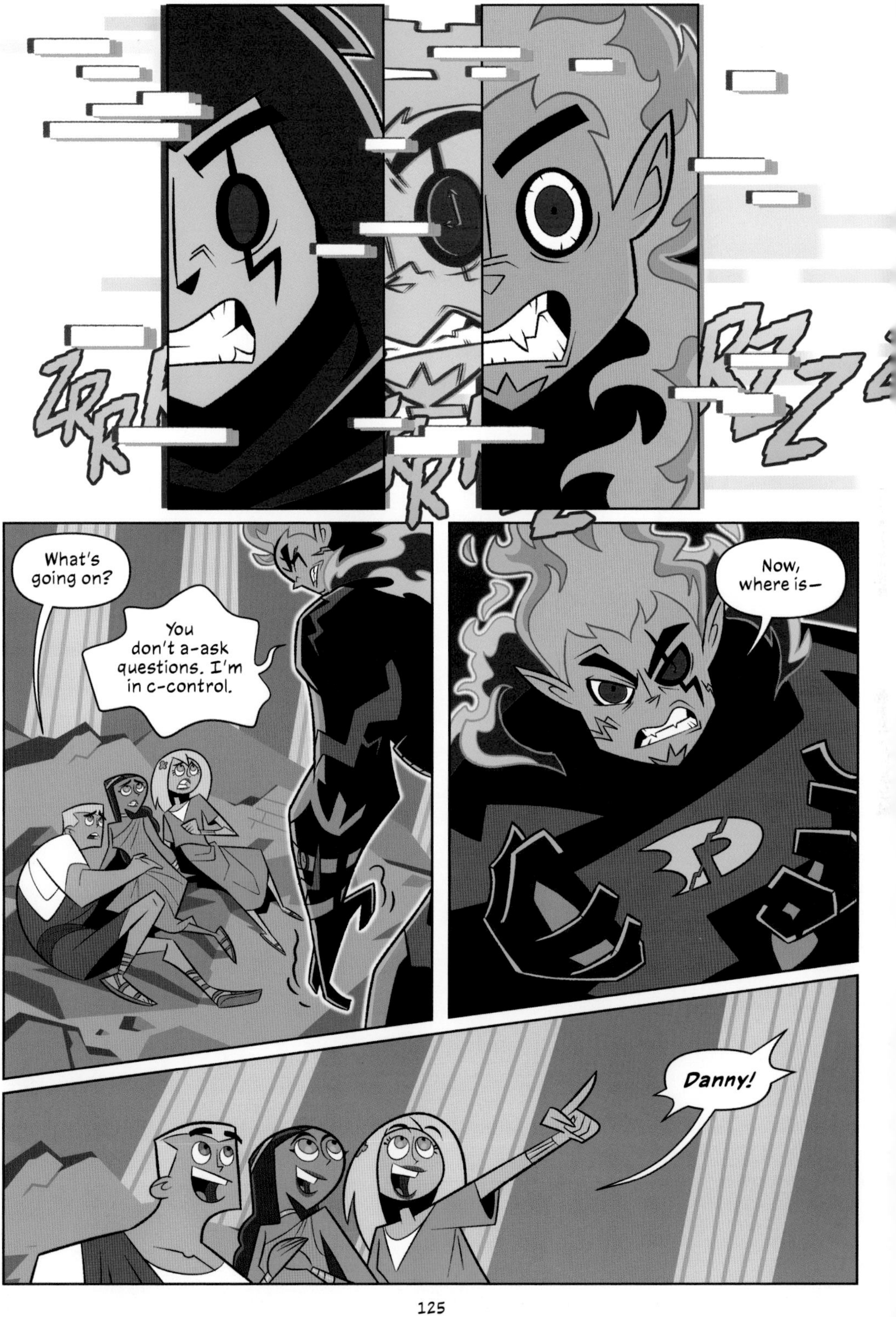
ZRRK
ZRRK
RZZZ
What's going on?
You don't a-ask questions. I'm in c-control.
Now, where is—
Danny!

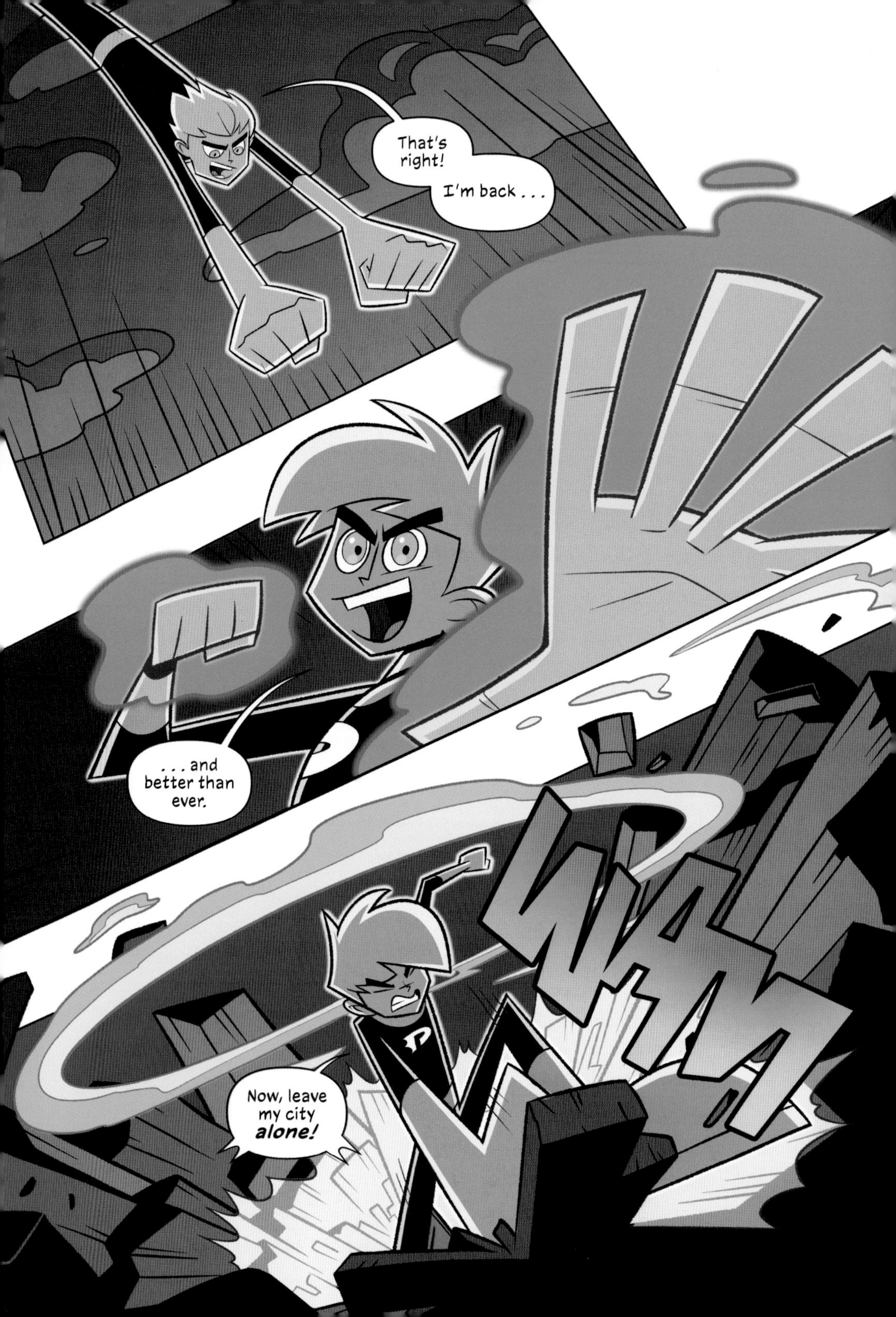
That's right!
I'm back . . .
. . . and better than ever.
WHAM
Now, leave my city *alone!*

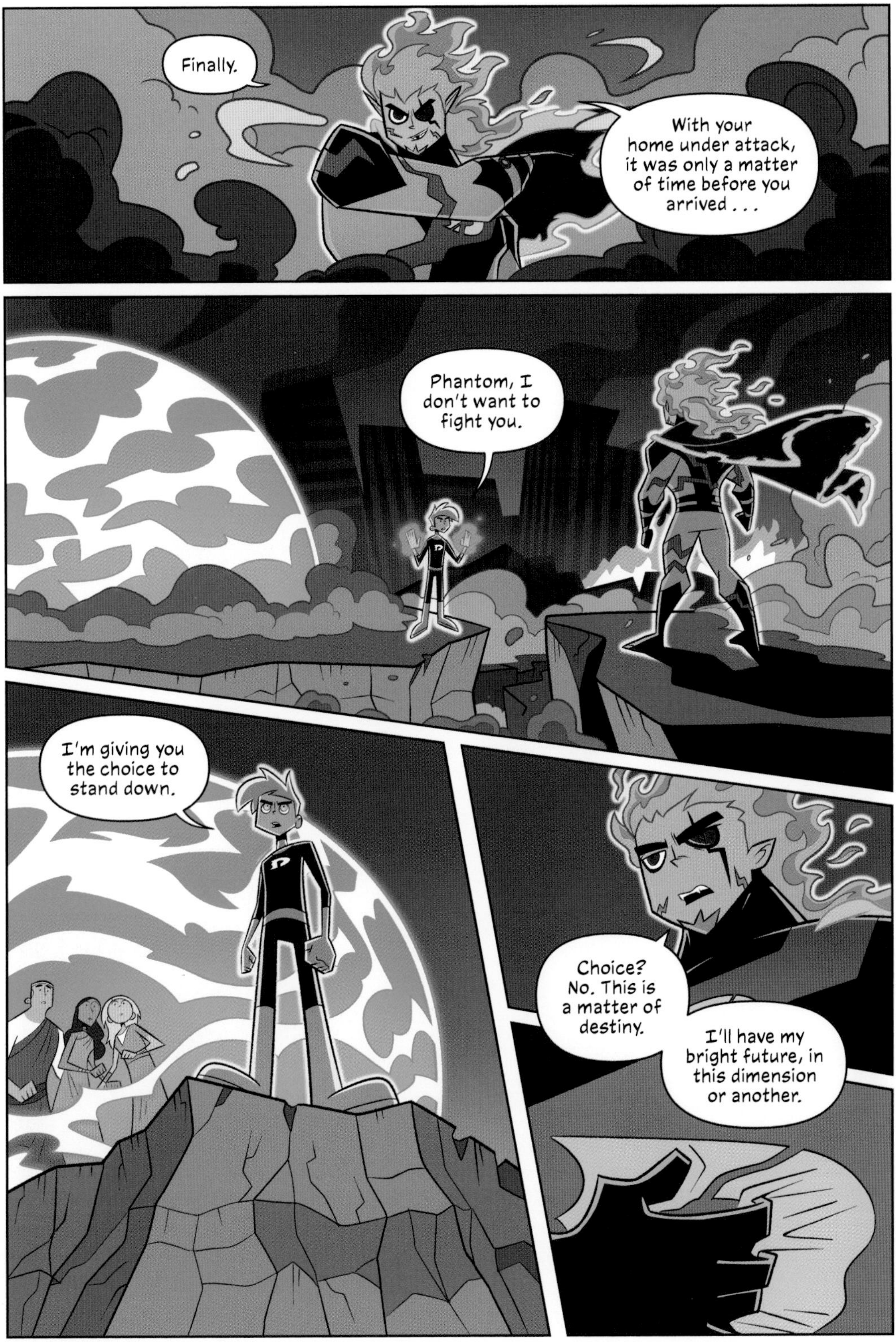

Finally.
With your home under attack, it was only a matter of time before you arrived . . .
Phantom, I don't want to fight you.
I'm giving you the choice to stand down.
Choice? No. This is a matter of destiny.
I'll have my bright future, in this dimension or another.

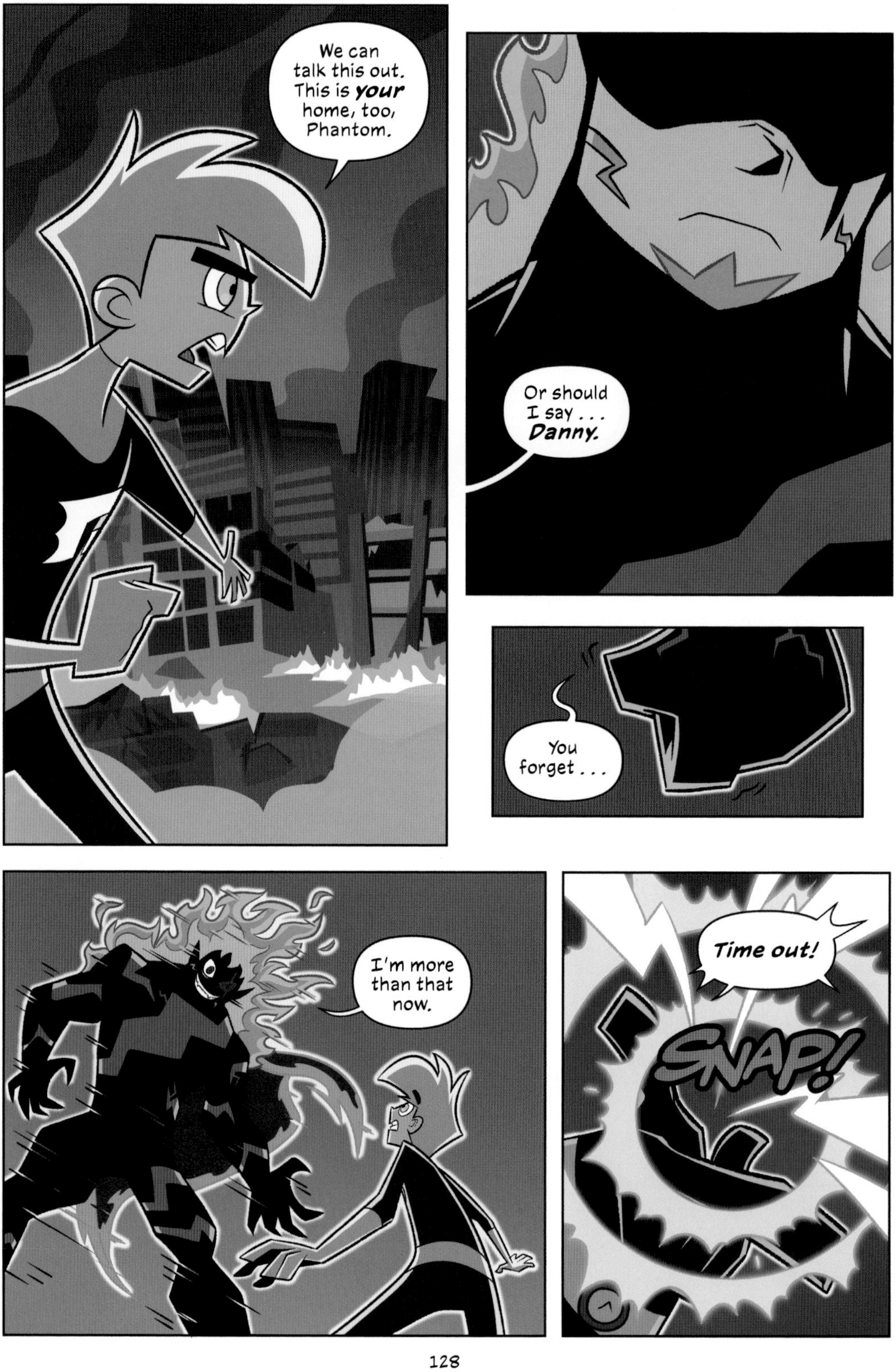
We can talk this out. This is *your* home, too, Phantom.
Or should I say . . . *Danny.*
You forget . . .
I'm more than that now.
Time out!
SNAP!

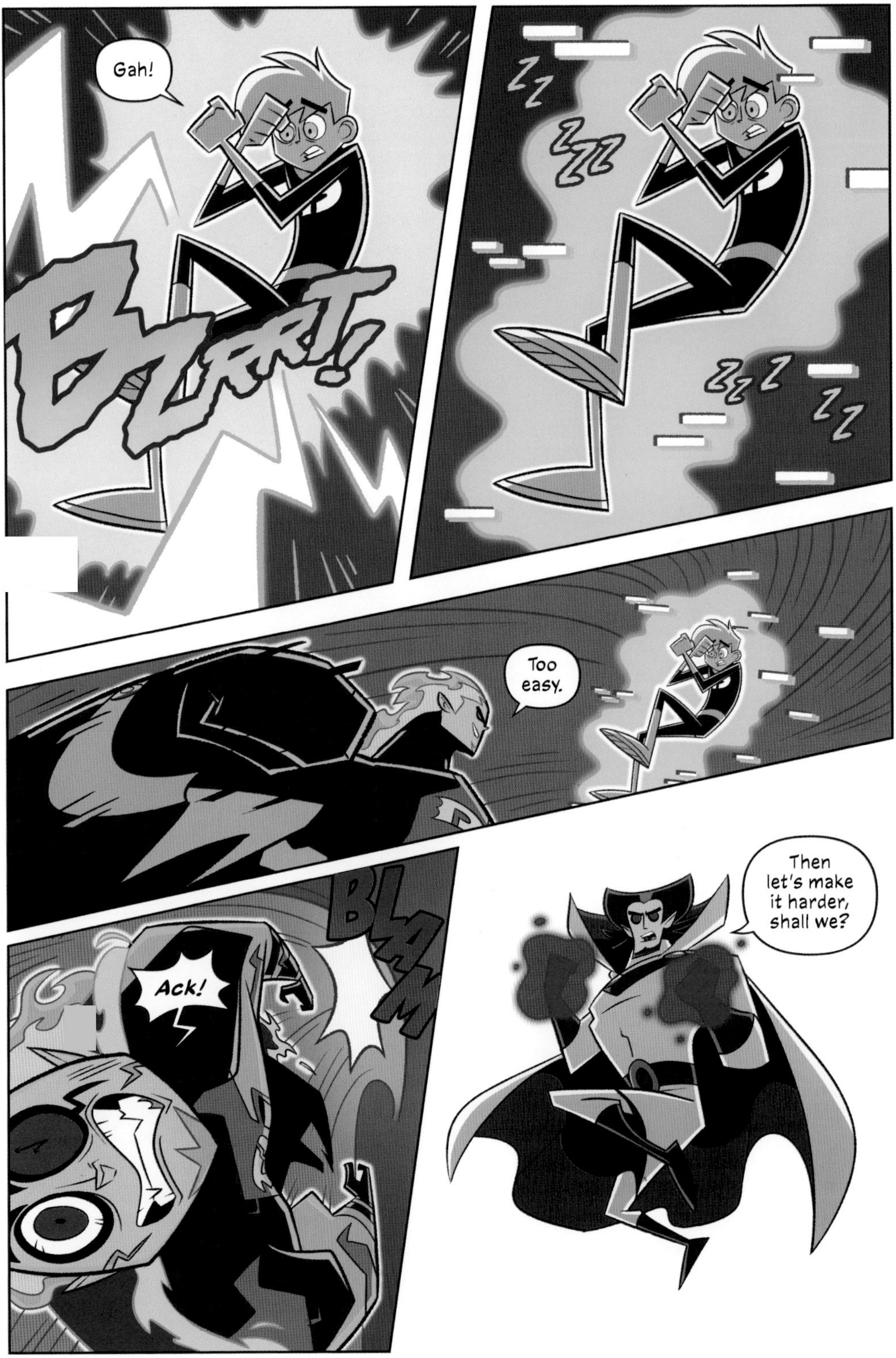
Gah!
BZRRT!
Too easy.
Ack!
BLAM
Then let's make it harder, shall we?

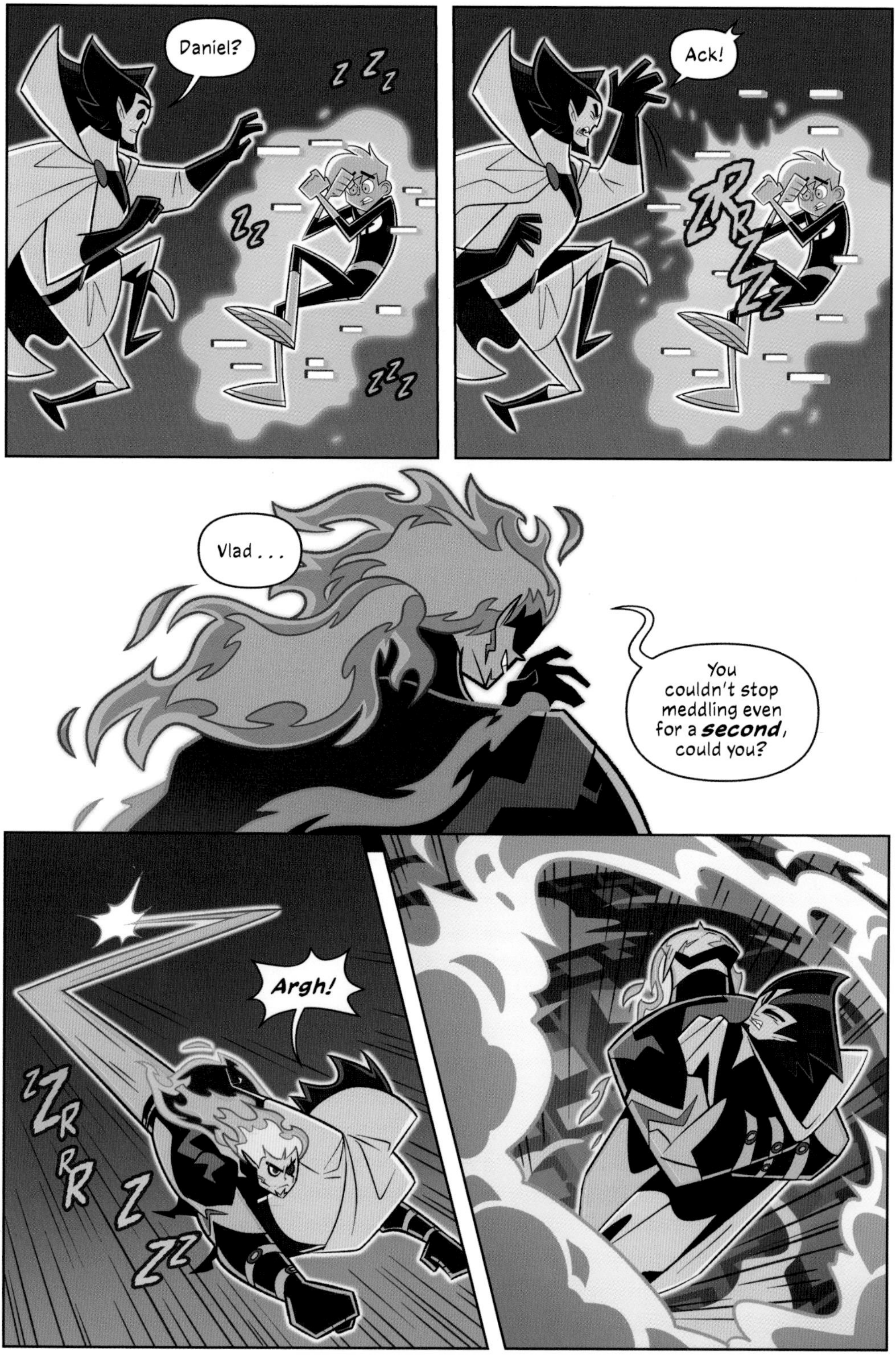
Daniel?
Z Z Z
Z Z
Z Z Z
Ack!
Z R Z Z Z
Vlad . . .
You couldn't stop meddling even for a ***second***, could you?
Argh!
Z Z R R R Z Z Z

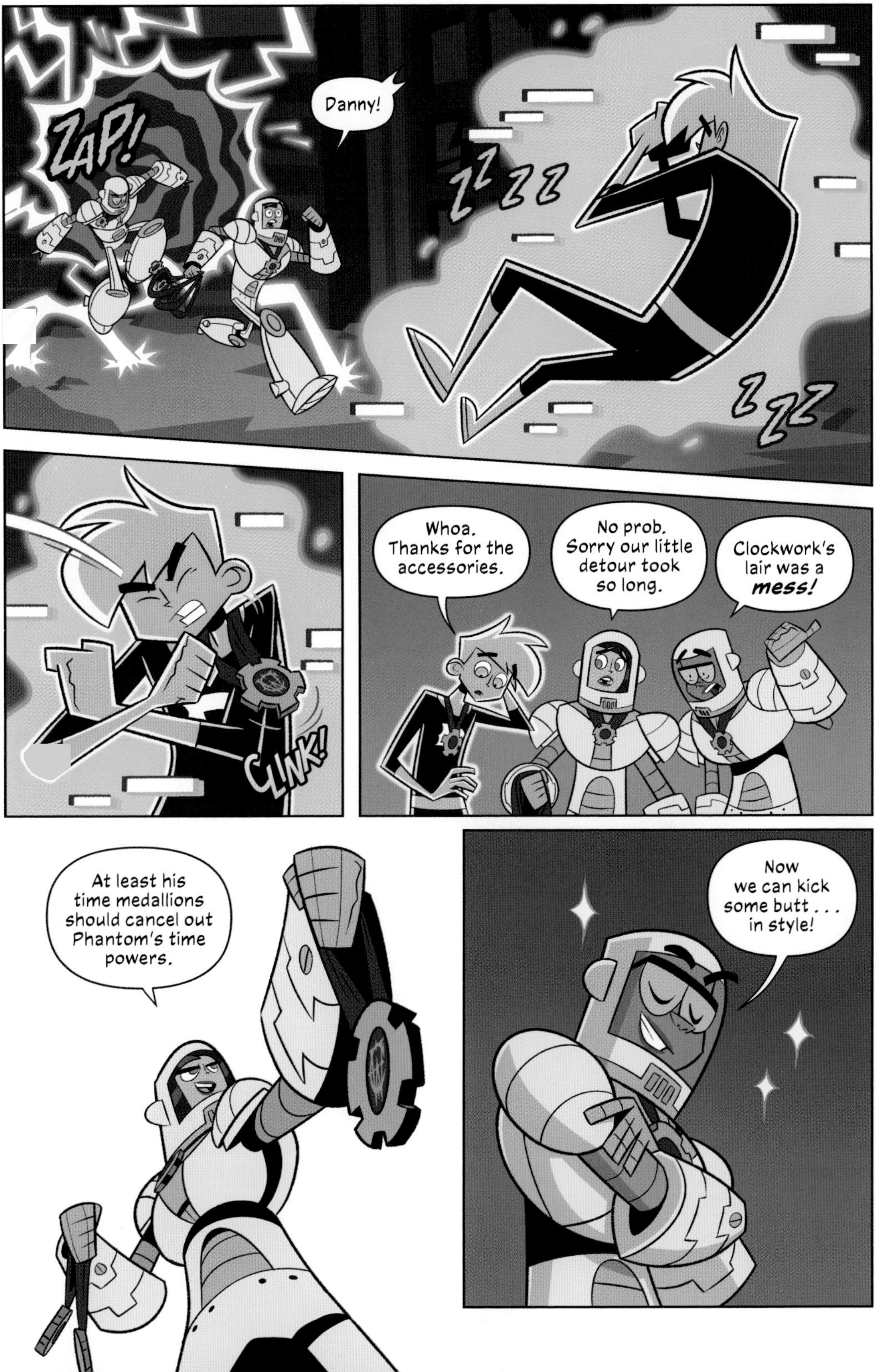
ZAP!
Danny!
ZZZZ
ZZZ
CLINK!
Whoa. Thanks for the accessories.
No prob. Sorry our little detour took so long.
Clockwork's lair was a ***mess!***
At least his time medallions should cancel out Phantom's time powers.
Now we can kick some butt . . . in style!

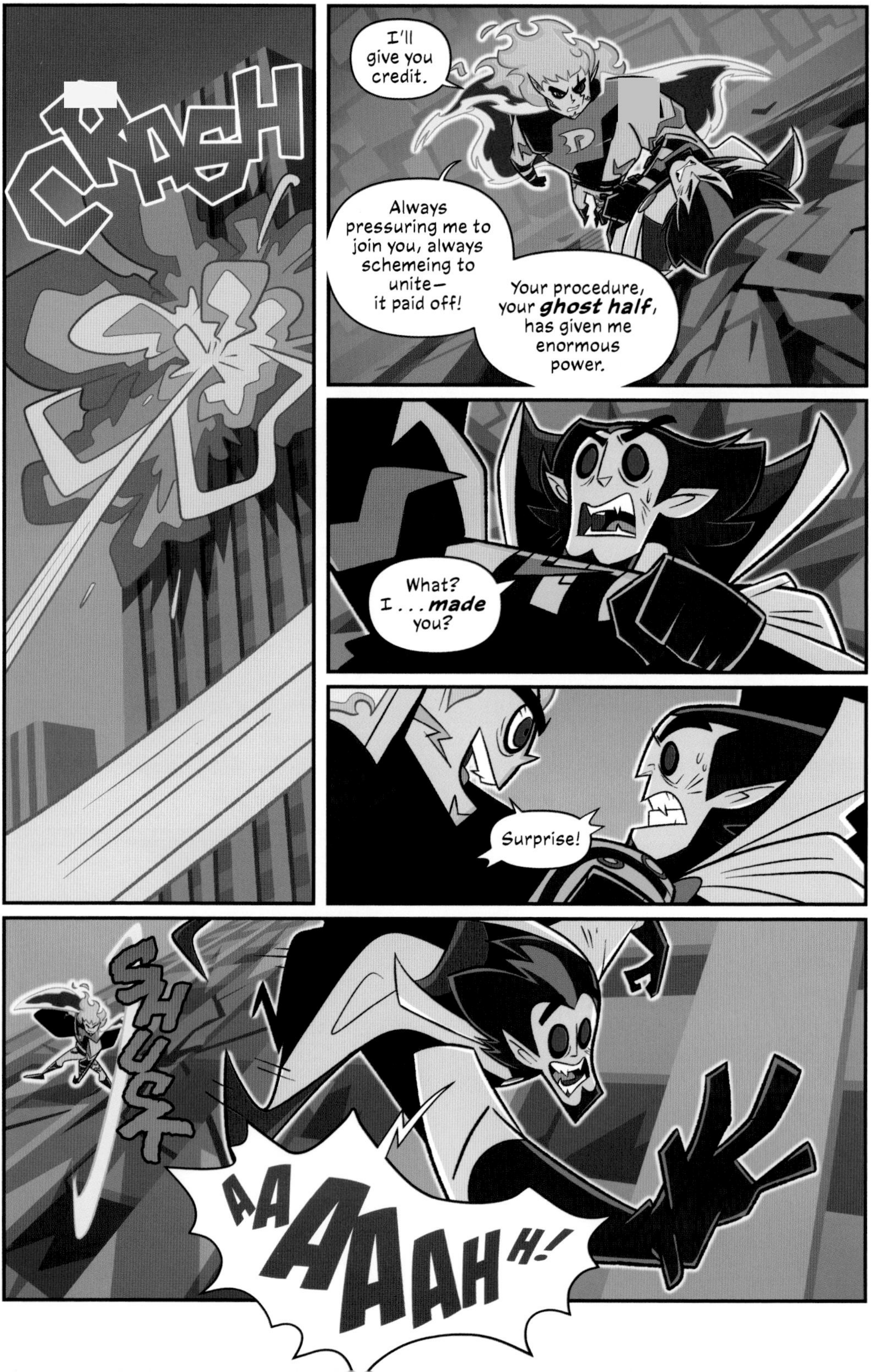
CRASH
I'll give you credit.
Always pressuring me to join you, always schemeing to unite— it paid off!
Your procedure, your ghost half, has given me enormous power.
What? I . . . made you?
Surprise!
SHUCK
AAAAAAH!

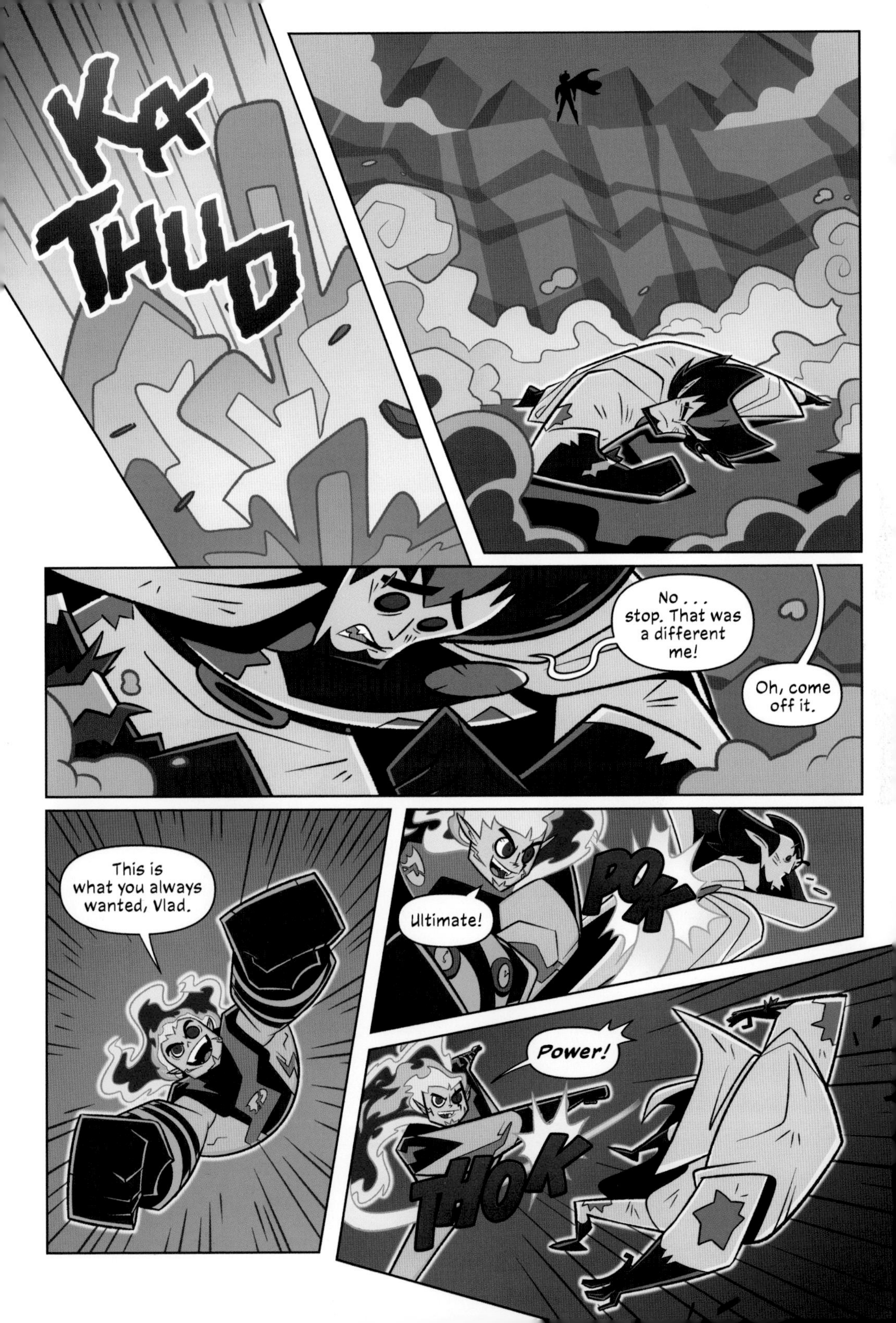
KA THUD
No . . . stop. That was a different me!
Oh, come off it.
This is what you always wanted, Vlad.
Ultimate!
POK
Power!
THOK

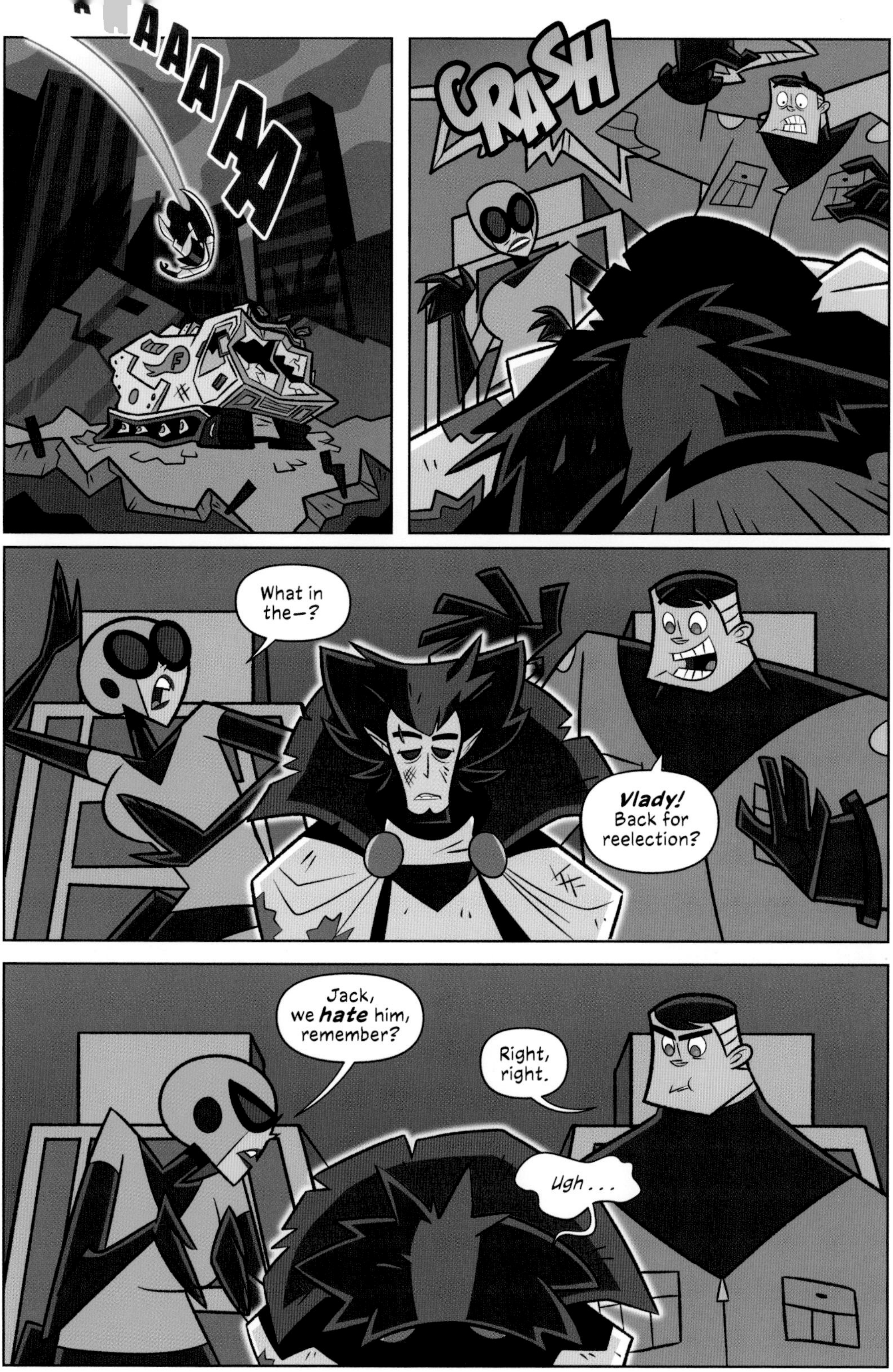
AAAAAA
CRASH
What in the—?
Vlady! Back for reelection?
Jack, we hate him, remember?
Right, right.
Ugh . . .

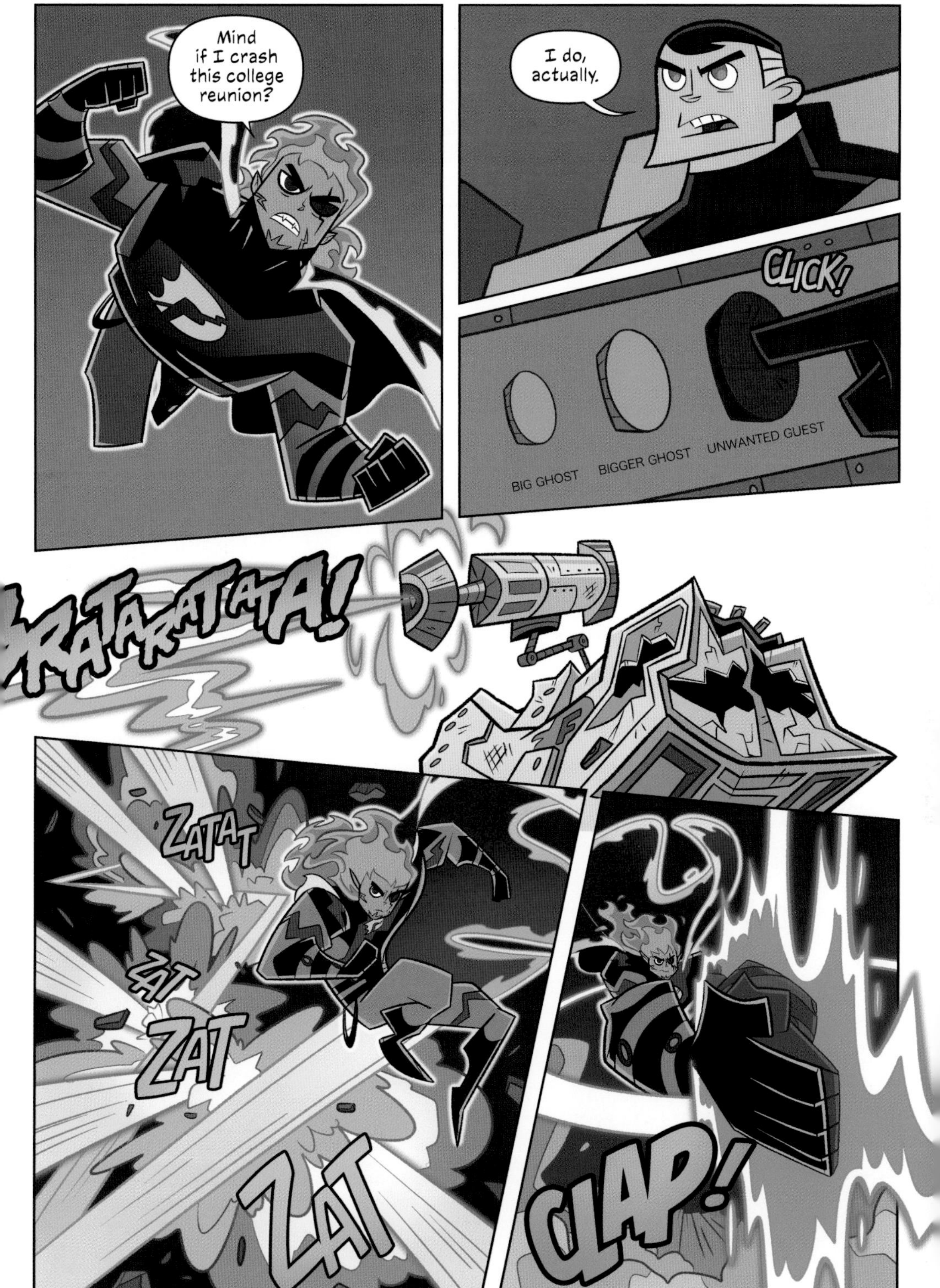
Mind if I crash this college reunion?
I do, actually.
CLICK!
BIG GHOST
BIGGER GHOST
UNWANTED GUEST
RATATARATATA!
ZATAT
ZAT
ZAT
ZAT
CLAP!

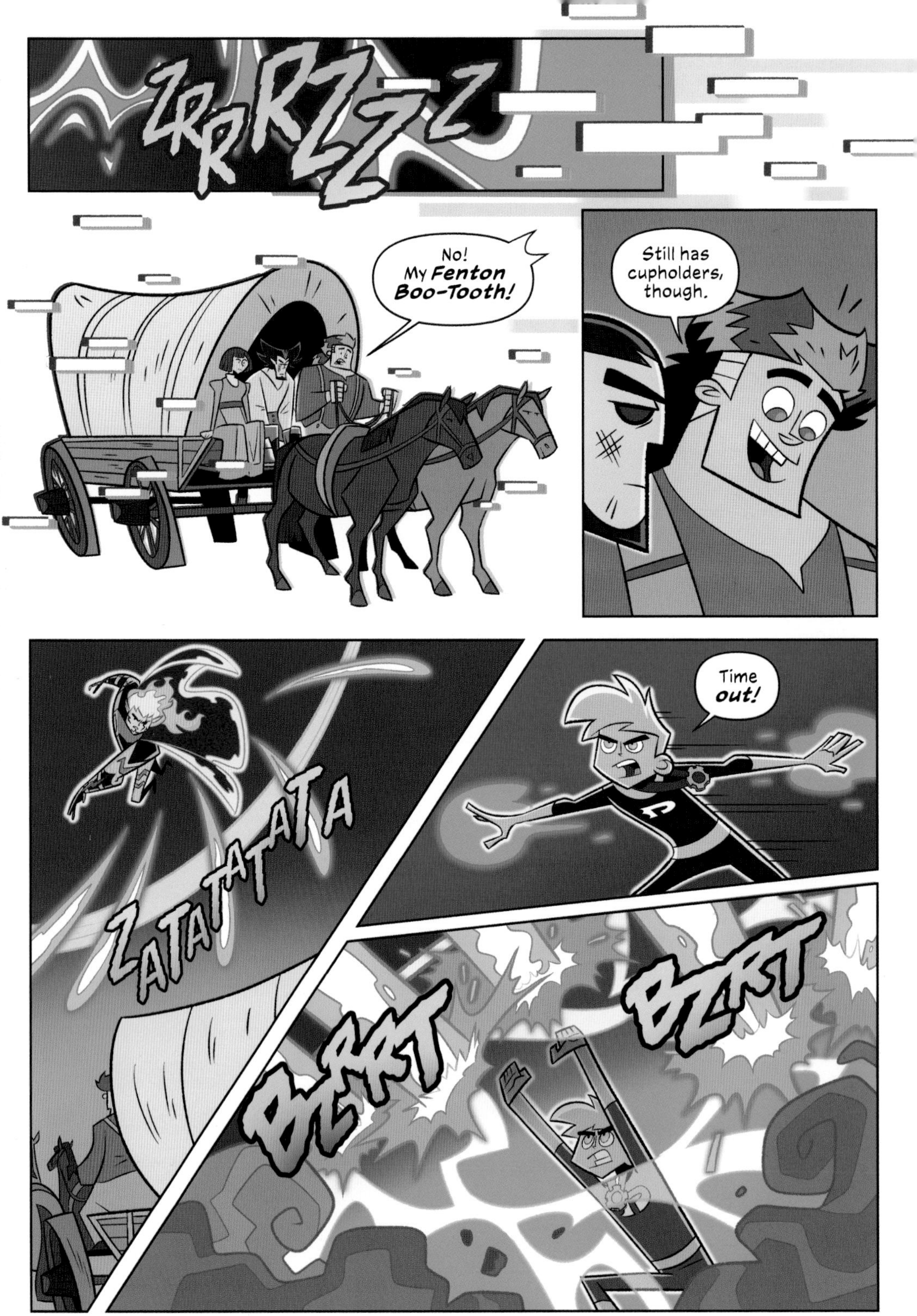
ZRRRZZZZ
No! My Fenton Boo-Tooth!
Still has cupholders, though.
ZATATATATA
Time out!
BZRRT
BZRRT

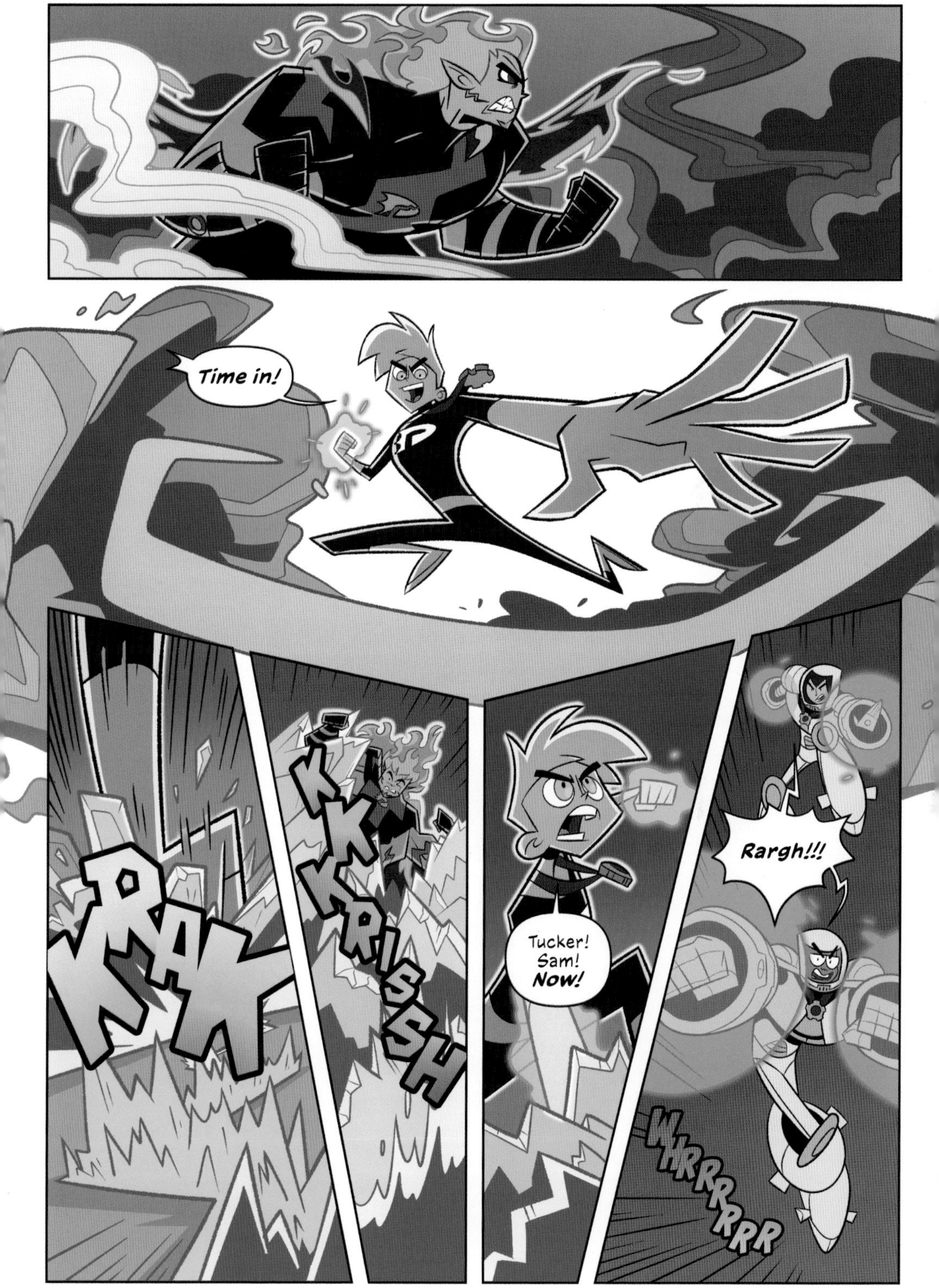
Time in!
KRAK
KKKRISSH
Tucker! Sam! Now!
Rargh!!!
WHRRRRRR

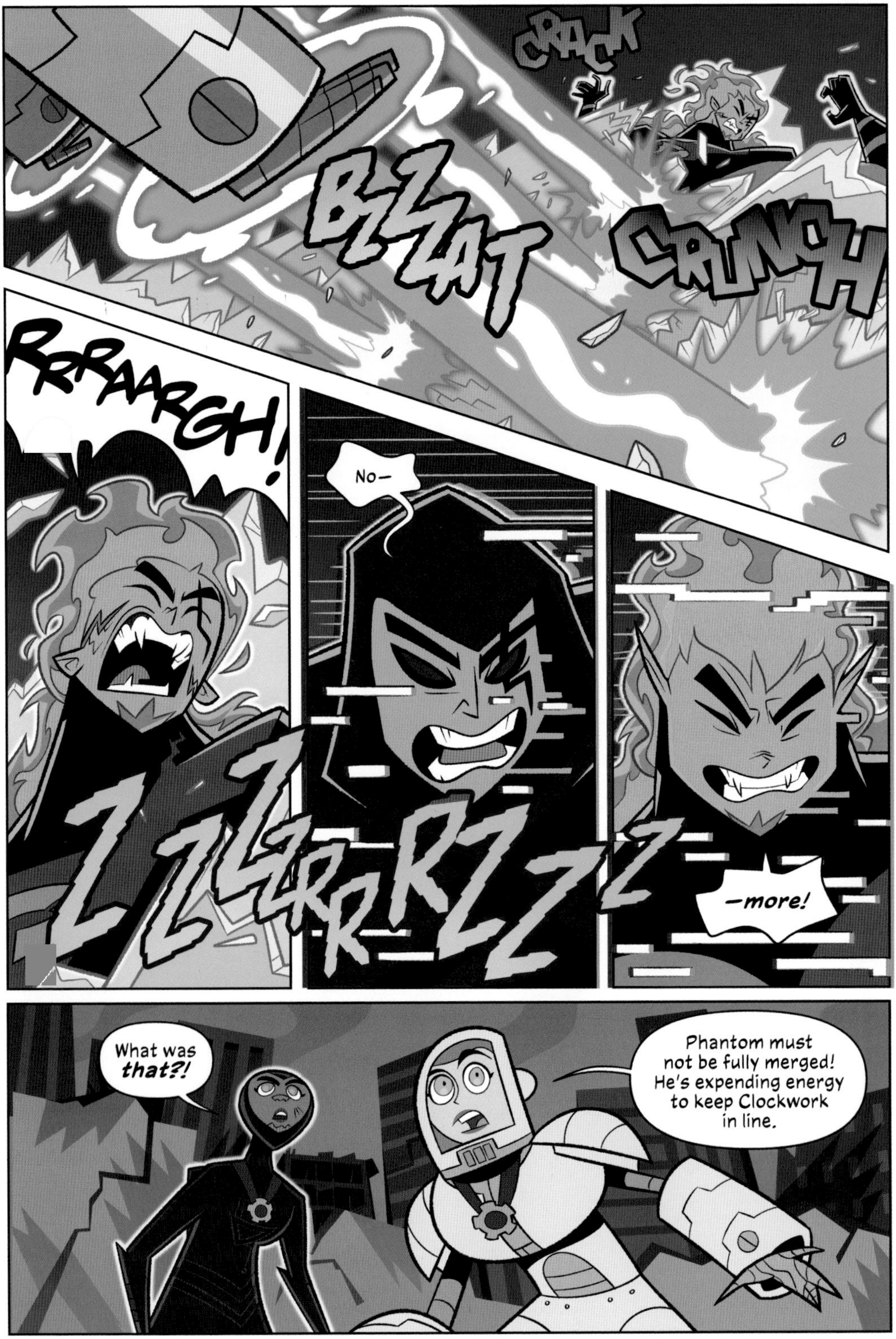
CRACK
BZZZAT
CRUNCH
RRRAARGH!
No—
ZZZZRRRRZZZZ
—more!
What was that?!
Phantom must not be fully merged! He's expending energy to keep Clockwork in line.

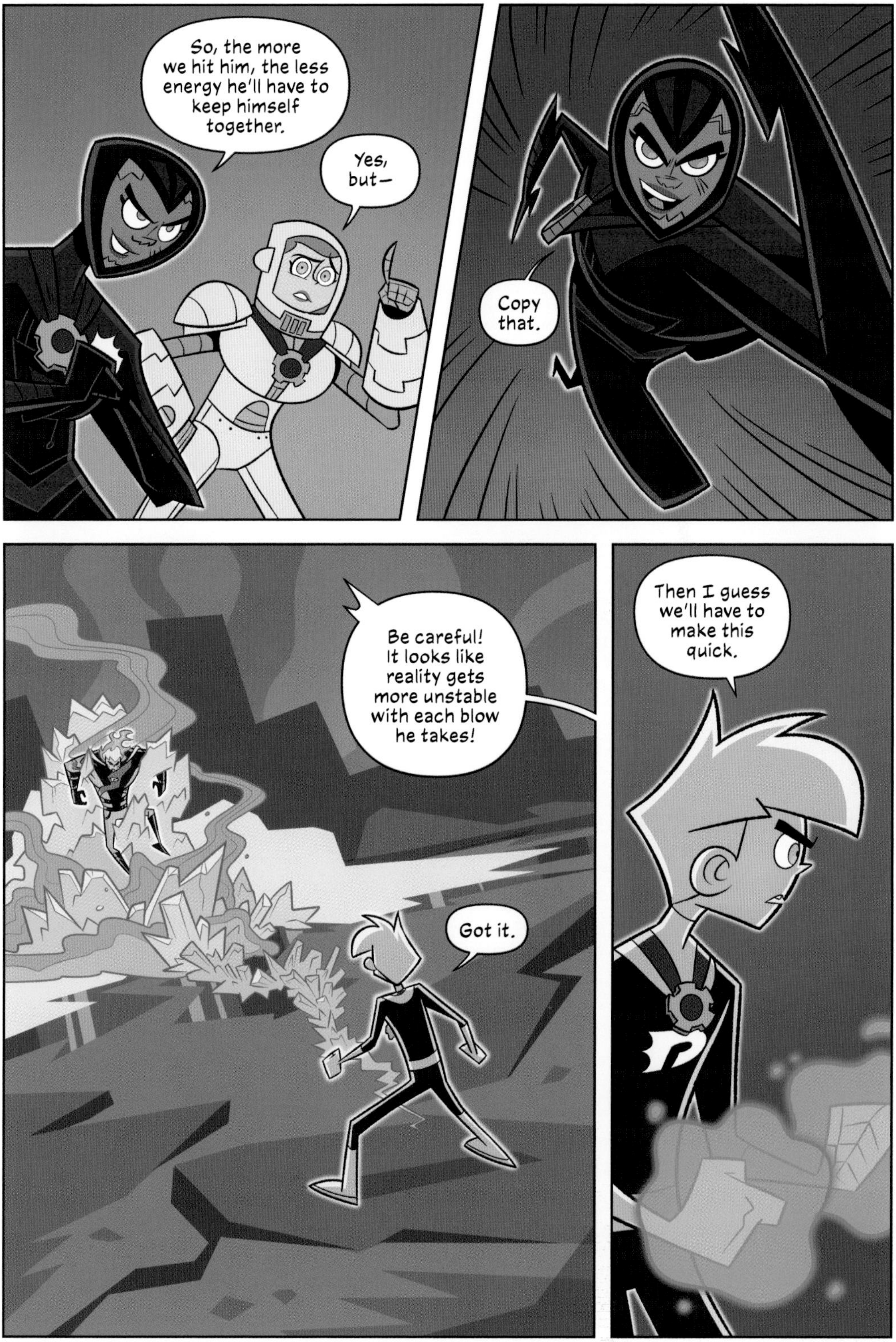
So, the more we hit him, the less energy he'll have to keep himself together.
Yes, but—
Copy that.
Be careful! It looks like reality gets more unstable with each blow he takes!
Got it.
Then I guess we'll have to make this quick.

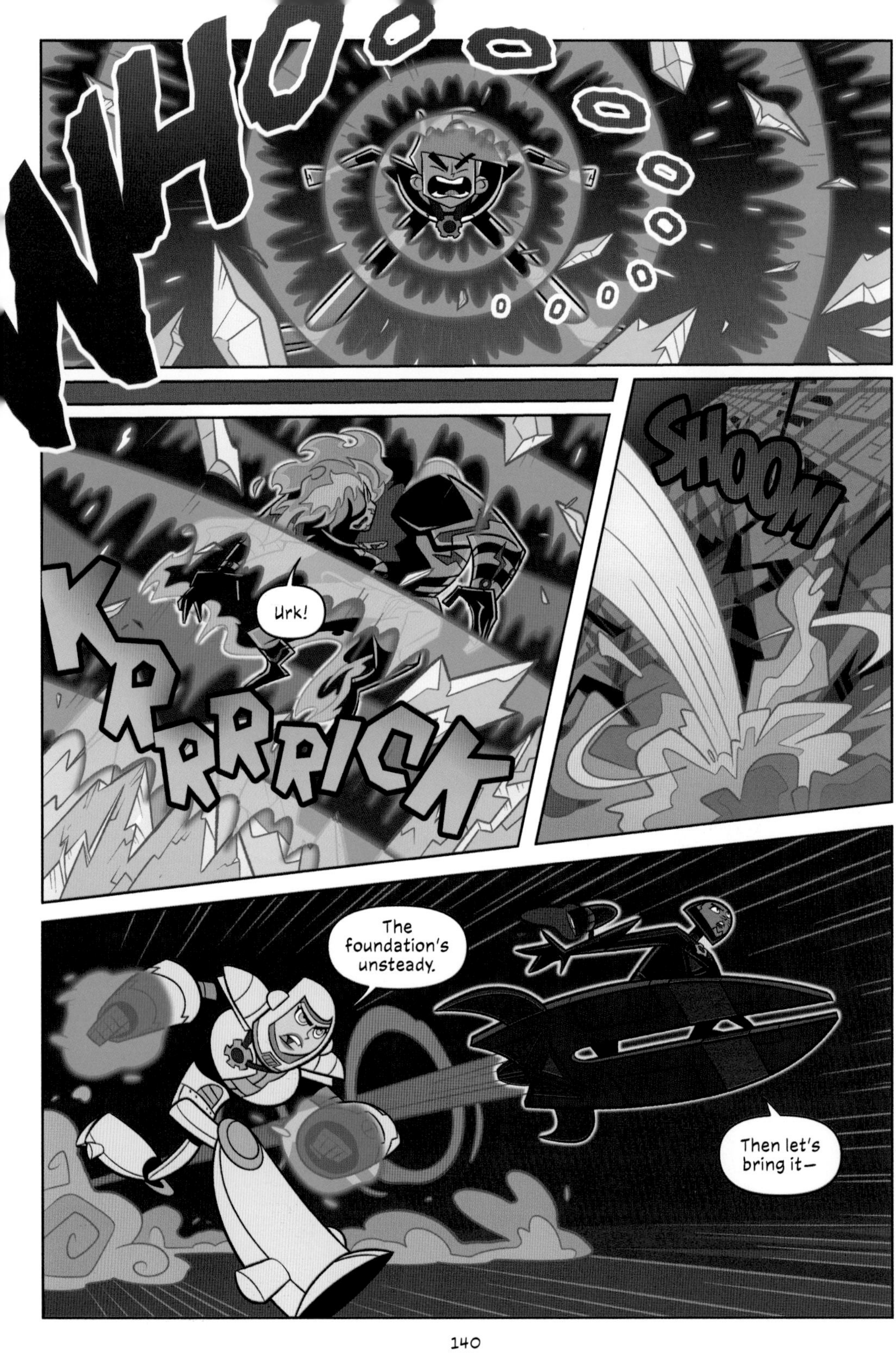
WHOOOOOOOOOOOOO
Urk!
KRRRRICK
SHOOM
The foundation's unsteady.
Then let's bring it—

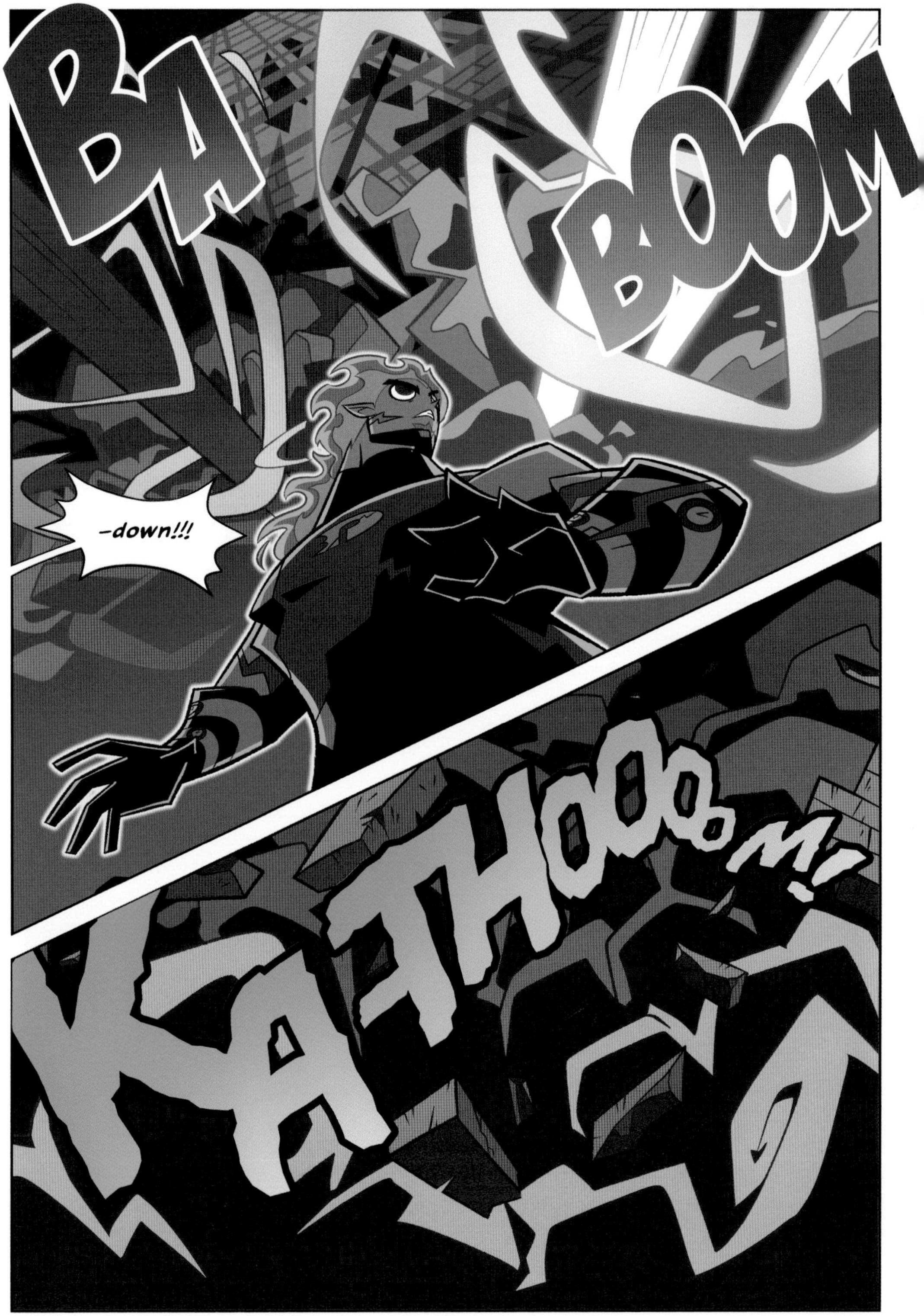
BA-BOOM
-down!!!
KA-THOOOM!!

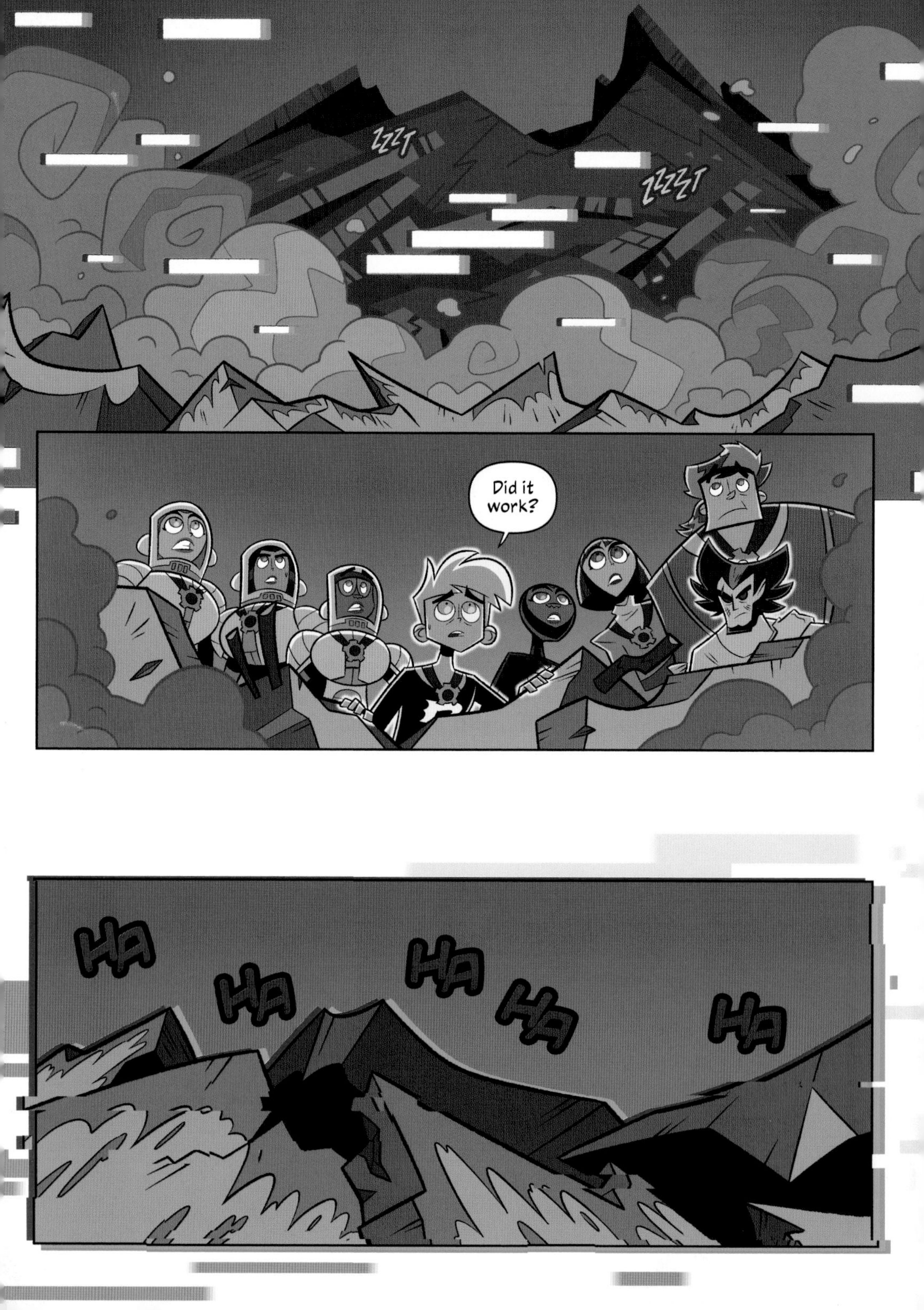
ZZZT
ZZZZT
Did it work?
HA
HA
HA
HA
HA

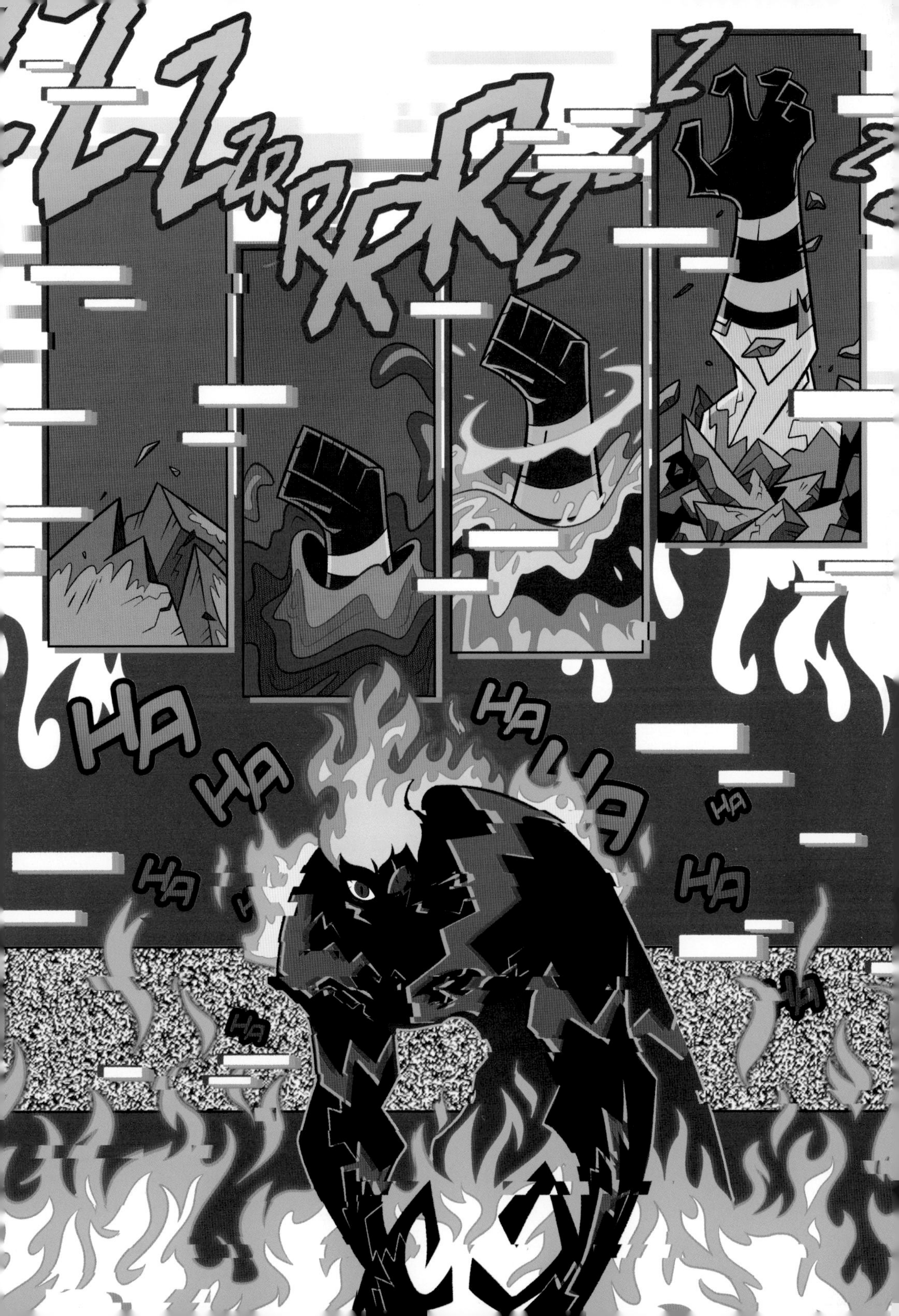
HA
HA
HA
HA
HA
HA
HA
HA

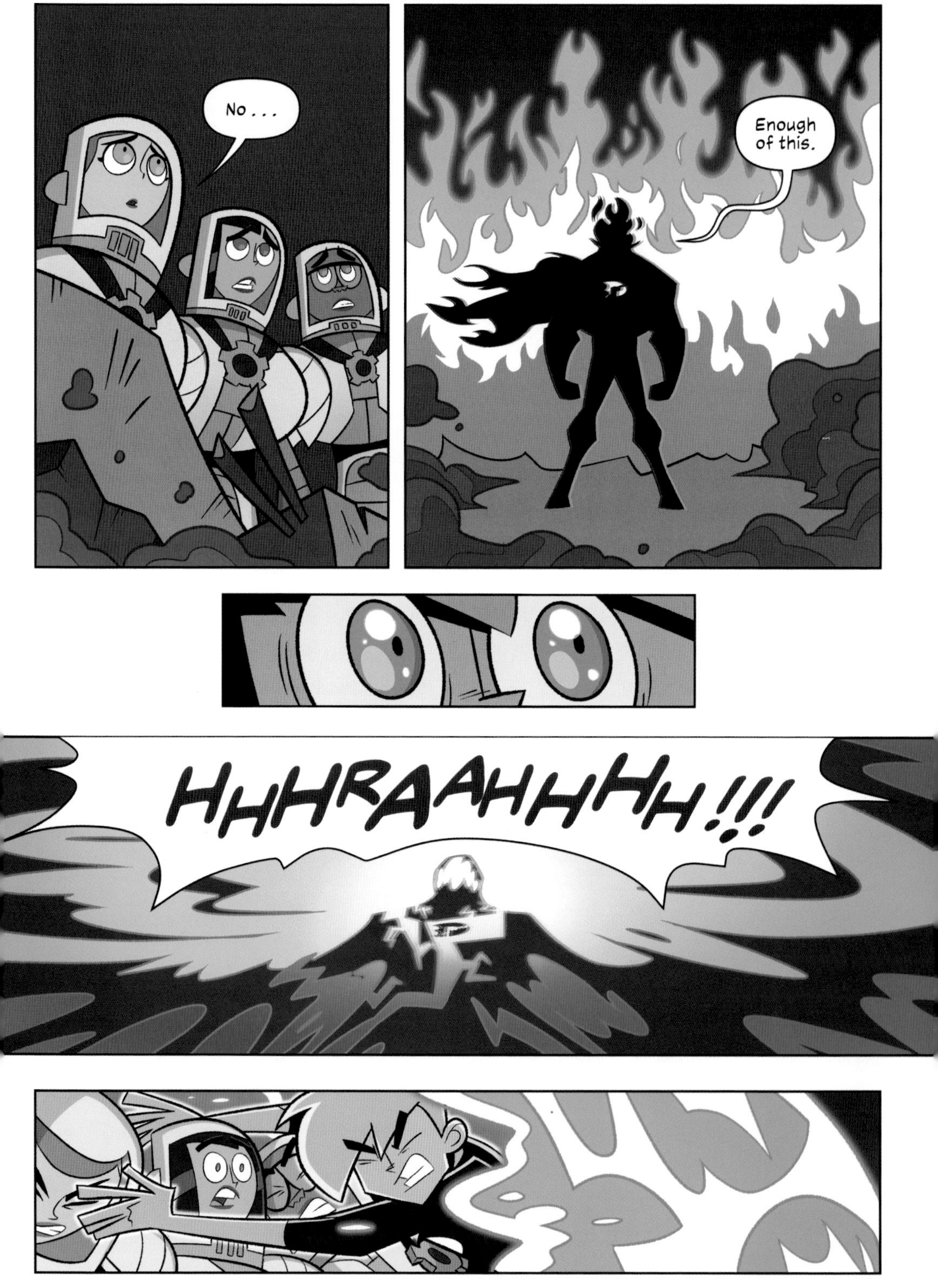
No . . .
Enough of this.
HHHRAAHHHHH!!!

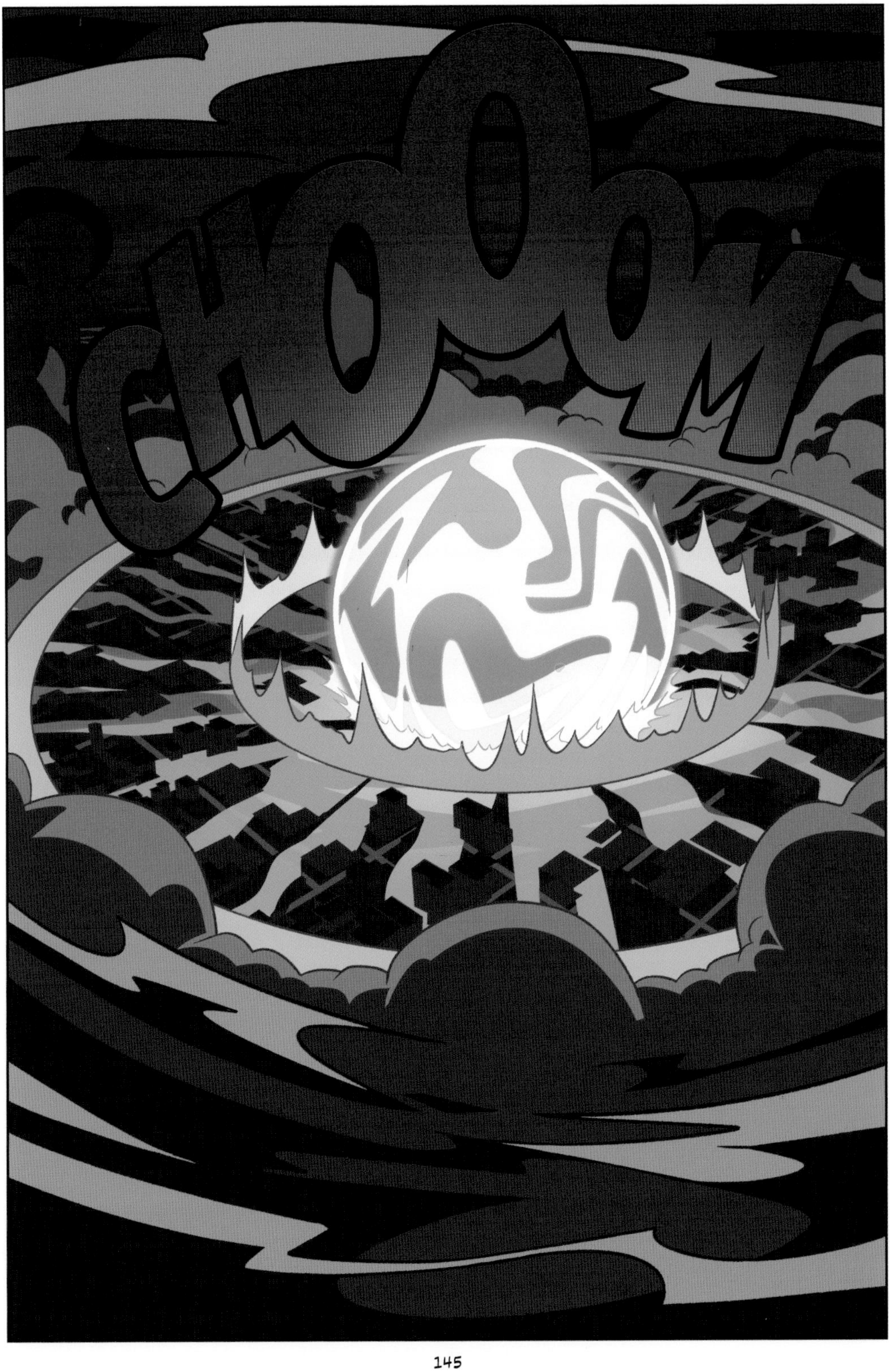
CHOOOM!

Ugh . . .

Sam?
Tucker?
Jazz?

They're
alive.

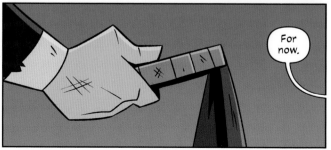

For
now.

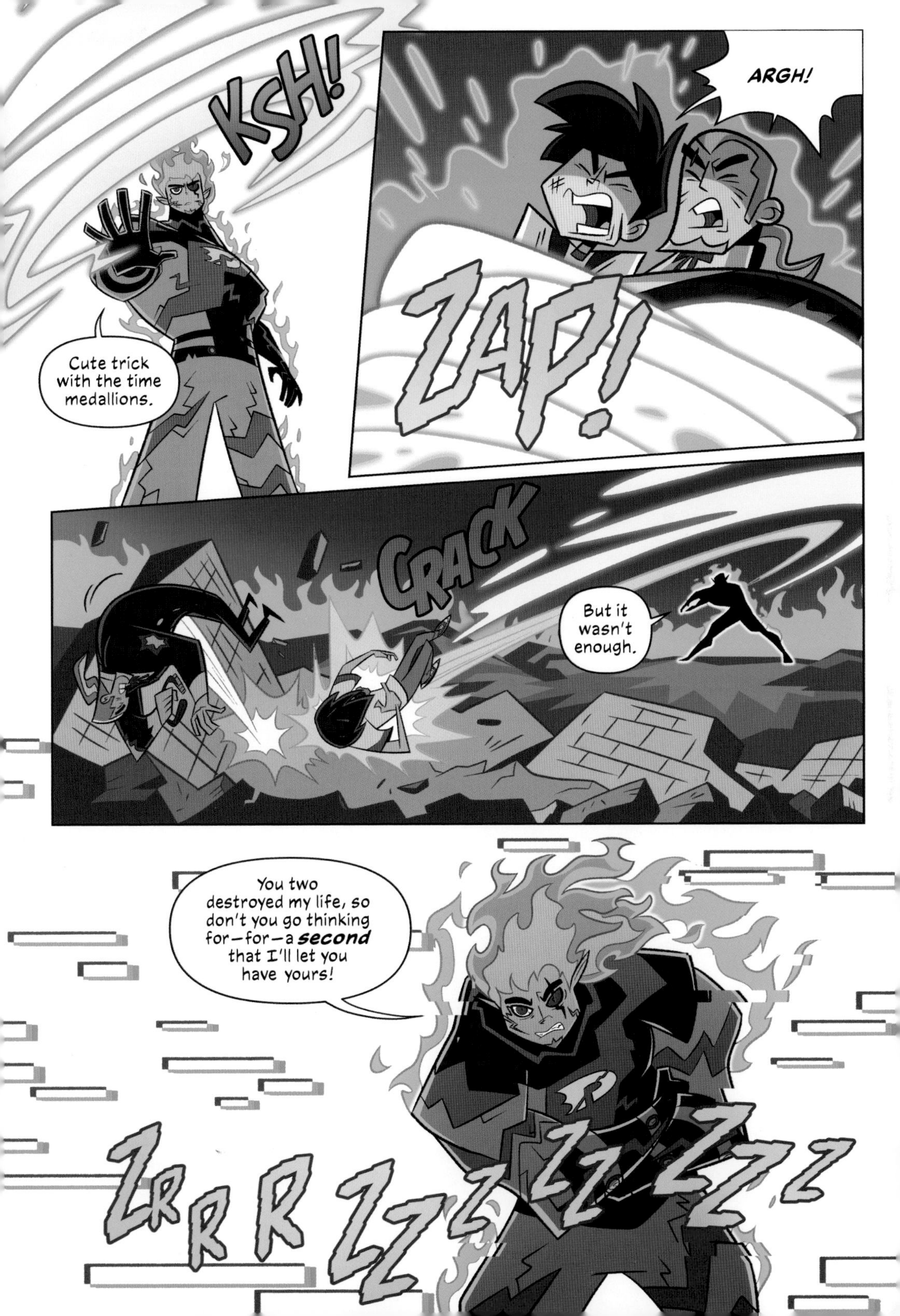
KSH!
Cute trick with the time medallions.
ARGH!
ZAP!
CRACK
But it wasn't enough.
You two destroyed my life, so don't you go thinking for—for—a ***second*** that I'll let you have yours!
ZRRRZZZZZZZZZ

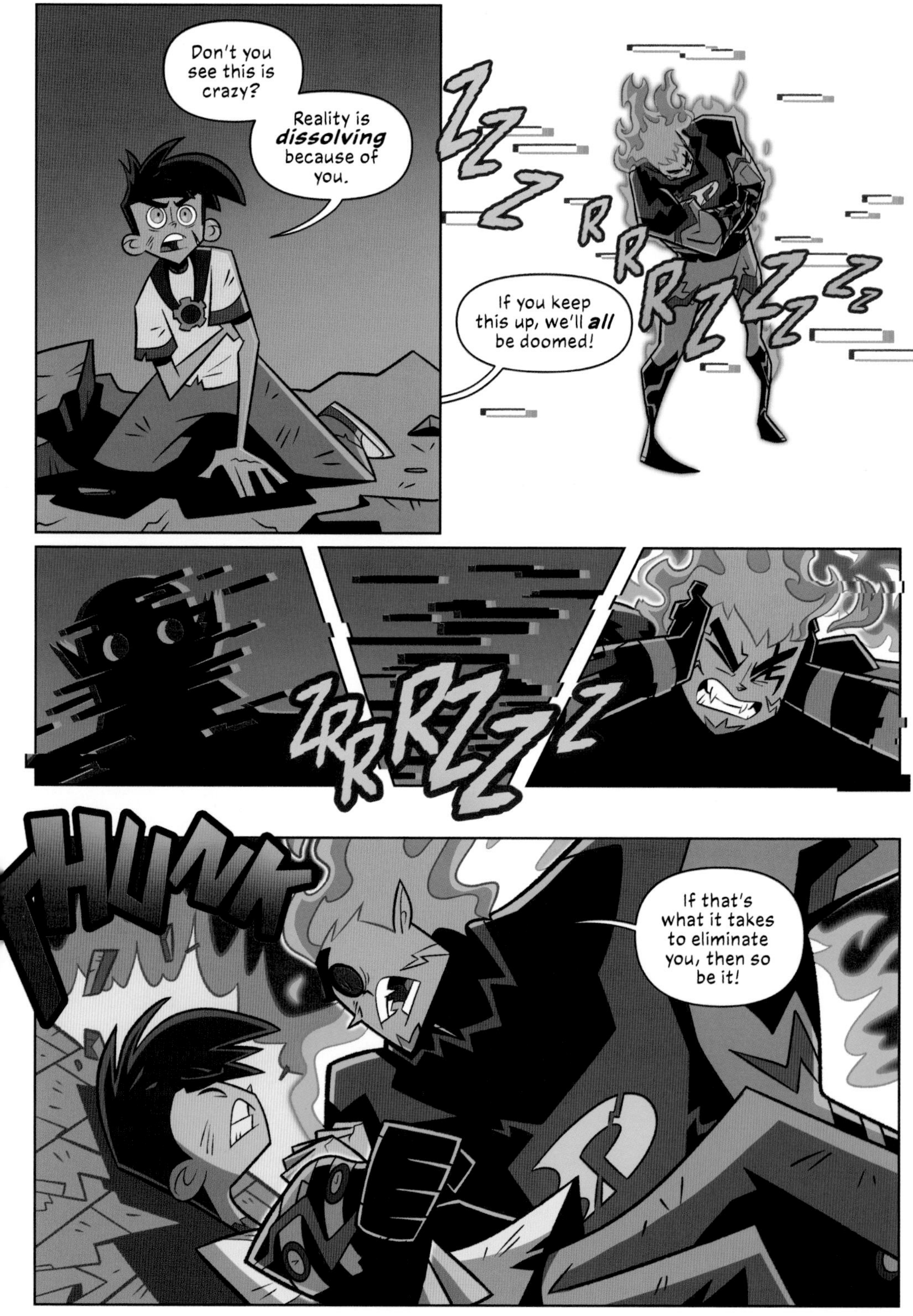

Don't you see this is crazy?
Reality is ***dissolving*** because of you.
ZZZRRRZZZZZ
If you keep this up, we'll ***all*** be doomed!
ZRRRZZZZ
THUNK
If that's what it takes to eliminate you, then so be it!

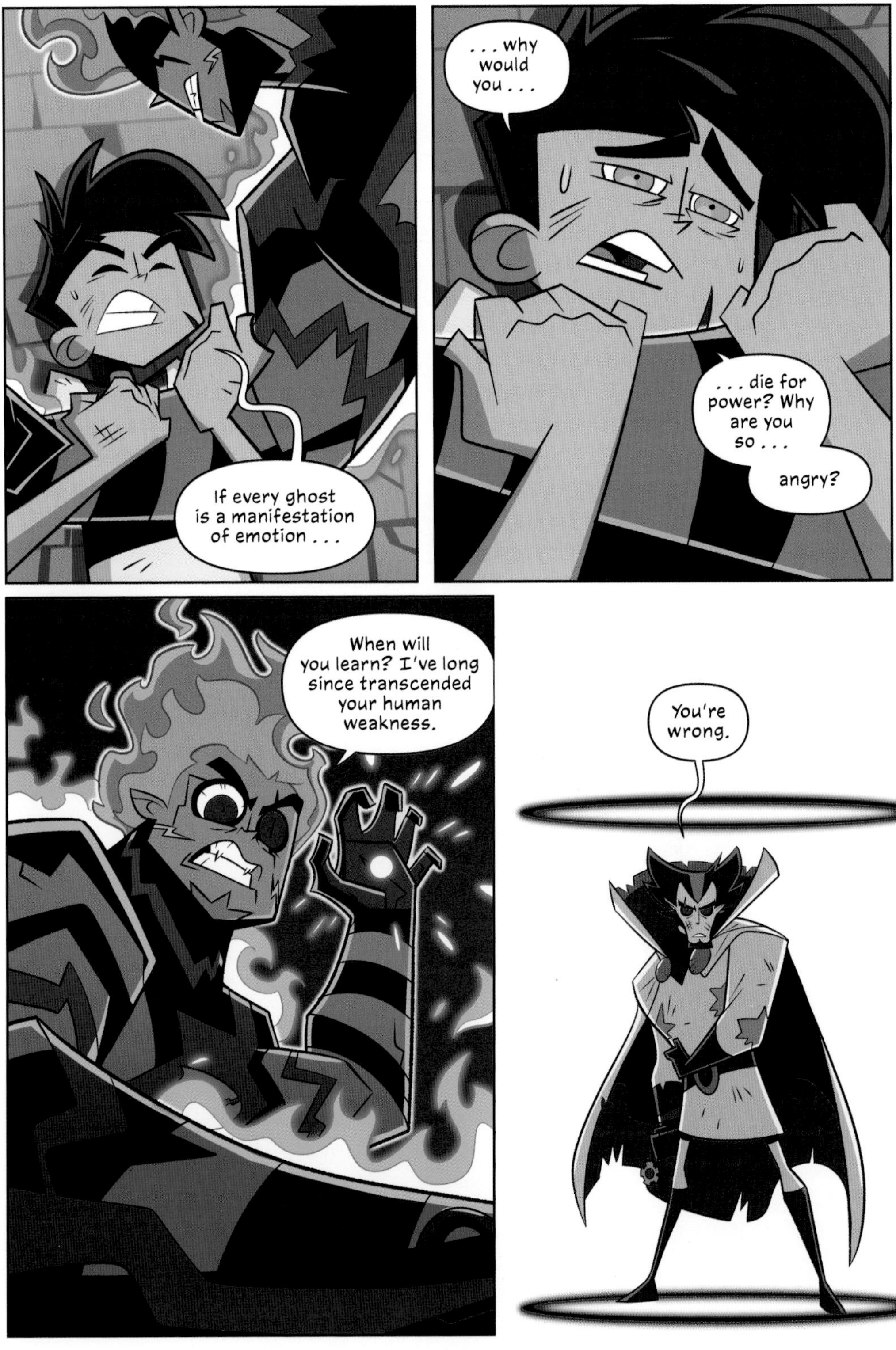
If every ghost is a manifestation of emotion . . .
. . . why would you . . .
. . . die for power? Why are you so . . .
angry?
When will you learn? I've long since transcended your human weakness.
You're wrong.

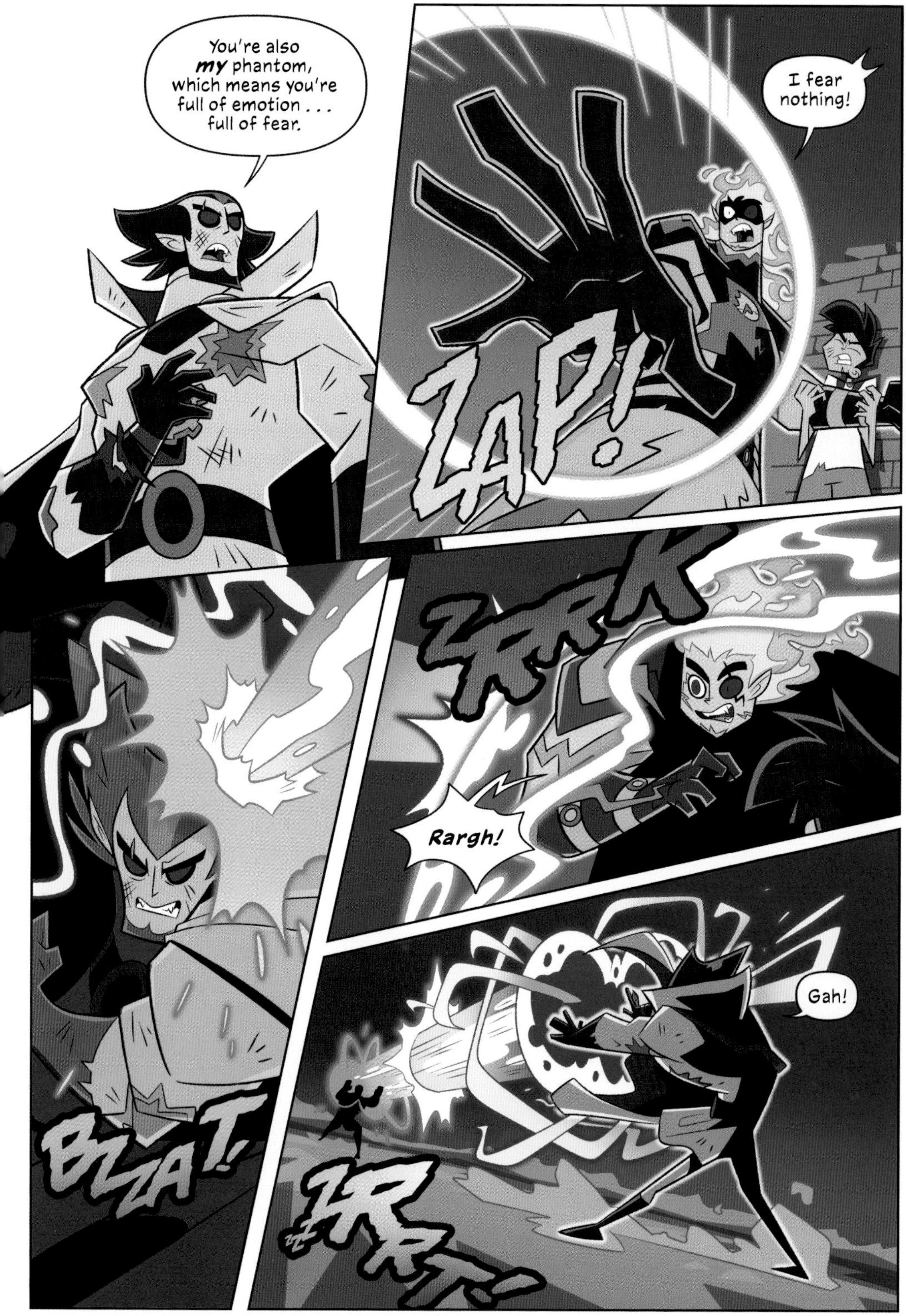

You're also **my** phantom, which means you're full of emotion . . . full of fear.
I fear nothing!
ZAP!
ZARRK
Rargh!
BZZAT!
Gah!
ZRRT!

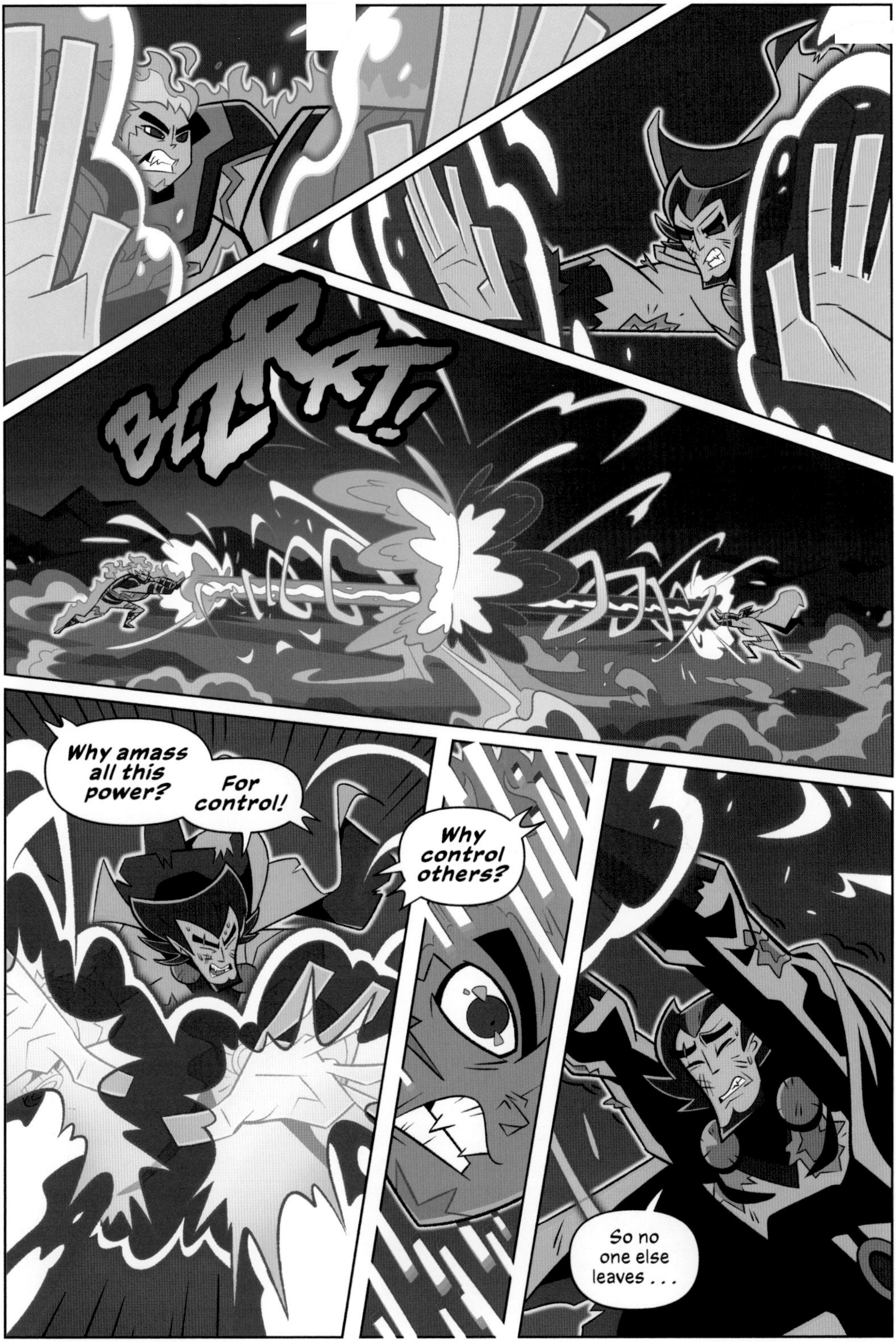
BZZRRT!
Why amass all this power?
For control!
Why control others?
So no one else leaves . . .

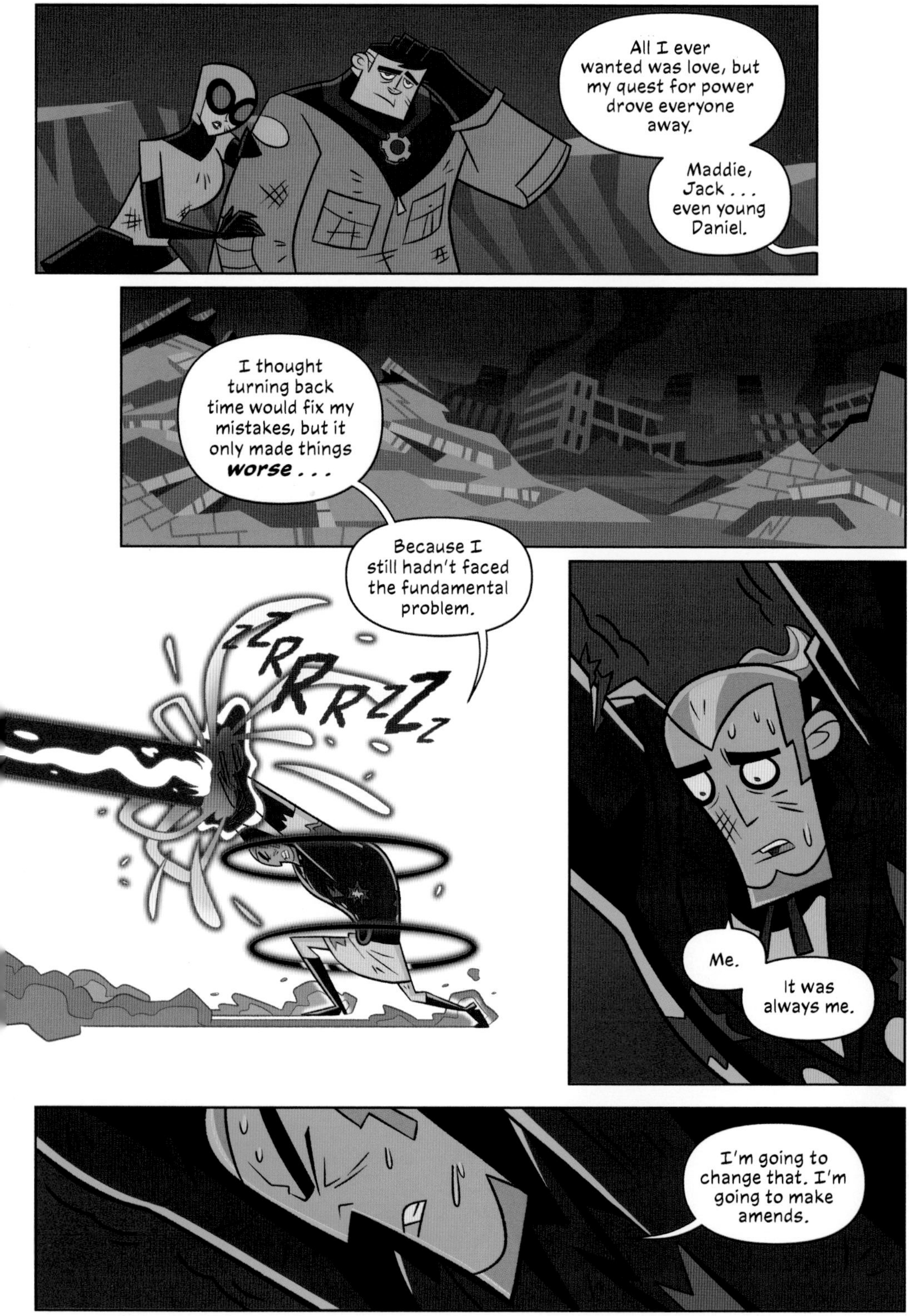
All I ever wanted was love, but my quest for power drove everyone away.
Maddie, Jack . . . even young Daniel.
I thought turning back time would fix my mistakes, but it only made things ***worse . . .***
Because I still hadn't faced the fundamental problem.
zZRRRRzZZz
Me.
It was always me.
I'm going to change that. I'm going to make amends.

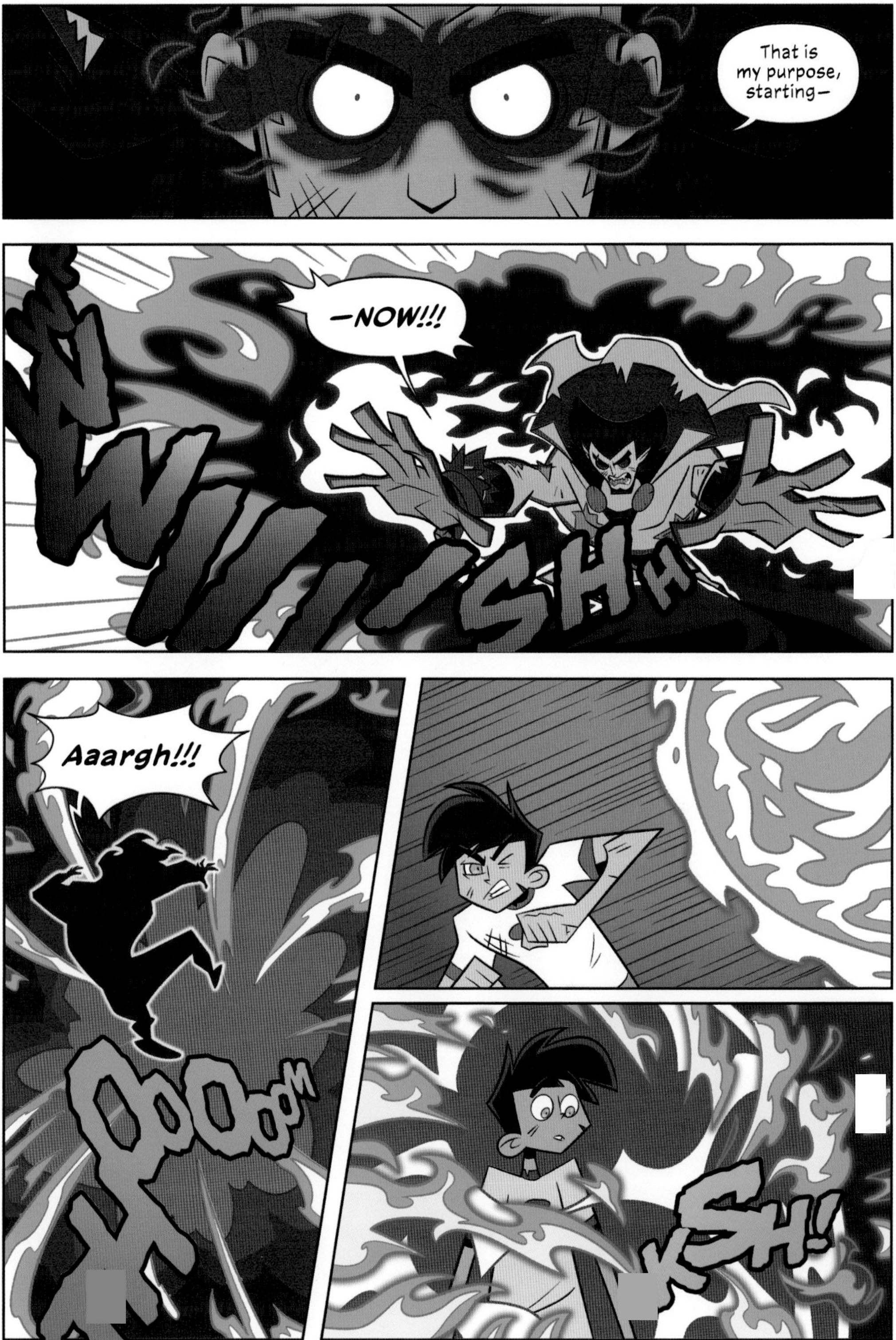
That is my purpose, starting—
—NOW!!!
Aaargh!!!
KSH!!

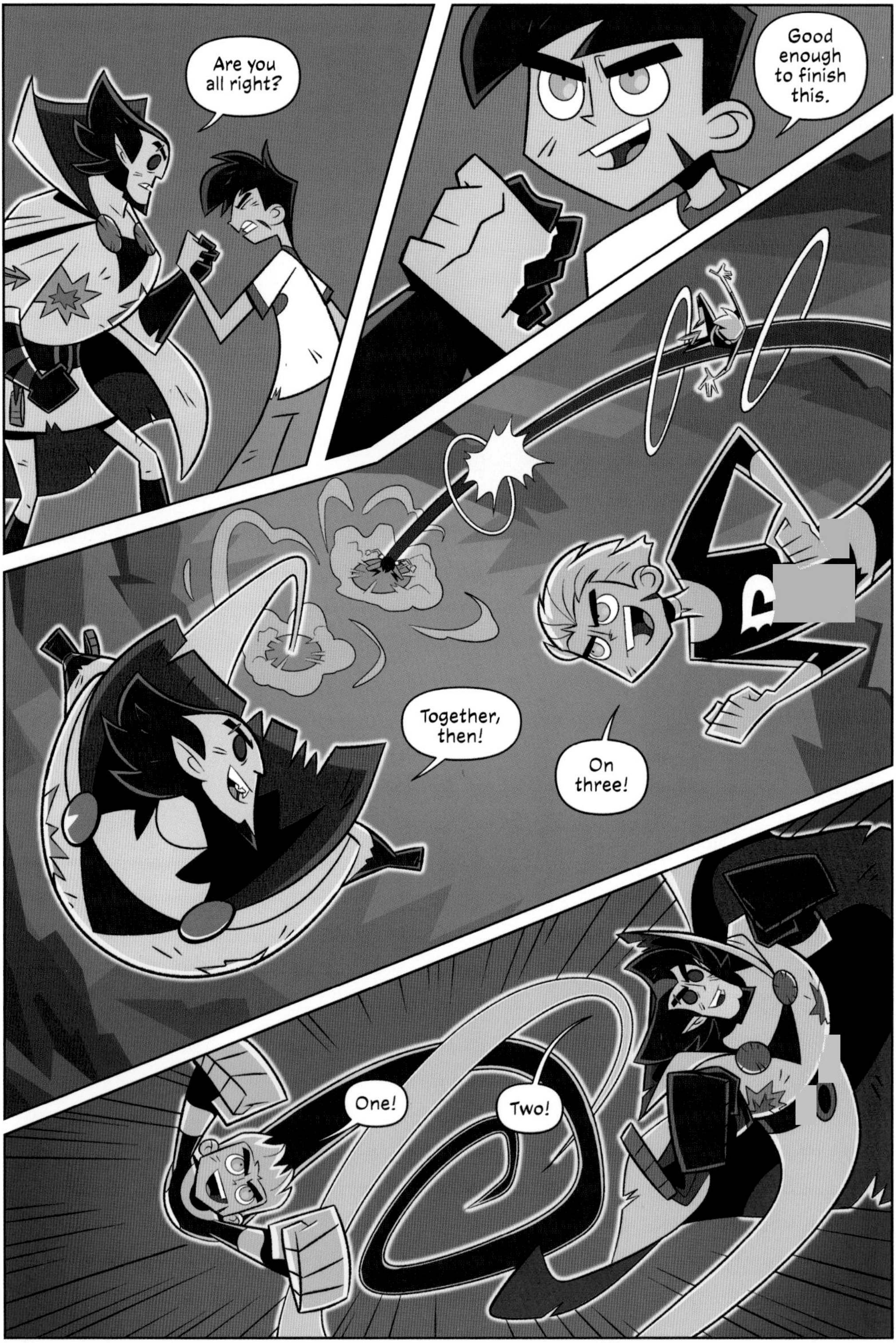
Are you all right?
Good enough to finish this.
Together, then!
On three!
One!
Two!

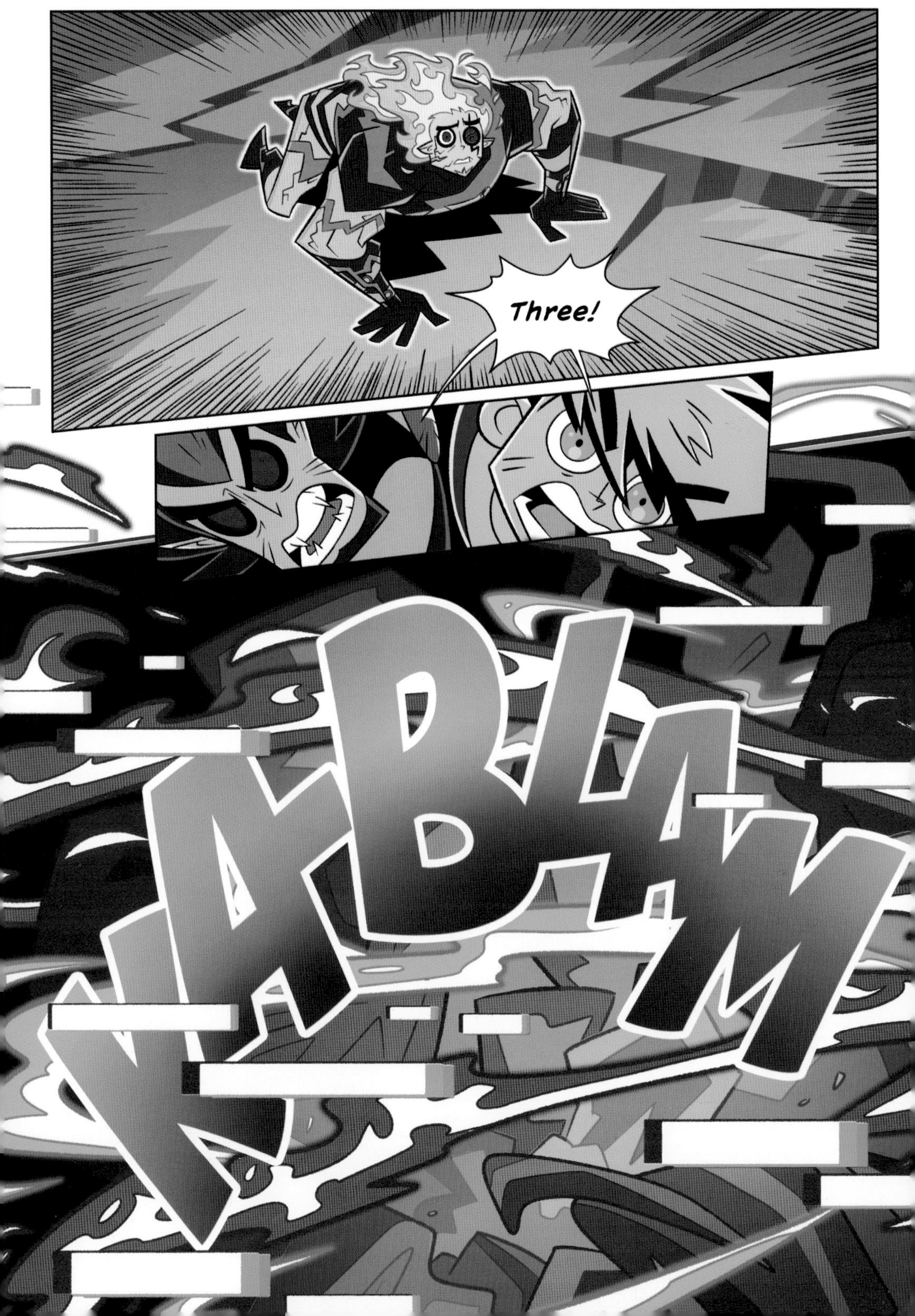
Three!
KABLAM

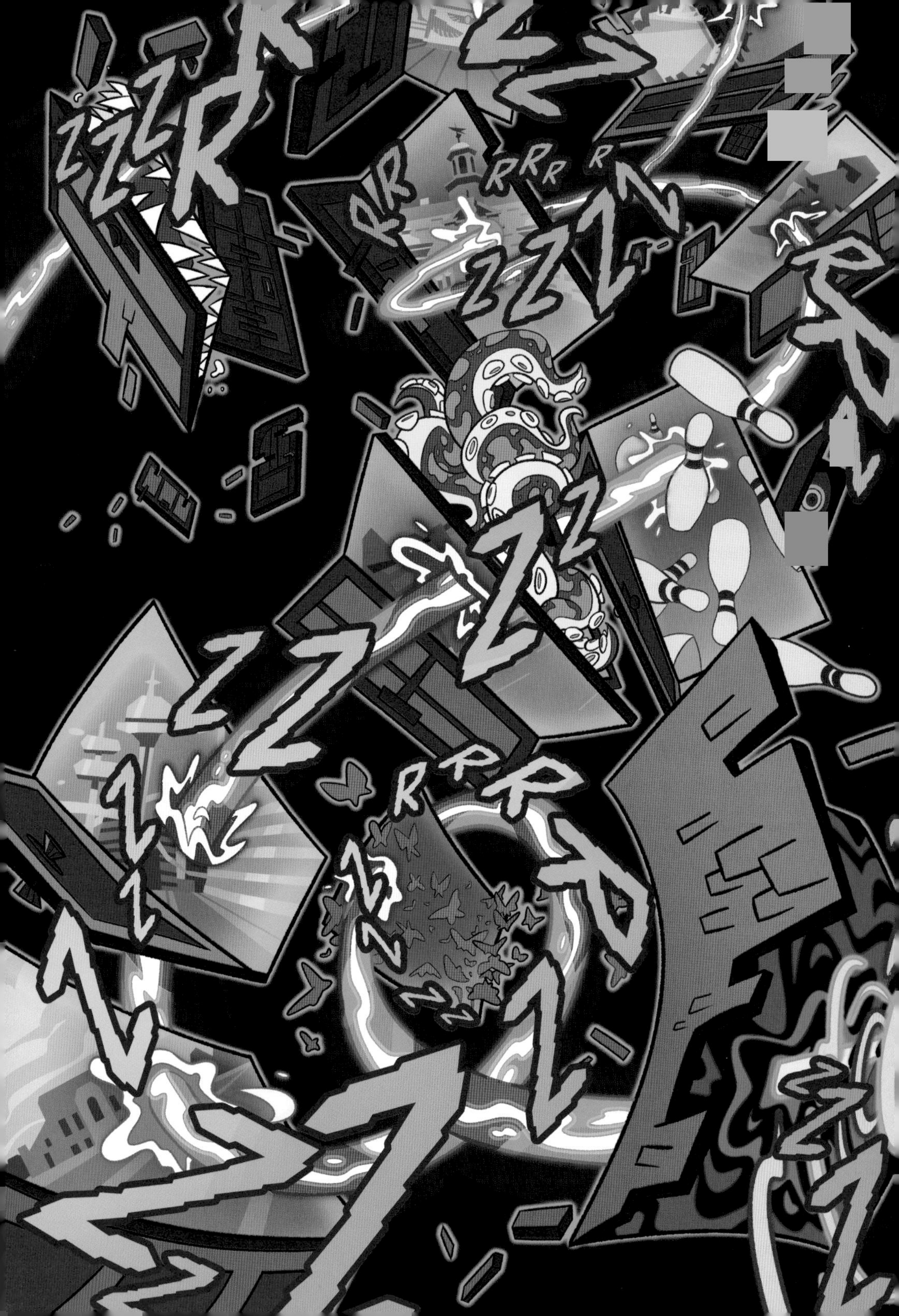

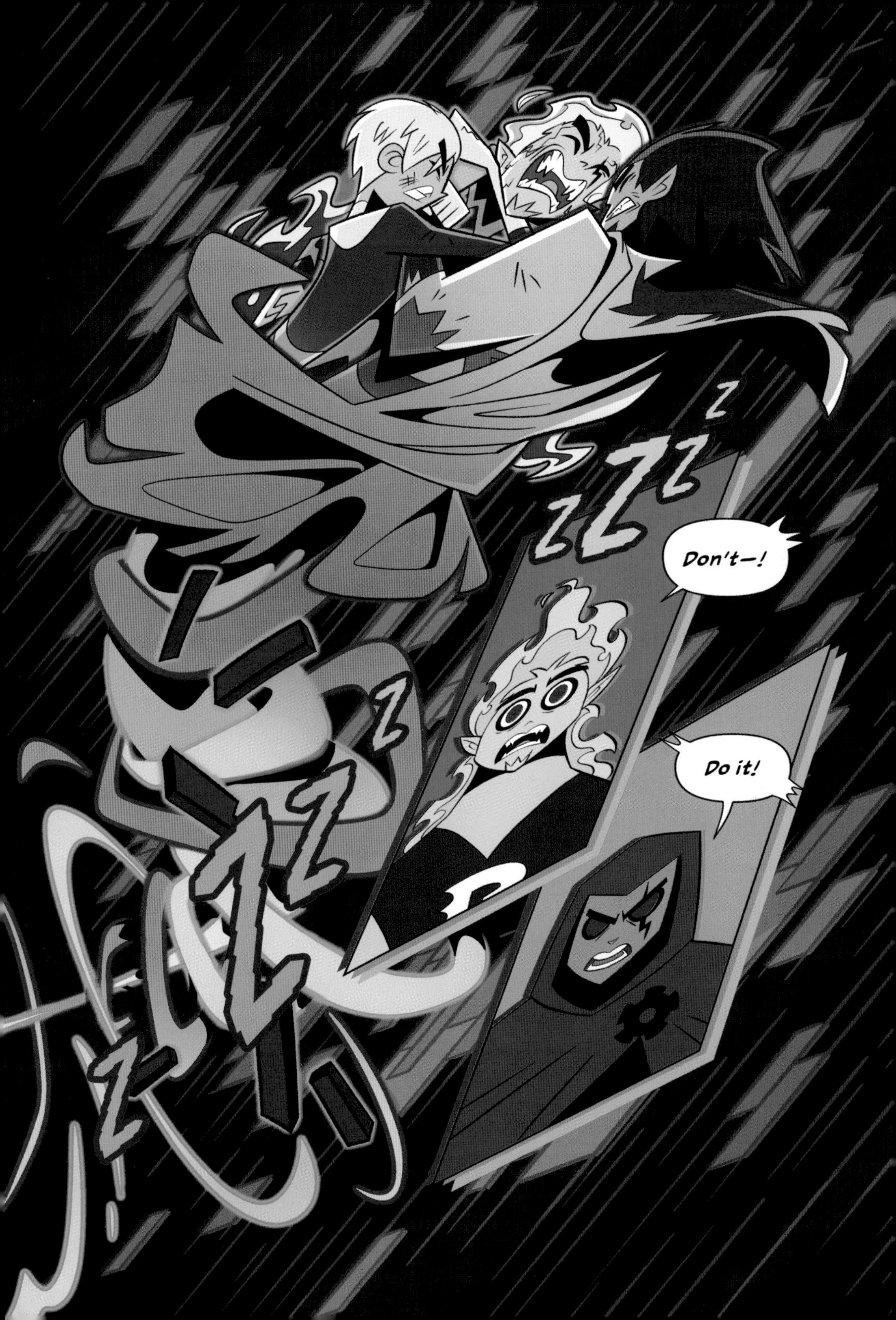
ZZZ
Don't—!
Do it!
ZZZ

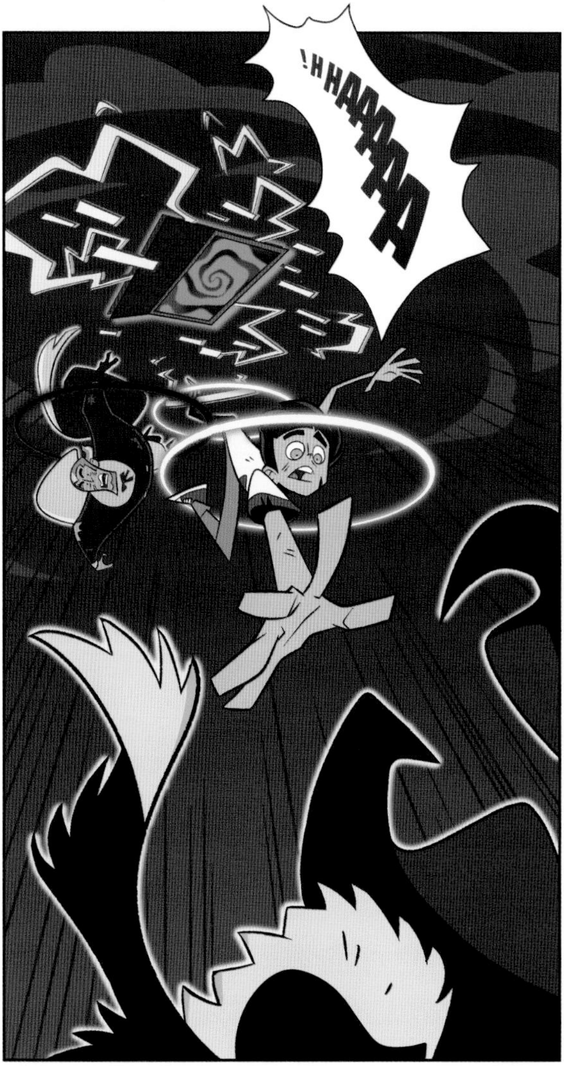
AAAAAAAHH!

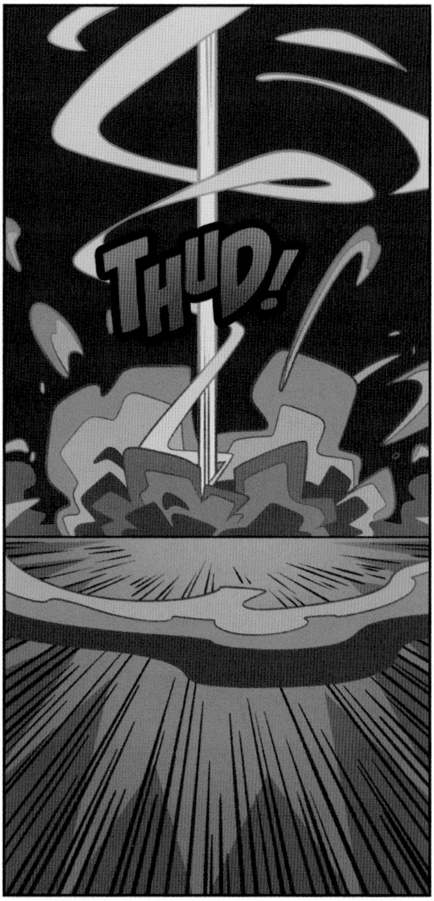
THUD!

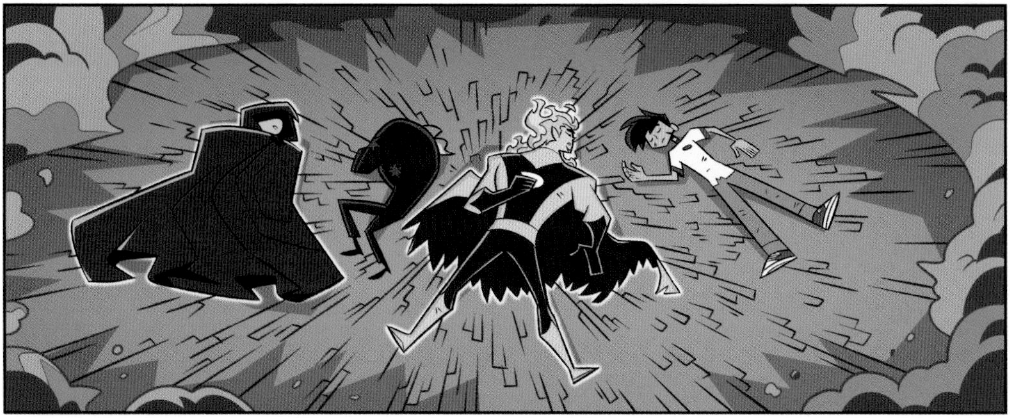

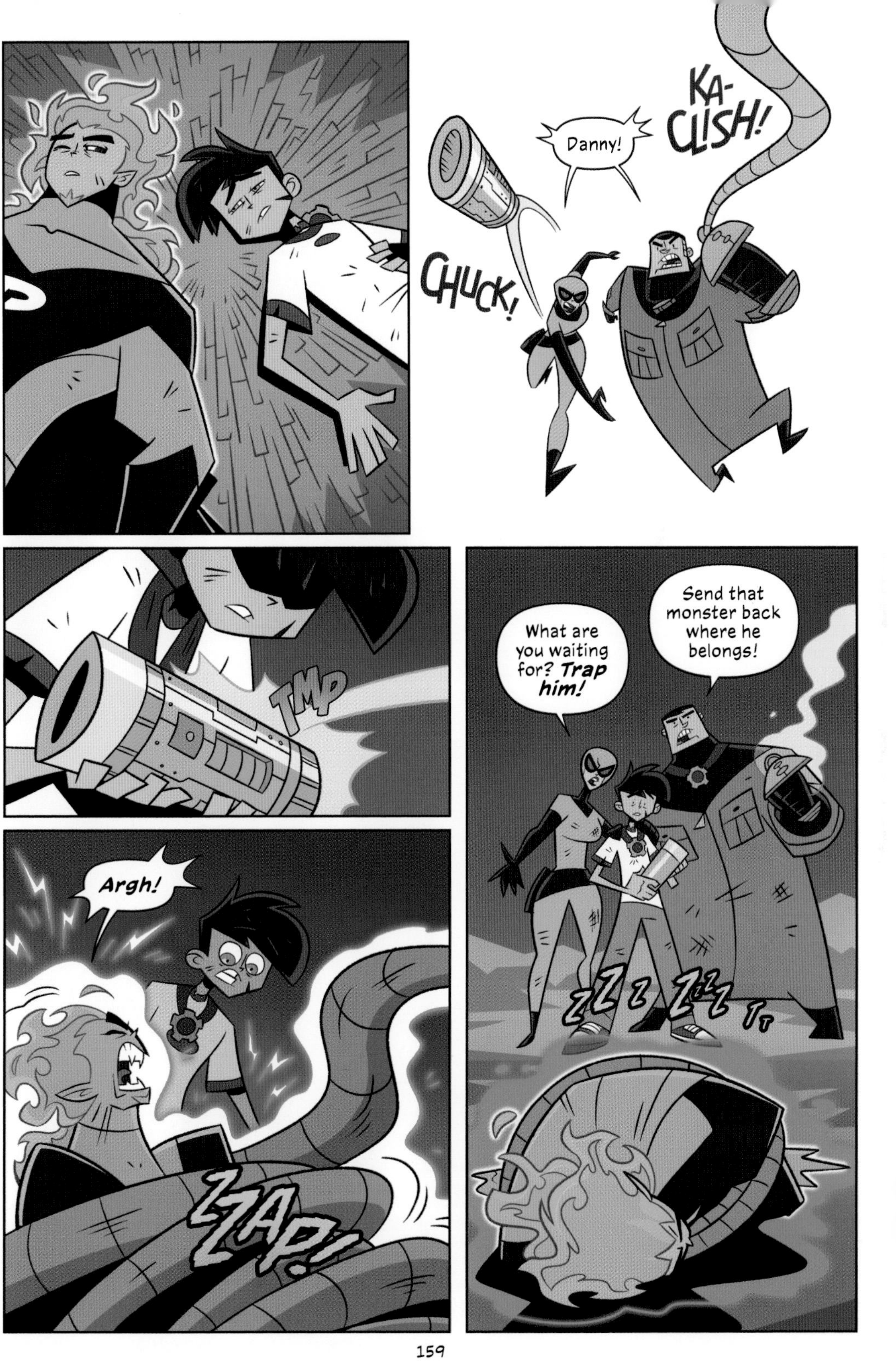

Danny!
KA-CLISH!
CHUCK!
TMP
What are you waiting for? ***Trap him!***
Send that monster back where he belongs!
Argh!
ZZAP!
ZZZ ZZZ TT

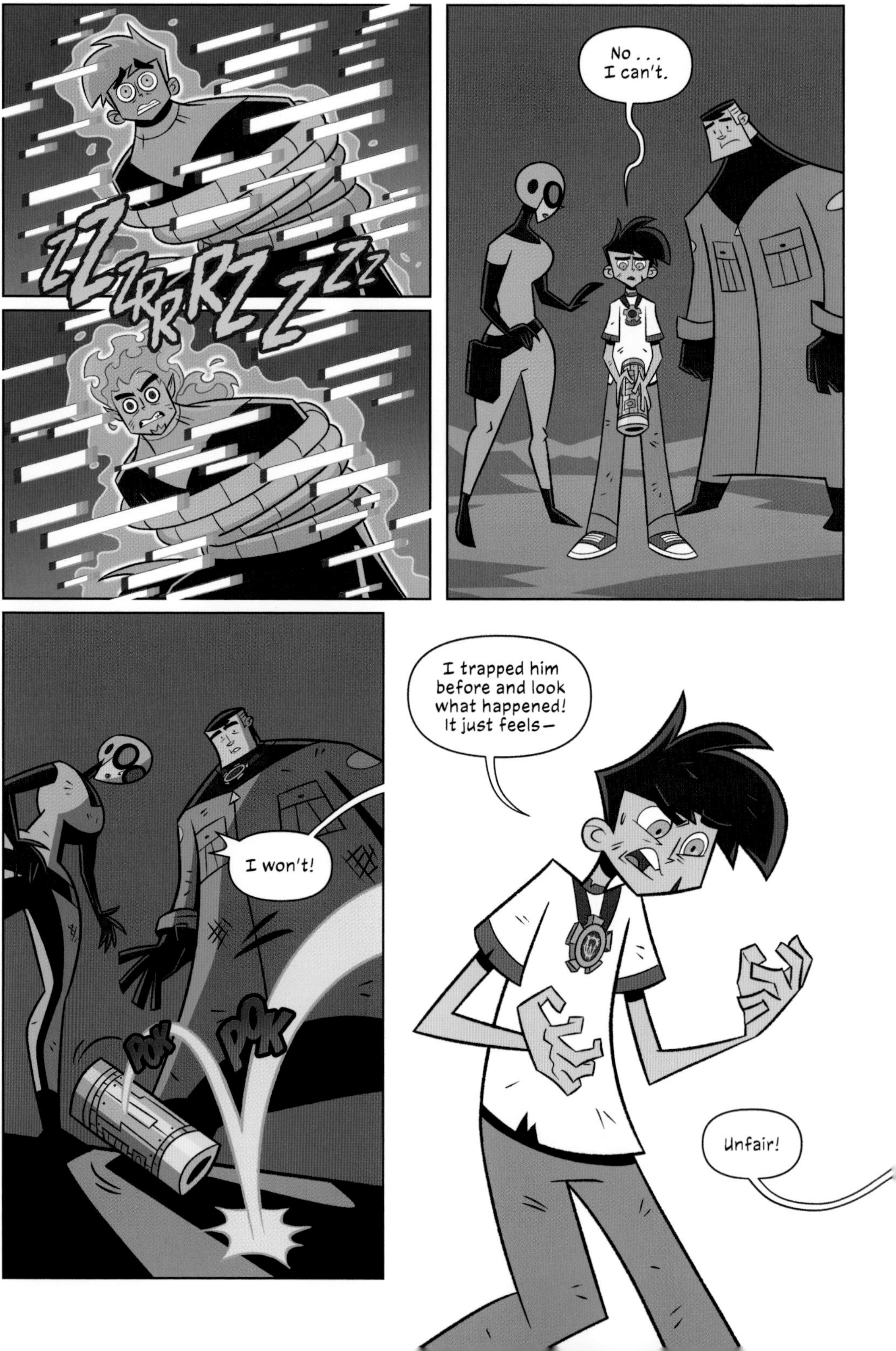

ZZZRRRZZZZZ
No . . . I can't.
I won't!
POK
POK
I trapped him before and look what happened! It just feels—
Unfair!

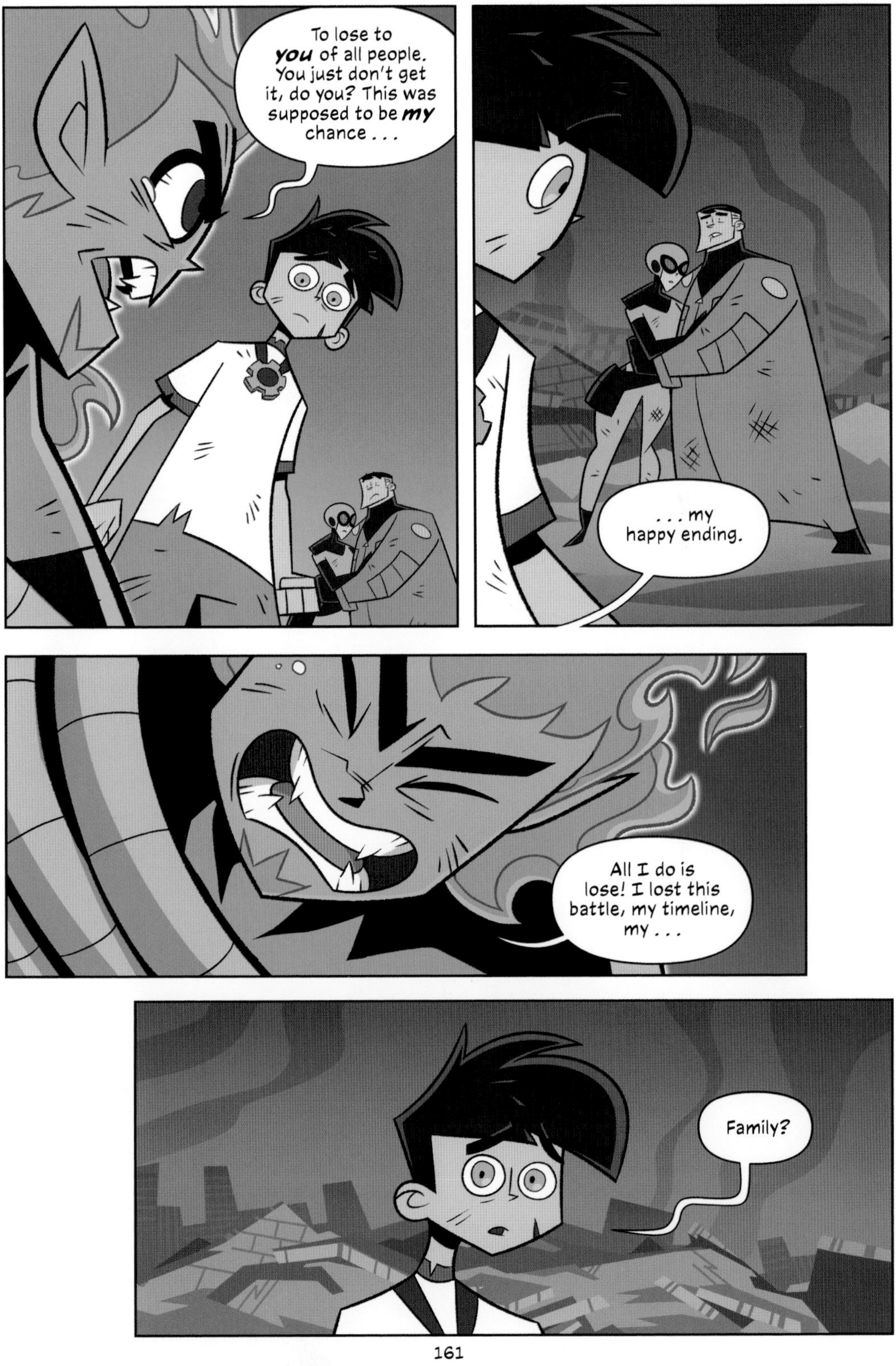
To lose to *you* of all people. You just don't get it, do you? This was supposed to be *my* chance . . .
. . . my happy ending.
All I do is lose! I lost this battle, my timeline, my . . .
Family?

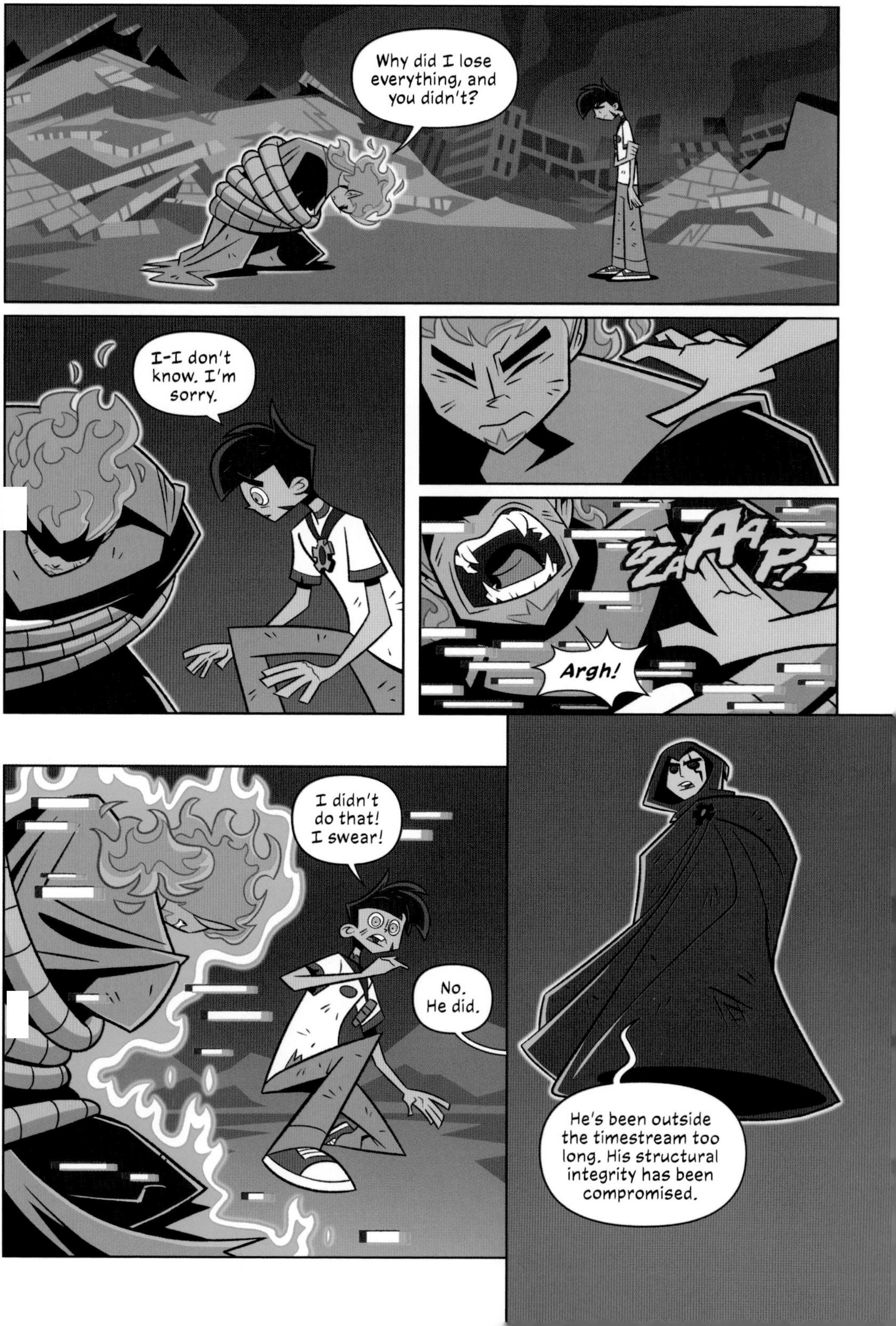
Why did I lose everything, and you didn't?
I-I don't know. I'm sorry.
ZZAAAP!
Argh!
I didn't do that! I swear!
No. He did.
He's been outside the timestream too long. His structural integrity has been compromised.

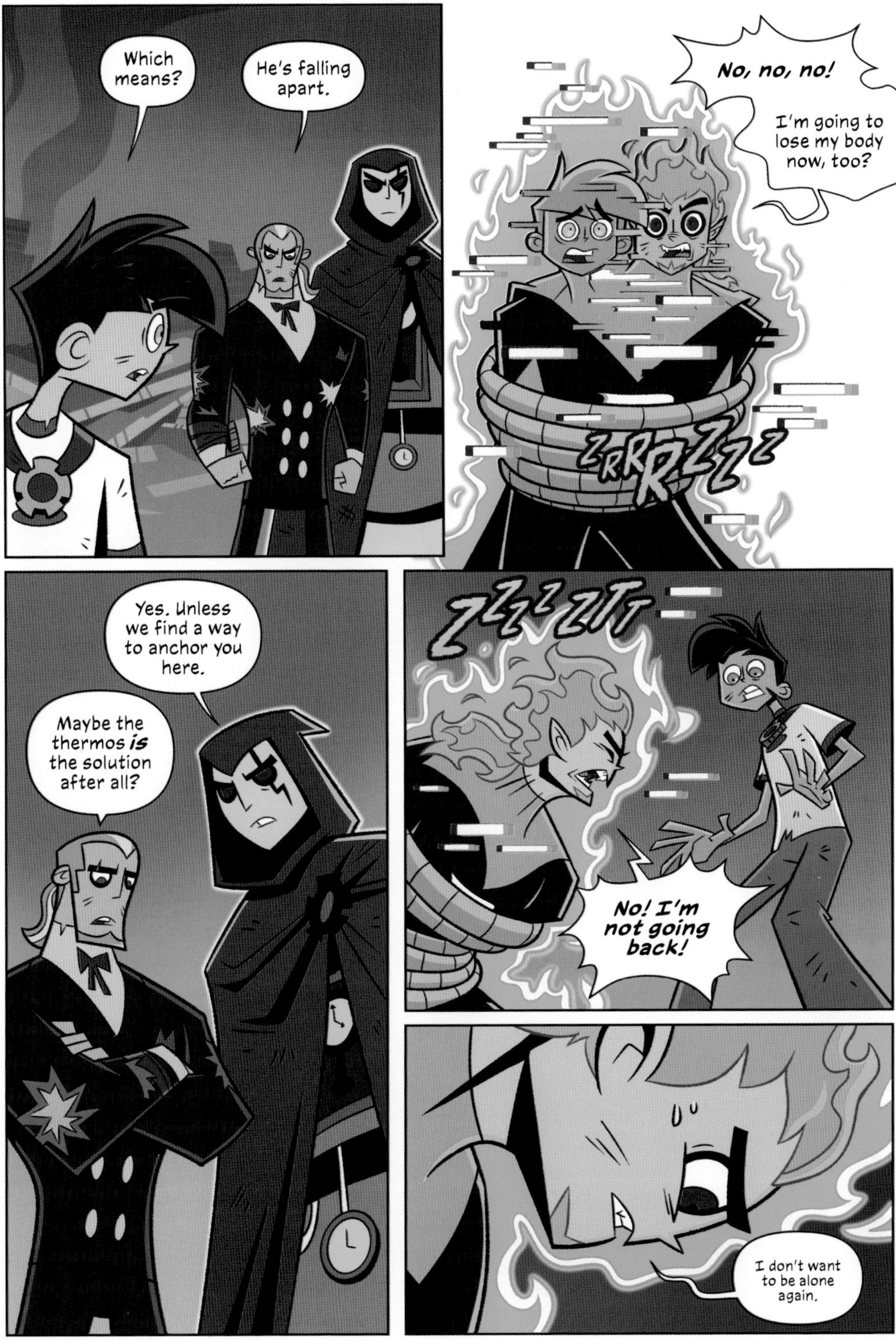
Which means?
He's falling apart.
No, no, no!
I'm going to lose my body now, too?
ZRRRZZZZ
Yes. Unless we find a way to anchor you here.
Maybe the thermos *is* the solution after all?
ZZZZZTTT
No! I'm not going back!
I don't want to be alone again.

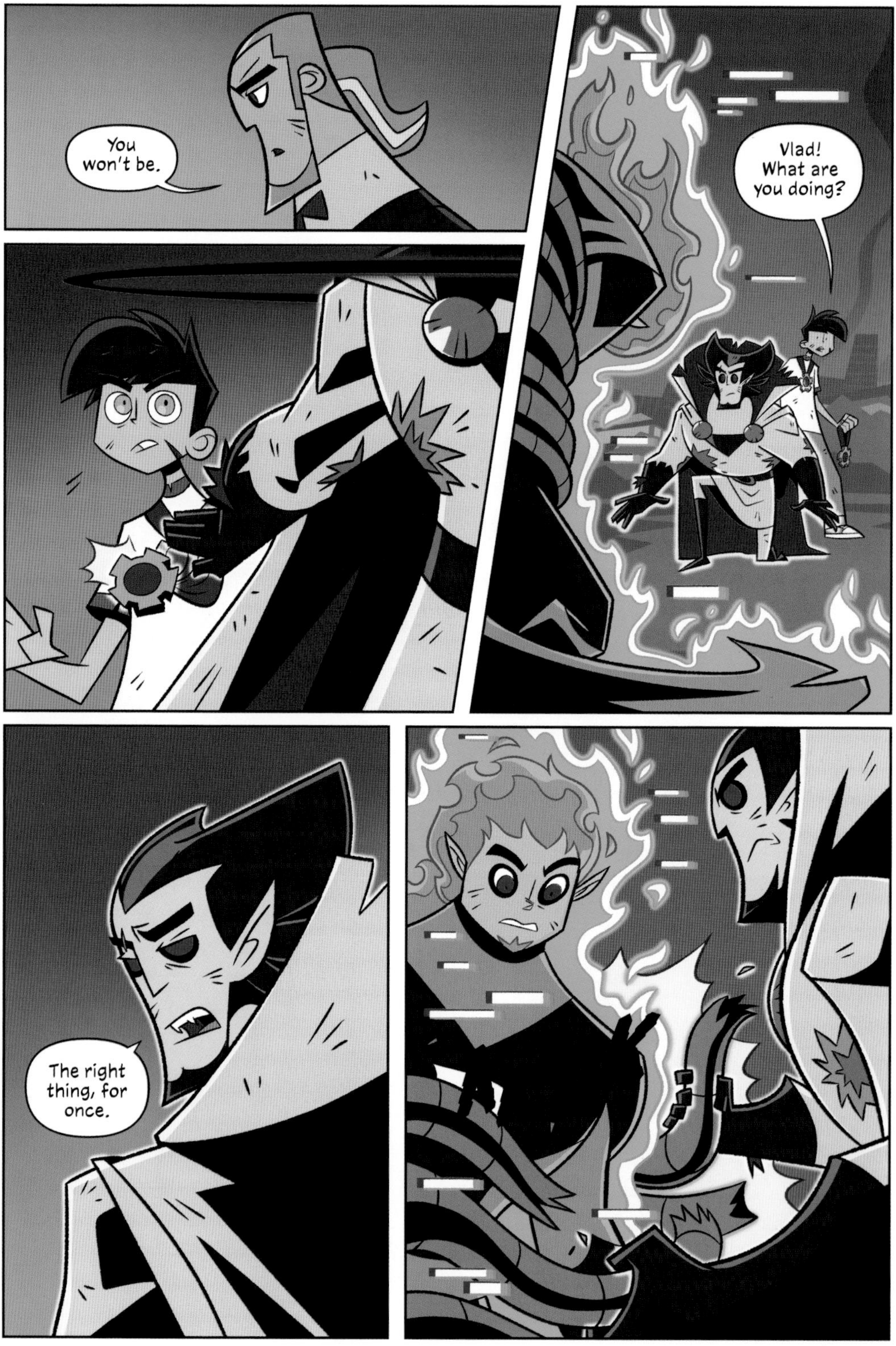
You won't be.
Vlad! What are you doing?
The right thing, for once.

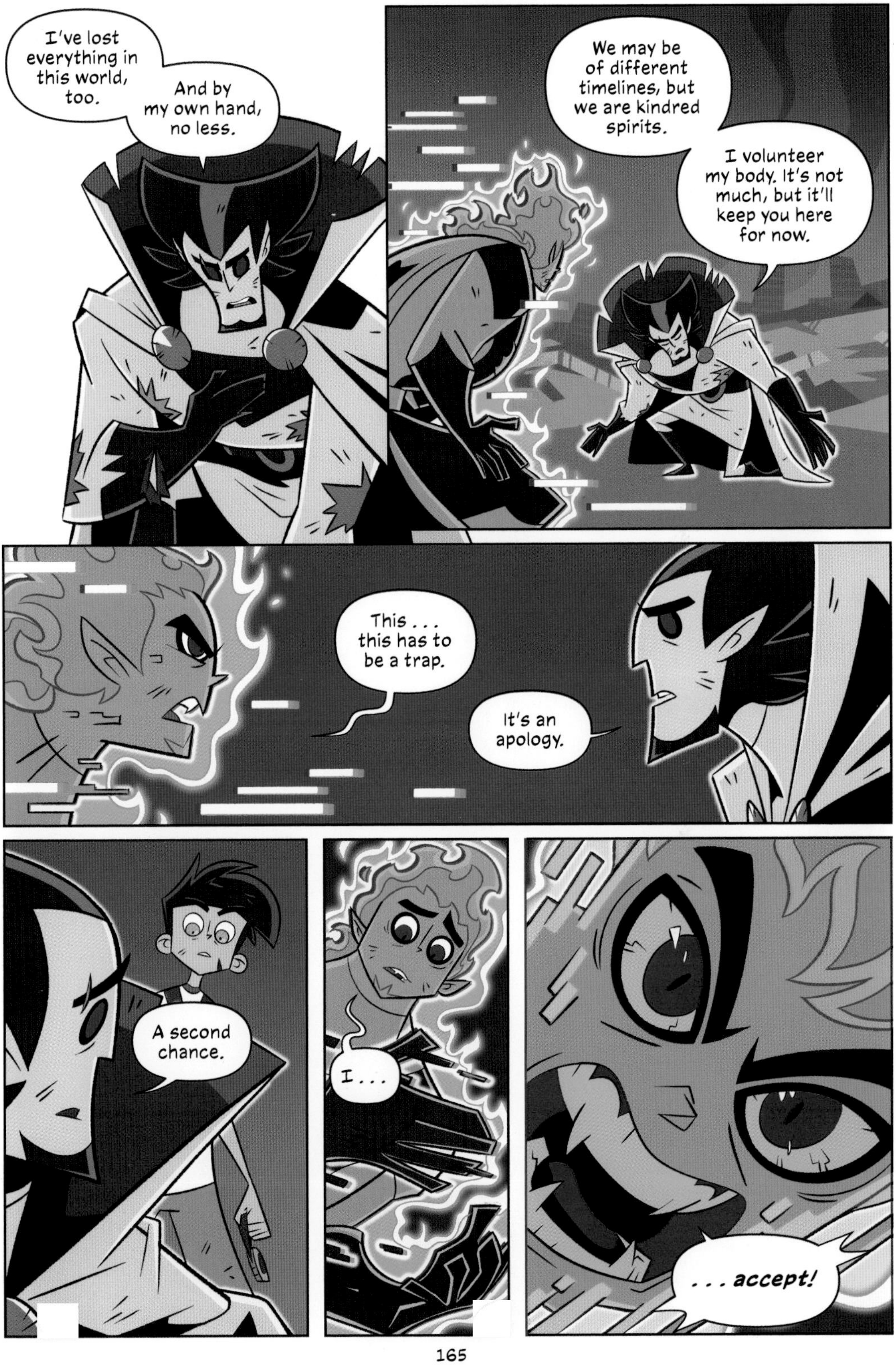
I've lost everything in this world, too.
And by my own hand, no less.
We may be of different timelines, but we are kindred spirits.
I volunteer my body. It's not much, but it'll keep you here for now.
This . . . this has to be a trap.
It's an apology.
A second chance.
I . . .
. . . accept!

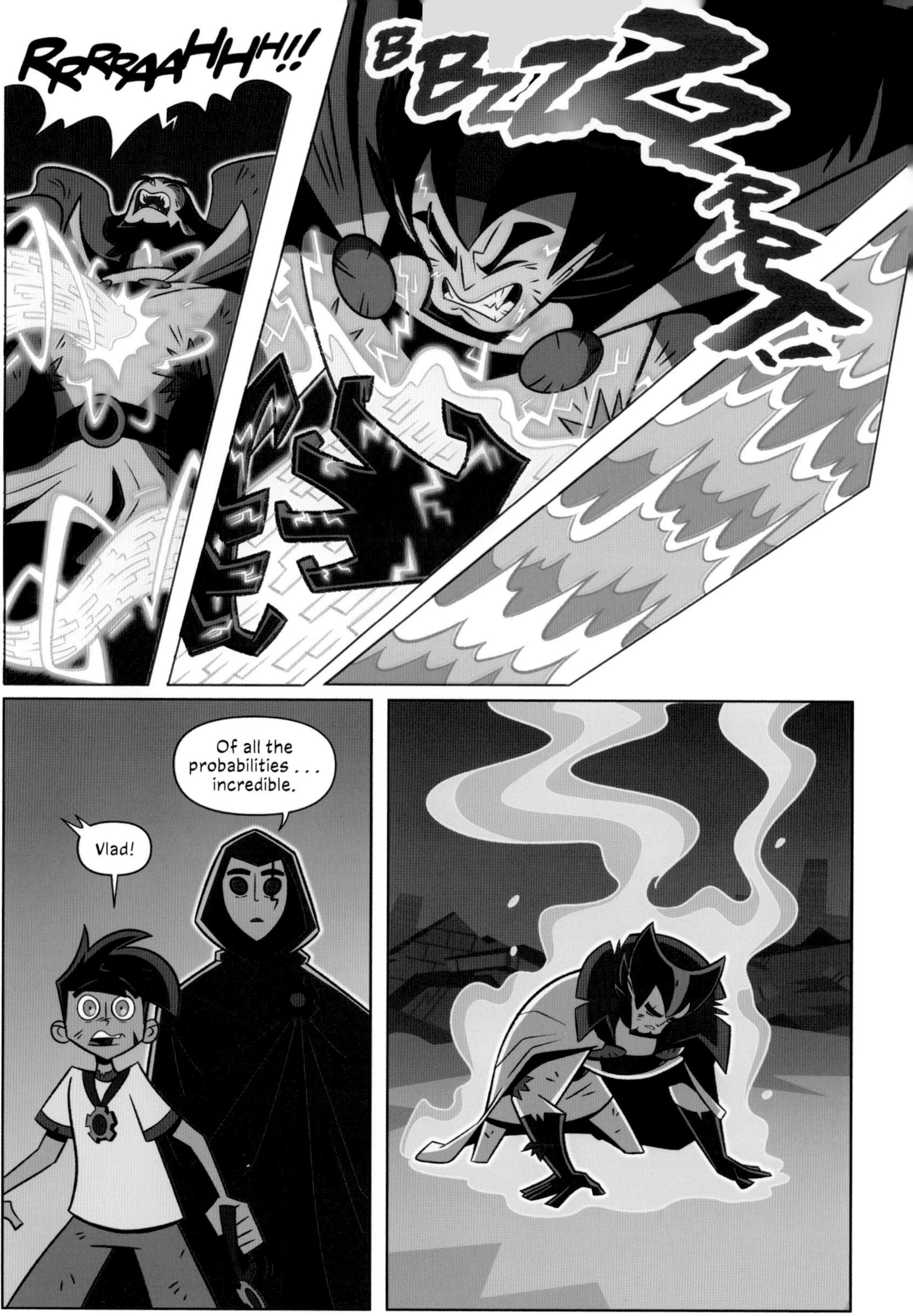
RRRRAAHHH!!
Of all the probabilities . . . incredible.
Vlad!

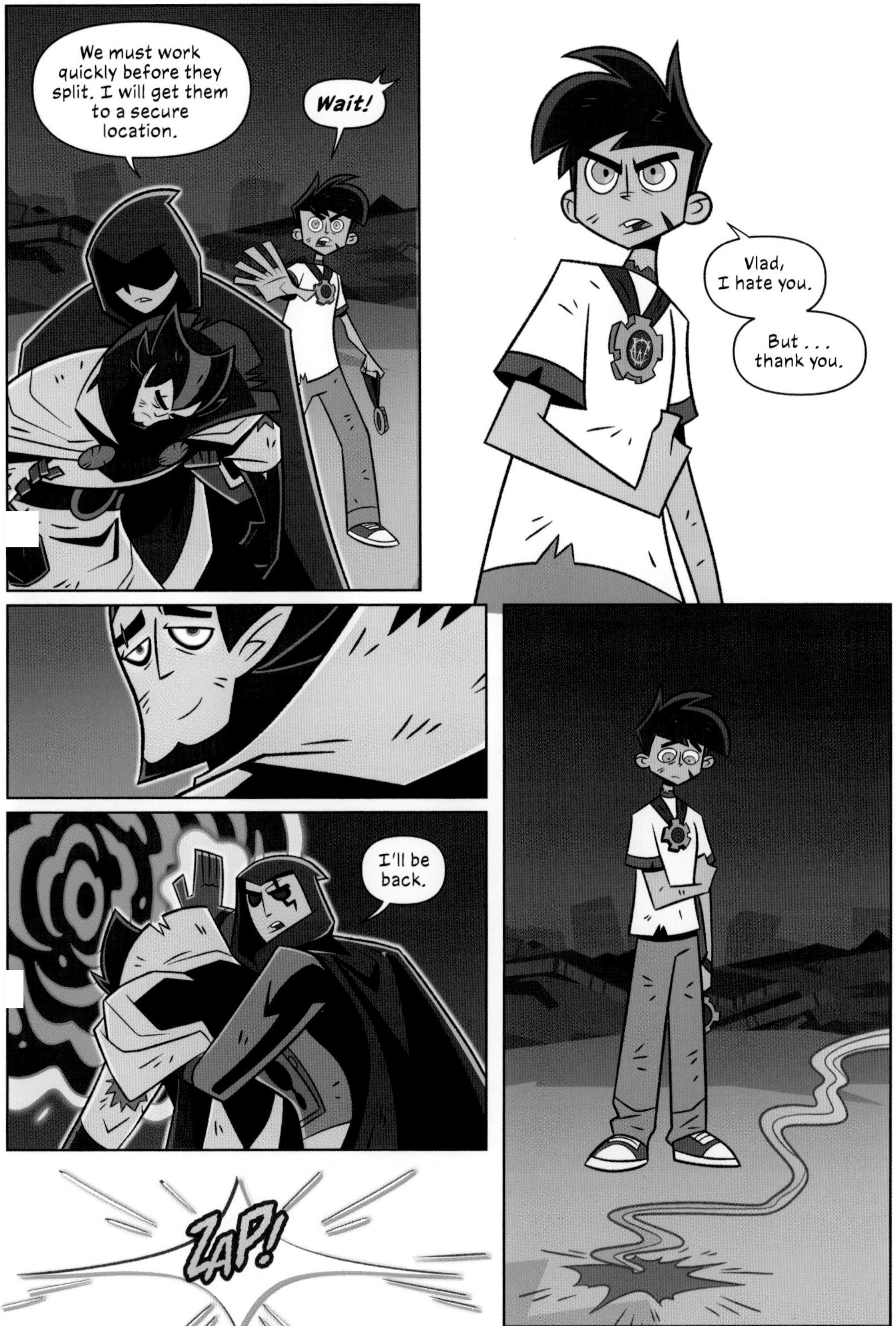
We must work quickly before they split. I will get them to a secure location.
Wait!
Vlad, I hate you.
But . . . thank you.
I'll be back.
ZAP!

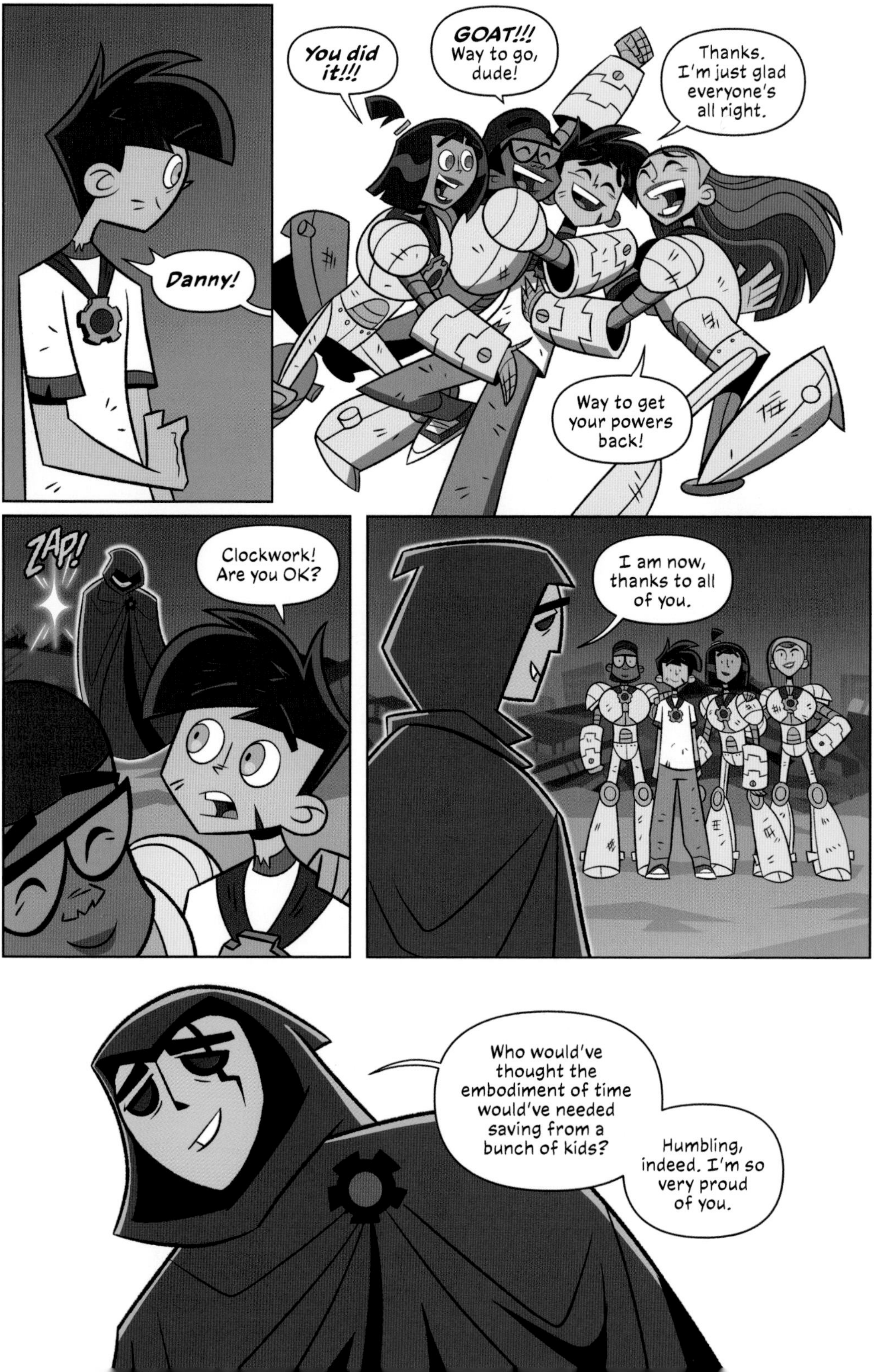
Danny!
You did it!!!
GOAT!!! Way to go, dude!
Thanks. I'm just glad everyone's all right.
Way to get your powers back!
ZAP!
Clockwork! Are you OK?
I am now, thanks to all of you.
Who would've thought the embodiment of time would've needed saving from a bunch of kids?
Humbling, indeed. I'm so very proud of you.

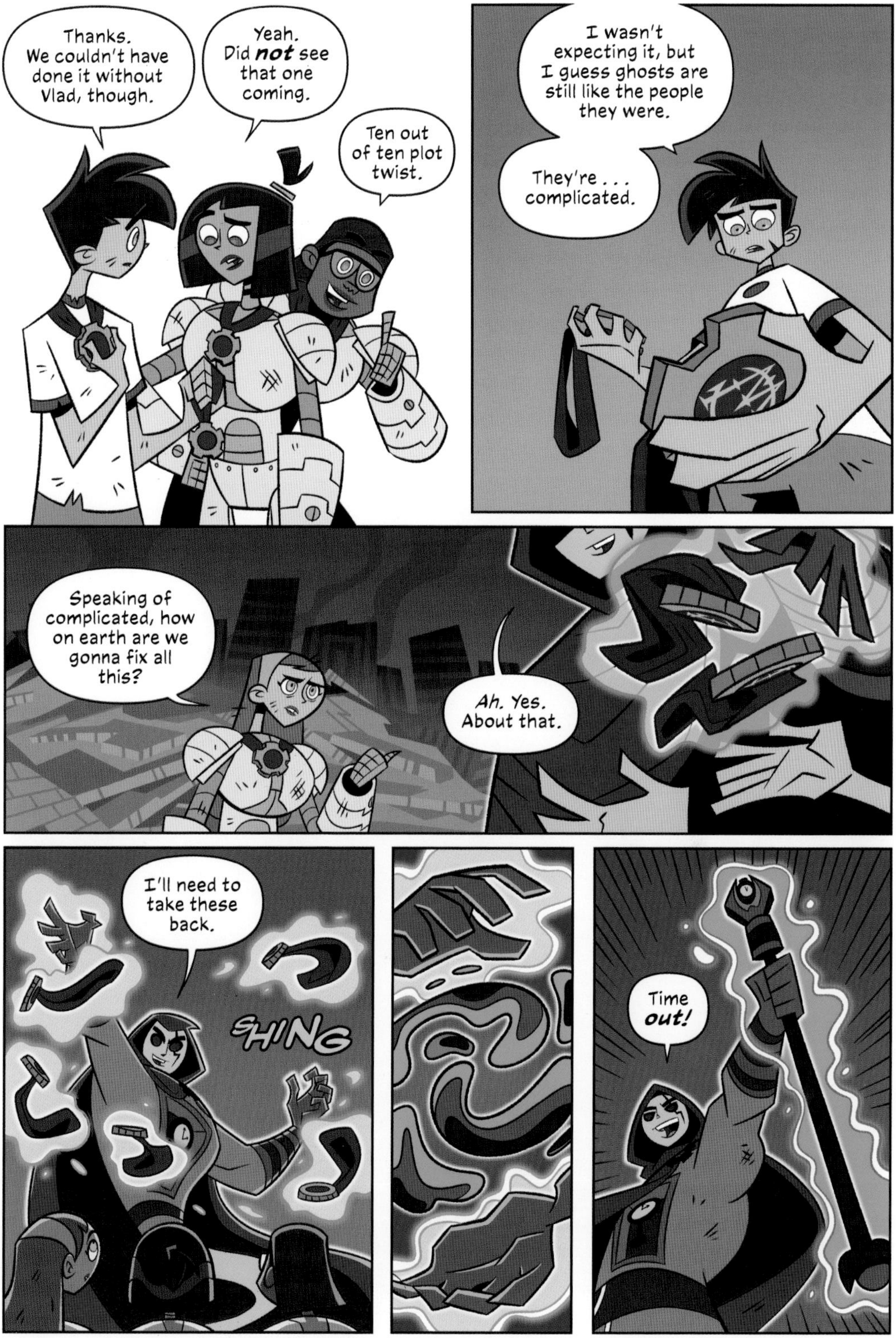
Thanks. We couldn't have done it without Vlad, though.
Yeah. Did **not** see that one coming.
Ten out of ten plot twist.
I wasn't expecting it, but I guess ghosts are still like the people they were.
They're . . . complicated.
Speaking of complicated, how on earth are we gonna fix all this?
Ah. Yes. About that.
I'll need to take these back.
SHING
Time **out!**

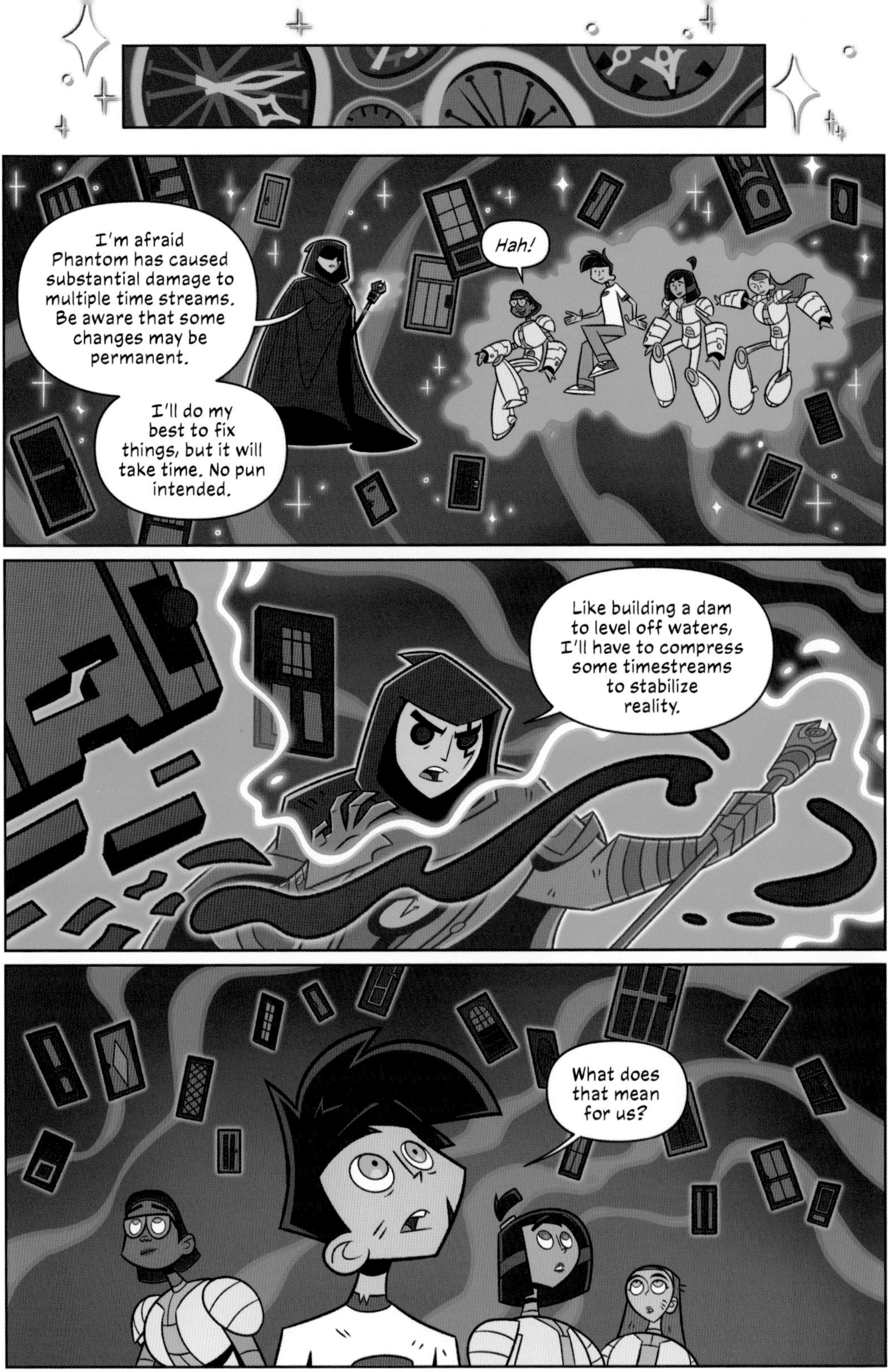
I'm afraid Phantom has caused substantial damage to multiple time streams. Be aware that some changes may be permanent.
Hah!
I'll do my best to fix things, but it will take time. No pun intended.
Like building a dam to level off waters, I'll have to compress some timestreams to stabilize reality.
What does that mean for us?

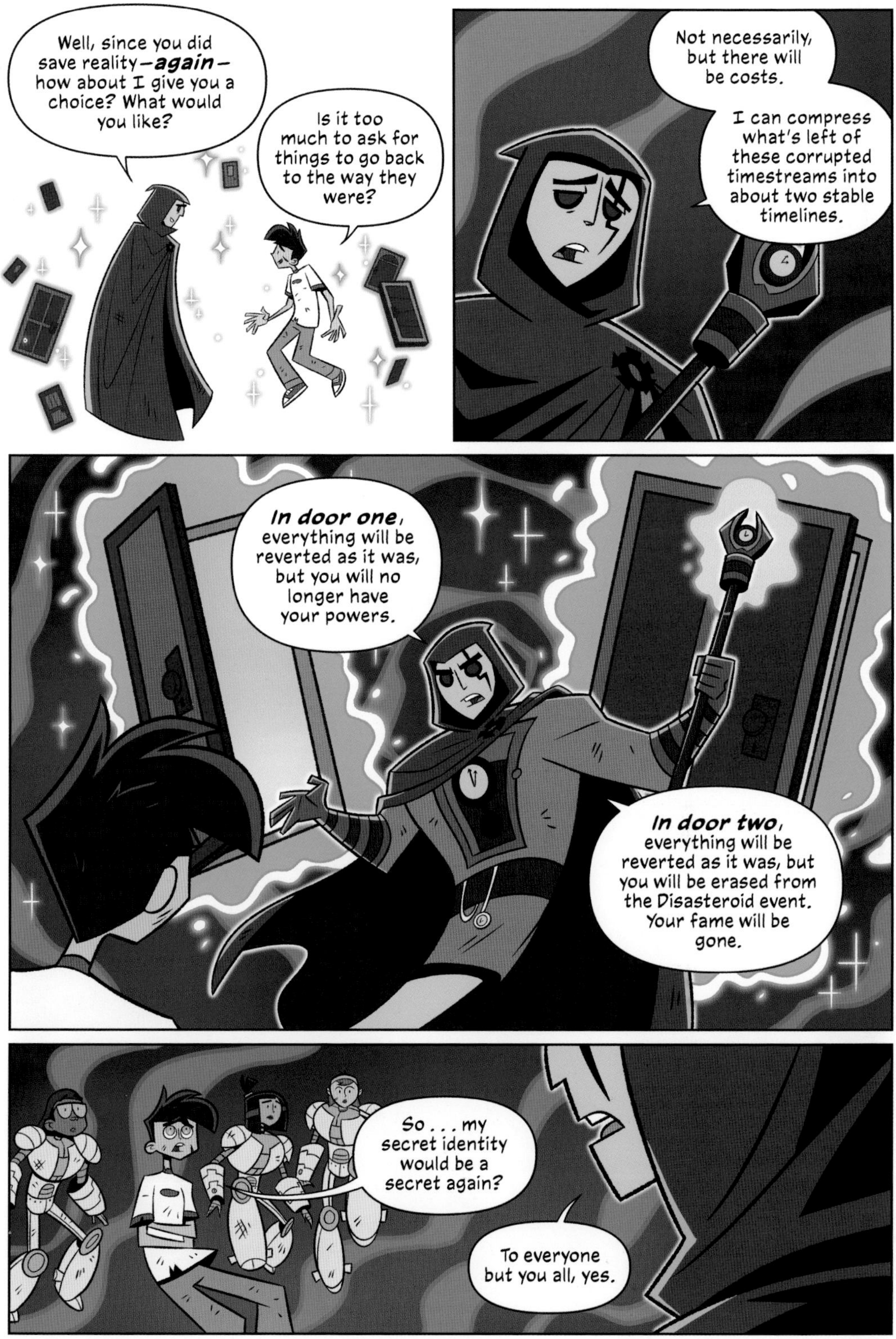

Well, since you did save reality—*again*—how about I give you a choice? What would you like?
Is it too much to ask for things to go back to the way they were?
Not necessarily, but there will be costs.
I can compress what's left of these corrupted timestreams into about two stable timelines.
In door one, everything will be reverted as it was, but you will no longer have your powers.
In door two, everything will be reverted as it was, but you will be erased from the Disasteroid event. Your fame will be gone.
So . . . my secret identity would be a secret again?
To everyone but you all, yes.

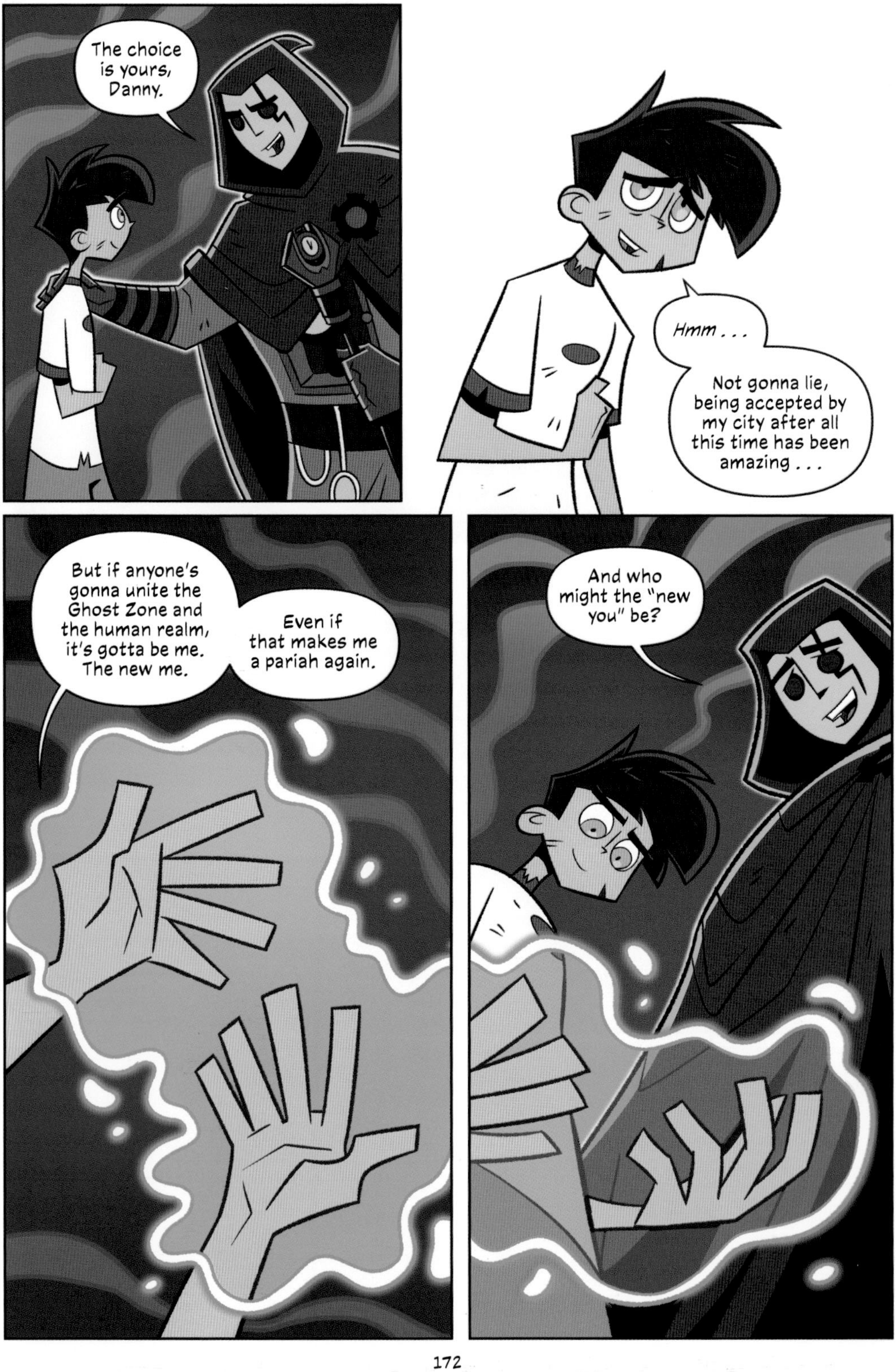
The choice is yours, Danny.
Hmm . . .
Not gonna lie, being accepted by my city after all this time has been amazing . . .
But if anyone's gonna unite the Ghost Zone and the human realm, it's gotta be me. The new me.
Even if that makes me a pariah again.
And who might the "new you" be?

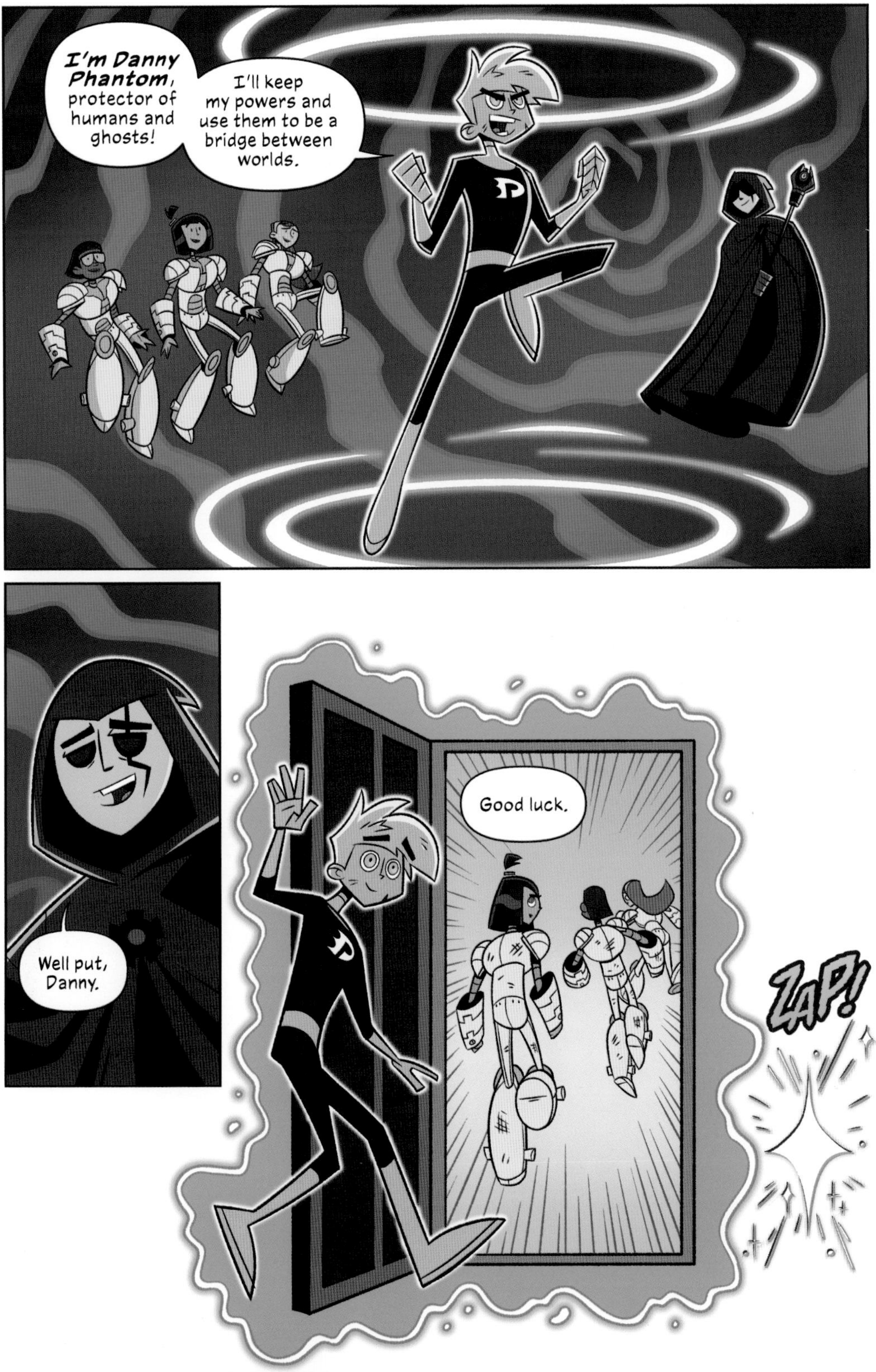
I'm Danny Phantom, protector of humans and ghosts!
I'll keep my powers and use them to be a bridge between worlds.
Well put, Danny.
Good luck.
ZAP!

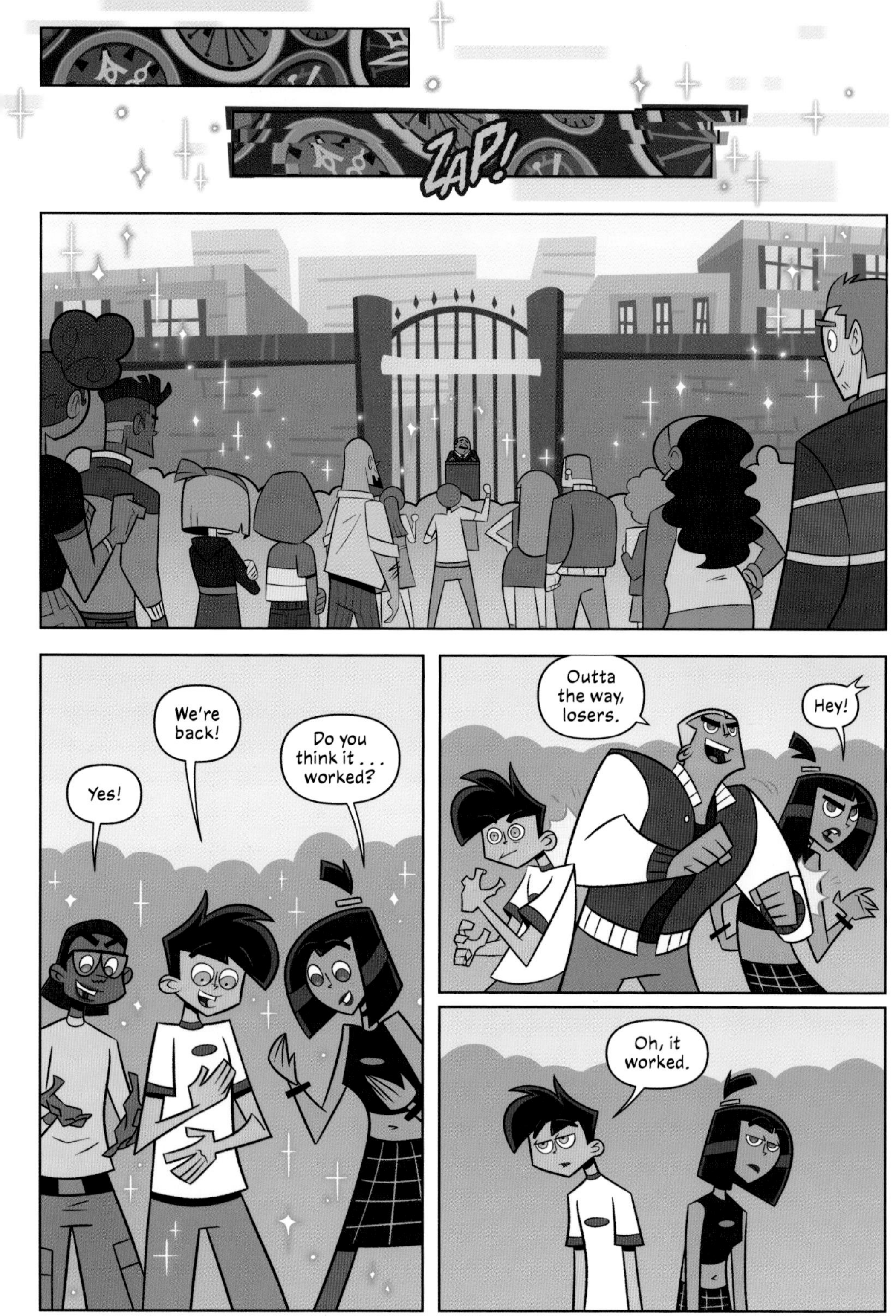
ZAP!
We're back!
Yes!
Do you think it . . . worked?
Outta the way, losers.
Hey!
Oh, it worked.

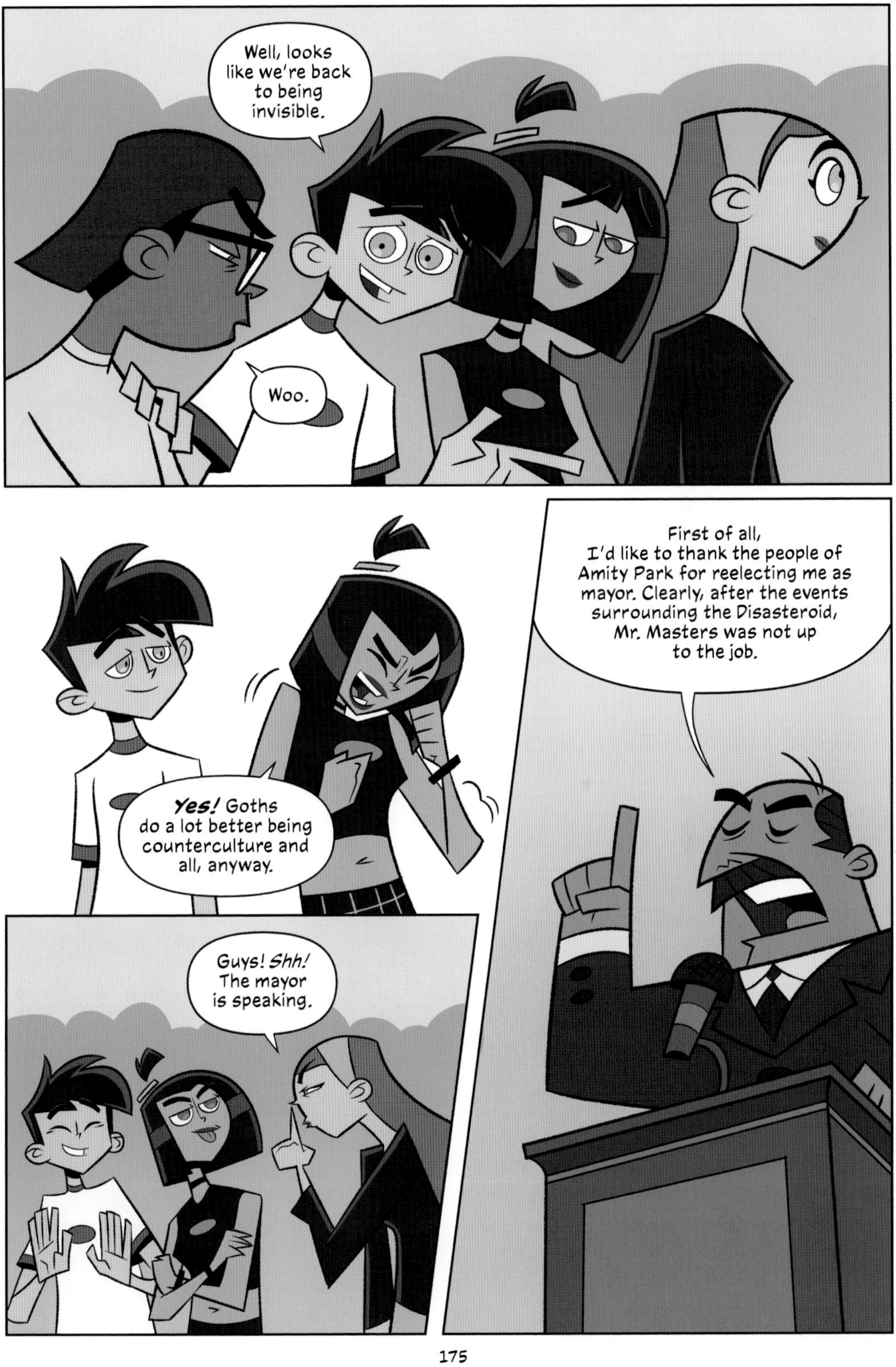

Well, looks like we're back to being invisible.
Woo.
Yes! Goths do a lot better being counterculture and all, anyway.
First of all, I'd like to thank the people of Amity Park for reelecting me as mayor. Clearly, after the events surrounding the Disasteroid, Mr. Masters was not up to the job.
Guys! Shh! The mayor is speaking.

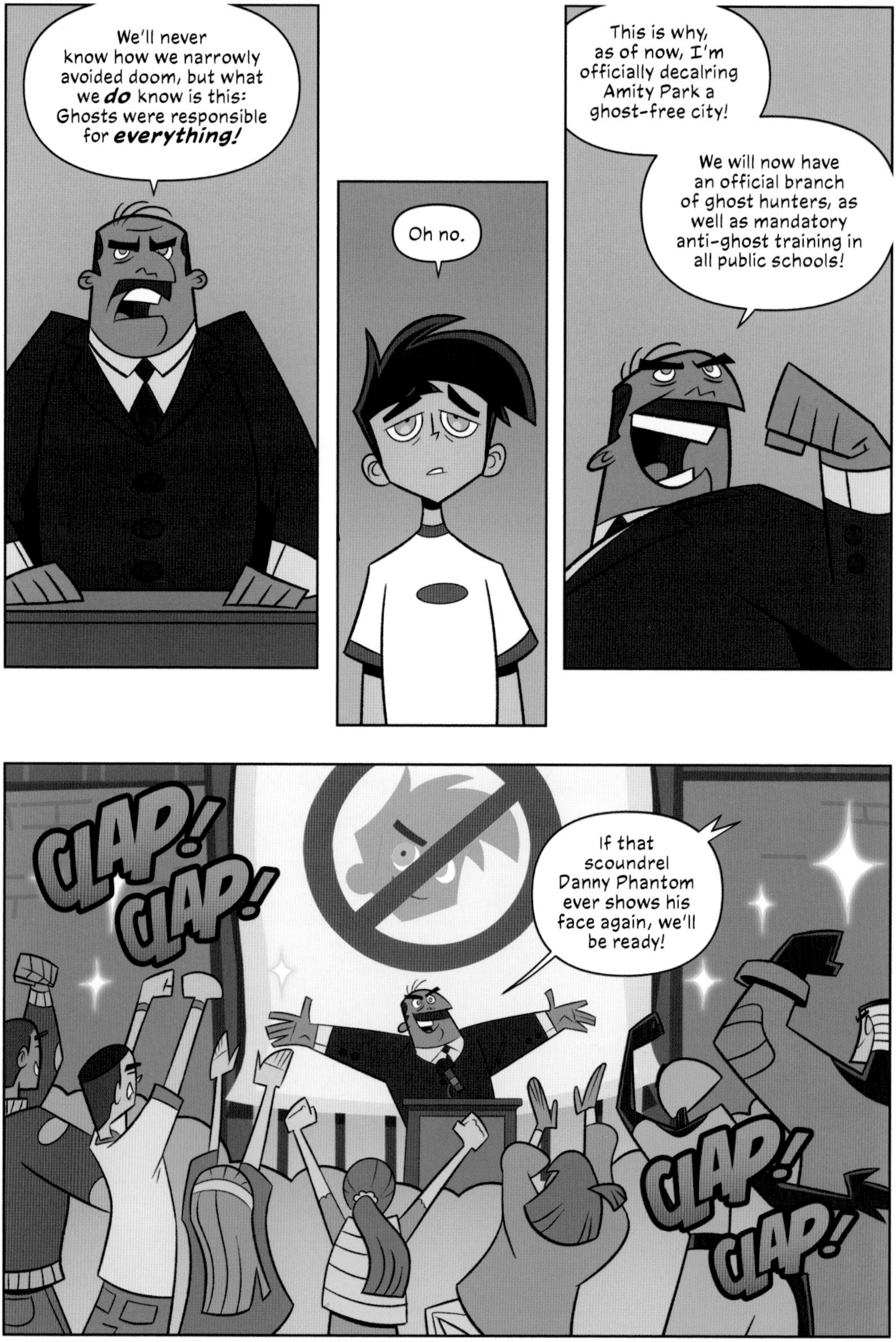
We'll never know how we narrowly avoided doom, but what we ***do*** know is this: Ghosts were responsible for ***everything!***
Oh no.
This is why, as of now, I'm officially decalring Amity Park a ghost-free city!
We will now have an official branch of ghost hunters, as well as mandatory anti-ghost training in all public schools!
CLAP! CLAP!
If that scoundrel Danny Phantom ever shows his face again, we'll be ready!
CLAP! CLAP!

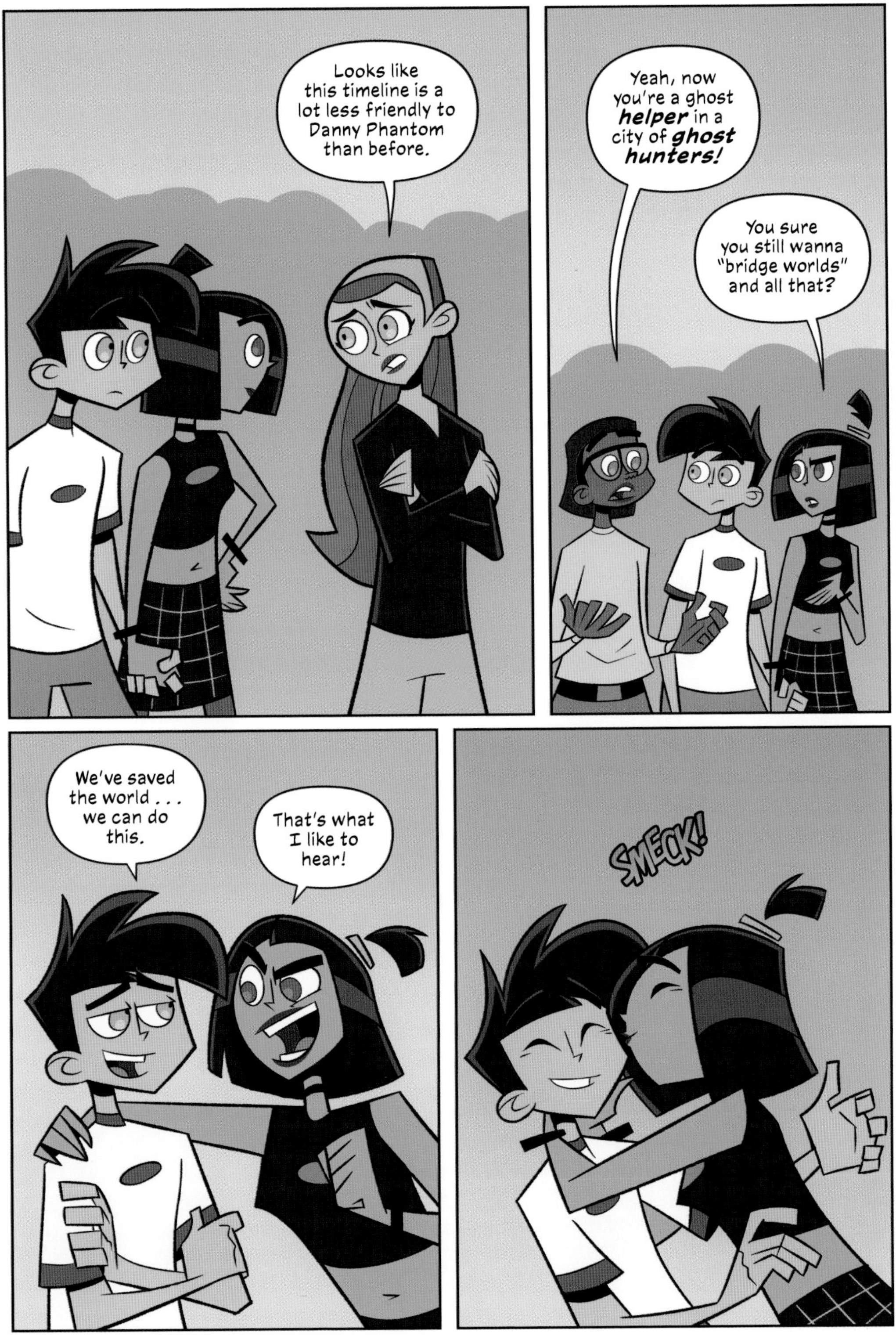
Looks like this timeline is a lot less friendly to Danny Phantom than before.
Yeah, now you're a ghost **helper** in a city of **ghost hunters!**
You sure you still wanna "bridge worlds" and all that?
We've saved the world . . . we can do this.
That's what I like to hear!
SMECK!

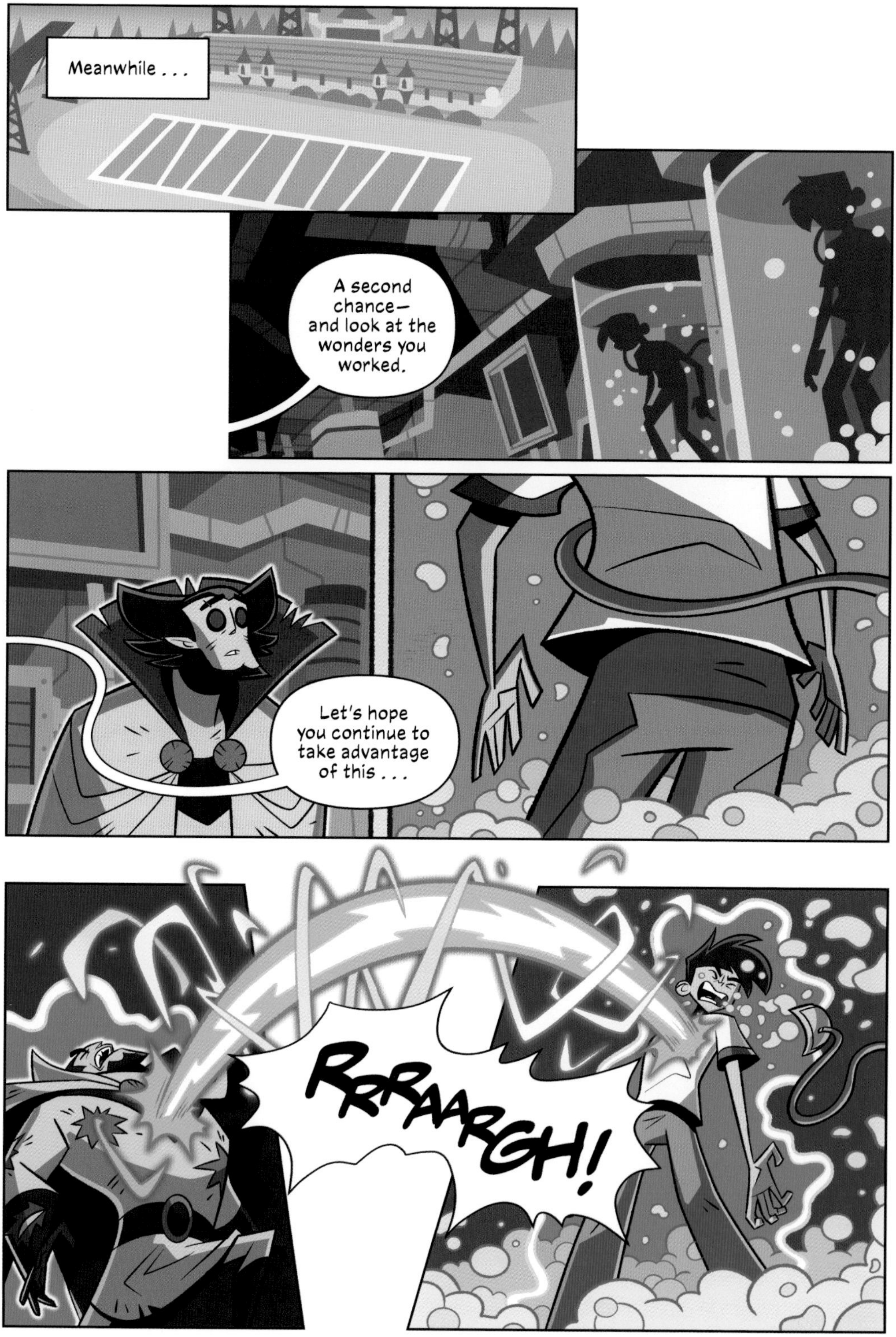
Meanwhile . . .
A second chance— and look at the wonders you worked.
Let's hope you continue to take advantage of this . . .
RRRAARGH!

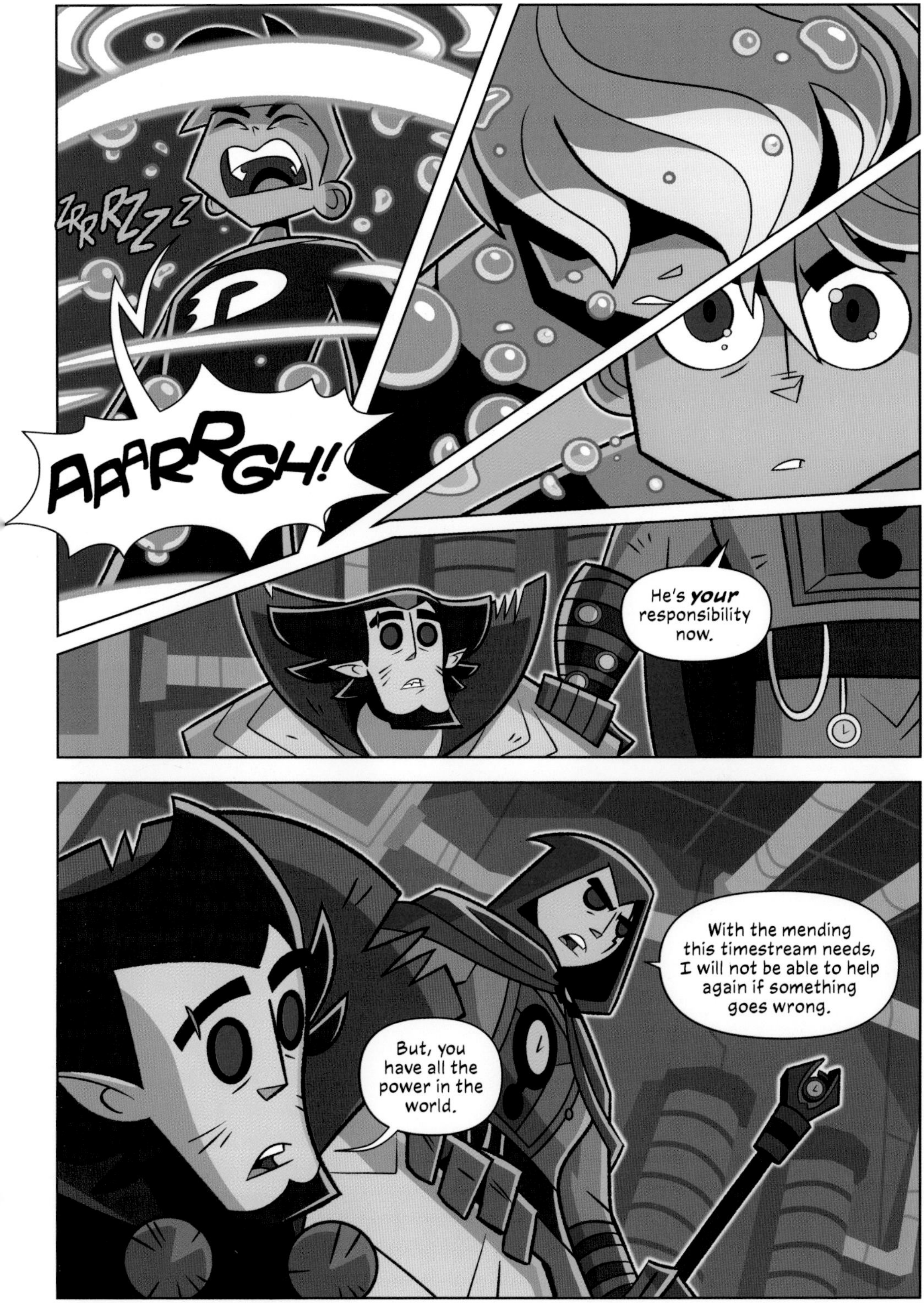
ZRRRZZZZ
AAARRGH!
He's ***your*** responsibility now.
With the mending this timestream needs, I will not be able to help again if something goes wrong.
But, you have all the power in the world.

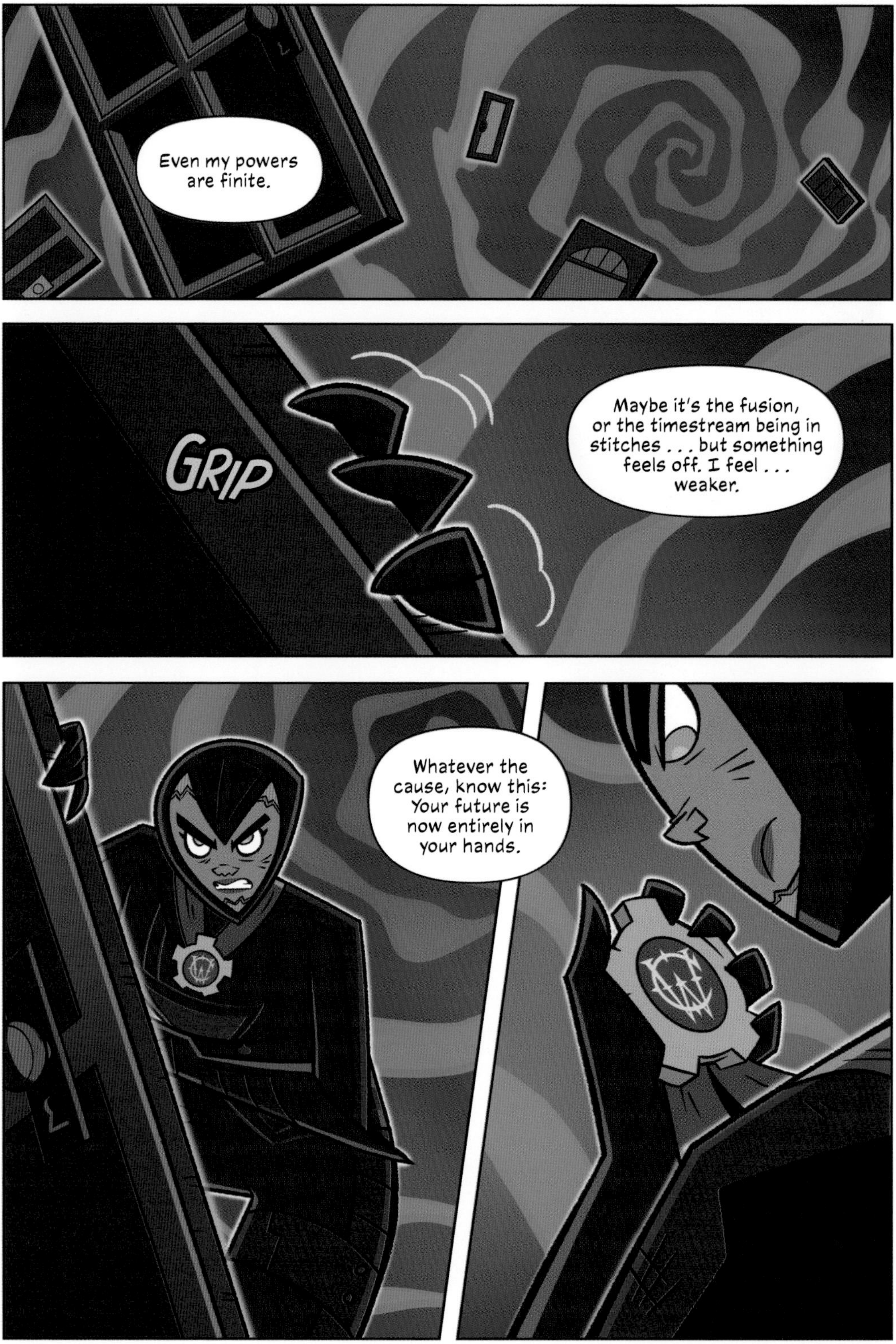
Even my powers are finite.
GRIP
Maybe it's the fusion, or the timestream being in stitches . . . but something feels off. I feel . . . weaker.
Whatever the cause, know this: Your future is now entirely in your hands.

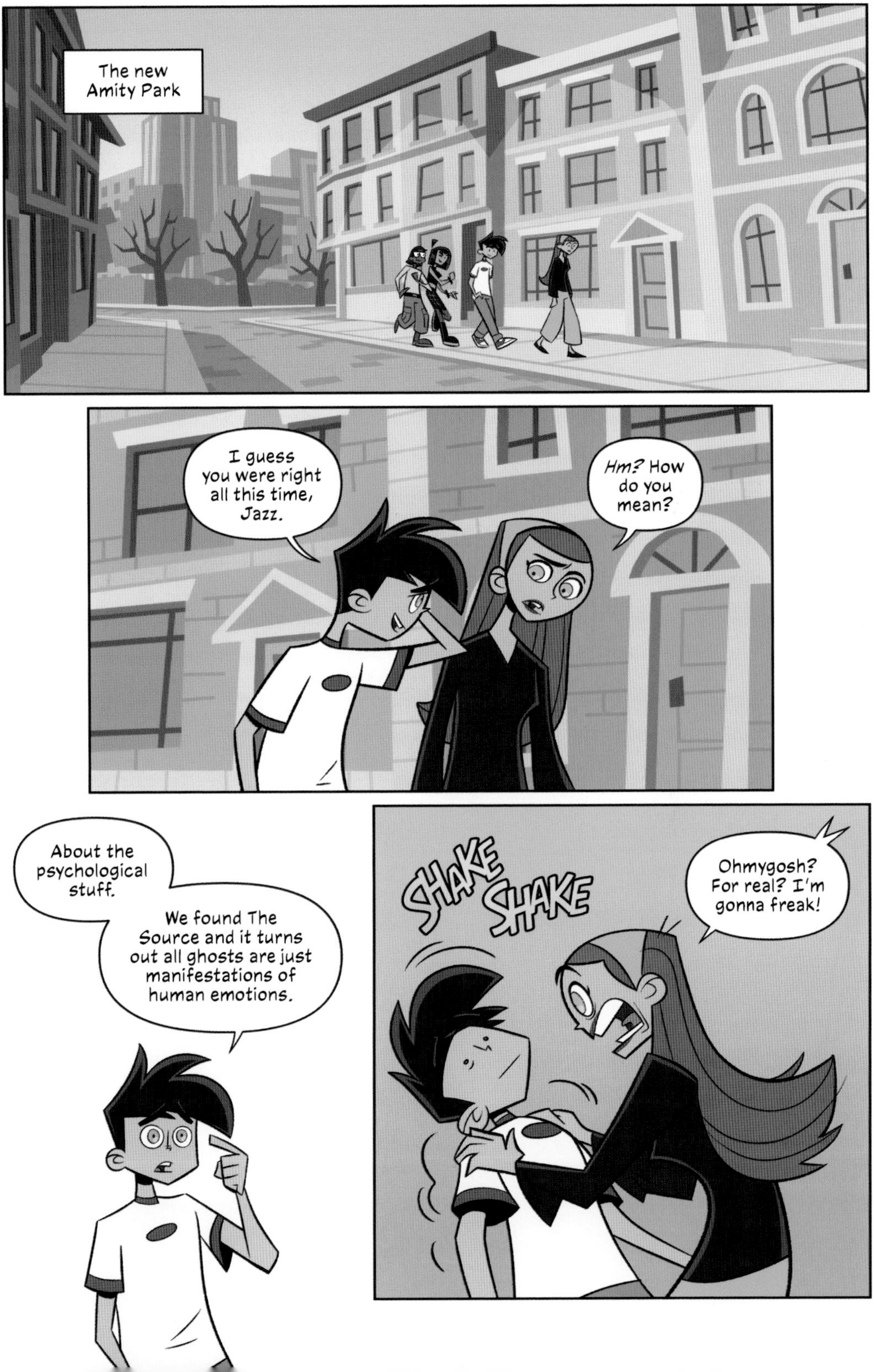

The new Amity Park
I guess you were right all this time, Jazz.
Hm? How do you mean?
About the psychological stuff.
We found The Source and it turns out all ghosts are just manifestations of human emotions.
SHAKE SHAKE
Ohmygosh? For real? I'm gonna freak!

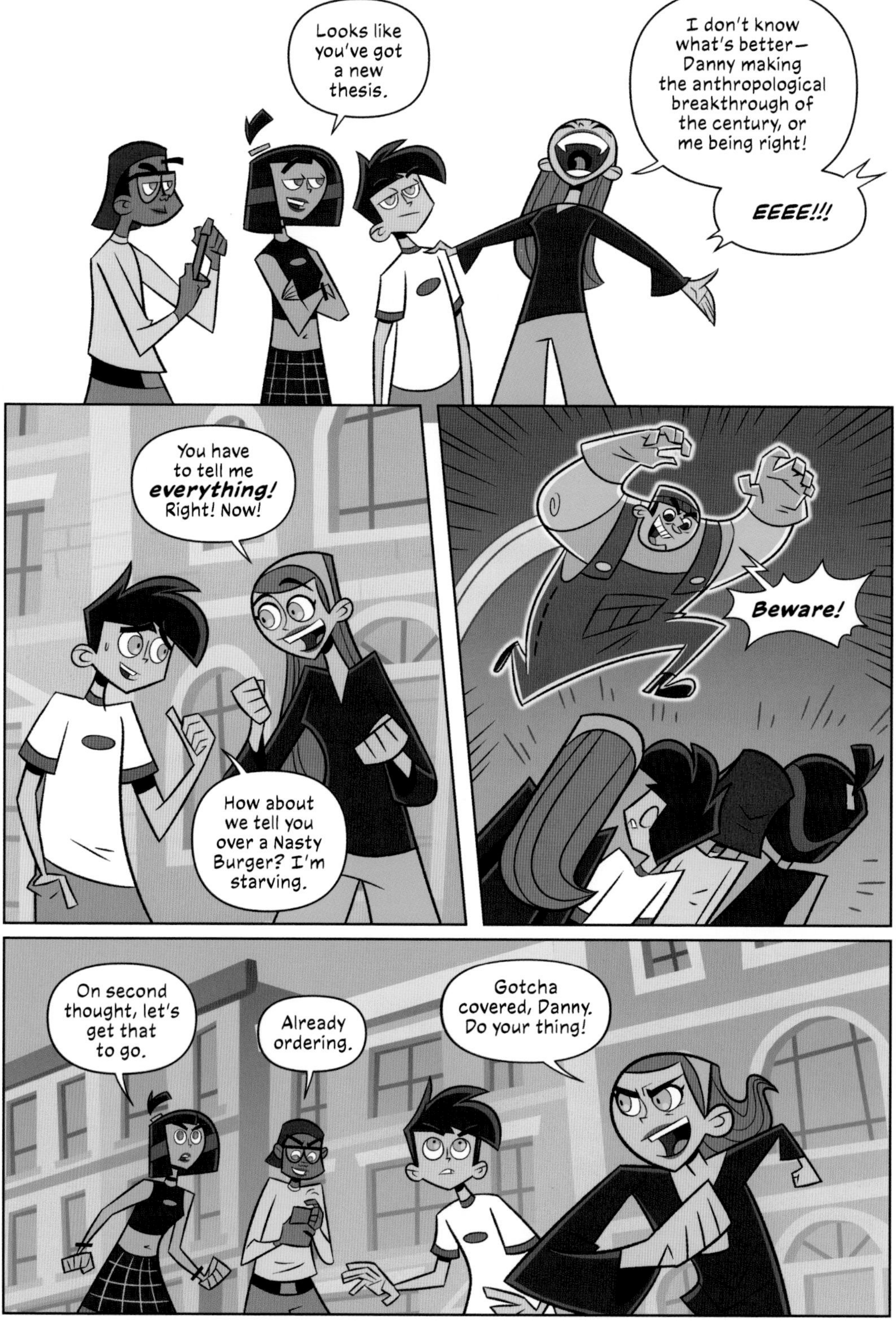

Looks like you've got a new thesis.
I don't know what's better— Danny making the anthropological breakthrough of the century, or me being right!
EEEE!!!
You have to tell me *everything!* Right! Now!
How about we tell you over a Nasty Burger? I'm starving.
Beware!
On second thought, let's get that to go.
Already ordering.
Gotcha covered, Danny. Do your thing!

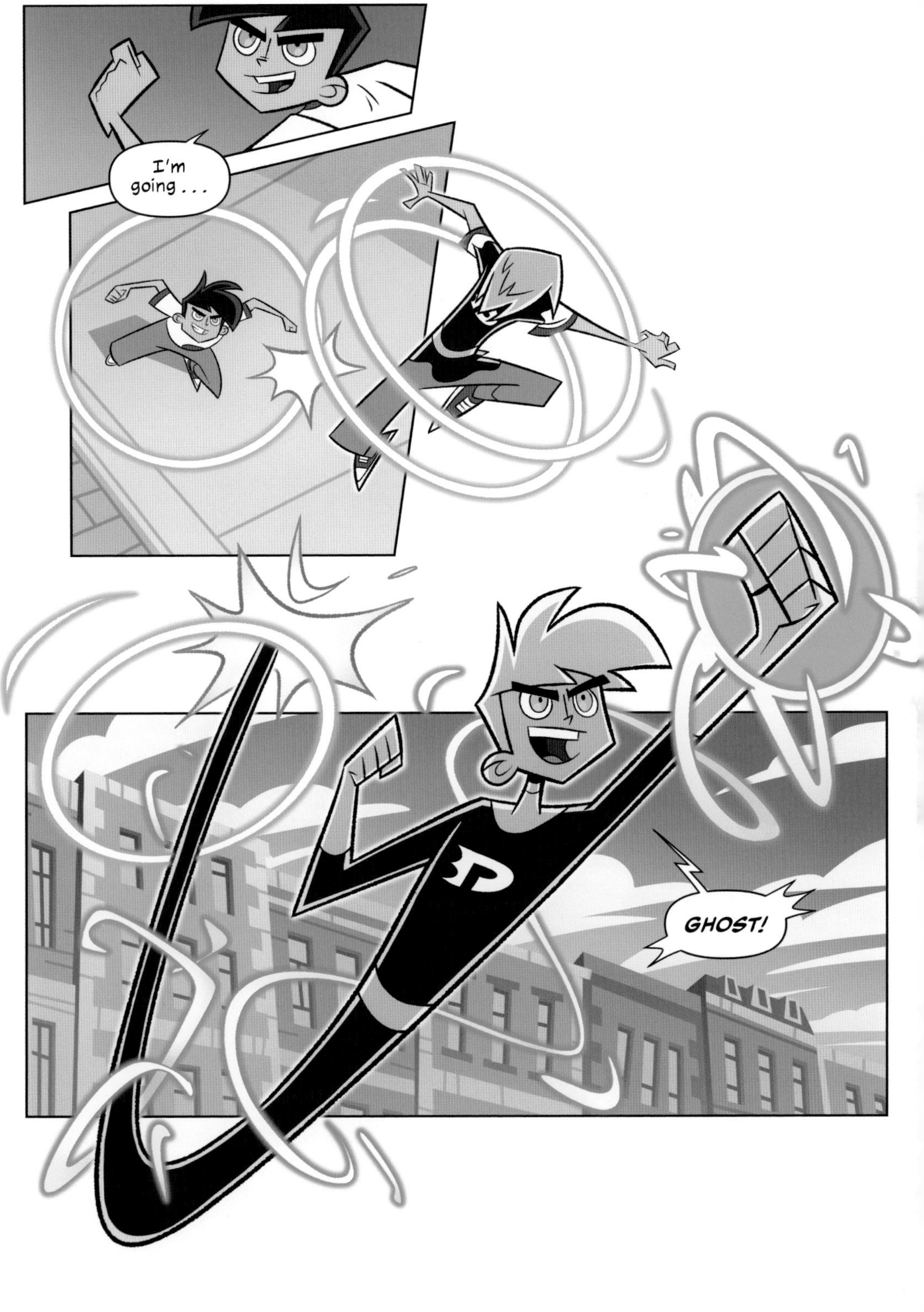
I'm going . . .
GHOST!

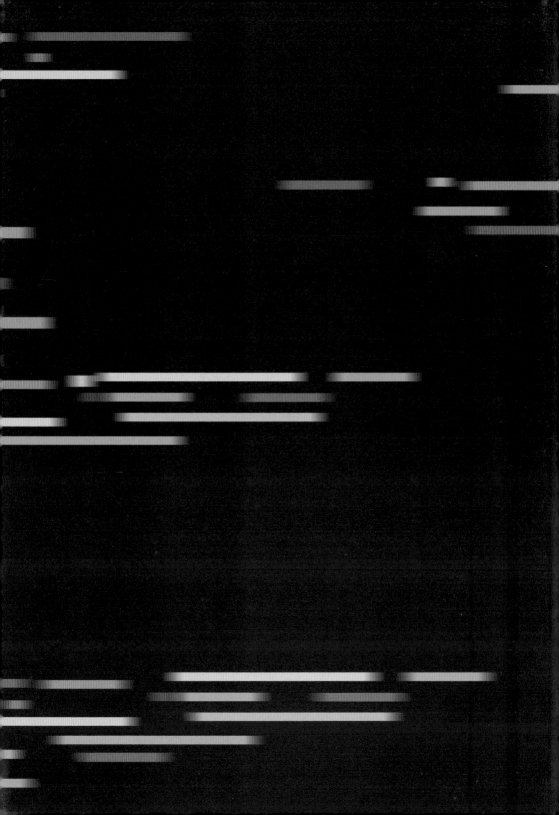

ABOUT THE AUTHOR

Gabriela Epstein is a *New York Times* bestselling illustrator based in Austin, Texas. She graduated with a BFA in illustration from Rhode Island School of Design and has since worked with clients such as Scholastic Graphix, First Second Books, CollegeHumor, Dreamworks TV, Powerhouse Animation, LionForge, Oni Press, and Image Comics. Currently, she is illustrating the Baby-Sitters Club middle grade graphic novel adaptations, including *Claudia and the New Girl*, as well as the young adult graphic novel *Invisibles* for Scholastic Graphix.

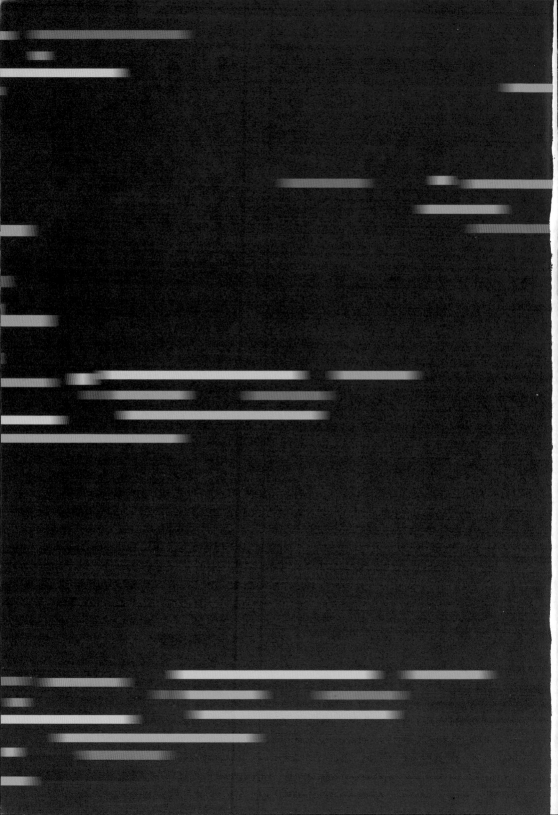